Praise for *Daniel's True Desire*

"Beautifully wrought characters, both good and stunningly wicked, interact with a knotty plot that will keep readers enmeshed... Touching and intense."

—*Library Journal* Starred Review

"The protagonists are perfectly matched for each other in a novel complete with touching romance and an undercurrent of suspense."

—*Publishers Weekly*

"Gifted storyteller Burrowes grabs the readers' emotions in this deeply moving and sexually charged romance. With an unconventional hero and heroine, a few familiar characters, touches of humor, and a few tears, this truly is a beautifully crafted love story."

—*RT Book Reviews* Top Pick, 4.5 Stars

"Burrowes continues her trademark portrayal of frank and loving families in her latest memorable romance."

—*Booklist*

Praise for *Tremaine's True Love*

"Burrowes is at the top of her game, and this latest offering is not to be missed."

—*Kirkus Reviews*

"A fast-paced love story with nuances of humor and poignancy, astute dialogue, passion, and sensuality. A definite keeper."

—*RT Book Reviews* Top Pick, 4.5 Stars

"The protagonists are brilliantly drawn, with plenty of romantic drama and witty repartee."

—*Publishers Weekly*

Praise for *The Duke's Disaster*

"An exquisitely crafted, intensely memorable romance. Another winner for the exceptional Burrowes."

—Library Journal

"An engaging read...very skillfully written...filled with suspense and intrigue."

—Fresh Fiction

"You managed to take [Regency romance] tropes and tweak them ever so slightly to turn what was merely very good into something magnificent."

—Dear Author

"Burrowes skillfully explores the importance of trust in a relationship, as well as love and passion, bringing a depth of emotion to her romance that resonates with readers."

—RT Book Reviews, 4 Stars

WILL'S
True Wish

GRACE
BURROWES

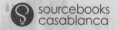

sourcebooks
casablanca

Copyright © 2016 by Grace Burrowes
Cover and internal design © 2016 by Sourcebooks, Inc.
Cover art by Jon Paul

Sourcebooks and the colophon are registered trademarks of Sourcebooks, Inc.

Published by Sourcebooks Casablanca, an imprint of Sourcebooks, Inc.
P.O. Box 4410, Naperville, Illinois 60567-4410
(630) 961-3900
Fax: (630) 961-2168
www.sourcebooks.com

Printed and bound in Canada
MBP 10 9 8 7 6 5 4 3 2 1

To those who have been bullied

Also By Grace Burrowes

One

"WE WERE HAVING A PERFECTLY WELL-BEHAVED outing," Cam said, though Cam Dorning and perfect behavior enjoyed only a distant acquaintance. "Just another pleasant stroll in the pleasant park on a pleasant spring morning, until George pissed on her ladyship's parasol."

The culprit sat in the middle of the room, silent and stoic as mastiffs tended to be, tail thumping gently against the carpet.

"Georgette did not insult Lady Susannah's parasol all on her own initiative," Will Dorning retorted. "Somebody let her off the leash." Somebody whom Will had warned repeatedly against allowing the dog to be loose in public unless Will was also present.

"Lady Susannah wasn't on a leash," Cam shot back. "She was taking the air with her sister and Viscount Effington, and his lordship was carrying the lady's parasol—being gallant, or eccentric. I swear Georgette was sniffing the bushes one moment and aiming for Effington's knee the next. Nearly got him too, which is probably what the man deserves for carrying a parasol in public."

Across the Earl of Casriel's private study, Ash dissolved into whoops that became pantomimes of a dog raising her leg on various articles of furniture. Cam had to retaliate by shoving at his older brother, which of course necessitated reciprocal shoving from Ash, which caused the dog to whine fretfully.

"I should let Georgette use the pair of you as a canine convenience," Will muttered, stroking her silky, brindle head. She was big, even for a mastiff, and prone to lifting her leg in the fashion of a male dog when annoyed or worried.

"I thought I'd let her gambol about a bit," Cam said. "There I was, a devoted brother trying to be considerate of *your* dog, when the smallest mishap occurs, and you scowl at me as if I farted during grace."

"You do fart during grace," Ash observed. "During breakfast too. You're a farting prodigy, Sycamore Dorning. Wellington could have used you at Waterloo, His Majesty's one-man foul miasma, and the French would still be—"

"Enough," Will muttered. Georgette's tail went still, for the quieter Will became, the harder he was struggling not to kill his younger brothers, and Georgette was a perceptive creature. "Where is the parasol?"

"Left it in the mews," Cam said. "A trifle damp and odiferous, if you know what I mean."

"Stinking, like you," Ash said, sashaying around the study with one hand on his hip and the other pinching his nose. "Perhaps we ought to get you a pretty parasol to distract from your many unfortunate shortcomings."

Casriel would be back from his meeting with the solicitors by supper, and the last thing the earl needed was aggravation from the lower primates masquerading as his younger siblings.

More aggravation, for they'd been blighting the family escutcheon and the family exchequer since birth, the lot of them.

"Sycamore, you have two hours to draft a note of apology to the lady," Will said. "I will review your epistle before you seal it. No blotting, no crossing out, no misspellings."

"An apology!" Cam sputtered, seating himself on the earl's desk. "I'm to apologize on behalf of your dog?! I didn't piss on anybody."

At seventeen years of age, Cam was still growing into his height, still a collection of long limbs and restless movement that hadn't resolved into manly grace. He had the Dorning dark hair and the famous Dorning gentian eyes, though.

Also the Dorning penchant for mischief. Will snatched the leash from Cam's hand and smacked Cam once, gently, for violence upset Georgette and was repellent to Will's instincts as a trainer of dumb beasts.

"Neither of you will take Georgette to the park until further notice," Will said. "If you want to attract the interest of the ladies, I suggest you either polish your limited stores of charm or take in a stray puppy."

"A puppy?" Cam asked, opening a drawer into which he had no business poking his nose. "Puppies are very dear."

Nature had intended that puppies of any species be very dear, for they were an endless bother. Ash, having attained his majority, occasionally impersonated a responsible adult. He ceased his dramatics and perched beside Cam on the desk.

"Shall you apologize to Lady Shakespeare or to Effington's knees?" Ash asked. "At length, or go for the pithy, sincere approach? Headmaster says no blotting, no crossing out, no misspellings. I'm happy to write this apology on your behalf for a sum certain."

Ash had an instinct for business—he had read law—but he lacked the cunning Cam had in abundance.

"Ash makes you a generous offer, Cam," Will said, stowing the leash on the mantel and enduring Georgette's but-I'll-die-if-we-remain-indoors look. "Alas, for your finances, Ash, you'll be too busy procuring an exact replica of the lady's abused accessory, from your own funds."

"My own funds?"

Ash hadn't any funds to speak of. What little money Casriel could spare his younger siblings, they spent on drink and other Town vices.

"An exact replica," Will said. "Not a cheap imitation. I will expect your purchase to be complete by the time Cam has drafted an apology. Away with you both, for I must change into clothing suitable for a call upon an earl's daughter."

Into Town attire, a silly, frilly extravagance that on a man of Will's proportions was a significant waste of fabric. He was a frustrated sheep farmer, not some dandy on the stroll, though he was also, for the present, the Earl of Casriel's heir.

So into his finery he would go.

And upon Lady Susannah Haddonfield, of all ladies, he would call.

❧

"A big, well-dressed fellow is sauntering up our walk," Lady Della Haddonfield announced. "He's carrying a lovely purple parasol. The dog looks familiar."

Though dogs occasionally accompanied their owners on social calls, men did not typically carry parasols, so Lady Susannah Haddonfield joined Della at the window.

"That's the mastiff we met in the park," Susannah said. "The Dorning boys were with her." A trio of overgrown puppies, really, though the Dorning fellows were growing into the good looks for which the family was well-known.

"Effington said that mastiff was the largest dog he'd ever seen," Della replied, nudging the drapery aside. "The viscount does adore his canines. Who can that man be? He's taller than the two we met in the park."

Taller and more conservatively dressed. "The earl, possibly," Susannah said, picking up her volume of Shakespeare's sonnets and resuming her seat. "He and Nicholas are doubtless acquainted. Please don't stand in my light, Della."

Della, being a younger sister, only peered more closely over Susannah's shoulder. "You're poring over the sonnets again. Don't you have them all memorized by now?"

The genteel murmur of the butler admitting a visitor drifted up the stairs, along with a curious clicking sound, and then…

"That was a woof," Susannah said. "From inside this house."

"She seemed a friendly enough dog," Della replied,

taking a seat on the sofa. Della was the Haddonfield changeling, small and dark compared to her tall, blond siblings, and she made a pretty picture on the red velvet sofa, her green skirts arranged about her.

"She's an ill-mannered canine," Susannah said, "if my parasol's fate is any indication."

Though the dog was a fair judge of character. Lord Effington fawned over all dogs and occasionally over Della, but Susannah found him tedious. The Dornings' mastiff had lifted her leg upon Lord Effington's knee, and Susannah's parasol had been sacrificed in defense of his lordship's tailoring.

Barrisford tapped on the open door. One never heard Barrisford coming or going, and he seemed to be everywhere in the household at once.

"My ladies, a gentleman has come to call and claims acquaintance with the family."

The butler passed Susannah a card, plain black ink on cream stock, though Della snatched it away before Susannah could read the print.

"Shall I say you ladyships are not at home?" Barrisford asked.

"We're at home," Della said, just as Susannah murmured, "That will suit, Barrisford."

She was coming up on the seventy-third sonnet, her favorite.

"We can receive him together," Della said. "If Nicholas knows the Earl of Casriel, he very likely knows the spares, and Effington fancied that dog most rapturously."

"Effington fancies all dogs." The viscount fancied himself most of all. "You'll give me no peace if I turn our caller away, so show him up, Barrisford, and send along the requisite tray."

"I've never drunk so much tea in all my life as I have this spring," Della said. "No wonder people waltz until all hours and stay up half the night gossiping."

Gossiping, when they might instead be reading. Was any trial on earth more tedious than a London Season?

"Mr. Will Dorning, and Georgette," Barrisford said a moment later. He stepped aside from the parlor door to reveal a large gentleman and an equally outsized dog. Susannah hadn't taken much note of the dog in the park, for she'd been too busy trying not to laugh at Effington. The viscount prided himself on his love of canines, though he was apparently fonder of his riding breeches, for he'd smacked the dog more than once with Susannah's abused parasol.

Barrisford's introduction registered only as the visitor bowed to Susannah.

Will Dorning, not the Earl of Casriel, not one of the younger brothers. Willow Grove Dorning himself. Susannah had both looked for and avoided him for years.

"My Lady Susannah, good day," he said. "A pleasure to see you again. Won't you introduce me to your sister?"

Barrisford melted away, while Della rose from the sofa on a rustle of velvet skirts. "Please do introduce us, Suze."

Della's expression said she'd introduce herself if Susannah failed to oblige. The dog had more decorum than Della, at least for the moment.

"Lady Delilah Haddonfield," Susannah began, "may I make known to you Mr. Will Dorning, late of

Dorset?" Susannah was not about to make introductions for the mastiff. "Mr. Dorning, my sister, Lady Delilah, though she prefers Lady Della."

"My lady." Mr. Dorning bowed correctly over Della's hand, while the dog sat panting at his feet. Like most men, he'd probably be smitten with Della before he took a seat beside her on the sofa. Only Effington's interest had survived the rumors of Della's modest settlements, however.

"Your dog wants something, Mr. Dorning," Susannah said, retreating to her seat by the window.

Mr. Dorning peered at his beast, who was gazing at Della and holding up a large paw.

"Oh, she wants to shake," Della said, taking that paw in her hand and shaking gently. "Good doggy, Georgette. Very pleased to make your acquaintance."

"Georgette, behave," Mr. Dorning muttered, before Susannah was faced with the riddle of whether manners required her to shake the dog's paw.

Georgette turned an innocent expression on her owner, crossed the room, and took a seat at Susannah's knee.

Presuming beast, though Georgette at least didn't stink of dog. Effington's endless canine adornments were the smelliest little creatures.

"My ladies, I'm here to apologize," Mr. Dorning said. "Georgette was in want of manners earlier today. We've come to make restitution for her bad behavior and pass along my brother Sycamore's note of apology."

"Do have a seat, Mr. Dorning," Della said, accepting a sealed missive from their guest. "At least you haven't come to blather on about the weather or to compliment our bonnets."

Bless Della and her gift for small talk, because Susannah was having difficulty thinking.

This was not the version of Will Dorning she'd endured dances with in her adolescence. He'd filled out and settled down, like a horse rising seven. Where a handsome colt had been, a warhorse had emerged. Mr. Dorning's boots gleamed, the lace of his cravat fell in soft, tasteful abundance from his throat. His clothing *fit* him, in the sense of being appropriate to his demeanor, accentuating abundant height, muscle, and self-possession.

Even as he sat on the delicate red velvet sofa with a frilly purple parasol across his knees.

"This is for you, my lady," he said, passing Susannah the parasol. "We didn't get the color exactly right, but I hope this will suffice to replace the article that came to grief in the park."

Susannah's parasol had been blue, a stupid confection that had done little to shield a lady's complexion. That parasol hadn't made a very effective bludgeon when turned on the dog.

"The color is lovely," Susannah said, "and the design very similar to the one I carried earlier."

Susannah made the mistake of looking up at that moment, of gazing fully into eyes of such an unusual color, poetry had been written about them. Mr. Dorning's eyes were the purest form of the Dorning heritage, nearly the color of the parasol Susannah accepted from his gloved hands.

Willow Dorning's eyes were not pretty, though.

His eyes were the hue of a sunset that had given up the battle with night, such that angry reds and passionate oranges had faded to indigo memories and violet dreams. Seven years ago, his violet eyes had been merely different, part of the Dorning legacy, and he'd been another tall fellow forced to bear his friend's sisters' company. In those seven years, his voice had acquired night-sky depths, his grace was now bounded with self-possession.

Though he still apparently loved dogs.

"My thanks for the parasol," Susannah said, possibly repeating herself. "You really need not have bothered. Ah, and here's the tea tray. Della, will you pour?"

Della was effortlessly social. Not the reserved paragon their old sister Nita was, and not as politically astute as their sister Kirsten. Both of those ladies yet bided in Kent, either recently married or anticipating that happy state.

Leaving Susannah unmarried and abandoned as the Season gathered momentum.

Exactly as she'd felt seven years ago.

"Georgette likes you, Susannah," Della said, pouring Mr. Dorning's tea. "Or she likes that parasol."

The dog had not moved from Susannah's knee, though she was ignoring the parasol and sniffing at the sonnets on the side table.

"Georgette is shy," Mr. Dorning said, "and she's usually well mannered, save for occasionally snacking on an old book. Her mischief in the park was an aberration, I assure you. Lady Della, are you enjoying your first London Season?"

For the requisite fifteen minutes, Della and Mr.

Dorning made idle talk, while Susannah discreetly nudged the sonnets away from the dog, sipped tea, and felt agreeably ancient. Without Nita or Kirsten on hand, Susannah had become the older sister suited to serving as a chaperone at a social call.

And upon reflection, she didn't feel abandoned by her older sisters. She was simply taking her turn as the spinster in training before becoming a spinster in earnest.

Thank God.

"I'll bid you ladies good day," Mr. Dorning said, rising.

"I'll see you out," Susannah replied, because that was her role, as quasi-chaperone, and having Barrisford tend to that task would have been marginally unfriendly. Mr. Dorning, as the son of an earl, was her social equal, after all.

"Georgette, come." Mr. Dorning did not snap his fingers, though Effington, the only other dog lover in Susannah's acquaintance, snapped his fingers constantly—at dogs and at servants. He'd snapped his fingers at Della once, and Susannah had treated Effington to a glower worthy of her late papa in a taking.

Georgette padded over to her master's side, and Susannah quit the parlor with them, leaving Della to attack the biscuits remaining on the tea tray.

"You didn't used to like dogs," Mr. Dorning observed.

"I still don't like dogs," Susannah replied, though she didn't *dislike* them. Neither did she like cats, birds, silly bonnets, London Seasons, or most people. Horses were at least useful, and sisters could be very dear. Brothers fell somewhere between horses and sisters.

"Georgette begs to differ," Mr. Dorning said as

they reached the bottom of the steps. "Or perhaps she was making amends for her trespasses against your parasol by allowing you to pat her for fifteen straight minutes."

Susannah took Mr. Dorning's top hat from the sideboard. "Georgette ignored the new parasol. I think my wardrobe is safe from her lapses in manners, though the day your dog snacks on one of my books will be a sorry day for Georgette, Mr. Dorning."

Despite Susannah's stern words, she and Mr. Dorning were *managing*, getting through the awkwardness of being more or less alone together.

"You're still fond of Shakespeare?" Mr. Dorning asked as he tapped his hat onto his head.

A glancing reference to the past, also to the present. "Of all good literature. You're still waiting for your brother to produce an heir?"

Another reference to their past, for Mr. Dorning had confided this much to Susannah during one of their interminable turns about Lady March's music parlor. Until the Earl of Casriel had an heir in the nursery, Will Dorning's self-appointed lot in life was to be his brother's second-in-command.

"Casriel is as yet unmarried," Mr. Dorning said, "and now my younger brothers strain at the leash to conquer London."

He exchanged his social gloves for riding gloves, giving Susannah a glimpse of masculine hands. Those hands could be kind, she hadn't forgotten that. They'd also apparently learned how to give the dog silent commands, for at Mr. Dorning's gesture, Georgette seated herself near the front door.

"I'm much absorbed keeping Cam and Ash out of trouble," he went on, "while allowing them the latitude to learn self-restraint. Apparently, I must add my loyal hound to the list of parties in need of supervision."

The dog thumped her tail.

Did Will Dorning allow himself any latitude? Any unrestrained moments? He'd been a serious young man. He was formidable now.

"We'll doubtless cross paths with your brothers, then," Susannah said, "for Della is also determined to storm the social citadels." Once Della was safely wed, Susannah could luxuriate in literary projects, a consummation devoutly to be wished, indeed.

"You have ever had the most intriguing smile," Mr. Dorning observed, apropos of nothing Susannah could divine. "Thank you for accepting my apology, my lady. I look forward to renewing our acquaintance further under happier circumstances."

Having dispensed such effusions as the situation required, he bowed over Susannah's hand and was out the door, his dog trotting at his heels.

An *intriguing* smile? Susannah regarded herself in the mirror over the sideboard. Her reflection was tall, blond, blue-eyed, as unremarkable as an earl's daughter could be amid London's spring crop of beauties. She *was* smiling, though…

And her hands smelled faintly of Georgette. Perhaps she *had* stroked the dog's silky ears a time or two. Or three.

"Though I don't even *like* dogs."

❧

"Our younger brothers are in awe of you," Grey Dorning, Earl of Casriel, said as Will's mare was led out. "Over their morning ale, they ridicule me, a belted earl with the entire consequence of the house of Dorning upon my broad and handsome shoulders. You, they adore for strolling down Park Lane swinging a purple parasol as if it's the latest fashion edict from Almack's."

Rather than reply immediately, Will took a moment to greet his bay mare. He held a gloved hand beneath her nose, petted her neck, and before Casriel's eyes, the horse fell in love with her owner all over again.

"I took Georgette calling with me," Will said, scratching at the mare's shoulder. "She can be both charming and menacing, which is why Cam and Ash like to take her to the park. She impresses the fellows and attracts the ladies, rather like *you're* supposed to do."

The stable lad led out Casriel's gelding, a handsome black specimen whose displays of affection were reserved for his oats. The groom gave the horse a pat on the quarters, and the horse wrung its tail.

"Don't scold me, Willow," Casriel said, climbing into the saddle. "The Season is barely under way, and an earl must tend to business. The impressing and attracting can wait a few more days."

"Your only prayer of avoiding matrimony evaporated when Jacaranda married Worth Kettering," Will said, taking a moment to check the fit of the bridle and girth before mounting. "Without a sister to serve as hostess, you are doomed to wedlock, Casriel. Marry for the sake of your household, if not for your lonely heart. Dorning House needs a woman's touch if the staff isn't to continuing revolting twice a quarter."

"You are such a romantic, Willow," Casriel replied as their horses clip-clopped down the alley. "I can barely afford to educate our brothers, and that rebellious household must eat. I will marry prudently or not at all. How did the visit to the Haddonfield ladies go?"

That question ought to deflect Will from sermonizing on the need for every unmarried earl to take a wife posthaste, though like many questions put to Will, it met with a silent reception.

They reached the street, where the surrounding traffic meant Will would remain civil, despite an older brother's well-meant goading, so Casriel tried again.

"Did Lady Susannah receive you? She has an entire litter of siblings, doesn't she?" Casriel did too, but lately he felt like a stranger to even his only full brother.

"Lady Susannah was most gracious," Will replied, "as was Lady Della. Lady Della has the misfortune to be the only petite, dark-haired Haddonfield in living memory."

"A runt, then, in your parlance. If she's a pretty, well-dowered runt, nobody will bother much about her shortcomings." Will was partial to runts.

Perhaps he'd marry the Haddonfield girl.

"Our own runt has taken to gambling," Will said. "Though if Cam keeps growing, he might soon consider a career as a prizefighter."

Sycamore, for shame. "All young men attend cockfights."

"No, Grey, they do not. Duchess of Moreland coming this way."

Casriel tipped his hat.

The duchess waved.

Her Grace—a pretty, older lady with a gracious smile—probably knew Casriel's antecedents back for six generations, but without Will's warning, Casriel would have forgotten that he'd seen the woman at the previous evening's musicale.

Financial anxiety played havoc with any man's concentration. No wonder Papa had retreated to the conservatory and the glasshouse rather than take the earldom in hand.

"How do you keep it all organized, Will?" Casriel asked. "How do you keep track of Cam's mischief, the duchesses, the purple parasols, the stewards?" Will didn't run the earldom, but he made it possible for Casriel to run it and still be head of the family.

"A purple parasol is rather difficult to lose track of," Will replied, possibly teasing. One could never tell for sure when Will was being deep and when he was being ironic as hell.

"Am I to worry about Sycamore's gambling?" Casriel would worry, of course, about the sums lost, and about Sycamore, who well knew the family had no coin to spare.

"Yes, you should worry," Will replied, "though not about the money. I've bought Cam's vowels, and will deduct a sum from his allowance from now until Domesday. You should worry because he was at a bear-baiting, because Ash could not stop him, because last week it was the cockfights. The company to be had in such locations is abysmal."

Cam should be at university, in other words. All young men in the awkward throes of late adolescence should be at university, though finding tuition for such an undertaking was three years of a challenge, when yet more younger brothers were busily inspiring insurrection among the maids back in Dorset.

"What does Ash say?" Casriel asked.

"That he can't control Cam, so he simply keeps an eye on him. This is how young men become spoiled or worse. My Lady Heathgate, her sister-in-law Lady Fairly beside her, with the matched chestnuts."

"Wasn't there some scandal involving Lady Fairly?" Casriel asked, when his hat had been dutifully tipped.

"She was a vicar's daughter taken advantage of by a scoundrel," Will said in the same tones he'd report on a Drury Lane play seen last Tuesday. "She managed Fairly's brothel, though she never entertained clients, and he's since divested himself of that business. The titled ladies in the family treat her as respectable, though she and Fairly live very quietly."

"Willow, no wonder the boys are in awe of you. Thank God our papa forbade me to buy any commissions, or Wellington would have turned you into an intelligence officer and shortened the war considerably."

Will drew back, allowing Casriel to ride first through a gap between a stopped curricle and the walkway.

"I would never have managed in the military," Will said. "Bad enough they kill boys who've barely learned to shave, but they also kill horses by the thousands."

This was the problem with Cam's bad behavior. Not that the youngest Dorning brother was wasting money, for an earl's younger son was bred to waste money, and not that he was making friends in low places.

Earls' sons did that too.

From Casriel's perspective, the problem was that

Cam sought entertainments involving harm to animals. Blood sport was supposed to be part of a young gentleman's diversions, true, but Will had no patience for entertainment based on inflicting misery on animals.

Cam had known that from the cradle.

Will did not have friends, though he knew everybody and was well liked. He had his brothers and his dogs. Casriel could not have said which Will would choose to save, if the choice were forced upon him.

"I can send Cam back to Dorset," Casriel said, "but we're better off keeping him where we can supervise him." Where Will could supervise him.

"He might be trying to get sent back to Dorset," Will replied as the green oasis of Hyde Park came into view. "One of the Dorset housemaids had her eye on our youngest brother, and has had her hands on him too."

"Angels deliver me," Casriel muttered. "We don't dare leave him in Dorset without one of us to watch over him, and yet I'm not about to turn off a housemaid simply because Cam can be lured into the butler's pantry."

"Younger siblings grow up more quickly than heirs and spares," Will said. "I'll think of something." He tipped his hat to a flower girl and tossed her a coin.

The girl was plump, plain, and her apron was streaked with damp and dirt, but her smile was radiant as she passed Will a bouquet of violets.

"Thank you, Miss Allen," Will said, bringing his mare to a halt. "Can you spare a posy for his lordship too? He must make himself agreeable to the ladies who are thronging the park."

The flower girl shot Casriel a dubious look, then

selected a nosegay of lily of the valley. She handed the
flowers to Will, who passed them over.

"Excellent choice," Will said. "Good day to you,
Miss Allen."

The mare walked on, while Casriel dealt with
holding a batch of delicate blossoms in addition to
four reins.

"What am I to do with these, Willow? Carry
them between my teeth? Why does that flower girl
look familiar?"

"I've hired her to supply flowers for the house. She
rarely speaks because of a stammer, but she's quite
bright, and has the best prices. An earl's home must be
maintained according to certain standards, which of
course a countess would see to."

Oh, of course. The fate of the earldom rested on
flowers Casriel probably could not afford, but stam-
mering street vendors would have a fine Christmas.
Whatever was amiss with Will, it was getting worse.

The closer they drew to the park, the more
crowded the streets became, so the horses could
move only at the walk. Willow deftly braided his
batch of violets into the mare's mane, where they
somehow did not look ridiculous. Casriel, by contrast, felt the veriest fool riding through Mayfair,
flowers in hand, and horse likely to turn up mischievous at any moment.

"The Duchess of Moreland's two nieces," Will said
quietly. "Miss Bethan and Miss Megan Windham.
Their cousin, Lady Deane, the duchess's youngest
daughter, at the ribbons."

"How in God's name do you keep them all straight?"

"Flowers to the elder," Will murmured. "Miss Bethan, sitting on the outside."

Miss Bethan Windham was a lovely little creature with whom Casriel had not danced. He would have recalled that red hair, and those green eyes, and the smile that blossomed when he passed her the flowers. The ladies flirted and teased and generally made a man forget which direction the park lay in, and then traffic shifted, and Will cleared his throat.

"Ladies, good day," Casriel said, for he was as well trained to Will's cues as any hound. "My regards to your family."

"You can be charming," Will said when the carriage had pulled away. "Don't pretend you can't. Those flowers will end up pressed between the pages of the lady's journal, and the scent of lily of the valley will always make her think of you."

"Is that how it works?" Will seemed very convinced of his theory, and yet to the best of Casriel's knowledge, Will had never fancied a specific lady. "How is it, Willow, you know the names of all the women, right down to the flower girl? You earn the undying loyalty of horses and dogs, both, and impress our brothers daily, but the females never seem to notice you?"

Willow had the knack of becoming invisible, in other words. Of disappearing without going anywhere, just another tree in the hedgerow on a still spring day. He'd had this ability since boyhood, had slipped through university on the strength of it, and still used his invisibility to good advantage in ballrooms and gentlemen's clubs.

"My objective is to ensure the ladies notice *you*," Will said. "One of them might even notice Ash, who is a good-looking, friendly devil, and knows his way around figures. Once I get you two married off, I can enlist your wives to assist me in finding ladies for our other brothers."

Papa had despaired of Willow, though the late earl and his second son had had much in common.

"As usual, Will, you have an excellent plan, though I detect a serious flaw in your scheme."

They crossed Park Avenue at a brisk trot, and not until they were well within Hyde Park did Will take the bait.

"What is the flaw in my plan?" he asked. "You and Ash are both handsome and sons of an earl. I see to it that you're well dressed when it matters. You're passable dancers and considerate of women. With all the bankers' daughters looking to marry into the nobility, all of the viscounts and baron's daughters or even widows—what?"

Willow had doubtless made lists of these women, another worry added to Casriel's endless supply.

"I know you mean well, Will, but Ash and I can find our own ladies. The flaw in your plan is that you've made no provision for finding *a lady of your own*. Give me those violets. This park has become over-run with women, and an earl-without-countess must defend himself with whatever weapons he can find."

"The park is always overrun with women at the fashionable hour," Will said, "but as it happens, I have my own use for these flowers."

Will cantered off in the direction of a gig driven by

a blond woman with a petite brunette at her side. The Haddonfield ladies?

Casriel trotted after him, for this moment would go down in Dorning history as the first encounter with a proper woman to which Willow Grove Dorning would arrive bearing flowers.

Two

"DELILAH HADDONFIELD, IF YOU DON'T STOP TWIRL-ing my parasol," Susannah said, "I will smack you with it. You'll scare some gallant's horse, and he'll be ridiculed, and then talk will start that you like men to notice you."

The parasol slowed. "I am in my first Season, Suze. I am a legitimate by-blow, and my name is Delilah. If I encourage the notice of the men, I'm fast. If I don't encourage the notice of the men, I put on airs. As it happens, I am trying to attract the notice of somebody."

Effington often rode in the park at the fashionable hour, else Susannah would never have subjected herself to two outings in a single day. After the morning's debacle, Delilah was doubtless nervous of his lordship's regard.

"It's early in the Season," Susannah said, maneuvering around a parked phaeton. "You needn't attract anybody's notice. Simply enjoy a pleasant outing in the company of your devoted sibling."

"I love that about you," Della said. "Behind your spectacles and sonnets, you're tenacious and loyal."

When Susannah wanted to slap her hand over Della's mouth, she instead nodded cordially to the Duke of Quimbey, a jovial older fellow who could still gracefully turn a lady down the ballroom.

"You will please not mention my spectacles." Spectacles were for the elderly, for clerks, and men of business. For people who had trouble reading, not for ladies who devoured literature by the hour.

"Mr. Dorning," Della said, snapping the parasol closed and resting it against the bench. "A pleasure to see you again. What a lovely mare."

Susannah didn't intend to draw the carriage to the verge, but to the verge the horse did go, and there halt. Perhaps their gelding needed a rest, or had an overly developed sense of the social niceties.

"My ladies," Mr. Willow Dorning said, touching his hat brim. "I'm happy to see the new parasol put to use. I will refrain, however, from commenting on either bonnets or weather."

Della's brows drew down at Mr. Dorning's grave tone, but Susannah understood teasing when she heard it.

"See that you don't, sir," she said. "Has your dog been denied the privileges of the park for her earlier indiscretions?"

Susannah noticed Georgette's absence, for the mastiff was a part of Will Dorning's ensemble, like a carved walking stick or a particular signet ring, only larger and more noticeable. Susannah wasn't sure what the violets in Mr. Dorning's hand were about, though for the past seven years, violets had reminded her of his eyes.

And of his gallantry.

"Willow, you are remiss," said a fellow trotting up on Will's left. The newcomer rode a handsome black horse, had the Dorning violet eyes, and felt entitled to an introduction.

The earl, then. Susannah hadn't seen him for years. Beside her, Della preened, fluffing her skirts and twiddling her bonnet ribbons, exactly as a young lady might.

Exactly as Susannah never had.

"My ladies, this presuming lout is my brother," Will said. "Grey, Earl of Interruption and Casriel. Apparently, we're about to be joined by my younger brothers as well, for which I do apologize."

The last was aimed at Susannah, more drivel, but Mr. Dorning's eyes said he was also commiserating with her on the entire topic of siblings. More introductions followed, for Mr. Ash Dorning, and Mr. Sycamore—"though he will ignore you unless you call him Cam"—Dorning.

The earl seemed content to sit back and allow his younger brother to manage the entire encounter. Other carriages tooled past, other gentlemen rode by, and for the first time, Lady Della Haddonfield was seen to hold court in the park.

Della teased Ash Dorning about the fancy knot in his cravat, while Susannah tried not to stare at Mr. Willow Dorning's violets.

"Thank you," Susannah said, beneath the banter of their siblings. Will Dorning was the most perceptive man Susannah knew, for all he lacked charm. She needn't say more.

"You're welcome," he replied just as softly. "I have my own motives, though."

Something Della said caused the other three brothers to laugh, and up and down the carriage parade, heads turned. The Earl of Casriel smiled at Lady Della Haddonfield, ensuring the moment would be remarked by the ladies over tea and by the gentlemen over cards.

"We each have our own motives," Susannah replied. Shakespeare had made the same point in a hundred more eloquent turns of phrase.

Mr. Dorning fiddled with his horse's mane. "It hasn't grown easier, then? You haven't learned to love the dancing and flirting and being seen?"

He'd predicted she would. He'd been wrong, or kind, or both.

"I am content," Susannah said, which they both knew for a lie. She had never needed to dissemble with him, so she amended her statement. "I will be content, rather. Della has already attached the interest of Viscount Effington, and that portends a successful Season for her."

This merry, impromptu gathering in the park surrounded by four handsome fellows improved those odds considerably.

"May we call upon you, Lady Susannah? You and Lady Della?"

The question hurt. A childish lament—*I saw him first*—crowded hard against loyalty to Della. Willow Dorning had been honorable toward Susannah before she'd comprehended how precious such regard was.

He'd make a wonderful brother-in-law, damn him. She smiled brilliantly. "Of course you must call upon us, you and however many brothers or dogs you please. We're always happy to welcome our friends." A slight untruth, for Susannah resented any who interrupted her reading.

"Willow!" the earl called. "Didn't you bring those posies for the lady?"

Della Haddonfield, who could wield truth like a rapier and silence like a shield, *simpered*, and Susannah's heart broke a little.

A nuisance, to have a heart that could break. Susannah had thought herself beyond such folly.

"The violets go with his eyes," Cam Dorning said. "Willow is partial to violets, you see."

"As am I," Della said. "Such a delicate fragrance, and so pretty."

Violets did not last, though. Susannah had reason to know this. The horse in the traces took a restive step and shook its head.

Time to go.

"I am partial to ladies who forgive us our minor lapses," Will said, presenting the violets in a gloved hand.

Della reached for the bouquet, and the moment might have turned awkward, but Susannah realized at the last possible instant that the flowers were not for Della, *they were for her.*

She passed the reins into Della's hands as if the movement were choreographed, and accepted the violets.

"Thank you, Mr. Dorning. I'm partial to violets as well. I don't want these to wilt, though, so I'd best get them directly home."

Della recovered with good-humored grace as the men made their farewells and cantered away.

"Shall I drive us home, Suze? Your hands are notably occupied."

Susannah's heart was occupied too, bemused with feelings of pleasure and uncertainty. She was once again sixteen years old, growing too quickly, and terrified of tripping on the dance floor.

"Hold these," Susannah said, shoving the flowers at Della and taking the reins. "You can drive next time."

They left the park for the busy streets of Mayfair, Della holding the flowers, and occasionally—say, when a carriage full of young ladies passed—raising them to her nose as she waved or smiled.

"You are awful," Susannah said, proud of her sister's guile and pleased with the day. "The entire battalion of Dorning brothers has asked permission to call on you. There's a handsome, eligible earl in the bunch, and he seemed taken with you."

A reassuring thought, for reasons Susannah would examine once she'd put the violets in water.

Della waved to another group, this time holding the violets aloft. "The earl is probably ten years my senior, Suze, but they're a fine group of fellows. Effington is titled, and he and I get on well enough."

For all Della was smiling furiously, and beaming gaiety in every direction, her words were tired and hard.

"You'll have other choices." A woman always had choices, though often, she hadn't any good ones. "Give it time."

"He fancies you," Della said, touching a fragile violet petal. "Mr. Will Dorning fancies you, Suze. You might have choices too."

⤙⤚

"What was that all about in the park, earlier today?"
Casriel asked. He was the most inquisitive older
brother ever to inconvenience a busy younger sibling.
"All that gallantry beneath the maples and flirting
among the infantry?"

"You will accuse me of trying to marry you off,"
Will replied, and the accusation would have had
some merit.

The waiter bustled over to their table. Casriel
ordered his usual beefsteak, Willow a plate of fruit and
cheeses, because Georgette harbored a special fondness
for the club's cheddar.

"Please recall," Will went on, "that you intruded
uninvited on my conversation with the Haddonfield
ladies. I was making amends for Georgette's
misbehavior."

Mostly, and being a little sentimental too.

"You bought the woman a replacement parasol
and hand-delivered a written apology. What amends
remained to be made?"

Casriel thought in terms of crops and ledgers, sums
owed, and acres fallowed, so Will explained. He
would explain as many times in as many situations as
it took for Casriel to learn to think like an earl, rather
than a country squire.

"Lady Della is in her first Season, Casriel. Her
escort this morning—a handsome, eligible viscount—
was nearly pissed upon by my dog. The worse damage
was not to the parasol."

The earl wrinkled a nose euphemistically described
as aristocratic. On Will, the same nose was a sizable
beak. Ash and Cam had been spared the worst excesses

of the Dorning nose, as had their sisters, Daisy and Jacaranda. The remaining three brothers had yet to grow into the family proboscis one way or the other, though they had the Dorning eyes.

"I suppose the lady's consequence might have suffered," Casriel said, considering his glass of wine. "From what I heard, Effington delivered a sound beating to Georgette on the spot. I'm surprised she didn't dine on rare haunch of viscount for his presumption."

So was Will. Georgette was a peaceful soul, but she took a dim view of repeated blows to the head.

"The whole incident makes no sense to me, Grey. Georgette has better manners than our younger brothers. Something must have provoked her to misbehavior."

"Cam would provoke a saint to blaspheming. Will you join me for tonight's rounds?"

The Miltons' ball, a soiree at Lord and Lady Hamilton's, perhaps a round of cards back here at the club. Casriel had to be let off the leash at some point, and those were safe gardens for him to nose around in.

"I think not," Will said. "If you make yourself agreeable to the hostesses, they'll ensure you're introduced to all the ladies interested in becoming your countess. Don't dance with any of the marriageable women more than once, don't leer down their bodices no matter how they trip against you or lean too closely on the turns. If you must, smoke a cheroot on the balcony or eat some leeks, and breathe directly on the more presuming ones."

Casriel was handsome, and he'd make a loyal, if somewhat distracted, husband. Like Will, he indulged the manly vices rarely and discreetly. He was not wealthy, however, not compared to what many of the ladies on offer were accustomed to, and Dorset was not the most fashionable address.

Grey Birch Dorning was a good man, though, and Will was proud to call him brother.

"Willow, one fears for you," Casriel said, keeping his voice down. "The point of tonight's outing, the point of this entire sortie among the beau monde, is to secure the charms of a well-dowered lady. Without your excellent counsel, I won't know one of those from the impoverished sort when they get to leaning or pressing or any of that other business."

Weariness dragged at Will. Weariness of the body, weariness of the fraternal spirit. So many brothers, and Jacaranda was too enthralled with her knight to be of any use getting those brothers married off. Will's other sister, Daisy, was knee-deep in babies, and had her hands full with her squire back in Dorset.

"You will be married to your countess quite possibly for the rest of your life, Casriel, or for hers. If birds can mate for life without recourse to intelligence officers, belted earls ought to be able to manage it too."

The food arrived and conversation lapsed. When Will had eaten half of his selection of cheeses, and wrapped the other half to tuck away in his pocket, he excused himself and repaired with a newspaper to the card room. Cam and Ash were probably once again losing money at some gaming hell or cockfight, and that was so disappointing as to be nearly sickening.

Perhaps the earl could sort them out. Will was growing tired of trying.

"Playing a bit deep, aren't you, Effington?"

The question was friendly and infuriating. Frankincense Godwin Emeritus Effington, Eighth Viscount. Effington, rearranged his cards, then put them back in their original order.

"The Season is upon us, Fenwick," Effington drawled. "I must have my diversions, and your pin money too. What say, the loser of this hand goes directly to the Milton ball and submits himself to the mercy of Lady Milton and the wallflowers of her choosing."

"High stakes, indeed," Fenwick said, amid a chorus of "Done!" and "Hear, hear!" though the other four men around the table were smiling. Two were married, the other two were wealthy. They could afford to be amused at the ordeals of the impoverished, titled bachelors.

Two minutes later, Fenwick threw in his hand. "A plague on your luck, Effington. Perhaps I should start carrying around a little dog, and my cards would improve."

"Having a well-behaved canine prepares a man for the companionship of a well-behaved wife," Effington said, stroking a hand over the homely little pug in his lap. "Both must be pampered, fed, taken about, cosseted, and occasionally disciplined for naughty behavior, isn't that right, Yorick?"

The dog looked up at mention of his name, but knew better than to bark. They all learned not to bark, eventually. A lap dog made winning at cards ever so much easier, drawing attention from a man's hands at opportune moments.

"I heard your well-behaved lady was laughing in the park with no less than four Dorning brothers in attendance," Fenwick remarked as he downed the last of a drink. "The Dornings are prodigiously handsome, and Lady Della Haddonfield is too pretty for you by half, Effington. If she didn't have so many strapping, devoted brothers, I might pay my addresses to her."

Effington had got word of the scene in the park from one of the many who'd seen Lady Della tooling home, all smiles, and brandishing violets under the very nose of Polite Society. Fenwick was moderately handsome, in a rough, dark way, and said to be connected to one of the northern earls.

Some ladies were attracted to a lack of refinement. Della Haddonfield apparently had better sense.

"Lady Della resides with only the one brother," Effington said, gathering up the cards. "The newly minted Earl of Bellefonte, who needs to take his womenfolk in hand, if you ask me."

"Is that what you were doing with Dorning's dog this morning?" one of the other fellows quipped. "Taking the beast in hand by beating it with a parasol?"

If the women hadn't been present in the park, Effington would have done much more than swat at the damned mastiff. The dog had wanted a firm hand, but alas, the women *had* been present.

"I should have had Yorick with me," Effington said, grabbing his dog's nose and giving it a waggle. "He would have defended the pride of the house of Effington."

Or Yorick would have been reprimanded for his cowardice.

"The ladies do like a friendly dog," one of the married men observed. "Don't understand it m'self. If a beast can't chase down vermin, what good is it?"

Effington ought to have burst forth into an aria about the wonders of canine companionship, for he'd cultivated his reputation as a dog fancier assiduously. Alas, the hour grew late, and more pressing matters required his attention.

"I will share something with you gentlemen in confidence, for our conversation has unwittingly touched on a sensitive matter," Effington said, tidying the deck into a neat stack. He shuffled the cards, when he'd rather have flung them into the fire.

For the last hour, he'd been winning. For the hour before that, despite Yorick's slavish cooperation, he had lost.

"I'm for my penance," Fenwick said, rising. Had an inconvenient decent streak, did Fenwick. No uninvited confidences would keep him awake later tonight. "Gentlemen, good night. Yorick, pleasant dreams."

Fenwick patted the dog, and earned Yorick's signature hopeful look, which was doomed to failure, of course. Yorick would do the job he'd been trained for until Effington no longer had a use for him.

"We spoke earlier of Lady Della," Effington said, dropping his tones to the regretful register as Fenwick departed. "I favor the lady with my attentions because she's burdened by unfortunate antecedents, and most of Polite Society treats her accordingly. As an earl's daughter, they can't ignore her, but she's in truth her mother's by-blow, and the ladies will never let her forget it. One feels compelled by gentlemanly honor to champion such a creature."

Sympathetic murmurs followed, for women in

search of a well-placed husband were not permitted
unfortunate antecedents.

"Good of you to take notice of her," one older man
said. "She should be appreciative."

"Her family probably is," another noted. "Not so
easy to find a match for the bastards."

"You will keep this in strictest confidence, of
course," Effington murmured, thus guaranteeing that
every man present told at least one other fellow and
two women by morning.

"Of course," came the general reply. No one
questioned where Effington had come by this "confidence," which was fortunate. Lady Della's dark coloring, her petite stature, and her siblings' protectiveness
had fueled some unkind talk, and the rest was nothing
more than nasty speculation.

"Then I leave you," Effington said, rising with the
dog in his arms. "And bid you all good night. Yorick,
my darling, it's past your bedtime."

Effington made his exit, stroking and patting his
dear little doggy, and kissing endearments to the top of
Yorick's head, while nobody seemed to recall that the
evening's winnings and losings had yet to be totaled.

The other men were probably too preoccupied
deciding where to share the juiciest gossip of the
evening. Well done, if Effington did say so himself.

❧

Georgette picked up the stick at Will's feet and
dropped it again, directly onto the toes of his boots.
He grasped the stick as she'd requested and pitched it
off into the hedgerow thirty yards to the right. When

Georgette came trotting back several minutes later, tail waving, stick clutched in her jaws for the two-dozenth time, Will gave up the outing as a failure.

"They're not coming." He produced the bit of cheese that signaled an end to the game. "*All done*, Georgette. All done for today. Perhaps because Lady Susannah has a marriageable sister to show off, she no longer reads on the most secluded bench in the—"

A flash of purple stilled Will's hand on Georgette's head. Lady Della, possibly, who had a penchant for borrowing parasols and twirling them conspicuously— but, no. The figure coming down the path was too tall, and she had her nose in a book.

She was also unaccompanied by her younger sister.

For years, Will had known that during the London Season, he'd be able to catch the occasional glimpse of Lady Susannah Haddonfield in this quiet clearing in a vast and busy park. Lady Susannah also frequented Hanford's bookshop on Bond Street, though she never noticed the gentleman in the corner pretending to be absorbed in some zoological text.

"She has become part of my pack," Will said to Georgette. "One keeps an eye on pack mates. Simple biology. No harm in it."

And yet this Lady Susannah was different from the version Will had first noticed at Lady March's tea dances years ago. More confident, also more reserved, more brisk and sure of herself.

"Prettier too, or pretty in a different way?"

Georgette cocked her head. To greet the lady or not?

"Wish her good day, but watch out for that parasol."

Georgette licked Will's gloved hand and trotted

away toward Lady Susannah. The dog woofed once, an unusual exuberance for her.

Also a happy greeting, but still Lady Susannah trundled along, absorbed in her book. Will took a moment simply to behold her, so focused on her stories and poems that even the glory of Hyde Park on a spring day could not deflect her attention.

"My goodness," she said, stopping abruptly. "Georgette? Is that—it is you." Though her ladyship was wearing a bonnet, she shaded her eyes with her book and peered about. "Mr. Dorning, greetings."

"My lady, good day." Will could not bow over Lady Susannah's hand because she was still holding the book in one hand and the parasol in the other. "A pleasure to see you."

"Likewise, Mr. Dorning. Georgette has apparently regained her privileges in the park. Della and Lord Effington are strolling closer to the Serpentine. You might want to avoid them."

To blazes with his lordship, whom Lady Susannah also probably wanted to avoid. "Shall we bide here for a moment, my lady? What are you reading?"

"A critique of Shakespeare's tragedies. Does Georgette want you to do something with that stick?"

The same stick, of course. "If that stick were taken from her, and hidden in the farthest reaches of the most obscure hedge of the park, she'd find it. It's hers now."

"I feel the same way about my books. My sisters say I've grown eccentric."

Will enjoyed this about Susannah Haddonfield. She was honest, had no airs or affectations. When she spoke, she spoke the truth. He peeled off his gloves, stuffed them in a pocket, and held out his hand.

"May I see the book?"

She passed it over, though her gaze followed her treasure the way Georgette kept track of a beloved toy. The book had been read many times, the spine well creased. Pages were not dog-eared, though, nor was anything scribbled in the margins. One could tell a lot from a person by how they cared for what they claimed to value.

"This was your father's?" Will asked, reading the inscription.

"My mother gave it to him. She had a gift for reading dramatically. Shall we sit, Mr. Dorning? Della will make an entire morning's work of toddling around at Effington's side, and they have a maid with them to observe the proprieties."

Will snapped the book closed. "Leaving nobody to observe the proprieties on your behalf, my lady."

"You sound like my brother Nicholas." Her ladyship plucked the book from Will's grasp. "He's become a Puritan since the title befell him. You and I are old friends, Mr. Dorning, and nobody will remark our passing a few minutes together in a public park."

Will did not like the sound of "old friends." Lady Susannah was quite youthful, and he was…hardly doddering. He accompanied her ladyship to the nearest bench, which sat beneath a canopy of maples in their vernal glory. The park was at a grand pause, between tulips and irises, a few of each in evidence, but not enough to overpower the sheer, lush greenery.

"This place keeps me sane," Will said when he

and the lady were sitting side by side. "My dogs love it here, and for an hour at a time, I can pretend I'm back in Dorset, taking a long walk to work out some problem, or simply enjoying a pretty day."

Lady Susannah set the book aside and untied her bonnet ribbons. "The libraries keep me sane," she said, placing her bonnet on top of her book. "As do the Bard, Mr. Pope, Mr. Donne. Books, books, and more books."

"I've seen you from time to time," Will said as Georgette settled at Lady Susannah's feet. The dog commenced gnawing on one end of the stick, a habit that would content her by the hour, though she'd stop short of destroying her toy. "The last time was at Almack's. You dance beautifully."

Every time Will saw Lady Susannah turning down the room, he was pleased for her all over again. She had never been an ugly duckling, but she made an impressive swan. When he caught sight of her, he'd find a convenient pillar or palm to shield him from her view. He satisfied himself that she was faring well, and did not intrude on her happiness.

"I dance adequately *now*," she said, turning her face up to the sun. "I was a proper disaster at it as a girl. I've never thanked you for rescuing me."

"Hardly a rescue, my lady." Will had been dragooned by his university acquaintances into accommodating Lady March's demand for young men to partner the girls at her tea dances. These were the practice sessions held for prospective debutantes, the private entertainments that ensured the young ladies had some confidence before facing their first Season.

For Lady Susannah, the result had been quite the opposite of confidence.

"You still don't enjoy dancing, do you?" Will asked.

Her ladyship was risking freckles, enjoying the sun that way. For years, Will had told himself Lady Susannah Haddonfield was a sweet memory from his youth. Then another spring would come around, and he'd find himself leaning against another shadowed pillar as she twirled past with some other fellow.

She looked in want of something. A favorite toy, or…kisses, perhaps.

"I enjoyed dancing with *you*, Mr. Dorning."

Her eyes were closed, her expression serene. If she'd been a dog, a cat, a horse, or even a bird, Will might have gathered insights from her posture, her expression, her attitude, her breathing. She wasn't a dog, and neither was he, but the only conclusion thumping through his male brain was, "Yes, kisses. Lots of kisses."

He'd been away from Dorset too long.

"I'm expecting the Duke of Quimbey to come by directly," Will said, a reminder to himself, a warning to the lady if she wanted to put her bonnet back on.

Lady Susannah retrieved her book from under her bonnet by feel, her eyes remaining closed.

"You have an assignation in the park with a wealthy duke? You intrigue me, Mr. Dorning."

Will Dorning intrigued nobody, nor had he any aspirations to acquire that skill. "I have an assignation with His Grace's dog. The hound is young and rambunctious, not a good pet for an older fellow who hasn't owned a dog before. Quimbey's brother gave him the dog, a final gift before the brother's death, so Quimbey's determined to keep it."

"My father always had dogs," Lady Susannah said, opening her eyes and casting a glance at Georgette. "Muddy, smelly creatures. Not like Georgette."

Georgette paused in her gnawing long enough to toss Lady Susannah an adoring look.

Will slipped his pet a nibble of cheese. "Dogs needn't be smelly or muddy any more than little boys do. Perhaps you enjoy cats?"

They'd never discussed pets before. Why was that?

"Cats sit staring at one, their expression rife with condescension. Then they lick themselves in certain locations, and one must pretend not to notice, though how can one ignore *that*?"

She had liked cats, years ago. Had had a tom named Aquinas.

"What about birds?" Will asked. "Surely you can't take exception to creatures both pretty and musical?"

Lady Susannah peered at Will, her expression bewildered and grim around the edges.

"Surely, Mr. Dorning, you do not expect me to approve of birds, intended by God to soar across the heavens, but instead caged for our entertainment?"

Maybe this was why Will hadn't approached Lady Susannah, because she wasn't the sweet, shy creature he'd waltzed around Lady March's garden, and never would be again. Neither was he the young fool who'd waltzed with her.

"Not all birds are trapped in gilded cages, my lady." And not all earl's sons were forced to bide in London for months at a time. "Yonder robin looks happy enough."

Opera dancers looked happy too, though Will knew their lives were difficult and exhausting.

"I aspire to be like that robin," her ladyship said as the bird flitted from one branch of the maple to another. "Plain, unnoticed, cheerfully obscure in my high, leafy bower. I'll surround myself with books, and nobody will notice me."

At sixteen, Lady Susannah had been intimidated by London, but determined to take her rightful place among the other debutantes.

She was still determined, but determined to hide.

"Has someone tried to cage you up, my lady?" This close, Will could detect a slight redness to her eyes, a weariness. "Have the gossips been unkind?" Unkind again. The little debutantes and their mamas had torn Lady Susannah Haddonfield to shreds simply for sport, a pack of rogue bitches roaming without supervision.

He'd intervened on principle.

Lady Susannah patted Will's hand, her fingers cool against his knuckles. "I've missed you, Will Dorning, missed your gallantry. I no longer cry, but I read late into the night. My eyes reflect an excess of Shakespeare, not an excess of sentiment."

Her ladyship's touch was extraordinary, in part for being unexpected. She wore no gloves, probably the better to turn pages, but neither did she hurry her caress to his knuckles. Her fingers rested on the back of Will's hand, soft, gentle, breathtaking in their daring.

Animals learned one command after another, all simply to earn a pat on the back or a scratch between the shoulders. For an instant, Will understood why, understood the peace and pleasure that a simple, gentle touch could engender. Everything came right inside him for a moment, because Susannah Haddonfield had offered him a single caress.

Will turned his hand over and closed his fingers around Lady Susannah's, the gesture pure, baffling instinct.

"You don't cry, my lady, but do you laugh?"

"There you are, Mr. Dorning!" called a cheerful male voice.

Georgette left off chewing her stick, Lady Susannah slid her hand from Will's, and the Duke of Quimbey's dog yelped in greeting.

"Stay, Georgette." Will rose and put a hand on Susannah's shoulder. "Guard."

Georgette excelled at guarding. Her fixed position and calm would set a good example for Quimbey's youngster—and encourage Lady Susannah to remain on the shady bench, while Will paced off to search for his wits.

Also to greet the duke.

The pup capered about on the end of its leash, tail wagging madly. When a half-grown mastiff capered, elderly dukes were in danger of toppling to the grass, so Will took the leash from Quimbey.

"Good day, Your Grace. Comus, down." Will signaled the dog, lowering his hand, palm toward the earth.

The dog sat, a good try for a young fellow.

"You're close," Will said, petting the dog once with the hand Lady Susannah hadn't touched. "Try again. Comus, down."

Quimbey remained quiet while Comus cocked his big head, his expression suggesting he was trying to puzzle out what a fellow had to do around here to get a bite of cheese.

"Comus, down," Will said again, repeating the hand signal. One paw stretched forward as if the dog might be considering a lie down in the grass. "Good boy."

Down he went.

"You praise him, Your Grace," Will said, passing the duke a piece of cheese. "Tell him what a good, smart, clever fellow he is."

"He's a big, strong, energetic fellow." Quimbey patted the dog's head and dropped the cheese between enormous paws. "He's always a saint for you, Dorning, while for me, he's deaf, rambunctious, and stupid, rather like half the young men in London. I say, is that your Georgette keeping the young lady company?"

"Georgette is with Lady Susannah Haddonfield, Your Grace. A friend of long-standing."

Quimbey was a bachelor, universally liked, and more shrewd than he let on. When he died, a nephew would inherit the dukedom, unless a young bride caught the duke's eye and presented him with a son. Nearly a half century of debutantes had tried, and so far, Quimbey had remained charmingly impervious.

"I knew Lady Susannah's parents," Quimbey said. "The present earl seems a fine man. Too smart to acquire any unruly puppies."

Comus, who had been sprawled in the grass, rolled over to expose his belly. His tongue lolled, and his tail wagged even in that undignified posture.

"Comus is a happy fellow, Your Grace, and he likes you." Will liked the duke too, as did Georgette, and Georgette's assessment of character was faultless.

"Let's greet the young lady," His Grace said, tugging gently on Comus's leash. "Comus, heel."

After three tries, with Will reminding the duke to stride off as if he *expected* the dog to come along, Comus eventually recalled this command as well.

Lady Susannah rose and curtsied to the duke, with whom she was apparently acquainted. Comus and Georgette touched noses, for they were acquainted as well.

What would touching noses with Lady Susannah be like?

"I'll leave you gentlemen to your canine dame school," Lady Susannah said, gathering up her bonnet and plunking it on her head a few minutes later. Her tone suggested Lady Della and the viscount would not be an improvement over present company.

"A moment, my lady." Will repositioned the bonnet and tied the ribbons in a bow. "A pleasure to see you, Lady Susannah, and we will definitely be calling upon you."

We, meaning Ash and Cam, who needed to work on their manners, and Casriel, who needed to acquire a wife. Will's role would be supervisory.

Mostly.

"Good day, Your Grace. Mr. Dorning." Her ladyship curtsied prettily, kissed Will's cheek, and strode off.

Kissed his cheek, in public, out-of-doors, with a damned smirking duke and two dogs looking on. Then her ladyship disappeared down the path, not so much as a bush rustling in her wake.

"Down, Mr. Dorning," His Grace said. "A handy command to know in many circumstances."

Georgette woofed and Comus resumed trying to pull the duke off his feet. Will helped himself to a nibble of cheese and thanked God grown men were not, in most circumstances, afflicted with visibly wagging tails.

Three

Susannah wanted to run, to whoop and leap and yodel for joy.

She'd surprised The Honorable Mr. Willow Dorning, had caught him off guard, and left him smiling faintly in the shade of the maples, a duke and two dogs looking on. Will was devastatingly attractive when he smiled. She'd forgotten that about him.

When he smiled, all the affection in his nature bloomed in his gaze, and for a moment, he exuded such warmth of heart as not even the Bard could have adequately described.

"Well done," Susannah assured herself. Will Dorning had given her flowers after all, and in public. He'd called upon her at home, he'd laced his fingers with hers, and, oh, the park was indeed a lovely place.

Not that she had designs on Mr. Dorning, of course, though he *was* an old and dear friend, and his brother *had* taken notice of Della.

And that business with Susannah's plainest, oldest bonnet, while Quimbey had stood by, petting his dog and looking bemused.

Will Dorning had taken Susannah in hand so…so…
matter-of-factly, repositioning her hat gently, tipping
it back an inch to reveal her face and tying the ribbons
off in a jaunty side-bow. He'd simply put her to rights,
and affection for him, for a man who'd *see* Susannah
Haddonfield, had inspired her kiss.

Life was so lovely.

Susannah rounded a stand of lilacs past their prime,
and all her joy dimmed. Viscount Effington was standing too close to Della by half, his golden male beauty
a contrast to Della's darker coloring.

Effington held his little dog wedged between them.
Yorick always looked uncertain, but his expression
was…alarmed, and too frightened to let it show.

Georgette never wore a worried expression, though
Will Dorning didn't fuss and coo over his dog as
Effington did Yorick.

"Della, I thought you'd gone home without me,"
Susannah said, affecting great good cheer. "We'll be
late for our midday meal if we tarry much longer,
and I'm sure his lordship has a busy afternoon ahead.
Where could Jeffers have got off to?"

Effington stepped back from Della, slowly. He
was making a point of some sort, a nasty point.
Susannah was reminded of the Mannering twins,
who'd filled her first forays into Polite Society
with gracious, public assaults. Their voices echoed
in memory as gratingly as if they'd attended last
night's musicale.

"That ensemble disguises nearly all of your height,
my lady!"

"How clever, to let your blue eyes and blond hair

be the plain, ordinary attributes they are. Nobody else would be so daring."

"It's not that Lady Susannah has no conversation, you see, it's that she hopes her silences will make her more mysterious than witty rejoinders ever could. An intriguing strategy."

Their cruelty had been so unexpected, Susannah at first hadn't realized she was being ridiculed. Her older sisters, Nita and Kirsten, had explained the realities to her, though they had been helpless to intervene when Lady Mannering herself was apparently encouraging the twins.

Will Dorning had intervened.

"I suppose the maid is off making eyes at some footman," Effington said, stroking Yorick's head. "We will doubtless find her, cap askew, waiting at the park's entrance with a besotted smile on her face. Come, my lady. Never let it be said I kept you from your victuals."

He set the dog down, and laced his arm through Della's while Susannah resisted the urge to tug her bonnet forward.

"Will you be at the Darlington ball tonight, my lord?" Della asked as they wandered toward Park Lane. "Lady Darlington is said to have an excellent orchestra, and I've been given permission to waltz, you know."

A lure, an invitation for Effington to beg a spot on Della's dance card.

Susannah dropped back rather than listen to Effington's reply. Yorick, also trailing behind the couple, was trying to both lift his little leg on the pansies bordering the path, and hop along to keep up with Effington. The dog's efforts might have been amusing, had the result not been for the dog to essentially wet himself.

"Yorick, come along," Effington said, hauling on the leash. "Lady Susannah has expressed concern over our tardiness."

Effington could not have seen Yorick behind him, but that tug on the leash jerked the dog right off his stubby legs.

"I'll take Yorick," Susannah said, appropriating the leash from Effington.

Della untangled her arm from his lordship's. "Suze, you don't care for dogs. I'll take Yorick."

"Nonsense. Yorick and I will manage well enough."

Effington placed Della's hand back on his arm. "Far be it from me to deny a lady the pleasure of the company she prefers. Yorick is a very well-behaved and friendly fellow, much like his owner."

The viscount sauntered off with Della, while Susannah gave Yorick a moment to heed nature's call. He was an ugly, fretful, smelly little dog, but Susannah could not abide Effington's casual disregard for the pet he claimed to love.

❧

"Something isn't right," Will said softly, so that under the hum and bustle of the Darlington ballroom, only Ash would hear him.

"You're right. The hour approaches midnight and I'm not yet drunk, a sure sign the End Times are upon us." Ash snagged a glass of champagne from a passing footman. "As the Season drags on, my tolerance goes up. I suspect Cam can already outdrink me, though."

A dozen yards away, under the minstrel's gallery, Lady Susannah and Lady Della appeared to be chatting gaily with each other.

Very gaily.

"Sycamore is in his gin phase," Will said. "Drinking blue ruin to feel sophisticated, tough, and wicked. He'll tire of it in approximately three weeks and become a wine connoisseur for the remainder of the Season. That's not what I meant."

Ash passed Will the full glass. "You're not drinking, and that's sheer folly. This is a ball, which means free champagne for the bachelors, and I haven't seen you touch a drop. Casriel was last seen on the terrace in discussion with the Earl of Bellefonte, who, being both enormously tall and enormously blond, is hard to miss. Cam was smoking on the terrace steps, so Casriel will keep an eye on him."

Brothers present and accounted for, true enough, and yet the hair on Will's nape prickled disagreeably.

"Many of the ladies are smirking behind their fans," he said, "and everybody is casting glances at the Haddonfield sisters, but nobody is approaching them." *This again.* Next they'd be accidentally tramping on Lady Susannah's hems and apologizing for their clumsiness, even as they also spilled punch on the back of her skirt.

Ash took back the glass and sipped. "Scandal afoot, d'ya think? Suppose that's the other reliable commodity at balls. That and dancing. Sounds like a waltz coming next, and about time."

Lady Susannah had held the same glass of punch for five minutes without taking a sip. Lady Della had drained her glass too quickly, and she was tapping her foot, but not in time to the orchestra tuning up in the corner.

"Does Lady Della waltz yet?" Will asked, though even as he raised the question, he knew the answer. She was an earl's daughter and pretty. The patronesses would have already given her permission to waltz in hopes of getting her married off, so the less titled or less lovely would have a clearer field.

Ash peered at Will owlishly. "You're asking about Lady Della? I thought you fancied the older one, Lady Susan."

"Lady Susannah, and she's merely a friend." A friend who had kissed Will in the park. He'd come to a decision regarding what to do about that folly if the lady made further advances. "Somebody needs to waltz with Lady Della." How Will knew this, he could not say, but he was prodded by the same instinct that told him when Casriel's hounds were about to turn on one of their own.

"You waltz competently," Ash said. "Might do you good and she's a lovely little creature. Now why is Trudy Mannering twittering near the men's punch bowl and glancing at the Haddonfield ladies? Never a good sign, when a Mannering female gets to twittering."

"I cannot waltz with Lady Della," Will replied. "I'm the spare. Casriel should be leading her out, dammit." A perfect opportunity to be the gallant knight, and his earl-ship was off discussing foot rot or Corn Laws. Gentlemen were bowing before their partners, couples were taking places on the dance floor.

"You just swore," Ash marveled. "You swore and Cam wasn't here to gloat. This is what happens when people schedule their social occasions for the full moon. Sheer folly. Nothing for it, then, but I must leap into the affray."

Ash pushed his now-empty champagne glass at Will, shot his cuffs, ran a hand through flowing dark locks and sauntered across the ballroom. He fixed a blazing smile on Lady Della in a manner sure to draw attention.

When Ash Dorning focused on an objective, he made a good job of it. He'd be a fine solicitor, perhaps even a barrister. Ash bowed over the lady's hand and led her out, leaving Lady Susannah looking relieved and tired.

The compulsion to go to her, to lead her out—to ask her why she'd kissed him—had Will's feet moving in her direction.

"There's been another one," said a voice to Will's left. An acrid whiff of smoke came off Cam's clothes, and his excitement was palpable. "Just today, another one taken. Hendershot was gabbling about it." Cam wasn't drunk yet either, but he was in a lather about something—though a lather was Sycamore's natural state.

"Sycamore, calm yourself," Will said, in the same tones he'd used on an excited puppy. "Another what?"

"Another dog, this time stolen from the dowager Duchess of Ambrose. Poor old dear is distraught, and that's why she's not here tonight."

Will took Cam by the arm and steered him back out onto the terrace. "Firstly, arrange your features as if you were discussing Greymoor's new stud colt; and secondly, how did you hear of the duchess's misfortune?"

"Who's Greymoor?"

God save me from half-witted younger siblings. "Greymoor is an earl of our brother's acquaintance, one who had the sense to marry several years ago. The example has yet to bear fruit with Casriel, but I cling stubbornly to hope. Tell me about the missing dog, Sycamore."

Dogs went missing all the time in London. They ran loose in the streets, congregated in alleys, and could menace foot traffic in the meaner neighborhoods. They also kept the rat population down, and Will suspected dogs were hunted in their turn in the rookeries.

"Her Grace was devoted to the brute," Cam said. "Rather like you and Georgette, apparently. She talked to the dog, kept it in her bedroom on stormy nights, took it with her everywhere."

Will did not talk to his dog. Very much.

He led Cam across the terrace, in the direction of the torch-lit garden. "This was a large dog?"

"Mastiff, like Georgette, and very protective of the duchess. That's the second one this month, Will. The second big dog to go missing from a fancy household, and nobody has seen a sign of either of 'em."

This was not good, not good at all. Sycamore's determination rivaled that of a bloodhound, and made Ash look like a puppy with an old shoe by comparison.

"Sycamore, dogs run off. They chase rabbits, rats, and cats. They run out in front of coaches, and if somebody inadvertently killed a duchess's dog, he'd keep that to himself." Dogs also fell in love, or their version of it, and no amount of training prevailed against that biological imperative.

Though two large dogs from wealthy households was enough of a coincidence to make Will uneasy for the dogs as well as for his brother.

"Is this why you attend the bear-baitings?" Will asked when they'd moved out of earshot of the terrace. "You think you'll find the missing dogs in the pits?"

Cam tossed himself onto a bench near a blooming hedge of honeysuckle. By torchlight he looked about eleven years old, too young for the violence and gore of a bear-baiting.

"You're not supposed to know about that," Cam said. "I wasn't looking for missing dogs, though. Did Ash peach on me?"

Will came down beside his brother as the strains of the waltz wafted from the ballroom.

He should have asked Lady Susannah to dance with him once Lady Della's plight had been addressed. That would have given him a chance to ask her why she'd kissed him, and then invite her for a stroll in the dark, fragrant garden. In private, he'd explain to her that calling a man an old friend one minute and kissing him the next rather muddled a fellow.

Muddled him to the point where *he* was thinking about kissing *her*, which would not do.

"Willow, if you're trying to flagellate me with your disappointed silence," Cam said, "it's working quite well. I only went to the bear garden twice."

And yet Will's disappointment was infinite. "Did you learn anything?"

"I don't recall much, to tell you the truth. Had a bit to drink before. Bear-baiting is legal," Cam said, taking out a gold case and extracting a cheroot. He rose to use a torch to light his smoke, then leaned against the lamppost. He smoked not with the restless self-consciousness of a youth attempting adult vices, but with the careless grace of the experienced devotee. Now he looked not eleven years old, but a man full grown, and then some.

He really should be at university.

"Bear-baiting is legal," Will said, "so is wife beating and selling your children into bondage. So are opium dens, so is prostitution."

Cam studied his cheroot, the smoke wafting around him in the shadows. "Why do they go, Will? Why do the crowds go week after week, to see the same bear chained by the same back leg, the same dogs hectoring him? The dogs tear at the bear, the bear bites and claws the dogs, a great mess is made, and much suffering endured on the part of the poor beasts, over and over, until death do them part. I don't understand it."

Thank God. "Why do you think the crowds go, Cam?"

Cam took a long, thoughtful draught on his smoke. "To be more horrified at the fate of the animals than at their own lives? To see somebody who has it worse than they do? I don't know. A lot of the crowd is swells and cits, Will. They aren't living brutal lives. Queen Elizabeth liked a good, gory bear-baiting. The cockfights are just as bad."

"Bear-baiting is worse," Will said. "The cock who won't fight or doesn't fight well is gifted with a summary execution, not staked in the pit over and over. You know your Roman history?"

Cam's cheroot was growing short. He tapped the ash off, the movement competent and graceful.

"Bread and circuses?" Cam asked, taking another drag. "That's for the masses, Will. What is a duke's heir doing at a bear-baiting? A German prince and his cronies? Members of Parliament? Puking drunk and howling with mirth at a tormented bear, the lot of them."

Cam dropped the last of the cheroot and stubbed it out with his toe, then slouched against the lamppost. His posture signaled disillusionment and bewilderment, necessary acquisitions on the road to maturity.

"I don't understand the appeal of violence as entertainment, either," Will said. "Papa took me to a bear-baiting when I was twelve. I left in tears, walked seven miles home in a howling rain, and wouldn't talk to him for weeks. I never respected him quite as much after that."

"Yes," Cam said, straightening. "I can't respect it, but the fellows think it's quite the crack. Can't wait to go, must sit right up front."

Oxford had no bear gardens, not in the literal sense. "Next time somebody wants to attend a bear-baiting or a cockfight, Cam, you tell them a lady waits for you whom you're loath to disappoint. Tell them her company is preferable to a pathetic old bear, a pack of mangy curs, or a lot of drunken boys."

Cam pushed away from the lamppost. "You'd lie to your mates?"

Will rose, because the waltz had ended, and the conversation with Cam would take years to conclude. At least they'd made a start.

"I wouldn't be lying, and they wouldn't be my mates. Georgette is a lady, and I prefer her company to most anybody else's. Let's find Casriel and lecture him about his duty to the wallflowers, shall we?"

"Yes, let's," Cam said. "Casriel has been sorely remiss, and sets a poor example for my impressionable self. Hasn't danced yet this evening, or introduced me to any lonely widows, or even scolded me for over-imbibing."

Will shook Cam by the scruff of the neck and shoved him toward the terrace steps, though he'd really rather have hugged him.

⁓

"Della, I think you've found the best dancer among the Dorning menfolk," Nicholas said. "Perhaps you'd introduce us?"

Nick's question bore all the geniality of a French firing squad taking aim, but only some of his ire would be directed at Mr. Ash Dorning. The rest, Susannah knew, was for her—for letting Della waltz with a man whom Nicholas, as Earl of Bellefonte and head of the family, had not inspected, interrogated, and investigated.

To Ash Dorning's credit, his smile remained in place, his manner relaxed and sociable.

"Please do introduce us, Lady Della, that I might offer your family my compliments on your faultless waltzing."

Blather, but charming blather. The knot in Susannah's belly eased a fraction.

"I'll do the honors," she said, launching into the civilities. By the time she'd finished, the Earl of Casriel had joined the group, and where Casriel went…yes.

Willow Dorning lurked two paces away with the

other brother, Sycamore, at his side. Sycamore was young enough to have an element of beauty about his features, of refinement and innocence. He'd shave more out of vanity than necessity most days, and his prettiness might not ever blossom into handsomeness.

While Willow Dorning had sauntered past mere handsomeness years ago.

After further introductions, it was decided that the Haddonfield party and the Dorning party would walk home as a group, neither having brought a carriage for the evening. At the appropriate hour, good nights were offered to the host and hostess, dancing pumps exchanged for sturdier footwear, and wraps assembled.

By sheerest coincidence, Casriel offered his arm to Nicholas's countess, Leah. Della positioned herself between Cam and Ash Dorning, and Susannah was left to bring up the rear with Will.

Two brawny footmen from the Haddonfield household carried lanterns. The moon was full, and yet Susannah had a pleasant sense of sharing the darkness with her escort.

"Thanks seem to be in order again," she said as the larger party moved ahead down the Darlingtons' front steps. "I was growing frantic for Della. Once she waltzed with your brother, her card filled for the remainder of the evening."

Susannah walked arm in arm with Will, his gloved hand resting over Susannah's knuckles.

"Perhaps word of Lady Della's availability for waltzes hadn't reached the ears of the Eligibles yet," Will said. "She's a fine dancer, though. She'll be thronged at her next ball, I'm sure."

Will would do what he could for Della, in other words. Earlier in the evening, Nicholas had fumed and fretted and told Susannah she was imagining things, while Willow Dorning—without a word of discussion—had sent a dashing brother to the rescue.

"I hate London," Susannah said as laughter burst from the group ahead of them. "Hate the meanness of it, the hypocrisy, and pettiness. I almost think a woman is better off finding a husband anywhere else besides this social menagerie, where the animals turn on each other out of sheer boredom."

Her escort remained silent. Willow's silences were of geological proportions. Vast quantities of thought, regard, irony, disappointment, or consideration could weigh upon the moments when he said nothing.

"About the husband hunting, my lady."

"Wife hunting too," Susannah said, warming to the topic. "What woman shows to her best advantage when she's trying to dodge the Mannering twins' malice, or some aging baron's wandering hands? When she must sip the punch to be polite even though somebody has doctored her drink in aid of making a great fool of her in public?"

"They failed," Will said gently. "Nobody made a fool of you, though some poor fern probably had a bad few weeks when you dumped out your drink. Are you hunting a husband, then?"

Susannah had dumped her drink all those years ago at Lady March's tea dance because Will had taken a single, discreet sip and told her to. He'd tested all of her drinks after that.

"I am hunting for a husband," Susannah said. "One

good man. He doesn't have to be wealthy or hand-some, simply good and solvent, and his regard for his wife must be beyond question. Good birth would be nice, but even that isn't—what?"

Will had stopped walking. "I cannot be that man, my lady, not even for you. I'm sorry. I have respon-sibilities, duties, myriad obligations, and precious little coin with which to meet them. I esteem you greatly, but honor requires that the truth be aired sooner rather than later, however much it pains me. Make no designs upon my future, for I hardly make any myself."

In the moonlight, Willow Dorning had the qual-ity of a declaiming marble Apollo, and his voice was beautiful. Logical, balanced, articulate, and sincere, as if he'd rehearsed these sentiments like a speech.

"Mr. Dorning, what are you going on about?" Susannah injected amusement into her question, though she knew *exactly* what he was going on about. The Mannering twins could not have dealt Susannah a more stunning blow had they torn her ball gown from her very body.

"I cannot marry you." At least he had the decency to sound regretful. "I've considered the situation. Given it a great deal of thought, and while your charms are considerable, my means are not. You're an earl's daughter, and I'm...I'm very likely to end up as my brother's steward."

Only if Susannah let him live beyond this night.

"Mr. Dorning, I do not recall proposing to you." Susannah resumed walking, for the rest of the party was about to turn a corner, and the only safety on the streets of London at night lay in numbers.

"You kissed me," Will said, lacing his arm through Susannah's. "You called me an old friend, and you are looking for a husband. Have you kissed other old friends, my lady?"

No, Susannah had not, simply because she had no other old friends. Indignation threatened to become humiliation.

"Mr. Dorning, do you kiss your dog?"

"Georgette? What has she to do with anything?"

"Do you kiss your dog, sir?" Where was Susannah's dratted purple parasol when a man needed sense smacked into his handsome head?

They reached the corner before Will answered. "I have. Rarely. Georgette is not a demonstrative creature."

Bother the perishing dog. "Shall you propose to her, then? Does a friendly kiss signal addresses must follow? If so, I can assure you Lord Effington is about to plight his troth with any number of spaniels and at least one malodorous pug. My sister doesn't stand a chance. Perhaps His Grace the Duke of Quimbey harbors a *tendresse* for that exuberant mastiff, and Nicholas has given his heart to his mare."

Susannah slowed her pace, lest she catch up to the larger group.

"So you were not..." Mr. Dorning said. "That is, this husband you're looking for, he's—I beg your pardon, my lady. I have apparently misconstrued matters."

Susannah experimented with silence for about half a block, but she could not outlast Will Dorning's reserve. He had not misconstrued anything. She'd kissed him in the first act of hope she'd permitted her heart in years.

Also, apparently, the last. She hadn't gone so far as to *make designs on his future*, but the ache in her chest assured her she'd strayed past casual gestures onto the boggy ground of maidenly hopes.

"The husband I seek is *for my sister*, Mr. Dorning. My instincts when it comes to social ill will are not to be trusted, for my own experience skews my perspective, but Della's dance card has typically filled before the orchestra opens their violin cases. Tonight, she danced only three times before you intervened. I must see her married. I owe it to her."

"You suspect somebody wishes her ill?"

Will did not dismiss Susannah's fears out of hand, and he never had. He never would, and he would never return her kiss, either, apparently.

Rot this stupid evening.

"I suspect Della is about to be treated to the same polite cruelty I was," Susannah said. "Perhaps the same vile women are resuming the game with a different Haddonfield sister. Della is vulnerable, though."

Susannah ought not to have said that, but Will Dorning's discretion was as formidable as his silences.

"We all have weaknesses," he said. "Her lady-ship has strengths as well. She's comely, intelligent, graceful, witty. Compared to any number of young women, she's impressive."

"Compared to any number of *other* young women, she's plain, penniless, and—I suppose you'll hear it soon enough—from irregular antecedents."

Mr. Dorning's stride did not falter in the slight-est, and his hand remained relaxed over Susannah's knuckles, for which she could have kissed him all

over again—when she was through smacking him
with her parasol.

"Half the younger sons in that ballroom are similarly situated," Mr. Dorning scoffed. "My brother
Hawthorne is too. Sycamore and Valerian are proof
Papa and his countess moved beyond her ladyship's mis-
step, or perhaps beyond my father's neglect of his wife."

Will's words were a comfort, because his brother's
situation was not common knowledge—Susannah
would have heard of it—and thus a confidence
exchanged between friends.

"I am frantic for my sister. I can't bear that anybody
would hurt her, much less for something completely
beyond her control."

"As you were hurt, merely for the entertainment of
nasty young women and their nasty mamas."

The Haddonfield town house lay ahead, and yet
Susannah longed to walk farther in the company of the
man she'd never kiss again.

"My family doesn't know much about the circum-
stance surrounding my come-out," she said. Only
Will Dorning knew, because he'd been too decent to
ignore a girl crying in Lady March's garden. He had
passed Susannah his handkerchief, along with a stout
dose of courage, and a plan for enduring the remaining
tea dances with her dignity intact.

"Your family doesn't know what happened, but
you will never forget. Cruelty changes us."

Will stopped again, this time in the shadow of a
leafy maple. A hackney jingled past, and Susannah
wished he'd lend her his handkerchief again.

"If I had means," he said, "if I had fewer

responsibilities, if I had more time, if I had resources sufficient to support an earl's daughter…I might tempt you into considering a husband for yourself. But I do not. I have only my friendship to offer you, my lady, and the hope that you will forgive a friend the limitations of his circumstances."

A beautiful speech, a speech to break a woman's heart, if she let it.

"Thank you, Mr. Dorning, and good night."

Susannah would have marched off to join the larger group, but Will's hand on her arm stayed her. He took off his hat, kissed her gently on the mouth, then walked away into the darkness without another word.

Four

"Kettering, Andromeda is not your wife, that you should pet her and coo at her every instant." Will kept his tone friendly, lest Andromeda, a sensitive soul, think his impatience was directed at her rather than at his brother-in-law.

"But I want my dog to delight in my presence," Kettering replied, stroking Andromeda's head. "Not to the extent Jacaranda does, of course, but a man should be a delight to his dog, don't you think?"

No creature on earth could delight in Sir Worth Kettering to the extent Jacaranda Dorning Kettering did. Will's sister was smitten, besotted, top-over-tail, and in love with her dark-haired husband. Kettering's regard for Jacaranda regularly veered past all of those excesses into public adoration, at least in part for the pure joy of embarrassing Jacaranda's brothers.

"Think of it this way," Will said, dropping into a wrought iron chair on Kettering's shady back terrace. "If you randomly praised your clerks during business hours, for work done well, done poorly, barely done at all, or not even undertaken, what would happen?"

Kettering folded himself into another chair, the dog putting two paws on his knees as if to hop into his lap. She was a full-blooded Alsatian, one Will had coaxed from hiding in the mews one winter morning. Though she'd been starving, bleeding, and wretched, she'd allowed Will to tend her wounds and befriend her.

A creature of such courage and discernment deserved a second chance.

"If I handed out random praise, the clerks would think I'd finally gone daft," Kettering said, scratching the dog's ear. She was particularly fond of having her right ear scratched, but Kettering fondled the left. Though her tail was wagging, the dog kept moving her head to encourage Kettering to attend the other ear.

Will's patience, usually abundant, had lately been in short supply.

"Kettering, when you scratch her ears like that, even the wrong ear, you're telling her she's a good girl for trying to climb into your lap. She's nearly ten stone of teeth and claws, and not everybody will take her friendliness in the right light."

Andromeda had nearly reached her ideal weight, though she was only a few months into her recovery. Kettering cared for the dog with the enthusiasm of a boy, not the affection of a mature man taking responsibility for his dependents.

"Down," Kettering said to the dog, finally using the hand signal. "The archbishop says I'm corrupting your morals, my dear."

The dog, who'd probably been the head of her pack, removed her paws from Kettering's lap.

Will waited. One… Two…Three… Four… Five.

Hopeless. Kettering had something on his mind today, and no amount of figurative cheese would keep him focused on his pet.

"Kettering, if one of your clerks did a brilliant job, and you ignored his efforts…"

"Good girl," Kettering said. "Exactly right, Meda. Now can you sit?"

He forgot the hand signal, but she sat because she *was* a good girl, also patient and devoted to her charge. Kettering stroked the right ear.

"Now tell her *all done.*" Because Will's patience with his usually brilliant brother-in-law was *all gone*.

"I'm out of cheese," Kettering said, lounging back.

His terrace was a profusion of potted pansies, salvia, ferns, and lavender. Lady Susannah would love to read away a morning here. A hammock would be a perfect addition, and for her, a lap cat.

Will surrendered a morsel of cheese, though the moment had passed for teaching the dog a connection between her good behavior and her reward. She should have been given the *all done* signal before her master had settled on the terrace.

Kettering's schooling yet continued, however.

Kettering fed the dog her treat, stroking her head. "Well done, Meda. We'll be ready for the park soon, and then won't Jacaranda be proud of us?"

Will was not proud of himself. Last night, he'd delivered his stirring, correct speech to Lady Susannah, the oration that ensured she'd develop no marital designs on him. He'd thought himself very gentlemanly, to spare the lady embarrassment, when all he could think about was kissing her witless.

He, trainer to the Regent's puppies, had got the situation all wrong. Responded to the wrong command, read the signal incorrectly. Will had earned no treats for his honorable efforts. Lady Susannah's set-down had been a rolled-up newspaper smacked across the nose of his conceit. Cam and Ash would have howled themselves to flinders if they'd known.

Though Will felt rotten for having presumed to reject a woman who'd been rejected enough. If he'd had a tail, he would have tucked it between his legs.

"How are the other dogs doing?" Kettering asked when Andromeda lay panting at their feet.

"Comus is coming along. Had I known Lord Harold would suffer an apoplexy, I'd have placed the dog elsewhere. Quimbey understands leadership, though, and has a reluctant affection for his late brother's dog. They'll manage."

"Quimbey is a puzzle," Kettering said, snapping off a sprig of lavender and twirling it under his nose. He had a good nose, worthy of a Dorning even. Jacaranda was similarly endowed, and Will had wondered what their puppies—God help him—*their children* would look like. One child had recently arrived, with a darling baby nose and blue, blue eyes Kettering claimed were his contribution to the equation.

"Quimbey is a genial, wealthy duke," Will said. "He can be any damned thing he wants to be given those particulars."

Kettering brushed the lavender with his fingers, then held it down for Meda to sniff.

"You could have offered to take the dog back, Will, to find another home for it, but you knew the old boy would be lonely. You gave him a young, rambunctious dog when he was grieving for his only brother."

Kettering could be very attentive when motivated. His courtship of Jacaranda had been a blazing display of focus, though Will was uncomfortable being the object of Sir Worth's notice.

"I found a patient, even-tempered owner for a young dog who'd known much hardship," Will said. "Of the four of them, Comus was in the worst physical shape, but he's resilient and fair-minded by nature."

The poor brute had likely been beaten for the hell of it in an effort to teach him who was the superior species. Will had learned not to swear and curse, for it upset his dogs, but after Comus's wounds had been tended to, Will had taken Georgette out for two straight hours of fetch the stick.

"What about Hector?" Kettering asked. He rolled the lavender between his palms, then crushed it to dust and brushed his hands together. The terrace was perfumed accordingly, a soothing scent that put Will in mind of Lady Susannah.

"Hector will take a special owner," Will said, though every dog required a special owner, for every dog was special. "Somebody with a tender heart, who's fierce when the moment calls for it. His own man, but willing to laugh, even at himself."

Kettering propped his boots on the low table before them and crossed his ankles. He was like a long, lean purebred hunting dog who had the knack of looking elegant and appropriate wherever he was and whatever mood he was in. Jacaranda had chosen well.

Or Kettering and Jacaranda had.

"What about the fourth one?" Kettering asked. "I forget his name. Something heroic. Am I allowed to pet my dog now?"

"Yes, you may pet your dog. It's like business hours, Kettering. If you accosted your clerks at their breakfasts with some pressing memorandum, then failed to discuss business with them all morning, but talked only about the weather at your business meetings, you'd have very confused clerks." Will suspected Kettering did have frequently confused clerks, but they were loyal and hardworking too. "Meda needs to know when the training session starts and when it stops."

"Right," Kettering said. "When I wear my old plaid waistcoat, we're to learn doggy tricks. Always in the morning, always after our doggy prayers among the hapless bushes. Next you'll have poor Meda reciting vespers, matins, and lauds."

"Next, we'll have Meda behaving like a perfect lady in the park, despite all temptation to the contrary. Recall your own efforts to learn decorum, Kettering. The project wanted time and considerable effort, and has yet to reach its conclusion, though you're an exponent of a supposedly intelligent species."

As was Will, when not fuddled by Lady Susannah's kisses. He wished he'd kissed her back properly, not a mere gesture of apology and regret in the moonlight.

"What was the fourth dog's name?" Kettering asked. "It will bother me, like a snippet of Handel I can't place."

"Samson. He's coming along."

"Which suggests he went after the stable boys this very morning. Do you never give up on a dog, Willow?"

Not the stable boys, because Will allowed nobody but himself to handle Samson. He was not a pack leader by nature, but Meda had been weakening, and Samson had been distraught. He had not been treated as badly as Comus, but he was a mongrel, unsure of his place in the world, and easily upset.

The four of them—Meda, Comus, Hector, and Samson—had skulked about the Dorning mews for a week, rooting through the midden, terrorizing the cats, and scaring away even the birds. Ash and Cam had come upon one of the stable boys loading a pistol and fetched Will to intervene.

"Do you give up on a slow clerk?" Will asked. "A client who can't manage his money? If your son turns out to be backward at his Latin, will you turn him loose on the docks to fend for himself?"

"I have given up on clerks," Kettering replied. "A few. Not many. I mostly separate goats and sheep before taking anybody on as an employee or client. I can afford to be very choosy, especially now, and no power on earth could coerce me to do business with somebody I thought was crooked."

Kettering's reputation alone, for scrupulous dealings and scrupulous attention to details, was worth a fortune. A rapidly growing, immense-to-begin-with fortune.

"There are no crooked dogs," Will said, because Kettering comprehended business metaphors. "Only dogs we've broken, or dogs beset by illness and pain. The same is true, I believe, of every species we've appropriated for our comfort and well-being."

Will had not made up his mind regarding

humankind's inherent capacity for bad behavior. Crooked, rotten, mean people abounded, though, and woe to any—dog, bear, or debutante—in their paths.

"The stewardship lecture comes now," Kettering said to Meda. "Though I rather think you put me in Meda's keeping, not the other way around. Taking her outside every so often, going for a stroll with her in the evenings, seeing her lounging about the hearth at the office... One can't be quite as..."

Will waited, because Kettering was a smart fellow, and Will had had a strategy when he'd put Meda into Kettering's care.

"One is a happier, healthier person for accepting the companionship of a dog," Kettering said. "One must care for them responsibly, and learn to take pleasure in that. Owning a dog is good training for being a husband and father."

Will was so proud of his brother-in-law, he nearly reached for a bite of cheese. Meda was safe now, and Kettering and his little family were safe too.

"On that pleasant note, I'll take my leave of you until next week," Will said, rising. "Work especially on *that'll do*, on making Meda stop what she's doing and come to you no matter what task you've given her. I'm off to pay a call on the Duchess of Ambrose."

"Poor Annabella is in a state," Kettering said, Her Grace being one of his clients. He took on the affairs of many widows, and if the lady wasn't wealthy when she came to him, she often became wealthy. "She's in a taking over that missing dog."

"I know, which might be why she sent for me."

Kettering got to his feet, and Meda did as well,

remaining by her owner's side. Will always felt a pang to leave one of his dogs with their owners, but leave them he must. Casriel's coffers could not afford any additional strain, and Will's own means were limited.

"Let's go in through the office," Kettering said. "I have your last two quarters' earnings reports, but I keep forgetting to pass them along. Meda, come."

Good. She was training Kettering to give the commands, the word and the signal both. When Will reached the office, he jammed Kettering's reports in a pocket and checked his watch. One was not late to pay a call on an upset duchess, and Will had already done the pretty with his sister.

"The duchess has posted a reward for her missing dog, you know," Kettering said as they ambled toward the mews. "Her Grace is determined to find out what happened to her puppy."

Her puppy had been mean and starving when Will had found him. Her Grace, two years into lonely widowhood, had been in similar condition, though to outward appearances she'd been hale. She could still take a bite out of any who displeased her.

"A reward will bring out all the charlatans and swindlers," Will said. "Every retired coachman will be on her doorstep claiming his three-legged mongrel is her long-lost mastiff. I wish she'd asked me about this first."

"Willow, you can't save them all."

Will stopped by a pot of pansies, snapped off a yellow one, and tucked it into his lapel. He was soon to call on a duchess, after all.

"I can't save them all, and I can't ignore the ones

who need saving most. I know about your opera dancers, Kettering, which is why I entrusted Meda to you. You have many wealthy clients, and I suspect if you put your mind to it, you could find comfortable homes for a lot of deserving dogs."

Will stated his agenda baldly. He was not at all ashamed of his motives. Aristocrats had time, means, and room for canine pets. Wealthy households had assets worth protecting, and most of the wellborn were damned lonely too.

"My opera dancers?" Kettering mused, extracting the pansy from Will's lapel, and choosing another, this one a deep purplish-blue.

"Your opera dancers," Will reiterated. "The ladies whose tiny sums you invest, patiently, relentlessly, as you ensure they understand finances, as you ensure they can do the math necessary to not be cheated. The ladies whom you quietly set to tatting lace during their rehearsals, or doing piecework in their idle moments."

"They're Jacaranda's opera dancers now," Kettering said. "I'm allowed to help, but the project has out-grown my feeble vision for it. Do you ever read your financial statements, Willow?"

Will patted his pockets. He still had a few bites of cheese in the right one, and the reports were in the left.

"I'll read them when I have a free moment. I have a question for you, Kettering."

Kettering brushed a hand over Will's hair, smooth-ing it down. Cam and Ash weren't that familiar with him, though Kettering owned a dog now, and would be more likely to pet all in his ambit.

"You may trust my discretion, Willow."

"When you've bungled matters with a client, with one of your widows, say, how do you repair the damage?"

Kettering took up a lean against the garden wall. "I don't bungle matters, not financial matters."

He looked comfortable, elbow propped against the granite, pansies at his shoulder.

"What about other matters, Kettering? Perhaps the sort of matters that might have come between you and a lady prior to your marriage."

Kettering had been a flaming hound prior to his marriage. Half the bored wives and merry widows of Polite Society had gone into a decline when he'd taken Jacaranda to wife. The other half had followed when it became obvious Sir Worth was smitten with his lady.

"I never mixed business with that sort of bungling," Kettering said, "but I was a disgrace nonetheless. One apologizes, I suppose, and makes a public display of whatever flattering sentiments one honestly harbors for the lady. A man might have no interest in a woman's heart, but he must have a care for her pride. It's…delicate, and a damned lot of work."

"Hard work can pay dividends," Will said, finding a morsel of comfort in Kettering's words, one he'd consider at another time, in another place. "I wish Casriel would let you assist with his finances."

"So do I," Kettering said, pushing off the wall. "Keep at him, and we'll wear him down, then set Jacaranda on him. See you next week, and give my regards to Her Grace."

Kettering and Meda strolled up the garden walk, while across the alley, Will's mare was led out.

From an inside pocket, Will produced a lump of sugar for her, then swung up. He still had time to cut through the park on his way to see the duchess, which was the more agreeable route for the mare. She was a country horse, and Town noise and traffic did not appeal to her.

Of course, Will might also catch a glimpse of Lady Susannah reading on a bench at this exact hour, but that would be simply a coincidence.

⚜

Yorick trotted out from under the library sofa and licked Lyle Mannering's boot. When Mannering ought to have kicked the dog for displaying such bad manners, he instead picked Yorick up.

Mannering and the pug wore the same anxious, uncertain expression. They both had hopeful brown eyes too.

"I did what you asked, Effington," Mannering said, thumping the dog on its head. "Spread rumor, gossip, and innuendo in every available ear. Poor chit was left swilling punch and looking thoroughly bereft. A good night's work, eh?"

"An utter failure, I'd say," Effington countered, turning the page of his newspaper. "Put the dog down, Mannering." The society pages reported Lady Darlington's ball as a great success, a veritable crush, a lavish and lovely affair, et cetera, et cetera.

Effington remained seated, while Yorick planted himself at Mannering's feet—out of rolled-up newspaper range.

"What exactly did you say to people last night?"

Effington asked, leafing past the financial pages. Never any good news there.

"Pity about the girl's situation," Mannering said, wandering along the mantel, Yorick at his heels. "Such a shame people are so cruel about matters that are truly of no moment. Puts her family in an awkward position, but one must admire their loyalty to her." He peered at the painting above the mantel, an image of a fellow wearing a plumed hat and a lot of velvet, flirting with a portly wench. "Is this a Caravaggio?"

The morning was sunny and cool, as spring could be. Effington had not ordered a fire lit, the London coalmen having no sense of how to deal with their betters regarding accounts owed.

"Of course it's a Caravaggio." Or had been, before Effington had sold the genuine article and hung a copy in its place. "How did people react to your insinuations?"

"Odd about that." Mannering ran a gloved finger over the mantel, then wrinkled his nose at the resulting gray spot on the pale leather. "They mostly didn't react. Some made the predictable noises of false sympathy, others changed the subject. I gather Lady Della Haddonfield is well liked."

Too well liked. Effington began rolling the newspaper into a stout bat. Yorick scooted under the sofa, but Mannering wasn't as smart.

"Her dance card filled," Effington said, rising with the newspaper in his hand. "The plan was for Lady Della to be ostracized and pathetic, such that I could salvage her evening by dancing the last set with her. I didn't even approach her, once the Dornings started lining up."

"Bloody lot of Dornings, you're right about that. They left half the regiment back in Dorset too. I went to school with—ouch!"

Effington smacked Mannering again with the newspaper, and again and again. To hit something stupid and helpless felt good, as good as hearing Yorick whining under the sofa.

"I say, Effington," Mannering groused, rubbing his arm. "I followed your orders to the letter, despite having no call to speak ill of the lady, and this is your thanks? Are you mad?"

"You failed, Mannering. Your job was to ensure Lady Della was made pathetic, a pillar of bewildered shame. She became the toast of the bachelors instead."

"She's pretty," Mannering retorted, jerking down a peacock blue and green waistcoat that must have cost a fortune in embroidery alone. "In case you haven't noticed, she's also amusing to talk to, and she dances well. Not only that, she has a pack of enormous brothers, all in good health. What do you have against her, anyway?"

Mannering was proof of nature's whimsy. He was wealthy, handsome in a blond, pleasant way, rode well, and was universally tolerated. Effington had seldom met a stupider soul of any species.

"I have nothing against the woman and might well end up married to her, not that you need concern yourself with my motives. Concern yourself with redeeming your vowels, Mannering, in the coin of my choosing."

Mannering got down on his hands and knees and peered under the couch. "Yorick, there's a lad.

You can come out now. It's just us fellows here, after all."

"He'll cower under there until Domesday unless I bid him come out," Effington said. "You are to renew your assault on Lady Della's character. Enlist the aid of your sisters if you must, intimate that Lady Della has a gambling problem, a fondness for the poppy, a weakness for handsome footmen. By this time next week, she must be a pariah."

Mannering sat up, but didn't get to his feet. "This is not how you treat a woman you seek to marry, Effington. You ought to be raising her in the esteem of others, not wrecking her good name."

The greatest stupidity of all was good moral character, for those afflicted with that virtue attributed a similar weakness to everybody around them.

Effington laid the newspaper on his desk. "Violate my confidence at your peril, Mannering. I want Lady Della to have the most generous, outlandishly lavish settlements this side of Cleopatra's arrangements with Caesar. Her family must be strongly motivated to send her into my keeping. If I'm paying addresses to just another pretty, virtuous young lady, that won't be the result, will it?"

Mannering looked disgruntled, as if an application of logic disagreed with his digestion. "If she's in love with you, then the settlements won't matter to her."

In love. The two most ridiculous words ever used. "She's the daughter of an earl. The settlements will matter, particularly when she's one of several daughters not yet married off. If the family is shamelessly relieved to be rid of her, they're more likely to dower her handsomely, and that is entirely in the lady's best interest."

Mannering popped to his feet and dusted off his knees. "Then I'm away to assassinate the poor dear's character in the clubs, but I want my vowels back, Effington. Fair is fair."

Fair was more stupidity, usually. If Effington had played fair, he'd never have been able to put Mannering in his debt.

"Of course, Mannering. I always keep my word and I do esteem the lady very much. Sometimes needs must when the devil drives, though. By the end of the month, she'll be wearing my ring, provided you don't bungle your assignments. Yorick, come."

A single snap of Effington's fingers and the dog scurried, head down, tail tucked, to his master's side.

"I tell myself you can't be all that awful a fellow if little Yorick likes you," Mannering said. "But this is the most peculiar means of winning a fair lady I've ever come across. I'll be glad when Lady Della is safely wed to you, and I can explain to all and sundry that I must have been mistaken about her situation."

"I'll be glad to have my ring on her finger too, Mannering. Now, come upstairs with me while I choose the day's waistcoat. You always have such exquisite taste. Did you hear that the Duchess of Ambrose's dog has been stolen?"

"As a matter of fact, I did. Poor old dear is beside herself. Fellows in the park this morning say she's offered a reward too. Quite sizable, but then it was a sizable dog."

A sweet shaft of cheer pierced Effington's outlook,

which had been rank since his last meeting with his man of business.

"A reward? A sizable reward? That's pathetic."

"I find it touching, though only a rogue would collect a reward for finding an old woman's dog, don't you agree?"

No, Effington did not agree. "The dog is probably larking around at some shambles," he said, "gorging himself on pig entrails when it's not humping every bitch in the alley. I am endlessly fond of even the lowest canine, but they're like that, you know. That dog will come home to Her Grace when he's done being randy and sick."

❧

Nicholas had dragooned Leah into accompanying him to the card room, leaving only Susannah on guard duty, again.

"I know Leah's strategy," Della said, swaying gently to the evening's first minuet. "You mustn't blame them for it, Suze."

"We're abandoned here in the wilderness together," Susannah said, "because nobody will come near you if Nicholas is glowering like the Wrath of Haddondale come to London."

"Nicholas *is* the Wrath of Haddondale, also its biggest kitten. Oh my, don't they look lovely?"

All four Dorning brothers approached in their evening finery.

Susannah had sat that morning reading in the park for more than two hours, or pretending to read. She'd come to a sorry pass when *As You Like It* couldn't hold her focus. Nonetheless, her attention had wandered all over the park.

The Dorning brothers, by contrast, would turn any lady's head, and apparently had, for half the ballroom—dancers, musicians, wallflowers, everybody—watched them.

"Oh no," Della moaned. "Effington is coming this way too. Susannah, what do I do?"

"You enjoy them all. You be witty and charming, and let the gentlemen compete for your notice."

Though how tedious was that? Watching grown men flirt, flatter, and fawn?

"My ladies," the Earl of Casriel said, bowing over Susannah's hand, then Della's. "We're having a dispute, and Ash suggested you might resolve it for us. Willow says we shouldn't burden you with our squabbles, but I also need a lady to take pity on me for the supper waltz, so here we are."

Casriel was convincing in his charm, his grave smile genuine, but Susannah had the impression he was setting an example for his younger brothers rather than showing a real interest in her or her sister.

"Explain your dispute to us," Della said. "We'll happily sit in judgment of the lot of you."

Cam and Ash smirked while Will... Will was studying an enormous, feathery potted fern. He was so handsome, and so miserable in this ballroom, but he would not leave his brothers unguarded.

"We were talking about the Duchess of Ambrose's missing mastiff," Cam explained. "I said I don't think large dogs make good pets for ladies. Ash, of course, disagrees with me, and says a protective dog is an excellent companion for the frail sex. Casriel says the only good dog is a dog with a real job, such as hunting or birding, and Willow says we're all ridiculous."

"A conundrum, indeed," Della said, "when each man's opinion has something of sense in it, but none of you is entirely right—except for Mr. Willow Dorning. There, your dispute is solved, and somebody may now fetch me a glass of punch."

Della was managing, but like the Earl of Casriel's charm, her riposte was a performance. Susannah's head began to ache, and still Will had not so much as looked at her.

"I'll fetch drinks for both of you ladies," he said, bowing and withdrawing.

Lord Effington neatly took Willow's place in the semicircle that had formed around Della, his golden good looks contrasting with the darker Dornings at his side. Behind Effington, Lyle Mannering shifted from foot to foot, and even tried a little hop to see past the taller Dorning brothers.

"We're discussing the best breed of dog to serve as a lady's pet," Casriel said. "Your thoughts on the subject are, of course, welcome, Effington."

Effington studied Della, his expression pensive. The immediate company grew quiet, but Susannah realized others were also monitoring the conversation. Effington was unrelenting and vocal about his affection for dogs, so of course, his opinion would be noted.

The throb at the base of Susannah's neck threatened to climb higher, and if it reached her temple, then the entire evening was doomed.

"Not every woman is suitably matched with a noble

canine companion," Effington observed. "Dogs are sensitive creatures, and a woman so absorbed with her own consequence that she neglects the adoration of a loyal defender—a fellow who is at her side through all the vicissitudes of life, one who asks virtually nothing of her in return—that woman is sure to be unworthy of his devotion."

Murmuring reached Susannah over the bewilderment threatening her composure. Effington was apparently feeling peevish, and willing to vent his feelings publicly. A rotten whiff of disaster wafted on his languid condescension.

Others heard Effington's comment, though Susannah was at a loss to decipher its entire meaning. Behind Ash Dorning, the Mannering twins were fanning themselves, their gazes hard and eager.

"Seems to me," Ash observed, "if a fellow is truly a loyal defender, *noble*, handsome, and all that other twaddle, then his lady's happiness ought to matter more to him than the occasional pat on the head or kiss on his ear."

Casriel's eyebrows shot up, and another chorus of murmurs rose.

"Seems to me," Cam Dorning said, glaring at Effington, "if a man is a true devotee of the canine, then he ought to occasionally take his dogs to the park to run and enjoy themselves as dogs ought. That man should not be perpetually foisting his dear pets off on the footmen and grooms for quick trips to the mews, and he most certainly shouldn't treat the poor beasts as if they were interchangeable fashion accessories."

Figurative fur would be flying any moment.

"Gentlemen," Susannah said, "your opinions are all very interesting, but you're supposing every lady enjoys the company of dogs. I regret to inform you that assumption is in error. Perhaps we should discuss what sort of pets appeal to ladies who don't care for canines at all?"

Casriel put a gloved hand on Cam's shoulder and squeezed firmly. "Excellent question," the earl said, a bit too heartily.

"Irrelevant question," Effington countered. "If a lady has no respect for the companionship of canines, if she has no affection for the species that has been man's loyal companion since the dawn of time, the staunch defender of his hearth and family, then I have to wonder why anybody would associate with such an unfortunate woman. Wouldn't you agree, Lady Della?"

Five

In the silence following Effington's languid inquiry, Susannah was certain of only one thing: his lordship was offended. He was mortally, lethally offended, and Susannah's efforts to deflect his ire had only made matters worse. Where was Nicholas, where was *anybody* who might salvage a situation that had gone so wrong so quickly?

"I do love dogs," Della said with a desperate smile. "Everybody knows of my fondness for the noble hound."

"Your own sister professes to have no use for canines of any variety," Effington rejoined, adjusting the lace of his cuff. "I hope you weren't saving your supper waltz for me, my dear?"

The question had no good answer. *No* from Della would be an insult. *Yes* was an invitation for Effington to publicly reject her. In his present pique, his lordship would politely, publicly, inform Della she'd saved her waltz for nothing.

Will Dorning shouldered between Cam and Effington. "Casriel, weren't you intent on sharing supper with Lady Della?" He passed Susannah and

Della glasses of bright red punch, his manner simply friendly and curious.

"I certainly was," Casriel said. "Then we went chasing off on the topic of noble hounds, running riot like a pack of puppies. If Effington has spoken for the lady's waltz, then I must, of course, yield to an earlier claim."

Effington's regard for Della became subtly affectionate. He smiled slightly, his gaze warmed. Nothing effusive, but a relenting that allowed Susannah to breathe again.

"Lady Della must choose," he said, bowing elaborately. "Much about a woman's circumstances are beyond her control, but she can choose her partner for the waltz, as—happily—can we all."

"I must accept such a prettily worded invitation," Della said, giving Effington her hand, "and hope Lord Casriel will content himself with a dance at some other time."

Casriel bowed his acquiescence. "May I pin my hopes on the good-night waltz?"

"I'll save it for no other," Della said. She couldn't very well offer Casriel her hand, because Effington had yet to turn loose of it.

"And, Lady Susannah," Will said, "will you allow me to lead you out for the supper waltz?"

Susannah was too relieved to assess Will's motives, and too troubled. Something in Effington's entire bearing was off. Had he implied that Della could not help having a sister who disliked dogs?

Or that Della could not help who her family was?

"I would be honored to stand up with you, Mr.

Dorning, and thank you for the punch." Susannah took a sip, though the drink was awful. Syrup of strawberries mixed with lemonade, probably, and any ice had long since lost the battle with the ballroom's heat.

"We have another set before the supper waltz," Will said. "Might you favor me with a turn on the terrace, Lady Susannah?"

Bless him. "Fresh air would be lovely." She passed her punch to Ash Dorning and accepted Will's proffered arm.

And still Effington remained beside Della, her hand trapped in his.

❧

"I will find a muzzle that fits my brother Sycamore, and require him to wear it when we are in polite company," Will said. "Though he made a valid point."

Beside him Lady Susannah wore a pained smile. If she were a dog, Will would have suspected digestive upset, or the sort of bone weariness that came from being hunted too hard. In the park that morning, she'd looked at peace, and utterly absorbed in her book.

Also lovely. Will hadn't disturbed her with so much as a greeting because she'd always been happiest when absorbed in her books.

"I do not know what exactly that conversation was about," Lady Susannah said as they started down the corridor toward the terrace, "but Effington is offended."

Effington was a strutting buffoon whose dogs were to be pitied.

"The viscount is enamored of Lady Della,

nonetheless," Will said. Casriel clearly liked the girl too, though not enough that Will's hopes were stirred.

"Anybody should be charmed by Della." Lady Susannah stopped six yards short of the terrace doors. Behind them, the orchestra had swung into a gavotte, a lively, loud, stomping dance. Ahead of them, raucous laughter came from the torch-lit terrace.

"My lady, are you well?"

She untangled their arms. "A headache has got hold of me, Mr. Dorning. Men will be smoking out on the terrace, and people will remark that you and I both walked together and then later danced the supper waltz. I should not have tasted that vile punch, and—"

"In here," Will said, taking her by the hand. "The library is on the next floor up. This is the parlor set aside for Lord Holderby's maiden aunts. They over-feed their dachshunds, but love the dogs dearly."

The parlor was dark, so Will appropriated a lamp from the sconces in the corridor, lit a branch of candles, and replaced the lamp in the corridor.

"The cooler air is lovely," Lady Susannah said when Will returned. "How do you know Lord Holderby's aunts?"

Will closed the door, lest they be discovered and her ladyship forced to accept the addresses of a man who could barely support her.

"I'm not sure whether the heat or the noise is the greater challenge in a crowded ballroom," Will said, though the greatest challenge was keeping his brothers from trouble. "I know Henrietta and Helen Holderby because I gave them their dogs. Castor and Pollux were not faring well in the badger pits." The badgers, of course, fared far worse, but clearly those two dogs had not been raised to anticipate violence from any quarter.

The baiter, fortunately, had been one of the ones with a backward sort of conscience, at least as far as the dogs were concerned. He'd accepted coin for the dachshunds, though only after assurances from Will of utter discretion regarding the transaction.

Lady Susannah sank onto a sofa beneath the window. "Your brother Sycamore reminded me of a cornered badger. He's very fierce."

Will came down beside her, hoping they were past the more extreme demands of manners.

"He's young, but, yes, fierce as well. I owe you an apology, my lady."

Susannah rubbed her fingers across her brow. "For your brothers' behavior? They were simply trying to be gallant. I cannot fathom what queer start plagues Effington. He seems taken with Della, but last night, when she was on the verge of becoming a pariah, Effington was nowhere to be found."

Will had made inquiries on that very point. Effington had been in the card room, with a clear view of the ballroom's dance floor.

Now was not the time to cast aspersion on Lady Della's lone suitor. "The apology I owe you, my lady, is for my behavior as we walked home last evening. I presumed, and though a gentleman might mean well, when his words and actions—"

Two gloved fingers pressed against Will's lips. "Hush, Mr. Dorning. It was a simple kiss. I rather enjoyed it."

Will grasped those fingers in his own—drat all evening gloves to the dung heap.

"I wasn't apologizing for the kiss, *simple* though it might have been." His feelings for Susannah Haddonfield were *not* simple—longing, respect, desire, protectiveness, resentment, and sheer weariness blended to create a persistent sense of unrest.

Her ladyship retrieved her hand and rubbed her fingers across her brow again. "Your kiss was simple and enjoyable, which is apparently of no moment. If you're not apologizing for that kiss, then what does that leave?"

Should Will be heartened, that his marital unavailability had made no impression on a woman he couldn't stop thinking about?

Moonlight shone through the garden's trees to make shadow patterns on the carpet. As the breeze stirred the leaves, the patterns shifted silently. Will would have enjoyed watching those soft, shifting patterns while holding Lady Susannah's hand.

"Rubbing your ears helps," Will said.

"Mr. Dorning, have you had too much punch?"

Will's problem was a lack of kisses, not a surfeit of punch. "You have a headache," he said, tugging off his gloves. "Rubbing your ears… Hold still."

He knelt before Lady Susannah and gently grasped both of her ears between his thumbs and forefingers.

"Relax, my lady, and if you're offended two minutes from now, I will add this to the list of items I must apologize for."

He gently pressed her forehead to his shoulder, and tugged her on ears, moving his grasp outward, then repeating at a slightly different angle. Dogs were calmed by this particular caress provided it was done slowly and smoothly. For the first week in Will's care, Samson had refused to fall asleep unless Will had been stroking his ears.

"That is most...odd," Lady Susannah said. "But...soothing."

To them both, though Will still wanted to kiss her. "If you're ever around a nervous dog, try this. They'll love you for it. Just don't pinch too hard or move too quickly. The idea is to ease the worry away, to tug it free, not demand surrender of it."

A few more silent, peculiar moments passed. The thumping, stomping gavotte ended, thank the heavenly bodies, and beyond the door, people moved from the ballroom to the terrace.

Lady Susannah's gloved hands grasped Will's wrists. "You can stop now. I do feel better."

While Will felt like howling at the moon. He ceased his devotions to her ears, but cradled the back of her head against his palm.

"Last night, when I said I couldn't marry you, I presumed you'd want to marry me. That was arrogance on my part. I put you in an awkward position, and I'm sorry."

They were very close, Will kneeling before her ladyship, her hands on his wrists, her forehead resting on his shoulder. She smelled of good old English lavender, a country scent that made Will homesick for Dorset.

"We needn't speak of it again, Mr. Dorning," she said, straightening. "Your apology is accepted, though entirely unnecessary. Any woman would count herself fortunate to merit your addresses. I have put *myself* in an awkward position, however, and you might be the only person who can get me out of it."

❧

"Bloody big bugger to be hiding him under the very noses of the nobs," the first man observed.

"Bloody mean bugger," the second fellow muttered, using a rake to nudge the water pail closer to the door of the stall. "If 'e takes to barkin' again, don't expect me to put a muzzle on 'im."

In a maneuver the men had coordinated over the past several days, the first handler tossed food into one corner, and while the dog was devouring every scrap, the second quickly changed out pails of water. The stall reeked of soiled straw and dog urine, but more significantly of canine rage.

"Don't expect me to walk him down to Knightsbridge," the first fellow said as the dog snapped up the last of his food. Kitchen scraps weren't enough to keep a big animal like this fed, but they'd keep him mean.

"The baiters are used to dealing with the mean ones," his companion replied, double-latching the stall door. "They like 'em mean. The meaner the better."

"He's mean enough. He'll bring a pretty penny."

They fed the other dogs, none as large or as loud as the black mastiff, but then, the other dogs had been penned up longer. They all grew resigned eventually, even the big, mean ones.

"I'm for a pint," the first man said, "and then we'll get the nets and go for a walk. Come along, Horace. There's always a few strays about, and some of 'em are bound to be suitable for our purposes."

The new mastiff, the biggest and meanest of the lot, was already growling and pacing again before the men had even left the dingy, smelly stable.

∽

Susannah had on occasion studied her facial features in a mirror. They were adequate for their assigned tasks. Her eyes were blue, evenly spaced, where eyes were supposed to be. Nose in the middle, a fine place for a nose, even if that nose was a trifle more prominent than strictly necessary. Chin also in the middle, also a shade more pronounced than a lady's chin ought to be.

Mouth between nose and chin in the expected location, and of the expected size and particulars.

But her ears? *Her ears?* Her ears had been content to remain unnoticed for her entire life. They were simply ears, doing what ears did…until Will Dorning had grasped them gently and firmly, and…stroked them.

Susannah's ears apparently had a mysterious connection to her heart, which beat slowly and heavily against her ribs. Her ears also affected her body temperature, for she was abruptly warm all over. Her ears could control her intellect, which was having difficulty holding on to coherent thoughts.

Maybe that explained why she'd kept her hands around Will Dorning's wrists. Without anchoring herself to him, Susannah might have floated off on the moon shadows when she needed, for the first time in her life, to enlist a man's aid.

"I am at your service, my lady." Will sat back on his heels and dropped his hands from Susannah's shoulders.

"Though I cannot imagine any great difficulty has found you. You're a surpassingly sensible woman."

He'd meant it as a compliment, the daft man. Sensible women became sensible spinsters, which Susannah had only recently settled on as an ideal fate.

"I am a determined woman. Will you sit with me for a moment, Mr. Dorning?"

He shifted and was beside her, just like that. No careful choosing of his spot, no ensuring a foot of space remained between them.

Susannah resisted the urge to put her head on his shoulder. "Do you know the play *As You Like It*, Mr. Dorning?"

"Of course. A lot of running about in the forest, silliness, and speechifying about the meaning of life. Death, for once, plays little part in the entertainment."

Reality played little part in the entertainment. "I was reading *As You Like It* in the park this morning, natural sunlight being the best for reading, and it occurred to me: In what forest is the sun always shining? Orlando and Rosalind go cavorting and flirting and carrying on in the depths of an enormous forest, and all is bright days and soft air. In what forest does the cold or damp never make an appearance? In what forest does the sun shine relentlessly?"

"Do you liken the comedic forest to Mayfair ballrooms?" Will asked. "False illumination, false and flowery sentiments, pretty music and petty conceits, while outside the windows, the poor gather to gape at the spectacle?"

That very thought had held Susannah's attention until she'd become oblivious to her surroundings.

"If I put that analogy into a letter," she said, "and send it off to Professor Gillingham at Oxford, I'll see my fanciful notion expanded into a learned article in the next quarterly publication of the *Bodleian Crier*, which injustice has nothing to say to anything. I'm having trouble asking directly for your assistance, Mr. Dorning, and wandering off into my own preferred forest instead."

Susannah hadn't had to ask for Will Dorning's help the first time. She'd been so distraught that, simply by sitting beside her on a garden bench and proffering his handkerchief, he'd inspired her to a teary recitation of all the ills endured by one rather plain girl facing a rather boring come-out.

Petty tragedies for that girl, though, until Will Dorning had stepped in. Perhaps he could step in again.

"How may I be of service, my lady?"

Thank you. "I have offended Viscount Effington," Susannah said, tugging off her long evening gloves. "I made a comment in your absence, about some ladies having no liking for dogs, and he took that to mean *I* have no liking for dogs, which is true enough. He will hold my dislike for dogs against Della, whose fortunes will be decided on Effington's whim, whether he offers for her or not."

"His lordship does seem to command the notice of many gossips," Will said. "I've warned my brothers not to tangle with him, which was ill-advised on my part."

"Sycamore will now take his lordship into dislike?" Younger siblings engendered an odd blend of affection, protectiveness, and exasperation known only to older siblings, something Susannah shared with Will Dorning.

"Sycamore will make it his mission in life to torment Effington," Mr. Dorning said, "though I don't think the boy is up to his lordship's weight in nastiness."

When had Susannah taken Will Dorning's hand? Or had he taken hers? In any case, the contact was comforting.

"Effington is not nasty," Susannah said. "He's sophisticated and doesn't countenance fools. He's ideally placed to protect Della from the gossips, but I have antagonized him."

"He's easily antagonized."

Susannah's headache wanted to come back. She wished she could rest her forehead against Will Dorning's shoulder and have him stroke her ears again.

"I know Effington isn't the most pleasant fellow," she said, "but he's shown marked attention to Della, and he can't be all bad if his dogs like him, can he?"

Will's thumb brushed over Susannah's knuckles, a small, distracting caress. "What are you asking of me, my lady?"

Don't stop touching me. His hands were magic, bringing calm and quiet with them. No wonder the dogs, cats, and horses loved him.

"You're being gentlemanly," Susannah said, letting her eyes drift closed. "You dislike Effington."

"I've only seen him with the one dog, the little pug, and that fellow does not trust his owner. Watch carefully the next time Effington lifts a hand to pat the dog's head. The dog will never take his eyes off Effington, and will cringe away any time Effington raises his hand, even to pat the dog."

Some dogs were simply shy. Susannah was shy, though apparently not with Will Dorning.

"A detail, Mr. Dorning. How can I convince Lord Effington that I like dogs?"

Will patted her knuckles and withdrew his hand. "Isn't it more important that your sister like the viscount? If she doesn't care for him, what's all this posturing and running around in the forest in aid of?"

Della's position had become precarious, and Susannah's careless comment was at least partly to blame, a far weightier matter than simply running about in the forest of Mayfair spouting clever verse.

"Mr. Dorning, Lord Effington can ruin my sister or assure she's comfortably settled for life. I would do anything to see Della well situated. If I must pretend to like dogs, I will pretend to like dogs. If I must dance with Lyle Mannering while he sneezes on my bodice, I will dance with Lyle Mannering all night. I'll swill that horrible punch, smile, and look gracious until hell freezes—"

He kissed her. A quick little smack of lips upon lips that danced through Susannah like the leafy shadows danced with the breeze.

"A simple 'please be quiet' would have sufficed, Mr. Dorning."

"But it wouldn't make you smile, and you are apparently not one to take offense at simple kisses, so you might endure a few more from me. I don't like Effington, I don't respect him, and I don't trust him, though none of that matters."

Kisses mattered. Susannah was coming to believe they could matter a lot. "Then what is the difficulty? You teach me what dogs like, I'll do that, and Effington will see he's brought me to heel, so to speak."

"Is that image supposed to inspire my cooperation, my lady?"

Will Dorning would be a complicated dog to train. He was always thinking, and he missed little.

"You have the knack of disagreeing with a lady without arguing with her," Susannah said. "If more men cultivated this habit, social conversation might become interesting."

"Or the race might die out. Here's the problem: one can't fool a dog. If you don't like them, they know it. If you're frightened of them, if you disdain them, if you do like them, they know. Cats are the same, as are horses. I haven't met an animal who can be regularly fooled by somebody they've spent any time around."

"You're saying animals are smarter than we are?" Smarter than Susannah, in any case. She'd thought the Mannering sisters were her friends. She'd thought Edward Nash, former neighbor in Haddondale, would make a biddable husband.

She'd been howlingly wrong about Mr. Nash and the Mannerings, both.

"I'm saying animals aren't fooled by appearances," Will replied. "Maybe they can smell the fear and anger and love on us, maybe they see our actions more clearly for being unable to decipher our conversations. In any case, you can't fake a love of dogs."

Defeated by dogs? First by the petty intrigues of cruel girls, then the avarice of a greedy country squire, and now defeated by the honesty of dogs?

"I can go home to Kent," Susannah said, though abandoning Della was eighteen varieties of cowardly and wrong. "I can go home to Kent, and start on all the comedies, again. *As You Like It* is an excellent bellwether of the Bard's lighter charms. I haven't made a study of the comedies for nearly two years."

Had Will moved nearer? The urge to lean on him had certainly become more acute. He brushed a lock of Susannah's hair over her shoulder.

"You don't want to return to Kent, my lady. Or perhaps you simply can't stand to leave your sister to fend for herself."

Maybe, like an attentive hound, Will Dorning could discern truth beneath human babble.

"I have two older sisters in Kent, both recently spoken for by worthy men," Susannah said. "Both quite happy with their choices. I, on the other hand, attached the interest of a local squire. I should have consulted his dogs, perhaps, because Squire Nash was interested in my settlements, not me. I found this out rather later than I wish I had."

Three times later than Susannah wished she had: once in the saddle room, once in Edward's parlor, and once in his library, though how a room without a single copy of the Shakespeare sonnets could aspire to the name library defied explanation.

Susannah should have heeded that evidence.

"I'm sorry," Will said. "The man was an idiot and your brothers should not have let him near you."

"You're a brother. Brothers do the best they can, Mr. Dorning. So do sisters. Will you help me?"

For Susannah did not want to return to Kent. Wedded bliss for a sister was a fine, fine objective, in theory. Having one's face rubbed in that objective happily achieved twice over was purgatory.

"You'd tuck tail and scurry back to Kent?"

"I'd leave the field so Della's future is not jeopardized. The Bard and I have become excellent friends."

"Shakespeare is dead, Susannah."

"That is often a point in his favor, Willow Dorning."

This time, he kissed her knuckles, which helped a little, though he didn't try to keep hold of her hand.

"I can't make you like dogs," he said, "but there's hope, and I can work with that hope. You spend a great deal of time with books, and dogs like the smell of books, especially old books. That, among other factors, is in your favor."

"How refreshing, to have something in my favor besides a title and some settlements." Susannah ought not to have said that, for Will's smile was pained, and she would not for the world see him hurt.

"You're sensible, my lady. Also logical, not given to dramatic displays, you're persistent and orderly. You have many fine qualities that domestic animals appreciate."

Will was again offering backhanded compliments, though he couldn't know that. "To be found agreeable by the animals for the very qualities people find tiresome in me is a bit lowering, Mr. Dorning."

He rose, right when Susannah might have again reached for his hand.

Willow Dorning had excellent instincts.

"You are not tiresome, my lady, but Polite Society certainly can be. I don't expect everybody to like dogs, cats, horses, or nightingales, but you have an advantage many others don't, and for that reason I expect you will achieve your goal."

Susannah rose too. They'd been closeted for too long,

and not nearly long enough. "What is my advantage, Mr. Dorning? I can't see that an affinity for Shakespeare will gain me much notice among the canines."

Among anybody who counted. The occasional quote was entirely acceptable, but not entire memorized plays.

"The advantage you have, my lady, is that the dogs like *you*. They are discerning, and while tolerant of many, their affections are reserved for a few. If my own Georgette finds your company agreeable, then you may not be a dog lover, but the dogs apparently love you."

Susannah didn't know whether to laugh or cry at that pronouncement, so instead, she kissed Willow Dorning on the cheek—another simple, enjoyable gesture of affection between friends—and took his arm.

"We're probably in time for the supper waltz, Mr. Dorning. You may use that exercise in tedium to begin my instruction. I can think of no better use for time spent on the dance floor."

Six

"I COME BEARING EXCUSES," ASH DORNING SAID, flourishing a bow before Della. "Also an invitation. Casriel had to take Sycamore home. Something on the buffet didn't agree with Cam, and thus I was deputed to tend to your good-night waltz—if you'll have me?"

Della wished Susannah hadn't stood up with the Duke of Quimbey, because Susannah enjoyed a puzzle, which this invitation assuredly was. Why hadn't Casriel simply sent Sycamore home in Ash's company? Or in Willow's?

"You're wondering if Casriel abandoned you because of Effington's little drama earlier," Mr. Dorning said, setting aside the glass of punch Della had been holding for the last half hour. "You're thinking the innocuous younger brother has been sent to handle the waltzing, so as to avoid antagonizing your guard dog."

"Lord Effington is not my guard dog, Mr. Dorning." Not yet, though Della was supposed to consider herself fortunate to have his lordship's notice.

"Effington wants to be your loyal hound, but he's

off to his club where the play is more interesting than in Lady Holderby's card room. I'm here. Will you dance with me?"

Not even Della's older brothers talked to her like this, half dare, half in confidence. "Effington gambles?"

Dark lashes lowered over intriguing violet eyes. "We all gamble, my dear. I'm betting my heart this very moment."

"You are a flirt," Della said, placing her hand over his. "I like flirts, generally, though I'm not much good at flirting, myself."

"An excellent strategy. Be yourself. You'll confound the perishing lot of idiots who have nothing better to do than intrigue with each other all night long."

He escorted Della onto the dance floor and bowed correctly. Della curtsied, weary to her bones from a long evening of being witty, charming, and utterly false.

"I prefer the good-night waltz," Mr. Dorning said as the introduction began. "I like the slower tempo, the less crowded dance floor. If I weren't charged with keeping Sycamore out of trouble, I'd be home studying the calculus, truth be told."

Most men asked Della what her favorite dance was, and she was supposed to reply that *tonight* whichever dance that gentleman had stood up for was her favorite, though "she enjoyed them all."

She did not enjoy them all, but she was enjoying this one. "You're a scholar?"

Mr. Dorning had the look of the scholar. His gaze bore a calm equanimity that put Della in mind of settled horses and bachelor uncles. He smelled a good deal better than a horse even this late in the evening.

"I'm a younger son," he said, moving off with the music. "I hope to find a place in my brother-in-law's offices as a man of business. I like numbers, which is not the same thing as liking money, though money in its place is fine too. For now I'm pretending to be sociable in aid of setting an example for Sycamore."

Ash Dorning led beautifully. Considering that he was tall and Della petite, this was an enormous pleasure, for she spent most balls being hauled about like a sack of laundry.

"Susannah sets an example for me, though I wish she wouldn't," Della said. "She's fixed on marrying me off so she can retire to spinsterhood in the arms of Mr. Shakespeare or Mr. Pope or Mr. Donne."

"A woman of varied appetites. What about you? What is your objective?"

Della had several objectives, at least one of which she didn't share with even her closest sister. "I was mistaken, Mr. Dorning. Your flirtation needs work. What sort of question is that?"

"An honest one," he said, twirling her under his arm. "Are you looking for ten thousand pounds a year and a few thousand acres in the Midlands?"

No, Della was not. What she sought was at once easier and harder to find than that. "Is that your objective, Mr. Dorning?"

"Not particularly. I see how Casriel labors endlessly to keep up with changing agricultural science, changing laws, changing expectations from the tenants. I like fresh air and a hearty gallop as much as the next man, but give me a ledger or a good book, and I'm content."

How easy for a man to state his priorities and

saunter along in life, happily accepted by others on his own terms.

"I am a legitimate by-blow, Mr. Dorning," Della said *softly*. She wasn't daft. "My options are limited as a result. I must take no risks, must never laugh too loudly, never grimace too publicly. Ten thousand a year and an estate in the Midlands would be heaven."

Della hadn't risked this admission with any other man, though she knew there was speculation regarding her lamentably un-Haddonfield height and coloring. Mr. Ash Dorning was in a position to pass along Della's situation to the earl, though, and to save Casriel wasted courting.

"One of my brothers is in the same predicament," he said. "At least one, but he isn't half so pretty as you. He's not as quick as you are either, poor lad."

They twirled and dipped and turned along for another few bars, while Della dealt with a sense of reality tipping beneath her feet. She was more tired than she knew, and had probably drunk too much wine, the overly sweet punch being an affront to sound digestion.

"I ought not to have told you that," she said. "I'm sorry. I'm tired, and yet I can't be seen going home early. Not tonight."

Mr. Dorning guided her an inch closer. Nobody watching would have noticed, but Della felt the firming of his hand at her back.

"You may trust my discretion, my lady, and I'm not just saying that. Will and Casriel would beat me silly for violating a lady's confidences, and well they should. I can use a friend in these shark-infested waters, somebody who won't be horrified if I prose on about profit and risk. Shall we be friends?"

"I'm not offended by a discussion of profit and risk, Mr. Dorning." Was he implying something else?

"I'm offended when I see Effington posturing and sneering, dripping innuendo and sarcasm into the punch bowl. Cam's instincts were on the mark in that regard."

Della had forgotten what the company of an honest gentleman felt like, she'd spent so much time lately around the polite variety.

"Lord Effington is protective. You mustn't goad him."

"Where is his protectiveness now?"

Excellent question. "His lordship and I are to walk in the park tomorrow afternoon, so stop goading *me*, Mr. Dorning."

The music's final refrain was softer, slower, appropriate to a good-night waltz. Mr. Dorning twirled Della one final time, so she could sink into a curtsy, holding his outstretched hand. She wanted to keep right on going, to settle onto the floor in an exhausted heap, for she'd made no progress tonight with any of her objectives.

Mr. Dorning drew her gracefully to her feet. "I'm not goading you. If we're friends, we'll be honest with each other. I honestly do not like your viscount."

Said without malice, also without a smile. "He's not my viscount," Della said, placing her fingers over Mr. Dorning's proffered hand.

Right now, she did not much like Viscount Effington either. Della kept that to herself as well.

❧

"That is not a dog, that is a mastodon," Lady Susannah said, stopping short four yards from Will and Samson.

Georgette gnawed on a stick over in the shade of the maples, and on the far side of the lilac border, children yelled about a kite stuck in the trees. Lady Susannah had worn a lovely periwinkle walking dress for this outing and apparently left her parasol at home.

"His name is Samson," Will said, stroking a gloved hand over the dog's head. "He's shy and reserved, but well mannered." Much like present company. Samson needed to learn to make friends too, also like present company.

"He is to be my teacher?" Lady Susannah asked, coming not one step closer.

Will would be her teacher, because he was an idiot. He'd already stolen too many kisses from her ladyship, though she seemed to enjoy his thievery.

"You and Samson will learn together. I've only had him for a few months, but he's ready to enlarge his social circle. Come make his acquaintance."

"He's quite sizable, Mr. Dorning. I suppose he has all of his teeth?"

Samson was studying Susannah, women being something of a novelty for him. He seldom came into the house during daylight hours, now that the weather was moderate, and thus spent most of his time with the grooms in the mews, with Will, or napping in the garden.

"His nickname is Sam," Will said. "You must not smile at him." Not that her ladyship had been on the verge of any such display.

"He'll pounce on me and lick me to perdition?"

"He'll think you're showing him your teeth, and he's easily unnerved by aggressive displays."

Throughout the exchange, Samson had been sitting calmly at Will's feet, which was a testament to the dog's steady nerves.

"I'm unnerved by aggressive displays too," Lady Susannah said, taking a few steps closer. "Oddly enough, those do tend to be accompanied by bright, toothy smiles. Good day, Samson."

The dog's ears twitched, for he knew his name.

"Hold out your hand," Will said, "but remain relaxed, and look at me, not the dog."

Her ladyship complied, more easily than Casriel's head groom would have. Some women had an innate sense of how to avoid confrontation, and that served them well with powerful, nervous animals.

"He's breathing on my glove," Lady Susannah said, studying Will's lapel. "Exactly like a presuming gentleman. That pansy is the same color as your eyes, Mr. Dorning."

While Lady Susannah's eyes were the same shade as… Some cats had eyes that blue, that steady and noticing.

"When you're out late dancing, you can't be reading by candlelight," Will said. "Your eyes aren't as tired this morning."

"The rest of me is tired enough. Do you think those children will ever rescue their kite, and do you suppose Samson is done sniffing at my glove?"

Yes, Samson had sniffed her ladyship's glove to his satisfaction, while Will wanted to list the colors of blue that matched Lady Susannah's eyes.

"You can pet him, a pat on the head, a tug on

his ear, nothing effusive. Then we're taking a walk. Georgette, come."

Georgette gave up her stick and ambled over, while Lady Susannah offered Samson the minimal overtures necessary to establish friendly relations.

"If this dog decides to go bounding off, Mr. Dorning, I will either drop the leash or be yanked off my feet."

"Dropping the leash is the wiser alternative in many situations, my lady. Today, you'll have Georgette, and I'll take Samson."

They kept to the less traveled trails, but Hyde Park was popular even on a quiet morning, and so inevitably, they crossed paths with other people walking their dogs.

"I thought dogs always had to sniff each other, and growl and paw," Lady Susannah said. "Georgette and Samson barely notice the other dogs as long as the other dogs are well behaved."

While Will could not stop noticing Susannah. She and Georgette made an adorable picture, a fetching pair of ladies out taking the air.

"Georgette and Samson will react to overt threats," Will said, "but they'll notice first how we react. If you and I are not upset by the approach of another dog, then neither will Georgette and Samson be."

They were walking in a large circle, and the hour was such that the gentlemen on horseback had retired to their breakfasts, while the governesses with children were not yet out in force. The air bore the scent of greenery, and that alone soothed Will's nerves.

"Della notices my mood in much the same way," Lady Susannah said. "When we attend a social event, if I am in good spirits, if Nicholas and his countess are in a congenial mood, then Della worries less."

"Lady Della doesn't strike me as the nervous sort." In truth, Will hardly noticed Lady Della when she was in Susannah's company.

"She's…canny, almost deceptive. I love her dearly, but Della seems to know what's afoot before anybody else does, and she always has an air of private plans in train. I fear she's up to something even now, under the very noses of her siblings."

"Deceptive isn't good," Will said, though walking beside Lady Susannah, the park in its vernal glory, the dogs happily padding along, was a slice of heaven.

Also a slice of hell, for Will was simply showing another aristocrat how to get on well with a dog. He'd done this dozens of times, and at no point did the proceedings allow him to steal kisses from his pupils.

"Della is the soul of discretion," Lady Susannah said. "Whatever she's about, she won't be caught. Is this the extent of my schooling today, Mr. Dorning? Strolling the paths and sniffing at bushes?"

They'd returned to the clearing where they'd started, but Will did not want to part from the lady, even though they'd done much more than stroll along and sniff at bushes. They had started leash manners, they'd got the dogs accustomed to her ladyship.

They had also sorely tried Will's ability to focus on anything other than the soft curve of Lady Susannah's cheek, and how she smiled with her eyes rather than her mouth.

"Let's try some commands," Will said. "If you're working with dogs, you'll want to have a few nibbles of cheese with you at all times. We can't explain with words when a dog has guessed correctly or behaved properly, so we explain with affection and rewards."

"I am not affectionate by nature, Mr. Dorning. This undertaking could prove challenging."

Lady Susannah *was* affectionate by nature, and the undertaking had already proved to be a challenge ten times over.

"We'll start with *down*," Will said. "A very useful command, though one many dogs have trouble perfecting."

❧

"That's Comus," Sycamore hissed. "I'm almost sure that's him."

Ash remained on his horse, gaze on the dog, who was being half dragged, half led down the alley behind the Earl of Casriel's town house.

"Comus isn't that large," Ash said. "He's brindle, but his coat is smoother."

Cam trotted ahead, while Ash kept his horse to the walk. Cam tipped his hat to the man wrestling with the dog, but didn't pull up until his horse had reached the street.

"I told you: not Comus," Ash said when his horse was alongside Cam's. "But a very large and unhappy dog, nonetheless. Willow would have known what to say."

"The stupid blighter should stop yelling at the poor beast for starters, though Will never interferes uninvited. There's two of them now."

The last thing, the very last thing Ash Dorning wanted to do was play nanny to the younger brother who'd nearly got himself called out the night before.

Again.

"I have no idea what 'two of them' you're talking about, Cam, but if anybody asks you how you're feeling today, you tell them you're much improved."

The fellow with the dog disappeared around the corner, down the alley that ran at right angles to the one housing the Dorning mews. The animal had had all four paws planted, and the leash between its jaws as it was dragged along.

Even Will might have intervened, for the beast was clearly close to attacking its handler.

"I'm to say I'm much improved? Hard to improve on perfection," Cam said, taking a sniff of the rose affixed to his lapel. Cam was a bit of a dandy, and aspired to become more than a bit of a rake.

"Especially if perfection is lying dead in some woodland clearing," Ash observed. "Why the hell would you antagonize Lyle Mannering?"

Why antagonize anybody? The Dornings were an old family, but not a particularly prosperous or influential one, drat the damned luck. Cam was one of a herd of younger sons who'd be lucky to find work as a steward, factor, clergyman, or man of business. Casriel refused to buy military commissions for his brothers, and subduing the Corsican had left India as the most likely posting anyway.

The heat alone could kill a man there, and the calculus wasn't of much use against tigers.

"I didn't antagonize Mannering," Cam said, turning his horse to the left. "I contradicted him. Mannering was muttering about Lady Della being a trial to her family, and I took exception to that."

"Lady Della is not a trial to her family," Ash said. "What could Mannering have been about? He's not only harmless and decorative, but also usually benign." Of late, Mannering had also been a very poor card player, though he could afford to be.

"My point exactly, as I've already explained to Willow, who, in a rare and dazzling show of fraternal common sense, has agreed with me. What does it mean to be a gentleman, after all, if a woman you know, a woman to whom you've made your bow, can be maligned in the men's retiring room, as Mannering was maligning Lady Della, while all the other fellows do nothing but stand around waving their—that's the same dog."

Such was the labyrinth of Mayfair's streets that the man with the disobliging mastiff was emerging from the mouth of an alley.

The dog was now bleeding from a gash to its head.

"I don't like this, Ash. You beat a great beast of a dog like that, and the dog won't like it either."

"We're not Will, and that's not our dog. We're supposed to pay a call on Jacaranda and Kettering, then I'd like to drop in on the Haddonfield sisters. Sycamore, what the hell are you doing?"

Cam was already off his horse and passing Ash the reins.

"There are two *rewards*," Cam said, shoving his gold watch at Ash, but keeping his riding crop. "Two rewards for missing dogs, both great brutes. That man is not the dog's owner, and whatever is afoot, somebody will get hurt much worse if it's allowed to continue. Do you have any cheese?"

Ash fished in his pocket and passed over two

misshapen, linty lumps. "For God's sake, be careful and do not bring that damned dog home unless you want Casriel to send you back to Dorset at the cart's tail."

"My regards to the ladies," Cam said as the dog was dragged across the street thirty yards ahead. "Don't worry about me."

"Right," Ash said as Cam fell in step with the throng of people bustling about in the middle of a Mayfair day. "You're impulsive, temperamental, on your own, without much coin, and pursuing a man who beats dogs—oh, and you're in pursuit of a large, hostile canine in a foul mood too. Why should I worry?"

Ash turned his horse around, Cam's gelding coming along docilely. Before paying any calls, he'd have to drop the horse off, and hope neither Will nor Casriel was around to notice.

Two rewards would be enough to send the last pretention to sense Sycamore Dorning possessed clear to France.

❧

As You Like It weighed down Susannah's reticule, an awkward anchor that bumped against her leg as she and Georgette strode along. She'd carried the book with her for most of the last week, never quite finding time to finish the play.

Walking with a dog was different from mincing about by oneself. Georgette turned heads, drawing notice with her sheer size, but she also gave off an air of happy dignity, of being a lady about her business with no time to tarry over polite chitchat.

Susannah approved of that approach to life, and

walked beside the dog, in charity with the day. Then too, Willow Dorning made a handsome picture with Samson, who was an all-black, shaggy mastiff-mongrel with an enormous head and substantial paws. His coat was longer than Georgette's, and he took greater notice of his surroundings.

Which was to say, he lifted his leg frequently and sniffed the ground, the bushes, and *himself* at every opportunity. He fascinated Susannah, and intimidated her a little.

Samson was larger than Georgette, which should not have been possible, but Will Dorning controlled the dog easily. Or maybe he didn't control the dog, but used some other means of conforming the dog's behaviors to the owner's desires.

"Let's review a few commands," Will said when they'd made their usual circuit of the path. "Did you bring your cheese?"

This business of conversing with the dogs by means of rewards and affection sat awkwardly with Susannah. Some people explained matters to a pet with stout blows and scathing set-downs. While Susannah abhorred such behaviors, she did not relish the moment when she half tossed, half dropped a morsel of food in the vicinity of Samson's jaws.

Will set his hat on the only bench in the clearing as Georgette settled on her haunches and rested her weight against Susannah's side. The dog leaned casually, as if Susannah were as solid and dependable as a cast-iron hitching post.

"Is she tired?" Susannah asked, stroking a palm over Georgette's head. Georgette was hard *not* to pet, for her height put her head and shoulders in the same vicinity as Susannah's hand.

"Georgette isn't tired, she simply likes you," Will said. "Samson will lean if he's especially happy, but that doesn't happen often. Samson, sit."

The command was accompanied by a movement of Will's hand, from about an inch in front of Samson's nose to the spot between his ears.

Down he sat.

"Good lad."

Susannah had to look away when Will tugged on Samson's ears. Fortunately, when working with a dog, Willow Dorning was oblivious to all else, much like Susannah when in the grip of good literature. She'd learned the commands for sit, stay, down, and come, all of which Georgette dealt with amiably.

"Shall we try some fetch the stick?" Will asked.

Willow Dorning had a well-thought-out progression of exercises for his dogs, and a highly structured approach to their education. The sons of lords were not tutored with any more care, and the orderliness of the undertaking reassured Susannah that all was in hand.

More than the logical sequence of the commands, she liked Will's patience, liked the endless effort he took to make sense of everything from the dog's perspective.

"Fetch the stick will suit," Susannah said, for she enjoyed these outings with Will. "Though I know Georgette to be accomplished at it."

From the standpoint of Susannah's indoctrination into dog appreciation, fetch was a big step. The big steps were vaguely worrisome, because at some point,

Will would pronounce her a bona fide facsimile of a dog fancier, and then…

Then she'd thank him.

"Fetch the stick seems much like 'fetch me a glass of punch,'" Susannah observed. "You toss out a compliment, allude to a task, and the fellow who wants more compliments goes off on his mission. When he comes back, glass of punch in hand, you pet him, verbally at least, and he'll sit at your feet, wagging his tail for the rest of the evening."

Though the gentlemen of Polite Society were not as well trained as Will Dorning's dogs. The fellows also nipped from a lady's drink on occasion, or got lost in the card room en route to the punch bowl.

"We can conclude our session now if you've had enough for today," Will said. "Perhaps you're missing the Bard?"

The dogs panted gently, the rhododendrons were nearly in bloom, the squirrels were jabbering and leaping overhead. Shakespeare would be waiting for Susannah, even when Will Dorning was once again immured in the Dorset countryside, teaching another young collie "Away to me" and "come by."

Even when Susannah had read through all of dreary Milton and silly Sheridan.

"I'm happy to toss a few sticks," Susannah said, "though I'm sure you have other places to be, Will Dorning."

Quimbey and his pet had come along at the conclusion of Susannah's sessions twice in the past week. Comus seemed to grow between one day and the next, while the duke's affection for the dog came along more slowly.

Will ceased casually tugging on Samson's ears and Susannah's sanity. "There is no place I'd rather be, Lady Susannah, nobody I'd rather while away the morning with, and fetch is a reward for the dogs. They enjoy it, and so do I."

The same breeze that snatched away errant kites tousled Will's hair, and the same affection he frequently turned on his dogs laced his voice. Susannah pretended to survey the nearby hedgerow rather than try to fathom what she saw in Will's lovely eyes.

"Shall we find the very best sticks in the entire park, Mr. Dorning?" She marched over to the bracken beneath the rhododendrons, Georgette at her side.

Willow Dorning even had requirements for a fetch stick. Sturdy, not too heavy, still a bit green, not long enough to cause difficulty for the dogs. Susannah nudged a toe through last year's leaves beneath the ferns and bracken, pretending to look for a stick when she was instead trying to gather her wits.

Why must Will Dorning be poor and honorable? Why must he be devoted to his younger siblings at the expense of his own ambitions? Why must he be so handsome and dear and kind?

"This one will do," Will said, plucking a stout length of wood from the undergrowth. Samson hopped about as Will passed Susannah the stick. A little hop from a dog of that size was enough to make a lady uneasy.

Will, however, took no notice of Samson. Ignoring misbehavior figured prominently in his training scheme. He never raised a hand to the dogs, never shouted, but he ignored mistakes and expressed disappointment on occasion, rather like a very patient governess. He praised good behavior often, even the simple good behavior of quietly waiting.

"Have you ever lost your temper with a dog?" Susannah asked, pushing aside more dead leaves and ferns with her boot.

Georgette snuffled among the leaves as well, and Samson could not seem to hold still.

"Once I lost my temper, when I was about Cam's age. My dog, the one I'd raised from puppyhood, chewed a corner of the family Bible to bits. I hadn't realized he was trapped in the library for most of the day, so the fault was mine. My stepmother was in hysterics, and my father—who did not care a whit for the Bible—was wroth with me because of her upset."

Samson got his jaws clamped around a protruding piece of deadfall twice as long as he was.

"Samson, drop," Will said.

Samson looked at his owner without turning loose of his prize, mischief and longing in his doggy eyes.

Will met that hopeful gaze. "Drop, Samson."

With the air of a small boy forced to sit still in Sunday services, Samson let go of the branch.

"You lost your temper over the incident with the Bible?" Under the trees, the morning was cooler, the shade welcome.

"I shouted at my dearest companion," Will said. "Called him every name a gentleman doesn't use before ladies. Kicked him hard, once, in the shoulder, and then couldn't believe I'd done that. He forgave me before the sun went down. Slept at my feet that night, and woke up, tail wagging, ready to join me in the garden the next morning, the same as any other day."

Let not the sun go down on your wrath was a biblical proscription from Ephesians. Susannah had never had much luck with that one.

"You didn't forgive yourself," Susannah said. "Sit, Georgette."

Georgette obeyed, then leaned against Susannah's leg. The dog's weight was comforting, an I'm-here sort of presence, patient and solid.

"Samson, sit," Will said, though the dog only half obeyed. "I didn't forgive myself. I'd betrayed the trust of an animal in my care, first by leaving him in the library, where temptation was all around, then by punishing him for behaving simply as a bored dog will. Samson, sit."

Samson settled in the leaves, but with a quivering, "where's my stick?!" reluctance.

"We make mistakes," Susannah said, twitching a wrinkle from Will's cravat. His dress was conservative to the point of plainness, and yet understated tailoring only made his good looks more apparent. "I made mistakes, in Kent. I thought a fellow was about to offer for me, and I was hasty in surrendering my trust to him."

She wanted Will to know this. Wanted him to understand that she wasn't a pillar of virtue, innocent of what went on between men and women.

Susannah was not innocent, and she was not *good*, for regret had kept her up many a night. She did not regret the loss of her virtue per se, but why, if she had to yield her favors outside of marriage, couldn't she have yielded them to Will Dorning?

"I'm sorry," Will said, trapping her hand in his

own. "Sorry your trust was abused. You deserve much better than that."

His eyes, so surprising in their color, were grave, and that annoyed Susannah. "You're not sorry my trust was given to another, rather than to yourself."

She was about to berate him for being honorable, berate him for finding Edward Nash's bumbling self-ishness inappropriate.

"You do trust me, Susannah," Will said, letting go of her hand. "I hope you always will, and as for my regrets—"

Something flashed by immediately overhead. A squirrel, a bird, Susannah knew not what, but Samson lunged straight up from his position at Will's side, twisting in midair so his leash wrapped around Susannah, and pulled her hard against Will.

Will struggled to hang on to the leash, but Samson kept leaping and whining, and then Georgette abandoned her post by Susannah's side, tangling her leash around Susannah from the other direction.

As Samson let out one excited bark, Susannah and Will went toppling amid the ferns.

Susannah landed mostly on top of Will, a very agreeable place to find herself. She was like that young dog in the library, temptation on all sides, and nobody to ensure decorum held the upper hand over her instincts.

Knowing she ought not, knowing she'd deserve endless scolding for yielding to her impulses, Susannah bent her head and kissed the daylights out of Will Dorning.

Seven

SHEER ANIMAL DELIGHT COURSED THROUGH WILL, from his toes to the top of his head. Lady Susannah Haddonfield had plastered herself to him at most points in between, her lovely feminine weight pressing gratifyingly over Will's falls.

And by God, the woman could kiss. No chaste friendly peck, this; no polite gesture of regret. She was playing a serious game of fetch, determined on her objective, plundering and seeking, and oblivious to all else.

Will gave her what she wanted, kissed her back like a man who'd lost what mattered to him most, because twining through his delight was regret.

He and Susannah ought not to be kissing like this. Ought not to be kissing at all, but God in heaven, Susannah Haddonfield's tongue could steal a man's very prayers. She asked, she entreated, she demanded—she tasted like peppermint and sunshine and hope.

"Something's digging—" Susannah shifted, which tightened the leash wrapped around Will's wrist. "Dammit, Will Dorning."

"Susannah, settle."

He used the same command on the dogs, and it didn't work any better on her than it did on Will's cock.

"I don't want to dratted settle, Willow. I want to avail myself of your charms, and you will think me a strumpet."

She tried to raise herself up on her arms, but just as a dog tipping its nose up will naturally lower its quarters, this only pressed her closer below.

"I think you—" Will began as Georgette decided to have a seat right near his head. "I can't think. Samson, sit."

Now the daft dog turned up biddable.

"Susannah, if you don't get off of me, I will soon be trying to get under your skirts, and we are in Hyde *Park*, with two *dogs* looking on, and my *hat* sitting on a bench nearby signaling to all that somebody has gone arse over teakettle into the bracken—are you laughing at me?"

"Yes," she said, climbing off of him to sit beside him. "I do believe we've found the comedic forest."

Georgette licked Will's ear. Samson looked like that might be a fun game to join so Will sat up.

"Perhaps you've learned enough about dogs that you can appease Effington's worries," Will said, yanking Georgette's leash from under his fundament. "Stay, Georgette."

He fished through the leaves and weeds for Samson's leash and instead found Lady Susannah's hand.

"Willow Dorning, I want to ruin you. Thoroughly and repeatedly."

"A fellow can't be ruined, but I do appreciate the

sentiment. The problem is, I want you to succeed in your folly."

Leaning back on her hands amid the ferns and leaves, Susannah smiled—not a smile Will had seen from her before.

"Progress," she said. "What must I do to get you to take the treat, Willow?"

She had to marry him, or the next thing to it, and that meant Will had to find a way to support her. He brushed a green oak leaf from her hair.

"Stop smiling at me like that," he said as she winnowed her fingers through his hair, though he was smiling back. Besottedly, unreservedly, adoringly.

"No, Will Dorning. I will not stop smiling. I like you exceedingly, and I like kissing you. You cannot scold me or ignore me out of my sentiments."

A rock made itself known beneath Will's backside, and Georgette was watching him with a look he couldn't decipher. Pitying, perhaps. Georgette was the mother of seventeen, having had three litters.

"I think we're setting a bad example for the dogs," Will said. Or perhaps Georgette was laughing at him. Samson simply looked bewildered, as if to remind Will that kissing in the undergrowth was not what came after looking for a stout, stiff—

God help me. "We can't tarry here in the hedges without inviting scandal, my lady."

Though Will couldn't exactly parade about the park in his present condition, either, riding breeches leaving little to the imagination.

"Let's sit on the bench and discuss literature," Lady Susannah said. "That might cool your blood."

She scooted around and kissed him again, her hand settling on his falls and squeezing gently. Twice, as if to assure Will her actions were intentional.

Then she rose and picked up Samson's leash. "Samson, heel. Georgette, stay. Mr. Dorning, I will await you on the bench."

Away her ladyship strolled, grinning like a fiend, Samson trotting obediently at her side.

❧

"Three rewards now," Mannering marveled, scooping Yorick up, and stroking his head. "Great, fat, generous rewards. Lady March said she loved her little bowwow at least as much as the Duchess of Ambrose loved hers, and so must post an equal reward. The third is more modest, from some baron or other."

Effington disliked the look of Yorick, cradled trustingly against a waistcoat that had probably cost as much as an entire winter's coal expenses for Effington House. Neither did his lordship like the look of Mannering, lounging in his finery on the library sofa.

"Put the dog down, Mannering, or he'll piss on your expensive tailoring, and then I won't let you accompany me on my calls."

Effington would pay a visit to Lady March and the poor duchess too, for appearances' sake, of course. Dog fanciers were a close-knit group, after all.

"Little Yorick is a consummate gentleman," Mannering said. "If he did have an accident, and piddle a bit where he oughtn't to, well, that's what laundresses are for."

Laundresses were for tupping on Monday

mornings out in the mews. A merry lot, and clean, not coincidentally.

"If you're so enamored of the dog, then you hold the leash," Effington said, tossing the length of leather at Mannering's chest. "What do you hear regarding my intended?"

"I have other matters to manage besides assassinating the character of your beloved," Mannering said, affixing the leash to Yorick's collar. "M'sisters are forever plaguing me, and then Mama starts in. All very vexing."

"Get a wife. She'll bring wealth to the family coffers and manage your womenfolk, if you choose wisely." Effington was looking forward to the clashes between Lady Della and his own mother. Too bad he couldn't take bets, the way bets were taken in the bear gardens and cockpits.

Lucrative places, both. Thank heavens.

"I shall get a wife," Mannering said, setting Yorick on the carpet and rising. "I look forward to it, in fact. This business of playing cards at all hours, waltzing with the wallflowers, and pretending politics interests me more than the ladies do is tedious. Yorick agrees with me."

Yorick agreed with anybody whose boots were within dog-kicking range.

"Let's start with the Duchess of Ambrose," Effington said. "She's always glad to see me."

She was always glad to see Yorick. Fed the little beast tea cakes and held him in her lap.

"I like Her Grace," Mannering said. "Plainspoken, doesn't suffer fools. Always a fine quality. She's nice."

Her Grace had a nasty streak to go with her weakness for dumb animals.

Effington headed for the door. "Yorick, come." He snapped his fingers, but the stupid dog remained sitting at Mannering's feet.

"I don't suffer fools either," Effington said, snapping his fingers again. "Mannering, come. When I'm done trotting you around Mayfair on a leash, we'll pop down to the cockfights in Kensington. I can always use a bit of the ready, and I have an instinct for which bird is likely to win."

Lady Della, alas, would be left without an escort for her afternoon stroll in the park. Such a pity.

Mannering made a face. "Cockfights. Don't care for 'em. Not the best company. Bloody lot of noise, bloody lot of bloody feathers."

Bloody lot of money changing hands too. That thought kept Effington smiling as he endured the snappish and trying company of the Duchess of Ambrose, who appeared to have no idea what might have become of her dear Caesar.

Yet another great pity. Effington consoled her effusively, as did Mannering. She served excellent cakes, and made delicate mention of the reward she was offering for her missing darling.

Effington pulled Mannering away from the tea tray after half an hour of that tripe, and steeled himself for more of same from Lady March. Her Grace's butler escorted them to the front door and waited, nose in the air, while the footman found their hats and walking sticks.

"One feels sorry for the duchess," Mannering said. "Who would have thought she set such store by a dog?"

"Many do," Effington murmured, tapping his hat

onto his head, then tilting it a half inch to the left.
He scratched Yorick's ears, mindful of the butler. "I
certainly value my canine friends. Always have. People
are fickle, but a dog's loyalty is the genuine article."

Before the butler could open the door for them,
a knock sounded. The gentleman admitted was tall,
broad shouldered, and dressed with about as much style
as an impoverished Quaker, though he looked familiar.

He took off his hat and passed a card to the
butler. "Her Grace should be expecting me, Pinkney.
Mannering, Effington, greetings."

The gentleman bowed, and Yorick's little tail
wagged furiously.

"Dorning," Mannering said, extending a hand.
"A pleasure. Is Her Grace already on the hunt for
another dog?"

Dorning. One of the Dorset Dornings. The troublesome lot who'd made it their mission to dance
Della Haddonfield off her feet.

"I doubt anybody will replace Caesar in Her
Grace's affections," Dorning said. "I flatter myself Her
Grace won't mind me occasionally stopping by until
Caesar is found."

Dorning's face was not friendly, though he wasn't
exactly bad looking. Serious, certainly, and his eyes
were an odd color.

"We must be on our way, sir," Effington said. If
Mannering had worn a leash, a stout tug would have
been in order. "Come, Mannering. Our next destination lies five streets over, and time is flying."

After the requisite bowing and farewelling,
Mannering came along, Yorick at his heels.

"Why would a Dorning be calling on a duchess?" Effington asked. "They're sheep farmers, aren't they? Not much blunt, and even less consequence." Which was why Casriel's attentions to Lady Della were not worth fretting over—much.

"Effington, for a fellow who professes to adore dogs, you surprise me," Mannering said, stopping so Yorick could lift his leg on a lamppost. "Willow Dorning does magic with dogs. His collies are famous throughout the realm for working with sheep. He's trained the Regent's spaniels, and he's the fellow who matched Caesar up with the duchess."

"He's an earl's spare and he trains dogs—himself?" Effington didn't know whether to be amused or appalled.

Yorick finished watering the lamppost, and Mannering picked him up. "Wellington said if his troops had been as well trained as Will Dorning's dogs, then Waterloo would have been an afternoon's romp."

Messy business, Waterloo. Had Effington's title not limited his options, he would have been in the thick of it, surely.

"Dorning trains the animals himself, in person?"

"Every one. Some are strays. The collies, he breeds in Dorset. Worth a pretty penny too, but he's very particular about who he'll sell them to."

Ah, well then. No need to fret at all. "He's an earl's spare, and he not only trains dogs, he sells them for coin. I suppose his brothers trade in chickens, geese, and cheeses. How splendid. Mannering, you have quite made my day. You will please ensure Lady Della understands the caliber of swain she'll have slobbering at her heels should I quit the field."

❧

"I don't think his lordship's coming, milady."

Jeffers twirled the parasol Della had appropriated from Susannah for this visit to the park. Susannah herself had taken to spending most mornings reading in the fresh air, and thus Della had brought a maid with her to wait for Lord Effington near Park Lane.

All of Polite Society was assembling for the farce that was the fashionable hour, and Effington was nowhere to be seen.

"We'll give his lordship five more minutes," Della said. "Perhaps he came down with a megrim, or his horse threw a shoe."

Jeffers's sigh spoke volumes, about earls' daughters who'd become smitten with the dubious charms of sunshine, large trees, and green grass; about the pleasure of strolling around town when a maid's highest ambition was to get off her feet for five minutes.

"Horses do lose shoes, my lady. At least hold the parasol. A woman can't be too careful with her complexion."

"What is the point of avoiding freckles if my doting swain has decided to avoid me?" Della asked.

Jeffers was several years Della's senior, and worlds more experienced with what mattered. Hard work. Holding one's tongue. Men. She did not deserve to be the object of Della's exasperation.

"Gentlemen are a trial," Jeffers said. "This is your first Season, milady, so the frustrations of dealing with the gentlemen are new to you, but the parasol is ever so pretty, and with that green dress, it's quite fetching."

The green dress would have looked better on a

woman with blond hair. The lacy purple parasol was intended to be eye-catching, to make sure all and sundry knew that Lady Della Haddonfield was enjoying the park on the arm of Viscount Effington, and that a match was said to be in the offing.

"I hate that parasol," Della muttered.

Diplomatic silence greeted her admission.

"I hate London, I hate the Season, I hate every—"

And there he was, the man Della had been discreetly inquiring after and searching for from ballroom to bookshop to bridle path. Jeffers must have seen him too, lounging against a sturdy oak, his regard neither subtle nor particularly respectful.

He touched one gloved finger to his hat brim.

"We should go, my lady," Jeffers muttered. "I do believe it feels like rain. I'm sure of it, in fact. The London weather can be so fickle, don't you know? Wouldn't want Lady Susannah's parasol to get a soaking, now would we?"

In the middle of a sunny afternoon, thunder and lightning threatened from the dark-haired fellow beneath that oak. He was exquisitely attired in dark gray breeches, a silver waistcoat, and black riding coat. His boots were polished and well fitted, his top hat brushed to a shine.

He was intimidatingly magnificent, exactly as a ducal heir should be.

"Take these bread crumbs," Della said, shoving the bag at Jeffers. "Feed the fowl on the Serpentine, and take the parasol with you. I'll stay here in the shade, so you needn't fret about my complexion."

Jeffers made a noise of exasperation and defeat,

snatched the bag, and stomped off toward the grassy bank of the Serpentine.

The gentleman pushed away from the oak and sauntered toward Della, or maybe he was swaggering. Had he been waiting for her, and what would Della do if Effington decided to belatedly keep his appointment to stroll at the fashionable hour?

"Lady Della Haddonfield," the man said, tipping his hat. "How easily you divest yourself of the only protection on hand to shield your good name. Shall I muster a mutual acquaintance to make a proper introduction, or can we dispense with that farce?"

He had eyes the blue of a winter sky over a deserted churchyard, and a voice that blended the erudition of an Oxford don with the dissipation of a royal prince. Della estimated his age near thirty, and the wealth he came from at nearly immeasurable.

She had been raised with five brothers, else she might not have known what to do with a man who was as handsome as every debutante's dream, unmarried, exquisitely attired, and very much in need of a set-down.

If Della had had the infernal purple parasol, she would have smacked him with it. Instead, she rose and walked away.

❧

Will could spot one of his brothers from a great distance, knew each one from his walk, his posture, the gestures used in conversation. Will could also identify his brothers from the clothes they wore, for those clothes often belonged to him.

"Lovely jacket, Cam," Will remarked as he came

even with Ash and Cam on Brook Street. "Surely, that's a new acquisition. No unraveling seams, no stains, no thin patches on the elbows. The style is severe for you and the cut somewhat loose, but sober. I like it."

"Ash took my best coat," Cam said, twirling slowly on the walkway. "I look more like a banker in your clothing, Will. Thanks for the loan."

They'd steal Will's horse except nobody else could ride the mare when she was in a mood. They'd steal Will's boots, except he was usually wearing them.

"Clean, understated, well-tailored attire really does flatter you," Will said, mostly in hopes of making Cam feel guilty. "You might try asking before you appropriate it, though."

"Cam is your brother, and you don't lock your wardrobe," Ash said. "That's an invitation to borrow. Be glad I at least made him surrender the contents of your pockets." Ash passed over a folded document that Will stashed out of sight before Cam could snatch at it.

"What inspired you both to stir before sunset?" Will asked.

"I'm hunting for my dog," Cam said, gaze roaming over the nearby square. "A great brute with a gash over one eye. Smooth brindle coat, not quite full grown."

"You haven't a dog, Sycamore," Will said. "If you want a dog, I can find you one that will bring some manners to the equation, not a street mongrel that snacks on rats and garbage all day."

Though the street mongrels often had good sense and enjoyed reliable health.

"My boy isn't a mongrel," Cam said. "He's a

bloody great mastiff, and some fool was stealing him and making a bad job of it."

Ash's gaze was resolutely to the fore. In the square across the street, children played with balls, house-maids flirted with footmen, young swells lounged about talking in groups, looking smart and useless.

While Will's responsibilities never seemed to end.

Sainted gamboling puppies. "I am on my way to pay calls, you two," he said. "I do not have time to deliver the appropriate lecture on England's property laws, which are quite strict. You are the one stealing the dog if you assume possession in the absence of legitimate ownership."

"You never listen," Cam said. "I know what I saw, and you're not the only one who can grasp when an animal's miserable. The dog was being stolen and beaten. The idiot trying to haul him down the alley didn't even try asking the dog to come, didn't offer a single treat, and yelled at the poor creature so half of Mayfair might have heard."

Beating a dog was unproductive, disgraceful, and just plain ungentlemanly. Beating a dog that weighed more than many grown men was also stupid as hell.

"Cam is right," Ash said. "The dog was in the hands of a fool. You don't own a dog that size without some notion of how to manage it."

While Will, increasingly, had no idea how to manage his brothers. "What did you do, Cam?" For he'd done something, and Ash hadn't been able to stop him.

"I followed them for about a mile, though it wasn't a pretty mile. The dog had a lot of fight in him, but he was quick too, and dodged most of the blows.

They stuck to the alleys, and ended up on a back street toward Bloomsbury."

"Let's keep moving," Will said, for his appointments mattered to him, as did shepherding his brothers in the opposite direction from Bloomsbury. "Tell me the rest of it, Sycamore."

"Not much else to tell," Cam said, jamming his hands in his pockets. "The man dragged the dog halfway across the West End, then tied him in an alley behind a tavern. When nobody was around, I tossed the poor blighter a bit of cheese, told him he was a good fellow, then untied the rope securing him. He gave me a great lick across the cheek, then bounded off. I let him go because I didn't want anybody to see me with him."

The dog might have killed Cam. Might have delivered fatal bites, might have created a commotion that drew the owner and his friends from the tavern, and seen Cam hanged or transported for theft.

"Sycamore," Will began in his sternest tones, "what you did was very, very—" Ash caught Will by the arm when he might have marched right across Upper Grosvenor Street. With that hand on Will's arm came a glance. *Cam meant well. He's trying his best. I didn't know what to do.*

Dogs needed no words to convey their sentiments to one another, but humans seldom paid the same degree of attention to their own kind.

Sycamore had been doing exactly what Will might have done at his age, exactly what Will's instincts goaded him to do even now: protect those who couldn't protect themselves, look out for mute beasts left to the mercy of humankind's fickle honor.

Will settled his top hat more firmly on his head. "What you did, Sycamore, was brave, clever, and bold. I'm proud of you and your quick thinking, as well as your willingness to risk your well-being to look after an unfortunate creature in need of rescue. If you ever do anything like that again"—Ash was grinning at his boots, Cam looked bewildered—"I will bankrupt myself paying for your legal defense, and black the eyes of anybody who says a gentleman should have done differently."

"Will can nearly afford the legal defense too," Ash said as they set off across the street. "Our Willow has entrusted his coin to Kettering, with encouraging results."

"Sycamore, please don't take similar risks in the future," Will went on, because what mattered Ash's teasing, when Sycamore could have been arrested or mauled to death? "Bring the problem to me, and we'll find a safer way to handle it."

The duchess had hinted that Will ought to be look-ing for the missing dogs, and Will had pretended to misconstrue her innuendo—despite the nagging sense that Her Grace was right.

"I couldn't see a safer way," Cam said. "Poor dog was being dragged to perdition. Ash didn't try to stop me, so he agrees with me."

"I never said—" Ash began.

"He's your brother, and you didn't tie him to the saddle," Will said. "That's resounding agreement, Ash, and I'll thank you not to bruit my financial status about in the streets."

They sauntered along, tipping hats to the ladies, and Will wished for a moment that Casriel might have joined them. The earl deserved to banter with his brothers, to be proud of them, to know they could get both into and out of scrapes without moment-by-moment supervision.

A sense of wistful hope wafted through Will, because the boys would grow up, Casriel would marry, and maybe someday…

"If a man leaves his financial reports in his coat pocket," Ash said, "where his brother, an aspiring solicitor, can find them, then that man is not very careful with his privacy, is he?"

"Will's rich?" Cam asked.

"Now you've done it," Will said. "The town crier has got hold of the news, but having two coins to rub together hardly makes me wealthy. One has dogs to feed, and coats to order from the tailor. Unlike you lot, I don't take an allowance from Casriel and never have."

"You live off Georgette's affairs," Cam said.

"Georgette does not have affairs," Will retorted. "She makes her visits to the stud dogs of my choosing, and when the puppies are old enough, and have sufficient training—why must every conversation with you eventually turn to the topic of procreation?"

"Here it comes, the procreation and self-restraint lecture," Ash muttered. "You have more than two coins, Willow."

"How rich is he?" Cam asked.

Ash, thank heavens, did not name figures. "Look on the third page, Willow. Kettering is breaking records to get your finances put to rights. I shall ask him about investing a sum for me. Cam, I'm sure, would rather spend all of his allowance on wenches and wine."

"Can't spend it on the opera dancers," Cam

lamented. "Kettering takes a dim view, and then Casriel starts clearing his throat, and Jacaranda peers down her nose at me so disappointedly even a lusty fellow such as my handsome self finds it difficult to muster a proper—"

"Sycamore!" Both older brothers spoke at once.

Cam grinned, stopped walking, and tipped his hat. "Right. Gentlemanly discretion and all that. I'll leave you two well-dressed old nuns to make your calls. I'm for an ice at Gunter's."

He strolled, off looking entirely too self-possessed and rakish for a mere boy.

"That went well," Ash said, resuming their progress. "That went very well, in fact, but what will you do when he decides his calling is rescuing the oppressed canines of London, because that's how brave, bold, honorable fellows occupy themselves of a drunken evening?"

Will stared at the figure on the third page of Kettering's report, though Ash's question conjured scenes of Cam beaten and incarcerated, like the very dogs he'd seek to rescue.

"If Cam insists on disregarding the dictates of prudence," Will said, "I might be forced to go out dog-rescuing with him, despite the danger to life, limb, and reputation. Ash, could this total be in error?"

"No, it could not. Kettering's people don't make silly mistakes. They don't even make brilliant mistakes. Kettering is shrewd, and you gave him a decent sum to start with."

Every penny Will could spare. Still the figure was larger than he'd anticipated. Not a fortune, but…not a pittance.

"Will it continue to grow at the same rate?" Will

understood the canine species as well as he understood his own. Agriculture was in his very blood. He could manage a ledger fairly well, and monitored conversations with the bankers mostly to ensure they weren't cheating Casriel.

This investment business, though… It wanted more than a piece of cheese and a pat on the head for Will to take an interest in it.

"The rate of growth can change, and even become a rate of loss," Ash said. "Kettering is the best though, and you're family. He'll ferret out the more profitable projects for you, and watch them like an old tabby with one kitten. Then too, as the principle grows, the interest has more to work with."

"Like when Georgette's daughters are old enough to breed," Will said, folding the paper and tucking it away. In a few years, the progeny of one bitch and one dog could number in the hundreds. Why hadn't Will seen that invested money had the same potential?

Between Grosvenor and Mount Street, a bright, sunny revelation beamed down through the clouds of Will's worry for his brother, and for several unfortunate dogs: *Someday, I might be able to marry Lady Susannah Haddonfield.* Not now, maybe not for several years, but someday…

"That is a dangerous smile," Ash said. "Makes you look more like Cam. So upon whom are we calling?"

"Lady Susannah Haddonfield. Who said anything about *we*, Ash?"

"Don't be difficult, Willow. I stopped Cam from appropriating your newest breeches, and I am owed some consideration for merely borrowing them myself."

Eight

"MR. DORNING HAS ASKED ME TO ACCOMPANY HIM ON a call to Lady March. Would you like to come with us?" Susannah asked, tying her bonnet ribbons beneath her chin.

"Suze, you have no sense of style," Della retorted, untying the ribbons and repositioning the hat. "A slight angle to the bow, a jaunty set to the brim does not make you a Haymarket streetwalker."

In the mirror over the foyer's sideboard, Susannah studied Della's adjustments. "You're not supposed to know about Haymarket streetwalkers, or speak of them if you do. Are you fretting over Lord Effington's lapse?"

For the viscount had failed to keep his appointment in the park not an hour ago, and Della's handling of Susannah's millinery was brisk to the point of agitation.

"In truth I'd be relieved were Effington to attach his interests to another lady," Della said. "I want my own household, of course, and a husband and children, but if this is how he behaves when trying to secure my interest, how will he act once we're married?"

Susannah picked up her reticule, felt the weight

of Mr. Shakespeare therein, and decided he need not accompany her on this call.

"Effington might simply be ill, or busy with his solicitors, or perhaps he got the days confused," Susannah said, the same excuses she'd trotted out for the few and fainthearted gentlemen who had made overtures to her years ago.

A knock sounded on the door, and Susannah answered it herself rather than indulge in the absurdity of waiting for the butler.

"Mr. Dorning, and Mr. Dorning, good day." Susannah was disappointed to see Ash Dorning at his brother's side, though they made a fetching pair.

"My lady and my lady," Will replied, bowing when he and Ash had been admitted to the foyer. "Lady Della, will you join this sortie?"

Would he be disappointed if she did?

"No, thank you," Della said. "I've just come back from taking the air in the park."

"Ah, then you'll be having a spot of tea," Ash Dorning said. "I could use a cup myself."

Bold of him, but after Susannah's own behavior beneath the rhododendrons, she could hardly judge a man for a bit of boldness.

"Come upstairs, then," Della said, "and we'll leave the social calls to our elders."

Will watched them go, his expression troubled. "Lady Della is not pleased to have a caller other than Effington. Perhaps he'll stop by, for I crossed his path at the Duchess of Ambrose's house."

Oh dear. "Lord Effington was due to walk in the park with Della and failed to keep the appointment.

Did he seem in good health?" Had the viscount known what day it was?

"His lordship was to all appearances in the pink of health. Had Mannering in tow, and that fretful little pug."

Yorick, or poor Yorick, to Susannah. "You might have dissembled, Mr. Dorning. Hedged, prevaricated, failed to note the viscount's state of health."

Will took Shakespeare from Susannah's grasp and set him aside. "No, I mightn't. You prefer the difficult truth to the convenient lie. I like that about you. Shall we be on our way?"

A compliment, however well disguised.

"Your note was mysterious," Susannah said as Will held the door for her. "Why are we calling on Lady March? My memories of her tea dances are hardly cheering."

"They should be fortifying memories. You foiled the Mannering sisters' attempts to wreck your standing in the eyes of the young fellows, and to destroy your confidence. Others would not have fared as well."

"I was too stupid for some of their schemes. If somebody complimented my dress, I took it as a compliment."

Such an unusual color, my lady. What an original way to draw the notice of the gentlemen.

You actually drink the punch! Ah, so you can send more than one man to fetch you a glass. Very clever, Lady Susannah! Though I suppose you might become tipsy…

"You were too innocent," Will said. "We're calling on Lady March for old times' sake, but also because her mastiff has gone missing."

Will would be interested in the missing dog,

though his tone suggested he wasn't exactly pleased to be out socializing.

Perhaps he'd scheduled this call to allow Susannah a chance to revisit the sight of her youthful challenges, but she was more absorbed with the pleasure of walking along with her arm linked through Will's. Maybe their sessions with the dogs had made a difference, maybe Will was simply accustomed to her company, but Susannah's escort felt more relaxed, possibly even friendlier than he had in their previous encounters.

Most of their previous encounters. Willow Dorning was a prodigiously skilled kisser when caught unawares beneath the maples.

Lady March welcomed them with the flighty, dithery manners she'd shown her daughter's friends seven years ago. She had aged, and apparently grown more nervous with the passing of time. Her dark ringlets showed not a hint of gray, though the years had dug grooves beside her mouth.

Susannah was abruptly glad Will had suggested this call.

Prior to Susannah's come-out, Lady March had loomed in Susannah's imagination like the social equivalent of the Fates, one of the hostesses who could destroy a young woman's prospects or assure them.

Her ladyship had held neither power, though Susannah could see that only now. Lady March was a creature to be pitied rather than feared, trapped in a boring, anxious, lonely life.

"I do miss my little bowwow," her ladyship said, drawing a handkerchief from her sleeve when the tea service had been dealt with. "Alexander was such a comfort, such a dear." She touched the linen to the corner of her eyes, then balled up the handkerchief in a be-ringed grip.

"When did you first notice he was missing?" Will asked.

"I can't clearly recall. Not long ago. Mere days, I'm sure. I miss him so, it feels as if he's been gone an age." More dabbing at her eyes. "How is your sister, Lady Susannah? Lady Delilah is such a pretty little thing, though her looks are quite unusual for a Haddonfield."

Susannah smiled, though she wished Georgette had been with them, to leave a damp spot on Lady March's carpet.

"Lady Della is enjoying her first Season very much," Susannah said. "Society has been most welcoming. I only wish our parents could have been here to see her make her bow. Bellefonte and his countess are inundated with invitations, and her ladyship's at home is an utter crush."

Not a complete lie. The afternoons when Leah received were well attended, though not by swains looking to curry Della's favor.

"But that dark hair," Lady March said. "Dark hair can be a trial."

"I've never found it so," Will said, when Susannah might have spared a pointed glance for her ladyship's curls. "Nor have my siblings similarly afflicted ever complained about having dark hair. Have you any idea what might have happened to Alexander?"

Her ladyship glanced down, and for an instant, her expression was exasperated. "Of course not. He was a very large dog, and if he went over the garden wall, or some careless servant left the gate unlocked, how am I to know of that? I'm too upset to dwell on the details of his disappearance, if you want the truth."

She poured herself another cup of tea and neglected to offer any to either of her guests. In the late afternoon sunlight, the rubies adorning her rings and bracelet had a flat, smudged quality.

The tea service she'd brought out was plain blue jasperware; the spite she'd served Susannah had been quite fresh, however.

Will tried again, gently, to pry details of the dog's disappearance from the aggrieved owner, until Susannah realized Lady March would not share anything further.

"Mr. Dorning, we must be on our way," Susannah said, rising. "Lady March, our thanks for a congenial visit, and I do hope your little bowwow comes home soon."

While her ladyship directed a footman to clear the tray, Susannah leaned close to Will.

"Forget your walking stick," she murmured.

His consternation showed only in his eyes, then he gave the barest nod. They left Lady March clutching her handkerchief at the front door.

"Keep walking in case she's watching us," Susannah said, threading her arm through Will's. "She's lying, Will, I'm sure."

"How do you know?"

Susannah *knew* with every instinct developed while chatting desperately with the other wallflowers for the dozenth time in two weeks. She sensed Lady March's mendacity the same way she'd sense when one of her brothers was troubled, though he'd never share a word of the problem with her. She knew Lady March had dissembled, the way she knew she must kiss Will Dorning again, and soon.

"Did you notice she never actually shed a tear?" Susannah asked. "She put on a performance worthy of Mrs. Siddons, but she never cried for her dog or shared any information about him that would lead to his return."

Will slowed as they reached the corner. "What are you suggesting?"

"She doesn't want that dog back. She's making a great production out of her loss, but she doesn't expect him to be returned."

Will drew Susannah into the alley that would lead to the mews of the various great houses along the bordering streets. Maples and oaks arched over the lane, and the noise of passing traffic was muted in the alley. A tabby cat lay on a high garden wall, sunning itself amid pots of red salvia.

"So I'm to retrieve my cane and interrogate the help?" Will asked.

"I'd wait for another half hour. Her ladyship is more likely to have taken her landau to the park by then. Now, we should ask the help in the stables what they know about the dog's disappearance."

"I am hearing the word *we* entirely too much today, my lady, and applied to the wrong endeavors."

"While I am not hearing it enough," Susannah retorted. "You tell me you lack the coin necessary to allow a woman expectations regarding your future. The reward for this missing mastiff is substantial, and you're ideally suited to find a missing dog, Willow."

The cat blinked at them, then hopped off the wall and strutted across the alley.

Will slapped his gloves against his thigh. "What else did you notice about Lady March?"

"Her rings are paste," Susannah said as the cat leaped up onto another wall and thence into an oak. Crows scattered from the tree amid a cacophony of avian scolding.

"If a lady is so bold as to show off her jewels during daylight hours," Susannah went on, "she should expect those jewels to be noticed. The settings might have been real, but the rubies were not."

"Ah, that explains it," Will said. "Lady March cannot afford the reward she has so ostentatiously posted. Her dog is genuinely missing, but she has no means to make good on the obligations his return would entail."

Susannah began a brisk progress down the alley. "You do not want to find that dog. Are you so happy to remain an impoverished bachelor, Willow?"

He remained where he was, clearly reluctant to heed the implied command to heel which her departure had signaled.

"Susannah, stop."

Ha. She stomped along, looking for the mews that would serve Lady March's horses. Will was so quiet, Susannah didn't hear him until he'd leaped in front of her.

"Not an hour past," he growled, "I was admonishing my hotheaded brother that poking into the fate of lost dogs is dangerous, thankless work. I must think, and so must you. Give me two minutes, Susannah, to sort fact from folly, to—"

Susannah kissed him, lest he forget about lost opportunities while considering lost dogs.

"Talk to the stablemen, Willow. I'll await you near the street. If anybody sees me, I'll be a lady waiting for my vehicle to be brought around. You can walk me home, then come back and chat up the butler or the porter."

Will untied the bows of Susannah's bonnet and reset it on her head, as Della had done, at nearly the same coquettish angle. The feel of his fingers brushing against Susannah's chin had strange repercussions in the vicinity of her knees.

"You aren't concerned for the dogs," he said. "I wish I were not, but I am concerned for the dogs."

What was he going on about? "The weather is mild, London abounds with dung heaps, middens, and all manner of sources of food for an enterprising dog. Of course I'm concerned for the dogs, Willow, but I'm concerned for you too."

The notion seemed to puzzle him. He cocked his head as Georgette might have, while Susannah nearly panted from the effect of standing so close to him.

"Wait for me. I won't be long," he said, striding off in the direction of the stables.

Susannah had taken exactly one step in the opposite direction before Will's hand on her arm gently but firmly turned her into his embrace.

"You are concerned for our future," Will said. "I am too." With that, he kissed the daylights out of her, then set her back, and resumed his march upon the mews.

❧

"I have landed in the midst of one hell of a tangle," Will said, quietly, lest the other men in the club's dining room overhear him.

Casriel topped up Will's wineglass. "You, Willow? Are Cam and Ash behind this? I don't recall you ever being in a tangle, not even with a woman, and they are the very definition of a tangle."

"Unless that woman is your wife," Will said, taking a sip of cool, fruity red wine. Susannah's kisses were like this vintage, startling in their verve and impact, but sweet, too, and full of subtleties.

"Willow, will you explain this tangle to me or not?" Casriel asked, setting the bottle on Will's side of the table. "I am the head of your family, also your devoted brother. I would be surpassingly gratified to solve a problem for you for a change, instead of the other way round."

Will might once have used that opening to lecture the *head of his family* on the necessity of acquiring a countess, but such single-mindedness—such simplemindedness—was beyond his grasp at the moment. The notion that Casriel was concerned, even eager to help, was quite odd.

Also reassuring.

"I'll lay it out as best I can," Will said. "Several large, handsome, well-cared-for dogs have gone missing from aristocratic owners, and I suspect there are more I haven't yet heard of."

"I know about the Duchess of Ambrose and Lady March's dogs," Casriel said, circling his wrist in a gesture reminiscent of Cam. "Impressive rewards posted by both women."

"Cam is determined to find the dogs," Will said. "I cannot see any good resulting from his involvement in such dangerous matters, but neither will common sense dissuade him. I am thus considering lending my expertise to the search, provided I can do so discreetly. The duchess and I are on familiar terms, but Lady March and I are not well acquainted. I enlisted Lady Susannah's company to pay a call on Lady March."

Storytelling gave a man a thirst, and Will's glass had somehow become only half full.

"This steak is undercooked," Casriel said, pushing his plate away. "I don't care for Lord March myself. Can't hold his drink, and must let all and sundry know he's a regular at the tables where the deepest play is to be had."

Will buttered a crust of bread and popped it into his mouth. Paste jewels, gambling markers, a reward that could not be paid…the bread was too dry, and the conclusion clamoring in Will's mind utterly sour.

"Between calling on Her Grace," Will went on, "and calling on Lady March, I ran into Cam and Ash. Cam related a tale of pursuing some fellow who showed every sign of having stolen the mastiff he was dragging along. Cam followed and freed the dog, and the animal matches the description of Lady March's missing Alexander."

Casriel refilled his own wineglass. "Shite."

"Shite, because Cam nearly got into a scrape, or shite because Cam let the dog go when he might have earned a reward?"

Casriel took a sip of his libation, while the club's candlelight flickered over dark hair, a shrewd gaze, and features that looked more like their papa's with each passing year.

Grey was the earl. In that single, mundane moment, watching Grey take a considering sip of good German wine, Will realized that the title had settled on his brother's shoulders more firmly in recent months. The earl was more focused, more in charge of the family's affairs.

He met with the solicitors not at their offices, but in his library. He sat in the Lords and took his responsibilities seriously, but did not become preoccupied with affairs of state to the detriment of the earldom's affairs.

The realization sent Will's emotions in several directions at once, like puppies spilling out of their whelping box.

"I am proud of you," Will said, though he hadn't intended to burden his brother with that sentiment aloud.

"How much wine have you had, Willow?" Casriel asked, sitting back with his glass cradled in his hand. "I'm proud of Sycamore. He needs to learn that a fellow can get into all manner of interesting contretemps as long as he can also get out of them."

"Yes, well, I'm proud of Cam too," Will said. "For getting out of the scrape, but also for setting the dog free. One can't know, of course, who the dog's owner is, but Cam saw an animal in need of aid and intervened."

Will's feeling went beyond mere pride, to a sense of gratitude, for Cam had taken the risk Will himself ought to have shouldered. If the dogs of that size were being stolen, their fates would be miserable—a short life of violence and deprivation, a bad end.

"He took a risk," Casriel replied, holding the wine

up to the light. "Cam excels at tackling risky ventures, and usually comes out the worse for it, as does my exchequer. Back to your recitation, Willow. I'm expected at some ball or other before the hour grows too late, and I cannot like that you'd embroil yourself in this matter of stolen dogs."

Casriel was scheduled to attend the Windham ball. "Any particular lady standing up with you?"

"She's not even expecting me," Casriel said. "Perhaps a sneak attack will serve me well, if I can get up the nerve to ask her for a dance. So there you were, dressing Cam down for his foolishness, and then you're off to take tea with Lady Susannah at Lady March's?"

The other emotion Will could put a name on was a sense of loss. When even Cam was showing good sense—for Cam—life was changing. Casriel was apparently interested in a woman, Casriel was the one helping Will sort through a trying day, and Ash was on his way to a position with Worth Kettering.

The Dorning menfolk were settling down, which explained the relief Will felt, to behold his older brother looking every inch the handsome lord. Grey, Ash, Cam, and the youngsters would manage if Will found himself a small estate where he could train dogs and raise sheep.

And raise a family.

"Lady Susannah's company is agreeable to me generally," Will said, "and she is acquainted with Lady March. Try though we did, Lady March would not disclose a single detail of her dog's disappearance, and Lady Susannah suggested I instead talk to the help."

Casriel finished his wine. "What aren't you telling me, Willow?"

"Lady March's rings are paste, her tea service less than grand, only the upper servants are paid on time, and the dog typically spent the night in a stall in the mews. He simply wasn't there one morning, though he disappeared during the stablemen's night for playing skittles at the corner pub."

"Shite and more shite. She sold her dog?"

Will had hoped to gather evidence that her ladyship had *not* sold her dog, because the ramifications of Casriel's conclusion were many, and all of them bad.

"She might have," Will said. "He was a handsome fellow, reasonably well trained, but very protective. Some squire down from the north might have taken a fancy to him." Will prayed that had been the dog's fate.

"Tell that bouncer to Georgette," Casriel said, crossing his knife and fork on the edge of his plate. "What do you think befell the dog?"

"I think he's bound for the bear pits. The bear gardens need a steady supply of big, aggressive dogs. The bears occasionally kill a dog, often wound them, and sometimes knock the fight out of them. The only fools who enjoy a bear-baiting are the ones not in the pit."

"I avoid them, and the cockfights too. A Mayfair ballroom is all the blood sport I can handle. You're still not telling me the whole of it, Willow. Proving ownership of a dog would be next to impossible, and thus anybody involved risks finding disfavor with the law—and with the thieves."

Disfavor with the law being a polite way to refer to

charges of theft; disfavor with the thieves might result in severe injury, or worse.

"Lady Susannah has got it into her head I can use the rewards," Will said. "She's not wrong."

"A gentleman never argues with a lady when he can get drunk with his brother instead. The Dorning hasn't been born who's truly wealthy, Willow."

Will signaled a waiter to wrap up the earl's uneaten steak, an eccentricity the waiters were accustomed to from him. While the food was removed, Will searched for a way to say what needed saying without jeopardizing his privacy.

And mostly failed. "I fancy Lady Susannah, and I believe my sentiments are reciprocated."

"To hear Ash tell it, they're reciprocated in the undergrowth of Hyde Park of a morning. Your breeches were dirty and grass stained in interesting locations earlier this week."

"Clothing that is less than pristine is unlikely to be pilfered," Will said. "A man who wants to take a wife must be able to support her. I conveyed my concerns in this regard to Lady Susannah."

Casriel to his credit neither laughed nor swore. "So she wants you to earn those rewards, while you only want to find a few hapless mongrels without being caught doing so."

"Purebreds, but yes. I cannot expect the rewards, Grey—a gentleman would not accept them, though Susannah doesn't seem to grasp that—and yet she expects me to locate the dogs. Dogs meet difficult fates, I know that, but now Cam and Ash expect me to join the search, and—"

"And you cannot sleep at night, knowing several overlarge, unsuspecting pets will be thrown into the pits. You want to find them too, Willow."

Will wanted somebody to find the damned dogs, and Susannah wanted that somebody to be him.

"I'm no longer penniless, much to my surprise, but neither am I wealthy," Will said. "Susannah's lot with me would be humble, compared to what she's accustomed to."

Casriel made a study of the wine bottle's label, though Will doubted the earl could decipher much German in the limited candlelight.

"Can you find these dognappers, Willow? Allow me to remind you that thief-taking is hardly a respected or safe profession." Casriel spoke with the distaste of a man was has a reputation to consider, siblings to provide for, and a prospective countess to locate, court, and marry.

"Finding the thieves is simple," Will replied, for he'd studied on the matter for two entire sessions of fetch the stick. "I'd simply put it about that I'm pockets to let—typical Dorning, you know—and have a bad-tempered dog or two I would sell for a good sum."

Casriel's wince was subtle. "That sounds like Cam's idea of a strategy. You'll use your dogs as bait, and then snabble the thieves. What if you don't catch the thieves and then your dog is condemned to some bear garden in Manchester?"

Then Will would die a thousand deaths, though thinking of Caesar in that bear garden had already cost him much sleep.

"It won't come to that," Will said, "because I can't be the one to earn those rewards."

Casriel left off pretending to read the bottle's label and tipped his chair back on two legs.

"Willow, dearest, you are not making sense. Gentlemanly scruples aside, you need money, you're the fellow who can find these unfortunate brutes, you detest the spectacle of the bear gardens, and Lady Susannah is expecting you to muster the old derring-do. What am I missing here, besides the opening sets at the Windhams' ball?"

Casriel was missing the entire point, probably because he was focused on a young lady's dance card—now, when Will needed his brother's attention.

"Think, Casriel. Somebody knows which aristo-cratic households have these large dogs. Somebody knows which owners have either a need for funds, or a lack of security where the dogs are concerned. Somebody knows household schedules."

The earl's expression turned to a frown, but clearly, he hadn't put the puzzle pieces together.

"Somebody knows a lot of specifics," Will went on, "enough details to pluck large dogs from the middle of Mayfair and cart them off to short and violent careers making money from a lot of bloodthirsty toffs. Who could such a somebody be, and how would my consequence compare to his?"

The earl's chair settled onto all four legs with a *thunk*. "You could bring scandal and ruin on some scheming, impecunious lordling," Casriel said slowly, "and thus…on your untitled and relatively impecu-nious self."

"The Duke of Quimbey sits over there," Will said, "in all his finery, not a care in the world, but I depend on him and his ilk to buy my collies, and refer me business. London is full of men like him, and any one of them can ruin me, or ruin anybody associated with me, if I spoil the wrong titled fellow's little dognapping business. If I don't spoil that business, then innocent animals suffer a miserable fate, and Lady Susannah will think I'm indifferent to their suffering."

"And yet you risk ruin from a titled quarter if you search for the dogs," Casriel said. "That assumes you—and Georgette—survive to endure that scandal, and aren't instead sent to a premature reward by some wealthy peer who thinks violence is great entertainment."

Both brothers spoke in unison. "Shite."

❦

"Where the hell have you been?" Ash muttered, under the lilting elegance of the Duchess of Moreland's orchestra.

"Good evening to you too," Cam replied, shooting his cuffs. "I was on an errand of mercy. Dispensing alms to the deserving, living up to the nobility of character for which I would soon like to become—"

No wonder Willow wore a constant air of vexation. Ash swiped Cam's cup of punch, sniffed it, then took a drink.

"You can't be foxed already, Sycamore. You just got here, and you're too cheap to pay for your drink when you can get it for free."

"I would not disrespect my hostess by arriving to the ball inebriated. Where are the elders?" Cam asked, taking back his cup of punch. "I can't believe they'd leave us here without supervision."

Ash had lost track of Casriel and Will. He was too busy with his own concerns.

"Willow was here, but he might be off in some corner with Lady Susannah. Last I saw Casriel, he was making sheep's eyes at the Windham ladies and trying not to be obvious about it." Which was touching, in a way, or pathetic.

"Willow would be pleased," Cam said, scanning the ballroom. "Casriel is over by the ferns, in full view of the dowagers, no less. Which Windham lady has caught his eye?"

"How should I know? Between the Duke of Moreland and his brother, there's an entire cricket team of them."

Cam set his glass of punch aside, then glowered at Ash's cravat. "You stole my stickpin, you plundering Visigoth."

"Borrowed, my boy. I only borrowed it. Besides, you owe me your allowance for the next four years. Maybe I'll take the stickpin as a small installment on the principle."

A younger Cam might have stepped on Ash's foot, dashed punch on his cravat, or at least lapsed into foul language. This Cam merely smiled sweetly.

"For your information, Ash, there are four unmarried Windham ladies remaining now that the ducal branch has all wed. All of Lord Tony Windham's daughters are out, they're all pretty, and they're all well dowered. You're simply too busy worshipping at the hem of Lady Della Haddonfield to inspect any other possibilities."

"You stole my best reading spectacles is the more likely explanation."

The music trilled along, Casriel remained among the ferns talking to some dark-haired fellow in a kilt, and still, Cam simply watched the passing scene, a smile playing on his lips.

"What have you done, Sycamore?"

Lady Della was on the dance floor, looking vivacious and delectable in forest green, and entirely too smitten with her partner, Viscount Effete-ton.

"Will brought home a steak from the club. When he went upstairs to dress, I took half of it to where I last saw my dog. I went around to the pub to ask a few questions, and when I came back, the steak was gone."

No wonder Will so seldom smiled. Sycamore was an ongoing threat to the sanity of any family, and there were three more brothers just like him at home in Dorset.

"What if some of the pub regulars had followed the young toff around back?" Ash asked. "What if they'd decided to lighten his purse and relieve him of a few teeth? Could you not have at least taken me or Will with you?"

Lady Della twirled past again, not three yards from where Ash stood. This close, her expression was more desperate than gay, her eyes haunted rather than vivacious.

"You're worse than Casriel," Cam said. "Stop glaring at the poor woman. If I'd asked, would you have come with me to Bloomsbury?"

Ash could no more stop watching Lady Della Haddonfield than he could avoid applying the Rule of Seventy to an interest calculation.

"Of course I would have gone with you," he said, "but, Cam, you must desist. Will has offered to help and he knows what he's doing. I get the sense there's more to the situation than you perceive. If Will advises caution, heed him."

Regarding most situations, Will knew what he was about. Lady Susannah Haddonfield appeared to have even the great and rational Willow Dorning stumped.

"Is she nice?" Cam asked, popping something into his mouth.

"Is who nice?"

"Lady Della. She's pretty."

Good God, not Cam too. "What are you eating?"

"Peppermints. The punch can leave a fellow with rotten breath and yet he can't very well stand around chewing parsley like a sheep in formal attire. I'd miss you, if you got married and set up a household. Will's a lost cause, though. If you're intent on raiding his wardrobe, you'd best help yourself now."

The dance ended, mercifully, and Effington led Lady Della back to her brother, the Earl of Bellefonte.

"What in the sulfurous, stinking hell are you going on about, Cam?"

Cam passed Ash a tin that was probably intended for snuff. "Help yourself. I'm talking about Willow rolling about in the underbrush with Lady Susannah and two enormous dogs. In America, vines grow wild that can give you an awful itch. Will and her ladyship were growing wild and suffering an itch, without benefit of noxious greenery. I've never stood in the middle of a path getting a pebble out of my boot quite so long or so quietly."

Ash took several peppermints, slipped one into his mouth, and three others into his pocket, then gave the tin back to Cam.

"That is Casriel's snuffbox, you Vandal."

"I'm borrowing it," Cam said. "About time old Willow stopped acting like a monk, but in the very park? My virgin eyes!"

Lady Della disengaged herself from her brother, and crossed the corner of the ballroom that led to the grand staircase.

"Your eyes might be the only virgin territory left on you," Ash replied. "The ladies' retiring room is upstairs?"

"Ash, are *you* foxed? I'll see you home, old chap. As many time as you've looked after me, a bit of turnabout is only the done thing. I mean, the ladies' retiring room—you'll give a fellow cause for worry, and the elders are apparently hors de combat, and even I know better than to—"

Cam's concern was real, and quite gentlemanly, for a change. "Shut it, Cam. I'm not going into the ladies' retiring room, I was merely—who is that dark-haired fellow crossing the dance floor?"

Cam peered around Ash's shoulder. "Quimbey's nephew, Jonathan Tresham. Travels a lot, but is home at the duke's insistence. His Grace wants the succession ensured, but the nephew's not the type to be told what to do. Not the type to share a drink with a fellow either. I don't care for him."

A duke's heir was being pressured to take a wife, and that same man was now all but following Lady Della Haddonfield from the room—*after* having watched her for half the evening.

"Stay out of trouble," Ash said, sidling toward the doors at the end of the room. "And thanks for the peppermints."

"Don't do anything stupid—stupider than I would do!"

Nine

"Step lively there, Horace," Jasper said, knocking Horace's booted feet off the corner of the table. "Time to go hunting. I'm none too happy about the last one getting loose, and the gin doesn't pay for itself."

The gin didn't drink itself either, and the bottle on the floor of the stable's saddle room was empty.

"Not tonight, Jasper," Horace moaned, cradling his head. "Damned carriages everywhere, Quality about their amusements, too many brawny footmen on the street with nothing better to do than break my 'ead."

"How are the dogs?" Jasper asked, passing Horace a flask. The flask was only a quarter full, which meant Horace couldn't get falling down drunk even if he drank every drop.

"Dogs are mean, stupid, troublesome brutes. The big one's getting worse. We need to get 'im out of 'ere. What is this? Cat piss?"

"Gin. We'll move the big one when the price is right. Don't do to make them bastards down in Knightsbridge think we have dogs coming out our arses. Trying to hurry that black brute along was how he got loose. Let's go."

They had to walk past the stalls where the dogs were housed. Two stalls were quiet, but from the third, where the newest mastiff paced by the hour, a low growl rumbled.

"Makes my 'air stand up, when 'e does that," Horace muttered. "I pity the bear 'e wants a piece of. Won't be much bear left."

Jasper checked both latches on the stall door. Wouldn't do for another valuable dog to get away.

"They pull the dogs off before the bear's hurt that bad. Bears are trouble to catch, dogs come less dear. Give me back my flask."

Horace took another deep pull, then handed back the empty flask. "What you got in that sack?"

"Ham bones. Figure we'd leave some where the last one got away. Never know when a dog might travel back the way he came, hungrier than a dog likes to be."

"You're brilliant, Jasper. A bloody genius."

Jasper was a bloody busy man, with too many mouths to feed, and a missus with a mean temper. The traps were unreliable—they attracted everything from rats to cats to children—but the prospect of stealing another dog from some wealthy nob who could bring down the law...

A man could swing for stealing a dog from a titled household. Jasper got out his second flask, took a discreet nip, and led the way into the alley.

"What did you learn?" Susannah asked, for she would not be put off.

Investigating the disappearances of the dogs had been her idea, and if Will Dorning thought she'd sit on her tuffet reading *A Midsummer Night's Dream* while he had all the excitement, he was daft.

"I learned that you will risk your reputation for a conversation that could wait until tomorrow, my lady."

Susannah paced away from him, though she couldn't go far because they were in a shadowed alcove at the end of a corridor. Their only other option was to step through the French doors onto the balcony, where anybody on the terrace below might hear them.

Susannah turned when she was far enough away that she couldn't touch Will. "The evening has gone cloudy, Mr. Dorning, and tomorrow might well bring rain, so waiting until I can meet you in the park will not serve. If you don't want us to be discovered, then I suggest you answer my question. What did Lady March's staff tell you?"

Will brushed a lock of hair back over Susannah's shoulder. Because they were both in evening attire, that meant her bare neck was caressed by the errant tress, and *that* caused her to shiver.

"You can be very formidable, my lady. One has suspected this about you."

"Willow Dorning, I will formidable you right over my knee if you don't answer my question."

He looked intrigued, the dratted man. From around the corner and down the corridor came the sound of young ladies gossiping and tittering, and older women scolding them for their talk.

Will stepped closer. "I learned that Lady March hasn't been paying her junior household staff timely, and her husband plays too deep. She'd be motivated to sell a valuable dog if approached quietly. The dog has likely not gone missing at all, and there's an end to it."

His eyes were beautiful, even in the low light of the sconces. Did he know that? Was that why he was gazing directly at Susannah, muddling her wits when logic was needed?

"Her ladyship has not withdrawn the reward, though," Susannah said. "If you returned her pet to her, she'd have to pay you." A goodly sum too. Enough that the poorer half of London should have been scouring the streets for the wretched dog.

"Susannah, my dear, if Alexander has been sold to some squire from the Midlands, then we'll never see him again. Lady March has her sale money, the dog has a good life, the squire is happy. Shall we return downstairs?"

Those beautiful eyes, full of sunset hues and patience, also held shadows.

"You're giving up, then? Willow, I blush to point out that several dogs of similar description have gone missing, and if a man kisses a lady as if she matters to him, the same man being in want of coin, then that man is likely to confuse the woman who kissed him back as if…"

He stood even nearer, and Susannah's command of English met the lump in her throat. Will Dorning was the best person to find the dogs and earn the reward. He needed the reward if ever he was to take a wife, *and he was giving up?*

Anger, bewilderment, and longing crashed through Susannah as more giggling girls went past down the corridor.

"Willow?" *Don't you want me?*

His arms came around her, gently but firmly. "I left you with the impression that I am an impecunious younger son, because I believed that to be the case. Worth Kettering has taken over management of my finances, however, and very slowly, my situation should improve to the point where I can afford a... family. My dogs sell for good coin, my investments are prospering, and I thrive on hard work."

The torrent of self-doubt and indignation in Susannah calmed to a current of hope, albeit turbulent hope.

She linked her arms around his waist and leaned against him. "What are you saying, Will Dorning?"

He kissed her, sweetly, maddeningly, and Susannah cuddled closer in retaliation.

"I can't ask any woman to wait for my prospects to improve, Susannah. Investments fail, hard work can come to nothing. Better offers come along for a woman of good birth and lively intelligence—"

She wedged a silk-clad leg between his thighs, the better to stop his foolish gallantry. "I can be patient, Will. I'm not feeling patient now."

Susannah was feeling...giddy, as if her attraction to Will Dorning was a vindication of the good judgment and prudence for which she'd become notorious. She'd developed a towering *tendresse* for him years ago, and that preoccupation had saved her from the distractions offered by lesser men of greater standing and fortune.

Edward Whatever-his-name had been a faltering of that judgment, a sign of weariness and loneliness, but Will was a good man, and he was *her* man.

Susannah twined her fingers in Will's dark locks and pulled him in for a resounding, tongue-tangling kiss. She wanted him in the lush undergrowth of desire, wanted him panting and quivering as she nearly was.

"Susannah, my love, this isn't—bloody hell." His mouth came back to hers, ravenous and uncompromising, and Susannah's back hit a wall.

Good, because she needed leverage if she was to—gracious, Will was aroused, and letting Susannah know he wanted her by pressing *himself* firmly against her. She pushed back, cursing all evening attire to eternal flames.

"Willow, if you don't right this very instant—"

He kissed the side of her neck. "Hush. I shall not ruin you."

Susannah's knees nearly buckled as Will's kisses whispered along her shoulder. "I've already been ruined, and it was nothing like this."

She'd endured Edward's fumblings, recited sonnets in her head while he'd breathed stale pipe breath and staler promises all over her breasts. Will could promise nothing, and the only quote Susannah could pluck from the Bard's endless verbal riches was something about love being a madness.

Will rested one forearm against the wall and remained in Susannah's embrace. "You took all the risk and saw none of the reward?" he asked, trailing the backs of his fingers over Susannah's cheek.

"I don't know what that means. I expected

marriage, and allowed him liberties. It was…mostly bearable, at the time."

Another caress, a single fingertip drawn along Susannah's eyebrows. She'd be begging Will to tug on her ears next.

"Bearable. It was *bearable*, Susannah?"

This was not a Willow she knew. This man could touch her eyebrows and have her body singing in places low and feminine. His voice was cool moonshadows and hot innuendo; his kisses stole reason and words.

"This is not bearable, Willow. I can't think."

"Good," he growled, sliding fabric up over Susannah's thigh. "Don't even try. If you can think, I'm failing you. I never want to fail you, Susannah, and I never want you *mostly bearing* my attentions."

He drew her skirts high enough to stroke his fingers above her knee, and she half turned, half collapsed along the wall. Will stayed where he was, Susannah's back to him.

"Lean on me, Susannah. Let me be your support."

Will's hand moved higher, stroking, petting, teasing, until Susannah could not have remained upright without resting against him. Nobody had touched her this way, nobody had called forth this longing and frustration.

She should stop him, but what danced across her mind was the realization that while she'd wanted Edward Nash to *just get it over with,* she wanted Will to caress her without ceasing. Susannah had mentally declaimed tragic soliloquies rather than attend Edward's furtive liberties. In this stolen moment with Will, all of Susannah's attention was focused on what

Will would do next, as if time itself waited for Willow Dorning's command.

His touch became intimate as he glossed a fingertip over a slick bud of flesh and sent sensation skittering across Susannah's nerves.

"Breathe, Susannah. Don't push the pleasure away, let it come to you."

Had Susannah been able to speak, she would have told Will the feelings were not pleasurable. The physical experience he conjured was shocking, intense, and unsettling.

And yet Will was all around Susannah, solidly at her back, his arousal obvious where she pressed against him. Susannah could bear the welling desire because Will was with her, in every sense. She could explore the growing tide of need, and as he'd bid her, let it come to her.

The lilt of the violins from the ballroom receded to the periphery of Susannah's awareness, the voices murmuring around the corner faded as Will's touch became diabolically delicate and…relentless.

Moment followed moment, and Susannah had all she could do to breathe and to remain silent, and then pleasure was upon her, consuming her from the center out.

"Willow—"

He bent his head to cover her mouth with his own, while his fingers kept up a rhythmic torment that sent white heat exploding behind Susannah's eyes. For an eternity, she hung suspended between "too much" and "God help me," while Will cradled her against his length.

Eons of pleasure later, Susannah's skirts brushed down over her knees, and she was left panting against the wall, Will at her back, his arm around her waist. He turned her in his embrace and held her loosely.

Every part of Susannah was renewed and exposed. The soft night air caressed her cheeks, the shadows flickering from the sconces danced across her vision. Will's heart beat against hers like a timpani of sheer life force that echoed between her very legs, and inside...

Inside she was poetry, ancient wrath, orchestral crescendos, and every rose ever to bloom unseen under a waning summer moon.

"Hold me," Susannah whispered, leaning her entire weight against Will.

His embrace became more snug, while Susannah's grip on him remained desperate. His hand smoothed along her back, bringing peace and sanity. Susannah's lover was in no hurry to leave her, he was not ashamed of what they'd shared.

And neither, by God, was she.

❧

Jonathan Landsdowne Farnsworth Verulam Tresham slouched against a pillar in the ballroom and allowed every iota of his antipathy for the assemblage to show in his gaze. He was in London contrary to his will, he was in evening finery contrary to his will, he was in this very ballroom contrary to his will, and contrary to his better judgment too.

The author of that last misfortune went dancing by in the arms of Viscount Effington, her smile ferociously bright. If Lady Della Haddonfield had seen Tresham, she did an excellent job of hiding her reaction.

Tresham suspected subterfuge was central to her ladyship's nature, though to be fair, she'd begun her blackmail attempts by writing to him discreetly, her note addressed as if from some fellow in Surrey.

Near the next pillar, the Earl of Casriel was commiserating with a kilted Scotsman about the price of wool and the necessity of taking a bride, and Tresham's mood went from surly to vile.

Earls might *consider* taking a bride, but a ducal heir committed an offense against God and nature when he reached the age of twenty-eight without marrying. Quimbey had made that increasingly apparent, though His Grace couldn't threaten Tresham with a tightening of the purse strings—Tresham's own purse was quite ample, no thanks to his immediate progenitor.

So instead, Quimbey—dear avuncular, mild-tempered Quimbey—wielded that most brutal of familial weapons, *guilt*.

An ironic coincidence, that Tresham's only living relative and young Lady Della should both attempt to coerce him, the duke with the leverage of a close family member and the lady with…

Tresham wasn't entirely sure what Lady Della had up her sleeve. Though she and Quimbey had nothing in common, she yet reminded Tresham of the duke, for nothing would stop His Grace when he'd fixed on a goal.

"Ah, there you are, my boy," said Quimbey himself. "Exuding charm in all directions, as usual."

"Your Grace." Tresham bowed, mostly to hide

the frustration of having been caught unaware. The old fellow had too much practice sneaking about in ballrooms. "Good evening, sir."

"Tiresome evening, you mean. Instead of glowering at all the demoiselles, you might consider standing up with one of them. You dance well enough."

Tresham abruptly wanted to soak his head in the men's punch bowl, which would likely result in blindness, at least, and rumors of bad blood in the Quimbey heir too.

"I dance passably, sir."

Quimbey had paid for the dancing master. He'd paid for tutors, for the obligatory years at Eaton, three years at Oxford, for a grand tour, such as one could make a grand tour with the Corsican misbehaving. The duke had also paid for every pony Tresham had sat upon, every cravat that had been tied around his neck, until he'd reached the age of twenty-one.

"You're accomplished at sulking too," Quimbey said equitably. "Your father excelled at the public pout. Drove your poor mama to Bedlam and gave me several bad turns as well."

They were in polite company, so Tresham could not retort with the truth. Papa's philandering had driven Mama to her various excesses and dramas, and her excesses and dramas had driven Papa to his philandering. All very symmetric, a *perpetuum mobile* of marital misery.

"Has it occurred to you, Uncle, that you urge upon me a course you, yourself, have eschewed? Why don't you take a bride? Snap up one of the fertile young things panting to become your duchess and leave me in peace."

Quimbey wasn't *that* old, and of all the loathings on Tresham's long and much-visited list of loathings, assuming his uncle's title was at the top. Quimbey had influence with half the courts in Europe, was universally liked, and commanded enormous wealth. Despite that ducal consequence, His Grace's most trusted companion was a half-grown, stinking, drooling mastiff cast upon him by Tresham's own departed father.

"My dear boy, even if I could stomach the notion of marrying one of these tender beauties, we have no guarantee the union would be fruitful. Your duty, irrespective of my own course, is to marry. If you prefer men, then you simply wed an accommodating woman, show the flag occasionally in the interests of ensuring the succession, and when the nursery is adequately—"

Two potted ferns closer to the door, the pair of earls had gone silent as the dancers left the floor.

"Uncle, for the love of God, stop. I know things were different in your day, but this is neither the time nor the place."

Thirty years ago, London must have been one unending bacchanal for a man of means, with the royal dukes and the heir to the crown setting a tone of competitive dissipation. Marriage for a man with a title had been a mere formality, and for his wife little better than that once she'd delivered a pair of sons.

How Quimbey, a decent, honest, dependable fellow, had emerged from such an era was a mystery.

"Very well," Quimbey said, "have your pout, though a bad mood only makes you look burdened and brooding. I'm promised to the Duchess of Moreland for this set. Lovely woman. Her Grace has been the making of Percy Windham too. She has at least four unmarried nieces, and they're all fine-looking young women. Don't let me trouble you, though, when you're having such a jolly time glaring daggers at Polite Society."

Quimbey sauntered away, greeting all and sundry with the casual good cheer of a man who made being a duke look easy.

Being a *good* duke was damned difficult. Tresham knew that. He also knew part of his resistance to marriage was simply a small boy's terror.

Not of marriage. Marriage could be civil enough, despite the example set by Tresham's parents.

His unreasonable, unbecoming obstinanteness was because Quimbey had been the only adult to show that small boy how a gentleman conducted his affairs, the only person to take an appropriate interest in a youth rudderless in a sea of parental drama.

And now Quimbey, unchanging, stalwart, lovable old Quimbey, was demanding that Tresham face a future that did not include his uncle. If anything happened to Quimbey, Tresham might be left with only his father's ill-behaved hound for company.

A man should not acquire a duchess simply to preserve himself from the company of a dog, however objectionable that dog might be.

Tresham's self-castigations were interrupted by a flash of green skirts and brunette curls moving in the direction of the stairs. Lady Della Haddonfield was without escort, and a second opportunity to accost her had at last dropped into Tresham's lap.

He waited the requisite sixteen bars of gossip and

laughter before striding after her, and to hell with whoever might have been watching.

❧

An earl's second son had options.

He could be embittered by his status as insurance against a title reverting to the crown, and go about in a perpetual ill humor in the church, the military, the diplomatic corps, or the academic disciplines.

He could indulge in a never-ending adolescence, leveraging biological utility into financial sustenance, wasting his allowance on the usual vices.

He could distance himself from the entire issue of the succession, finishing university as some sort of adult orphan, pretending no familial obligations limited his choices.

Will's father had disapproved of the typical occupations for a younger son, calling them either dangerous or frivolous, or both. The life of a tolerated wastrel was beyond Will's comprehension, as was the pretense that his family was an inconvenience rather than the center of his world.

Which left…protectiveness, and here Will's nature had long since settled his fate. He was protective of his siblings, their interests, and their ambitions.

He was not prepared for that protectiveness to pale in comparison to his regard for Susannah Haddonfield. In the dimly lit alcove, she clung to Will as if he were the mighty oak whose shelter would never fail her, as if in all the world, he alone held her trust.

The arousal throbbing through Will muted to

something rarer and equally fierce, even as voices drifted around the corner and Susannah stirred in his arms.

"That's Della," she whispered. "That's Della, and she's talking to a man."

Ballrooms were full of men. Every hostess ensured it was so, as did her bottomless punch bowl, congenial card room, and network of connections among the mamas and dowager aunts.

"She might be talking to Effington," Will said, his arms ignoring his command to release the lady from his embrace.

"Effington drawls, and whoever he is, he's not happy with Della. I must go, Will." Susannah kissed his cheek, and might have danced off to her sister's rescue, but Will detained her for a moment, tugging her glove up to her elbow, tucking a lock of golden hair over her ear.

"We were enjoying a bit of air on the balcony," Will said. "In plain view from the back terrace at all times."

Those lovely, delicately traceable, kissable brows drew down. "Perhaps you should wait here."

Not bloody likely. "Perhaps we should make haste. The conversation is turning acrimonious, and the retiring rooms are down the next corridor."

Susannah's posture shifted, shoulders back, chin up, expression serene. Will's lover disappeared into a precise rendering of an aristocratic lady who need not answer to anybody for anything. She took Will's arm and sauntered around the corner with him.

"I do not entirely agree that the sonnets are—oh, good evening, Della."

The younger lady was not happy with the fellow

glowering down at her. Her gloved hands were fists against her green skirts, her jaw set. Had she been a canine, her hackles would have been up, and her growl audible at twenty paces.

"Won't you introduce us?" Lady Susannah asked. "Sir, you look familiar, but my memory fails me."

Susannah was ignoring bad behavior, and making good behavior an attractive option for the combatants, one of the basic tenets of effective dog training.

"Jonathan Tresham," the fellow said, bowing. "At your service."

"My sister, Lady Susannah Haddonfield," Lady Della bit out, "and our friend, Mr. Willow Dorning, of the Dorset Dornings."

Tresham joined his hands behind his back, the gesture reminding Will of somebody. The name was damnably familiar too. Perhaps when Will's blood had finished returning to its usual locations, his intellect might resume functioning.

"Pleased to meet you," Tresham said, "my lady, and Mr. Dorning. Now if you'll excuse me, I'll return to the ballroom."

Tresham wasn't even trying to pretend he was pleased, about the company, about anything.

"I'll come with you," Will said. Until Susannah sorted her younger sister out, Will would be de trop. Then too, Tresham had provoked Lady Della—or she had provoked him—and he thus wanted watching.

Tresham tossed off another crisp bow and marched away, while Will wanted to kiss his lady farewell— clear evidence of besottedness, when he'd see Susannah within the next fifteen minutes, and probably dance with her too.

"Did that contretemps amuse you?" Tresham asked, stomping along. "Or do you smirk for some other reason?"

Growling and snapping were posturing behaviors in many species. "I'm having a pleasant evening, Mr. Tresham, though you apparently are not."

Tresham paused before they reached the main stairs. A bust of Cicero stared blankly at them from an alcove, though some wit had adorned the old fellow's marble head with a lady's green silk garter.

"What is your connection to the Haddonfields?" Tresham asked.

Such a fierce inquiry. "Friend of the family. What is yours?"

Tresham snatched the garter off Cicero's head. "Total stranger, and I'd prefer to keep it that way."

"They are an agreeable group, and the earl is noted for his geniality—also for his size. The other brothers are formidable as well, but gentlemen all."

Tresham looked as if he'd like to plant Cicero—or somebody—a facer. "Those brothers need to keep a closer eye on Lady Della, or send her back to the family seat on the next mail coach. She is a bold creature."

Tresham was the bold one, accosting a young lady when she was unchaperoned in a corridor.

"Your observation, sir, is unfair and unwise," Will said. "Lady Della is not bold. If she has been bold with you, then you did something to either encourage her or provoke her. She's enduring an awkward first Season due to circumstances beyond her control.

She's been the butt of undeserved censure, rumor, and rude behavior, and I'll not tolerate you adding to her burdens."

Cheering thought—Cam, Casriel, and most of all, Ash would have agreed with Will.

"Who are you to be tolerating anything?" Tresham muttered. "She's a thorn in my side, and the sooner she's gone from Town, the happier I'll be."

"Are you the one circulating the unkind rumors about her?" Will asked, for he'd caught the barest breezes of talk in the club. Cam's eavesdropping in the men's retiring room, and Lady Della's paucity of recent dance partners suggested those breezes were originating right here in Mayfair. "I will put a stop to your misbehavior if you are."

Tresham might be a handsome fellow if he ever bothered to smile. He looked positively thunderous now.

"Who in their right mind would circulate rumors about an earl's daughter who has five older brothers, any one of whom might meet a man on the field of honor?"

Will propped an elbow on the top of Cicero's head. "Interesting question, but the fact remains, rumors have made the rounds about Lady Della's antecedents. Unkind rumors that mean her ladyship is lucky to fill her dance card, and lately must rely on the good offices of family friends to get through every ball, musicale, and Venetian breakfast. I account myself among those friends, and you slander her at your peril."

Where was Susannah, and what would she think of this discussion?

"Rumors about her antecedents?" Tresham asked, twirling the green garter on the end of a gloved finger.

Will maintained a politic silence. He'd got Tresham's attention, and with the stronger light of twin sconces to aid him, Will recalled where he'd last seen Tresham. This was Quimbey's heir, the younger man who'd shared dinner with the duke at the club.

Lady Della had vexed Tresham sorely. Not well done of her, when her reputation already hung by a thread.

"The rumors are not my doing," Tresham said, "but I thank you for calling them to my attention. Whatever my private differences with the young lady, she is a lady, and deserving of every public courtesy."

"Every private courtesy too."

Tresham stuffed the garter into a pocket. "You won't say a word about my discussion with Lady Della, sir, or I'll let the world know Mr. Willow Dorning was sharing very personal liberties with the woman's sister. I took a wrong turning in my search for Lady Della, and happened upon a couple in a shocking embrace."

Will straightened and patted Cicero's head, for nothing and nobody would ruin Will's good mood tonight.

"Being a gentleman and a duke's heir," Will said, "you also took note that the lady was enthusiastically reciprocating the gentleman's attentions, and thus you did not intervene. Lady Susannah would probably have done you an injury otherwise. The Haddonfield women are nothing if not fierce."

And passionate, though where was Will's fierce, passionate lady? The musicians were tuning up after their last break, and Will needed to hold his lady in his arms.

"You're courting Lady Susannah?" Tresham asked.

"Yes, so don't come near her unless your manners are in excellent repair." Interesting—snorting and pawing could be great fun, something Cam was born knowing, and Casriel had yet to discover.

"I will maintain all possible distance from—ah, Lady Della, Lady Susannah." Tresham's tone was about as civil as a Highland winter night.

"Mr. Tresham," Lady Della said, twining her arm with Susannah's.

Will sensed Susannah was waiting, letting the young dogs sort themselves out, while the elders maintained an air of calm control.

"If you have the next set free, Lady Della," Tresham said, "I would be honored to partner you."

"Oh, do, Della," Susannah said. "If memory serves, Mr. Tresham has neglected to dance all evening, and his uncle, dear Quimbey, will be pleased to see a lady has taken pity on his nephew and turned down the room with him."

Oh, neatly done. Lady Della's smile boded ill for Mr. Tresham, but she snagged him by the arm before he could dodge off to glower amid the potted palms.

"I believe I shall," Lady Della said. "Even a man short on grace deserves the occasional turn about the dance floor. Come along, Mr. Tresham, and I'm sure we'll find something to talk about."

Tresham looked nearly amused, and oddly enough, so did Lady Della.

"My lady," Will said, sweeping a bow. "May I have this dance?"

"I think not," Susannah replied. "I don't trust myself if you take me in your arms again, Mr. Dorning, but let's keep an eye on Della and Mr. Tresham, shall we? Effington will be beside himself, and it's about time."

Before Susannah could abandon Will in the empty corridor, he kissed her fleetingly on the mouth. She could not trust herself in his arms, but she could trust him enough to make that admission.

How very exceedingly lovely.

Ten

"WE ALMOST HAD HIM," HORACE MOANED FOR THE fortieth time. "Great big bugger going at that bone like a dog on a—well, going at it nineteen to the dozen, and some toff has to come along and warn him off. Why'nt the Quality piss in the convenience, and leave the alleys to the regular folks?"

Because the alleys afforded privacy, and even the toffs needed privacy. What did the scent of the dung heaps and rotting kitchen slops matter when a man wanted to take a piss or parlay with a streetwalker?

"Toffs are stupid," Jasper replied as a skinny orange cat went streaking past and scrabbled straight up a brick wall. "The fancy gents don't know the alley's the most dangerous place to be. No matter. The brute comes around our alley regular, and the King's Comestibles serves good ale. We'll snabble the mutt, see if we don't."

They ambled through the night, keeping to the twisted lanes and side streets rather than the main thoroughfares. Far less chance of being spotted in the shadows, and far more likelihood of coming across a sizable stray, or even a poor doggy left tied in a nabob's garden. Mastiffs, terriers, Alsatians, wolfhounds—the baiters had jobs for them all.

"When do we get paid, Jasper? Me missus doesn't like me being out 'alf the night when I don't bring 'ome any pay."

These nocturnal rambles gave Horace time to sober up, and when he was sober, Horace was the sort to ask questions. Complaining he could do drunk, sober, and every place in between.

"We're paid when the baiters pay us," Jasper replied. "I've told you and told you, but his lordship says we're not to move the dogs until the baiters are willing to pay decently for them. We tried to deliver that big black devil to them, and look how that turned out."

"I heard about the reward," Horace said. In this part of town, May-*La-De-Da*-Fair, parties and balls went on until dawn, and the great ladies obliged the less fortunate by keeping the ballroom draperies open. The strains of violins—the nancy kind, not good, honest fiddles—drifted through the fetid darkness like perfume over the stink of an unwashed whore.

"The Quality treat us like dogs," Horace went on, "with their parties and dancing. We stand outside the windows like starving curs and gawk at them in their finery. I know 'ow the dogs feel, Jasper, and all I want is me money."

All the dogs wanted was their freedom, because unlike Jasper and Horace, the dogs could find their own food, and paid nothing for a place to lay their ugly, stupid heads.

"You cease that talk about the reward," Jasper said.

Three rewards, two of them sizable. "Here's how it works with the Quality, Horace, me lad. They post the rewards, and when their little doggies are returned to them, they'll cry and carry on, and thank you until the next Frost Fair, but they'll not pay you."

Horace stopped walking in the mouth of the alley they'd just traversed. "That's not fair, Jasper. If they say they'll pay, they should pay."

Loyal, simple, and half-drunk, Horace was twice the man his lordship would ever be.

"They should pay, but whoever finds the dog is supposed to refuse the reward because of his gentlemanly honor. He's supposed to pretend he had great fun tracking down a slobbering, stinking hound, and then pretend he don't need the money."

"That's cracked, that is."

"Aye, that's cracked, and I've had enough for one night. Let's have a wee nip, and find our beds. We can try again tomorrow, if his lordship doesn't want us to move the dogs to Knightsbridge."

"Say, Jasper?"

Like a dog on a bone, that was Horace. "Aye?"

"What if a woman finds the dogs? A woman don't 'ave no gentlemanly honor. Would a woman get the reward for finding the dogs?"

❧

Susannah stood at Willow Dorning's side, in charity with life—and with him. He'd shown her new intimacies, such as she'd not dreamed men and women could share. Later, in the privacy of her boudoir, she'd examine the emotions that had gone with the passionate sensations, and she'd decide what to do about them.

"They make a handsome couple," she said as Mr. Tresham led Della to the middle of the dance floor. "He might try a smile, though."

"Or Lady Della might."

Was Will off balance too? His tone was cool, possibly annoyed. Worry nipped at the heels of Susannah's well-being, for she hadn't exactly set a good example for Della, had she?

"You're tall enough to tell me if Effington's here," she said. "I want him to see that Della has attracted the notice of a ducal heir."

"I don't see Effington," Will replied in that same composed, unreadable tone, "but he'll hear of this dance. If the gossip at the punch bowl is to be believed, Lady Della is the first woman Tresham has led out this Season."

The introduction began, with men bowing and ladies curtsying in a graceful choreography of manners and fashion.

"That is the best news," Susannah said, her toe tapping. "Della deserves to be noticed in a positive sense, to have the hounds panting at her feet."

Will took a half step back. "Susannah, this is not a horse auction, with the broodmares going to the highest bidders. Those are people on the dance floor, with hearts and lives and hopes."

The orchestra was in good form, the first violin embellishing the melody with lively appoggiaturas and trills, while Will seemed determined to introduce a sour note.

"I know what you're about, Willow Dorning," Susannah said as the conversation around them grew louder in competition with the orchestra. "You are disconcerted by what happened earlier, and so you're on your dignity. I should be on my dignity too, but I'm happy for my sister."

Also worried, because Mr. Tresham's expression hadn't lightened in the least. He and Della were two lovely, grim dancers amid a sea of gaiety.

"I am not disconcerted," Will said as a warm caress whispered over Susannah's right shoulder blade. "I am in awe. Had the Bard shared passion with a woman like you, he would have written a hundred more sonnets, each so incendiary, the words would have caused the printing presses to spontaneously ignite."

All over again, Susannah's knees went weak, her heart beat faster, and her mind gave up forming thoughts. If she'd had a tail, she would have wagged it against Will's knees.

That caress came again, secret, soft, sweet.

"The world has gone daft."

Ash Dorning's unhappy observation several caresses later gave Susannah a start.

"Mr. Dorning, good evening. I hope you're enjoying the gathering?" Susannah's voice was even, but behind her, she could *feel* Will smirking, the rotter.

The handsome, passionate, *imaginative* rotter, whom Susannah could not wait to share a secluded alcove with again.

"Good evening, my lady, Will. And no, I am not enjoying myself. That's Tresham doing the pretty with our Lady Della, and it's my dance."

Damn and blast. Why must somebody's feelings always be hurt?

"I'm sure Lady Della will spare you another dance," Will said. "Tresham's invitation doubtless caught her off guard. Are we still in want of Sycamore's company?"

The music was whirling through a crescendo, and Ash merely nodded, his gaze on the dancers.

Drat all younger siblings to the nursery. Susannah had wanted to waltz with Will, but not until Della had turned down the room with her ducal heir. Now, the Dorning men, en masse, would exit stage left in search of their youthful prodigal.

"Are they arguing?" Ash Dorning muttered. "A gent doesn't argue with a lady. Perhaps Tresham needs a refresher on basic manners."

Will's hand clamped on his brother's elbow. "The lady might be the one in need of the refresher, and that's not your place."

"Willow?" Susannah half turned at the annoyance in Will's voice. "Della had little choice. If she'd refused Tresham, he would have taken that amiss."

"Somebody has taken something amiss," Ash said, shrugging off Will's grasp. "The talk in the men's retiring room is two cuckoos make a very interesting pair. Mannering mentioned seeing a green garter the same color as Lady Della's dress in the corridor upstairs, and Tresham followed Lady Della up the steps earlier this evening like a hound on the scent of a bi—of an attractive lady dog."

The violins broke into an ascending flourish followed by stirring, fortissimo down-bows, and Susannah abruptly wished she had stayed home.

A green garter the same color as Della's dress? Found in a conspicuous location by no less gossip than Lyle Mannering?

"Mannering said *that*?" Susannah murmured. Green was an unusual color for a debutante, but Della looked well in it, and she was older than most debutantes. The color had almost become her signature, in fact.

"My lady, people will talk," Will said in the same repressive tones he used on Comus when the dog was in an excitable mood.

"Men especially," Ash added. "Idle talk, much of it. You mustn't make anything of it, and I should not have spoken so freely."

The music came to its final cadence as Tresham bowed, Della curtsied, and again, scandal beckoned.

"You will have Lady Della's next dance, Ash Dorning," Susannah said. "Will, if you would find her an earl, a marquess, a baronet, or even a colonel for the dance that follows. Anybody with consequence, a decent reputation, and two functioning feet. This is a disaster, for Della to be gossiped about by the men, and I cannot think, I can't—"

Dread wrapped a cold fist around Susannah's windpipe, and where all had been warmth and wonder, the evening turned rank and anxious. Again, she felt like the too-tall girl with the punch spilled down the back of her skirts at Lady March's tea dance—bright red punch nobody had alerted her to until Willow Dorning had slipped her shawl around her shoulders and suggested she favor him with a turn on the terrace.

"It's talk," Will said quietly. "Nothing but talk. Lady

Della has attracted an eligible bachelor's notice, and talk is inevitable. Ash, fetch Lady Della. Susannah, breathe."

Not as easy as it ought to be, but Susannah managed. No less person than the Duke of Quimbey was soon at her side, while Will slipped off who knew where to find more dance partners for another Haddonfield sister who did not deserve the unkindness and slander hurled in her direction.

❧

"Your brother Will might tell you to speak to me in a stern tone, then turn away," Sir Worth Reverence Kettering informed his wife. "I have been a naughty knight."

Jacaranda passed him the baby, who was blissfully asleep after her last meal of the day. The sight of the infant at the breast provoked a riot of feelings in her papa. Tenderness, protectiveness, and a touch of... well, jealousy. Worth Kettering had admired those breasts before they'd provided sustenance to his daughter, and part of him longed to be their exclusive admirer again.

"Ready to go nighty-night?" he asked the child, nuzzling her downy crown while Jacaranda did up bows and ribbons and other armaments of maternal modesty. "Papa's ready to go nighty-night, and all those fussy, frilly distractions your mama thinks will keep him from having the sort of thoughts that resulted in *you* will only inspire him to prodigious feats of persistence. Papa can be a very determined fellow when he's missing Mama's special kisses."

"Worth Kettering, fatherhood has made you daft,"

Jacaranda said, kissing his cheek. "Let's tuck in your princess, and you can tell me all about your latest misbehavior. Come along, Meda."

While Jacaranda had dealt with the baby, Worth had taken Meda out for her last garden visit of the day. His little family had a routine now, though once upon a time, routine had loomed before Worth like durance vile, the tribulation a man tolerated for growing successful enough to misbehave with impunity at least some of the time.

"That child is always so good for you," Jacaranda observed as they reached the nursery, "and you never lose patience with her."

"Like your brother Willow never loses patience with his dogs? I wish wealthy dukes were as canny and self-disciplined as Will. But, no, Their Graces as a species expect the laws of finance do not apply to ducal coin."

Worth laid the sleeping child in her bassinet, and Meda curled up on the carpet. He put an arm around his wife, and took a moment to simply behold the little miracle they'd made.

Though the child wasn't so little anymore. He wasn't sure how he felt about that. If she kept growing, then someday, long before Worth was ready for such a trial, their daughter would have beaus and wear ball gowns.

Fatherhood had made him daft, indeed.

"You usually enjoy the company of your ducal clients," Jacaranda said. "The Regent earns your most colorful language."

Jacaranda was absorbed with motherhood, with her

opera dancers—they had once been Worth's opera dancers—with organizing the social lives of his clerks and his business associates, with organizing *him*. Had she studied on the matter, she would have realized the royal dukes and princes were more bothersome than the Regent himself.

Worth escorted his wife across the corridor, leaving both the nursery door and their bedroom door open a few inches. If the child stirred and Worth was slow to fetch her to her mother, Meda would wake him. When Worth was naked behind an almost-closed door, he drew Jacaranda's dressing gown off her shoulders and led her to the bed.

"A certain pair of wealthy dukes accosted me at the club this afternoon," Worth said, turning back the covers.

"Wealthy dukes are always accosting you," Jacaranda muttered, climbing into bed. "If you didn't make them even wealthier, they might leave you in peace."

"My besetting sin," Worth replied, joining his wife under the covers. "I like making money. Dukes want me to invest a sum and make it grow. Royal princes want me to conjure money from thin air, instantly. These dukes were looking for something different to invest in, not the usual French winery or Italian olive grove. My love, what are you doing all the way over there?"

Worth hopped and flopped across the bed, until he could tuck his wife against his side. Because Jacaranda was no delicate flower, and he no small fellow, the fit was marvelous.

"Well, if isn't my own husband," Jacaranda said, tugging her braid from between them and tossing it over her shoulder. "How very friendly you've become since the baby showed up."

"My friendliness is part of why she arrived sooner after the nuptials than strictest propriety would have allowed, my love."

"I've never heard it called friendliness," Jacaranda said, brushing a hand over Worth's chest and settling in with her head on his shoulder. "You want to help these dukes, don't you? They'll get up to mischief otherwise, and then their duchesses will expect me to have a word with you, and I do miss the country, Worth. We were not plagued by mischievous peers there."

"We all have our little crosses to bear," Worth said. "Dukes are mine, and—" His mind went blank as Jacaranda's hand moved lower, then lower still.

"You were saying?" Jacaranda prompted.

Worth's body was saying *please, please, please.* "They want something different, these two, something they can boast of in the clubs to the other dukes. Something besides the usual canal or— Madam, I caution you that unless you desist…" Worth's lady had the loveliest, most confident grip on the part of Worth most in need of gripping. "Jacaranda, what are you about?"

"Tell me about the dukes, Worth."

What dukes? "Compound interest," Worth nearly gasped. "They've finally got the notion of compound interest through their thick heads and… That is lovely, Jacaranda."

"I've missed you," she said, setting up a rhythm with her hand. "I do not want our daughter to be an only child, you know."

"Perish the notion. One of twelve, at least. Children,

that is. Of…ours." For the next twenty minutes
Worth spoke mostly in single words. "Please…
Damn… Again…" figured prominently, as did the
undifferentiated moan of pleasure, and then the more
singular groan of satisfaction.

"You've slain me," Worth murmured when
Jacaranda was dozing in his arms, and whole sentences,
short ones at least, were once more within his abilities.

"One should regularly slay one's spouse," Jacaranda
replied. "Puts one in a grand humor. What were you
prattling on about earlier, regarding compound interest and the dukes?"

Worth cast back over their precoital conversation,
as a man casts his line over a placid trout stream. At
first no mental fish bit at the lure, then he grasped the
thread of their conversation.

"My dukes want a profitable novelty, a project
that's gentlemanly, but not in the common way. A
gold mine, perhaps—there's gold in Scotland—a successful portrait artist to sponsor." A glimmer of an idea
quivered in the undergrowth of Worth's imagination,
but fatigue and the pleasurable muddling of a happily
married man dulled his ability to flush the idea into
the open.

An investment scheme was like a wife. Timing
counted for much, and most did not thrive when har-
ried, bothered, or rushed.

Jacaranda yawned, stretched, and ran her toe up
Worth's calf. "Twelve children is a lot of children, Sir
Worth. Do you know how many grandchildren we
might have? How many great-grandchildren?"

Worth knew, for this was the biological equivalent

of compound interest, like Willow Dorning's collies or the King's dozen living progeny.

"I can't do the math right now," Worth said. "Heaps and hordes of little darlings. Somebody must set an example for your backward brothers in this regard." Not a one of whom had wed yet, which Worth knew was a source of worry for Jacaranda. "Are you falling asleep on me?"

"Half on you. You're very warm, if rather bony in places."

Worth was very married, thank a merciful Deity. "Go to sleep, Jacaranda. Something suitable for keeping a pair of wealthy dukes in pin money will come to me by morning. Meanwhile, I'll dream of siblings for my princess, and compound interest."

Jacaranda's toe made another trip along the ragged border of Worth's sanity. "I'll dream of you."

"Why dream," Worth whispered, "when I'm here in the same bed, and your every wish is my dearest command?"

❧

"I intend to cause gossip," Lady Susannah announced.

Georgette's ears twitched at her ladyship's tone, while Samson sat at Will's side, bumping Will's hand with his nose. Susannah paced before the bench in the park, her hems swishing. The day was overcast, much like Will's mood, and thus the park was less crowded. Beyond the secluded clearing, no children yelled, no nursery maids called to their charges.

"We nearly did cause gossip," Will replied, stroking Samson's head. "I owe you an apology for that."

Susannah came to a halt, her skirts settling around her half boots. "You'd apologize for those private, shared moments?"

The grass at her feet apparently fascinated her. Her reticule and straw hat sat on the bench beside Will's leashes and his bag of cheese. Quimbey would not disturb them today. Will hoped His Grace was too busy scolding Tresham to spare time for training Comus.

"I do not apologize for private shared moments of bliss," Will said, "but I apologize for risking your good name. Until I'm in a position to offer for you—"

"Exactly," Susannah said, a finger jabbing the air. "A lady's good name is her most prized possession, and Della needs to bring Effington up to scratch before she has to endure another evening like last night."

Last night had been wonderful, until Lady Della and Tresham had begun their little drama.

"Susannah, might we sit for a moment? Samson is worried about you." Samson worried easily. Will was worried too, though.

Her ladyship marched to the bench, and perched as if the boards spanned a nest of vipers.

"I need to make a public impression, Willow, so that all and sundry remark what a dog lover I am. I've come a long way, wouldn't you agree?"

Will took the place beside Susannah, but didn't dare reach for her hand. "You have made great progress."

"Effington danced the good-night waltz with Della, but she said his mood was off."

Will's mood was going more off by the moment. "The viscount lost at the card tables, my dear. His disposition is often wanting, for he loses frequently."

Unless Effington had Yorick with him "for luck."
Will had his suspicions about the variety of luck
Yorick imparted.

Susannah yanked the strings of her reticule closed.
The bag was beaded and wouldn't stand up to much
rough handling.

"Is there something you're not telling me, Willow?
We're friends, right? Friends are honest with each other."

Will was not in the habit of pleasuring his friends in
private alcoves, not in the habit of kissing them until
his cock throbbed. He did not invite his friends to
work with his young dogs, he did not—

Susannah had asked him something.

"Tresham and I found a green garter last night,"
Will said. "Upstairs in the corridor that led to the
retiring rooms. Somebody had placed it on the head
of a bust of Cicero, as bold as you please. Tresham
pocketed the garter, but that bit of bright green fabric
had been sitting on old Cicero before Tresham and
I stopped to chat, as Lord Mannering so happily
informed half the world."

Georgette took up a lean against Susannah's knees,
while the humid breeze lifted the leaves in the surrounding trees. The air was warm, hinting of summer,
and summer storms.

"You're saying somebody spotted that garter and
left it in plain sight," Susannah said. "Or worse,
somebody placed that garter where all would see it,
knowing Della's wardrobe favors green."

"Somebody wants to ruin your younger sister."
That Susannah grasped the magnitude of the malevo-
lence Lady Della faced was for the best. Will had

considered bringing up the matter with Bellefonte, but the earl would either call somebody out or dismiss the situation as schoolgirl nonsense.

Schoolgirls did not gossip around the men's punch bowl.

"That is so…so…so *mean*," Susannah said. "This goes beyond talk to actions, premeditated, malicious actions. Willow, who would do such a thing?"

More to the point, *why* would they do it, when Lady Della already faced a difficult first Season based on her patrimony?

"What do you know of Jonathan Tresham, my lady?"

"I know he's Quimbey's heir, and Della won't say where they were introduced."

So Susannah had interrogated her sister. That did not make Will's next suggestion any easier.

"How would Lady Della feel about returning with you to the family seat for a few weeks?"

"*What?* You want her to turn tail and run, as if she's guilty of misconduct when she's been a pattern card of probity? You want all these interminable evenings and awkward waltzes to be for *nothing*? Effington would drop her before a week was out."

Georgette put her chin on Susannah's knee, and Samson whined.

Will wanted to take Susannah in his arms, wanted to kiss the frown from her brow, but she'd probably bludgeon him with her reticule and use the leashes to tie him to a tree if he made those sorts of advances now.

"I've done nothing but think about alternatives, Susannah, and a strategic retreat at least deserves consideration. I suspect one of three individuals has authored

Lady Della's difficulties, and she's not in a position to take on any one of them, much less all three."

"Say on," Susannah said, waving a hand. "I won't like it, but if I mention anything about this situation to Nicholas, he'll break heads first and apologize to his countess later."

As long as Bellefonte didn't break Will's head. "First, we must consider Tresham. He bears Lady Della antipathy, and told me last night he wants her gone from Town. I know not why, but those were his words."

"Perhaps he's simply a disagreeable gentleman," Susannah said, worrying a nail. "My fingers taste like dog." She withdrew a linen handkerchief from her sleeve and wiped at her fingertips, though that wouldn't make any difference.

"Tresham is a very wealthy disagreeable gentleman," Will said. "One who could have his pick of the debutantes. Lady Della is no match for him."

Will was no match for such a man, not in terms of worldly consequence or coin of the realm.

"Della should also be of no matter to Tresham," Susannah said, cramming her handkerchief into the reticule. "Who else do you suspect?"

"Lyle Mannering, though again, I'm at a loss for a motive. Mannering's sisters have antipathy toward you, they've been vicious in the past for the pleasure of bullying an innocent, and Mannering was in the vicinity of the men's punch bowl last night. He gossiped about Lady Della, but he's such an empty-headed gudgeon, no one much listens to him."

Will plucked Susannah's reticule from her grasp,

extracted her handkerchief, folded it neatly, tucked it back inside, then returned the bag to its owner.

"I would skewer my brothers for such presumption as you just showed," Susannah said.

"Lucky for me, I am not your brother."

That observation earned Will not a hint of a smile, as Susannah stroked Georgette's head again.

"Who is your final suspect?" she asked.

Now for the delicate part. "Lord Effington."

Susannah shot off the bench, and Georgette trotted after her. "Willow, have you taken leave of your senses? Effington is the only man to show Della marked notice. He was the first to waltz with her other than Nicholas's handpicked stable of married titles, and he's— Your theory is preposterous."

No, it was not, but expecting Susannah to view the matter objectively had been.

"Effington has allowed Della to suffer the nasty talk, to stand alone, when he might have stood by her side, literally and figuratively. Effington is, not coincidentally, Mannering's bosom bow. Effington has not championed Della's cause when she has badly needed a champion, nor has he set Mannering to doing the same."

Susannah muttered something from three yards away, her back half turned.

"I beg your pardon?" Will asked, rising.

"I said, perhaps Effington hasn't been as forthright as he might have been because that would only fuel more talk, and perhaps somebody else was already at Della's side."

Samson whined again, while Will wanted to kick something. "You imply that when Effington abandons the lady, and my brother Ash waltzes into the breach, Effington is to be accorded points for gentlemanly discretion, while Ash—what? I'm not fabricating the sequence of events, Susannah."

But Will was arguing with a lady.

"I'm sorry," she said. "I'm upset, and that's upsetting the dogs. Lord Effington is by no means an ideal suitor, but he's all Della has, and I've not endeared myself to him."

"You're reasoning with me," Will replied, letting Susannah lead him back to the bench, upon which he was heartily sick of sitting.

"Irksome, isn't it?" Susannah said. "You and I are the ones typically reasoning with our siblings. Tell me again why you think Viscount Effington is sabotaging Della's Season."

Because Georgette hadn't liked Effington, because Yorick didn't trust his own master not to deal him a blow when no blow was warranted. Because Effington used his innocent dog to cheat at cards.

"Effington says he cares for Lady Della," Will said, "then he leaves her to slay dragons on her own, then castigates her for accepting the help of the knights who come to her aid. I cannot abide a hypocrite. If Effington truly has Lady Della's best interests at heart, he ought to be thanking the other fellows, and never leaving the lady's side. He ought to be offering for her, in fact."

Nonetheless, Will did not want to see any woman shackled to a husband who'd needlessly beat a small dog.

Though Lady Susannah apparently regarded even Effington as better for her sister than no husband at all.

Eleven

To Susannah's relief, Will apparently grasped the central issue: Effington must offer for Della.

"You bring me to my original point," Susannah said. "The time has come for me to impress the world with my affection for dogs. Effington issued a challenge, and I'm ready to answer it."

Will tugged gently on Samson's ears—probably to comfort himself as much as the dog.

"Susannah, you have learned a great deal about how to interact with a canine, but if you had to choose between spending time with Georgette or with your volume of Shakespeare—for you are never without a volume of Shakespeare—which would you choose?"

"What a question, Willow." Unfair, really, to compare a dog with the greatest talent ever to put pen to paper, though Susannah was without the Bard at that moment. "I'd choose Georgette over *Titus Andronicus*." Old *Titus* was not Mr. Shakespeare's best work, of course.

"I don't like the look of that sky," Will said, rising and offering Susannah his hand. "Let's get you home, and please consider my suggestion. If Lady Della spent a few weeks in absentia, whoever has taken her into dislike might aim their spite elsewhere."

Now Will's tone was reasonable, and Susannah's mood took on the quality of the sky. Unsettled, unpleasant. Had he really expected her to choose Georgette over the Bard?

"Instead of leaving Town, tail between my legs," she said as she rose, "I'd like to show Effington that he was in error. I'm entirely comfortable around canines, and I will make him an ideal sister-in-law. The issue isn't the dogs, it's my willingness to bend to Effington's expressed preferences."

Last night, as Susannah had tossed and turned with anxiety for Della, insight had struck:

Effington was presenting Susannah with another version of the Mannering twins' challenge: fit in, duck, dodge, avoid the "slings and arrows of outrageous fortune," such as those that were hurled about by members of Polite Society.

A willow tree could live for decades, through storms that felled oaks, because the willow had broad roots and supple branches. Susannah lacked the roots, but she could be accommodating for a good cause.

Though the notion angered her in a way it hadn't seven years ago.

Will settled Susannah's hat upon her head—she would have marched off without it—and was tying the ribbons into a modest bow when Georgette growled. Samson rose from his haunches and aimed a glare at the undergrowth where Susannah had kissed Will only days ago.

"Willow, why are they upset?" Was everybody's mood unhappy today?

"I don't know."

The answer presented itself a moment later, as an enormous mastiff emerged from the bushes, head down, hackles up, a healing gash over its left eye.

"That is Sycamore's stray," Will said. "Cam borrows my clothing indiscriminately, and my scent must have attracted the dog from whatever hiding place it bides by day. Stay behind me, Susannah. Georgette, Samson, sit."

Both dogs sat, slowly, as if coiling for a launch at the intruder.

Susannah understood the male gender as well as any woman with five brothers could. "The poor thing is starving," she said, picking up Will's bag of cheese.

"Susannah." Will's pleasant tone sounded as if he'd forced her name through gritted teeth. "Please put the cheese down *right now*. If the dog wants the cheese, he'll hurt you to get it."

The mastiff hung back, uncertain and woebegone at the edge of the foliage. "No, he won't. He's a good dog, Will. Somebody's pet fallen on hard times."

Will slipped leashes on Georgette and Samson, though if both dogs charged at once, even he might not be able to control them.

"Stay," Susannah said, making the hand sign where both Georgette and Samson could see her. "We'll share with the less fortunate."

"Susannah, don't you dare go near that animal." Again, Will's tone was pleasant, while Georgette's sentiments were more honestly expressed in a low, rumbling growl.

"Maybe you'd like a snack," Susannah said to the stray, tossing a bite of cheese in the dog's direction. "I'm easily vexed when I'm peckish. We all are. Willow, mightn't you lead Georgette and Samson down the path? I'll follow when I've shared our cheese with the hungry fellow."

The cheese disappeared and the dog looked up, his gaze hopeful. Susannah hated to see a noble creature brought low, and yet the beast was not begging and wasn't threatening, either.

"Feed him one piece at a time," Will said, "and make him wait between nibbles. Toss them a few feet from where he's sitting, so he has to look for each one. When I've got Georgette and Samson out of here, toss several bites at once, and leave a few more where he can find them while you follow me to safety."

Georgette growled again, and the stray sat. Not a growl, not a bark—and not a retreat to the under- growth either. Susannah approved of this dog, though she couldn't fault Georgette's protectiveness.

"I'll be along in a moment," Susannah said. "My new friend and I will pass the time while Georgette and Samson take the air."

Will did not want to leave, Susannah knew that, but she couldn't control Georgette if Will's pet turned up headstrong; therefore, Will must be the one to remove Georgette and Samson.

"Don't approach him, Susannah," Will said, lead- ing the dogs to the path. "Don't pet him, don't make friends with him. He seems healthy enough, but if he's rabid, even his saliva on your skin could mean your death."

The look in the dog's eye was entirely sane. Sad, bewildered, and tired—Susannah knew exactly how that felt—but sane.

"I won't lay a hand on him," Susannah said. "Tell Georgette not to growl. She's setting a bad example for Samson."

Will led the dogs off, but of course he didn't chide Georgette. Mastiffs were protective by nature, as apparently was Susannah.

She wanted to pet the injured dog, wanted to promise him that if he gave her an ounce of trust, she'd make sure he had a cozy stable to sleep in and a juicy bone to gnaw on.

"You haven't done anything to deserve this rough patch," Susannah said as more cheese met its fate. "I'm sorry for that. Della hasn't done anything to deserve such a difficult start to her come-out, either. If you and I meet again, I'll do what I can to make matters come right for you."

The dog sat, as if somebody had instructed him that treats were only dispensed to canine gentlemen. Susannah did as Will instructed, and threw several bites at once, then sprinkled a few more in the grass nearer where she stood.

"He's ravenous," Susannah said, when she'd rejoined Will. "I strongly suspect that is Lady March's missing dog. His name was Alexander, if I recall correctly." A great warrior who'd died much too young.

"Yes, Alexander," Will said, blinking as a drop of rain hit the side of his nose. Susannah wiped the raindrop away with her fingers, for there wasn't another soul in sight. "I will remind Cam of the dog's name, in case you're right, my lady. Now, all I want to do is get you, my dogs, and myself home."

Will was being polite, straining at the leash of good manners. Susannah suspected he'd rather lecture her about repairing leases, stray dogs, and Effington's shortcomings.

About which, Susannah would think later.

"The temperature has dropped," she said. "I hate to think of that poor dog out in the storm, lost and hungry."

"Hold this," Will said, passing Susannah a leash and taking the treat bag from her. He passed her the second leash, and told both dogs to stay. "We can at least make sure he won't be hungry, if that's Alexander. I'll be but a moment."

Susannah waited, both dogs panting gently against her skirts, and more raindrops speckling the path at her feet. She'd become fond of her old straw hat, and a downpour would ruin it, but Susannah's mood had improved for meeting Will in the park.

She wanted to prove to Lord Effington that she'd become a dog fancier, and Willow Dorning, trainer of the Regent's spaniels, had just entrusted her with two of his most beloved canines.

Surely even Will had to admit Susannah was ready to meet Effington's challenge?

❧

"Lady Susannah has taken it into her head that Effington must offer for Lady Della," Will fumed as he walked along with his younger brothers. "Somebody else has decided that Lady Della's chances of a match must be thoroughly blighted, and thus *my* chances of a match with Lady Susannah, while not blighted, are certainly not uppermost in her mind. Where's Casriel off to tonight?"

A look passed between Cam and Ash, one that spoke to the novelty of Will asking them about anything to do with the earl, when Will had the job of keeping Casriel organized.

"Casriel is playing cards at the home of that Scottish earl, MacHugh," Ash said. "An excuse to dodge the matchmakers under the guise of gentlemanly bonhomie."

"Playing for farthing points, then," Will said as they crossed into the park. The fashionable hour had ended, and soon the park would become the playground of pickpockets, streetwalkers, and footpads, but light yet remained in the sky, and Cam and Ash were insurance against petty thieves.

"Have you offered for Lady Susannah?" Ash asked, ever so casually.

"I have not," Will replied. "Not that it's any of your business. My prospects are limited, and she's much taken with the idea of launching her younger sister first."

Will could not afford to offer for Lady Susannah. Should he dismantle the lucrative scheme of some aristocratic dognapper, he'd be lucky to afford Georgette's cheese snacks, and yet Susannah expected him to do just that.

"Coward," Cam said, giving Will an affectionate shove that nearly sent him sprawling on his arse. "The ladies usually marry in age order, oldest to youngest. If you'd like a few pointers, I've made a study—"

"He's being Will," Ash interjected, cuffing the

back of Cam's head. "Looking after everybody before he looks after himself. Your prospects are improving, Willow, and I've wondered if Lady Della is as keen on being married off as Lady Susannah is on marrying her off."

The park in the early evening was beautiful, despite the afternoon's showers. The birds caroled their end-of-day songs in the leafy canopy above, the last of the sun's light slanted through stately maples, and squirrels danced among the branches.

And yet Hyde Park wasn't Dorset, nor was it that perpetually sunny forest of Lady Susannah's imaginings.

"Lady Della is wellborn," Cam said. "Of course she wants to get married, but she can do better than the likes of you, Ash-Can Dorning. You'll recite the multiplication tables while you're—"

"Sycamore!" both older brothers shouted in unison.

"—wooing her," Cam went on, "and expect her to live in a poky little room in the City, darning your stinking socks and having your stinking brats, while you get squint-eyed and hunchbacked from— That's a dog."

A deerhound-mongrel sort of dog trotted purposefully across the path ahead of them. No collar, and the animal wasn't lost. Either an owner was somewhere close at hand, or the dog was in pursuit of dinner in a corner of the park that would yield game.

"That's not Alexander," Will said, "and that dog is doing reasonably well for himself." Unlike Will, who was so muddled after the day's exchange with Susannah, he wanted to play fetch the stick with Georgette for hours.

Which, in Dorset, he might have done.

"Shall we leave that fellow some cheese?" Cam asked. "Handsome dog like that could probably use a home."

"We're looking for Alexander," Will said, "because Lady Susannah expects it of me. If a lack of coin prevents my offering for her, and finding the dog will yield coin, then find the dog, I must—according to her."

Cam kicked a pebble straight into a puddle, starting a series of concentric rings that quickly doubled back on themselves.

"What about according to you, older-and-wiser-though-seldom-jolly brother?"

Excellent question. Will paused in the middle of the path, for here in Hyde Park, at this hour, he had privacy with his brothers.

"According to me, something is rotten in Denmark."

"Is Shakespeare contagious?" Cam asked.

Ash ambled over to a bench—the very bench Will and Susannah often occupied—and sat. "What do you mean, Will?"

"Three large dogs missing from aristocratic households," Will began.

"Three?" Cam said, tossing himself down beside Ash. "I'd only heard about two."

"Because you're too busy wenching and gin-ing," Ash said. "Worth mentioned something about this at luncheon. He heard it from another Alsatian owner he occasionally meets when he's out walking Meda."

"The most recent one's an Alsatian," Will said, "and the owner is the Earl of Hunterton. His children are particularly fond of the dog; consequently, there's—"

"—another reward," Cam said, helping himself to a bite of cheese from the sack Ash had carried. "This is getting out of hand, Willow. You're the Duke of Dogs. Somebody is stealing canines from people who can afford to pay to have them returned. Ransoming dogs is heinous. Make it stop."

"And make me rich and Cam sensible, while you're at it," Ash muttered.

"Are you in the wooing-but-not-courting business now too?" Cam asked, popping another bite of cheese into his mouth. "Maybe this is a new fashion: make violent love to the lady, but out of noble poverty, never offer for her."

"Sycamore," Ash said, snatching the bag from him. "If you eat any more of this cheese, your bowels will seize, and the prodigious flatulence upon which you pride yourself will fail you when you most especially seek to embarrass your siblings with it."

"You sound like Will," Cam said, punctuating his sentiments with an audible demonstration of the talent under discussion.

"You smell like a dung heap," Ash retorted.

"Quiet, both of you," Will said as another canine came down the path, sniffing at one bush, lifting a leg on another. Will took the cheese from Ash and remained standing. "That's him. That's the dog Susannah and I saw earlier. Neither of you move. Cam, is that the fellow you've seen behind the King's Comestibles?"

"The very pup," Cam said. "He's healing too."

"Alexander," Will called, opening the cheese bag. They were downwind of the dog, but this fellow was astute enough to recognize the bag, or perhaps to recognize Will.

"He knows his name," Ash said as the dog's gaze riveted on Will.

"He knows the smell of cheese," Cam retorted. "My boy is no fool."

Very likely, the beast knew the smell of Cam. Will shook the cheese bag. "Sit, Alexander."

Something distracted the dog, for he looked worriedly off to the left.

"Alexander," Will said again, more firmly. "Sit."

Alexander—if it was Alexander—turned in a circle, then lay down.

"A right genius," Ash observed. "Cam's dog to the life."

Will tossed the dog a treat. "Good boy, Alexander." The dog's training had probably been haphazard in the March household, so a reward for paying attention— for trying—was in order. "Sycamore, do not think of getting out that leash. If the last time Alexander was leashed, he was also beaten, injured, and dragged from his home, then a leash is the last—"

Alexander got up, his gaze going to the undergrowth. A rabbit, perhaps, and this dog could not afford to be indifferent to rabbits.

Will tossed three pieces of cheese at the dog's feet. "You'd have to work to bring down the rabbit, while the cheese is yours for the asking."

"Will is spouting courtship analogies," Cam said. "Or something."

"Will speaks dog, while you speak only nonsense," Ash retorted. "It's getting dark, in case either of you failed to remark the obvious. We need to either capture that dog, or live to befriend him another day."

"Ash wants to pant at Lady Della's delicate feet again tonight," Cam said. "I'm not leaving without my puppy."

Will worked steadily closer to the dog, the whole time talking to him, tossing out treats, and trying to establish a rapport. Alexander's owner had been a woman, while his trust had been abused by men, so progress was slow.

"There's a lad," Will said, taking two steps closer. "You're in need of sustenance, my boy. You'd best eat all the cheese I toss at you, because on Cam's allowance, you won't enjoy many feasts."

"What allowance?" Ash asked. "Cam owes every penny of it to you, me, or the corner pub."

Will extended a gloved hand a few inches toward the dog. The gash above the left eye ought to have been stitched, but appeared to be healing cleanly. The scar would disfigure an otherwise handsome countenance.

"Shall we be friends?" Will asked, scanning the undergrowth. "Casual acquaintances will do, provided you let me take you back to my stables. A few meals, a few sessions with the hand signals and the treats, and you'll be—damn."

The deerhound had come into the clearing, and Alexander's response was to look away, fleetingly at Will, then up the path.

The deerhound growled, and Alexander, being a sensible soul, loped off at a smart clip.

"Willow, you let him get away!" Cam yelled, coming off the bench. "You let that poor, injured, helpless dog simply run off. And, you"—he turned to the deerhound—"you're no help at all. Don't expect any treats from me, you great lout. You ought to be ashamed of yourself, acting the bullyboy to a fellow who's down on his luck."

The deerhound cocked its head, as if Cam were some incomprehensible creature that fit into neither predator nor prey categories. In the next instant, the dog was off through the undergrowth, running in the opposite direction Alexander had gone.

"And you," Will said, shoving the cheese at his brother, "ensured neither dog will come back for a good long while. Thank you for making the outing not only a complete loss, Cam, but a setback. Alexander might be fifty yards away, but he can hear you, and hear your threatening tone of voice. Badly done of you."

"I behold a miracle," Ash said, sauntering over from the bench. "Sycamore Dorning is silent, which happens occasionally when he sleeps, and—Willow, you are my witness—he's holding food without consuming it. Signs and wonders on every hand. Shall we be off, gentlemen? Casriel might be hiding at his little card party, but I intend to go dancing tonight with a dark-haired lady. She owes me a waltz, and I always collect my debts."

Susannah would expect a report on the evening's outing, and Will purely wanted to see her.

"The Breadalbane ball is tonight," Will said, though maybe it was the Henningtons'. "Cam, you'll doubtless want to pay homage to the punch bowl."

"Right," Cam said, tossing a bit of cheese into

the air, then catching it in his mouth. "Punch bowls and I get along famously. Alexander and I will get on famously too, starting tomorrow night."

While Will and Susannah were getting on…reasonably well, when she expected the impossible of him, and he knew not how to refuse her.

❧

"What do you mean, you ran into a slight difficulty?" Effington asked, stroking a hand over Yorick's bony head. "All I asked you to do was put a green garter in a location above stairs where it would be easily found, then remark upon it, and point out the similarity to Lady Della's dress."

Last evening had gone well, but the afternoon had been beyond tedious. The solicitors were coming at Effington in twos and threes now, armed with figures and innuendos about another firm being a better match for the Effington family's priorities in the coming years.

The lawyers were jumping ship, in other words, and that would signal the creditors, when everybody knew the trades weren't to be paid until December.

Soon, Yorick would have to go back to working for a living.

"I did what you asked," Mannering said, patting Yorick and tugging on a doggy ear. "Exactly what you asked. Green garter in a prominent location, remarks at the punch bowl. Drat the luck, m'sisters have stuck their oar in. I was trying to avoid that."

Effington put Yorick down, and gestured to the table near the windows. The drawing room was chilly, because a fire had become a luxury.

"Shall we play a few rounds of vingt-et-un, Mannering? Let you get back some of your own?"

"I have done my bit, Effington," Mannering said, taking a seat and flipping out the tails of an exquisitely stitched morning coat. "The little Haddonfield woman has been muttered about, gossiped over, and subjected to narrow-eyed glances from every corner of a half-dozen ballrooms. How about you hand over my vowels?"

Effington really should, but Mannering was both gullible and wealthy, a combination hard to come by among the beau monde.

Effington snapped his fingers. "Yorick, sit."

Down went a little doggy bottom with gratifying alacrity. Effington took the seat nearest the windows, and riffled through a deck of cards. The edges were minutely patterned, so Effington would know exactly how many points Mannering's hand held.

"Come here, Yorick," Mannering said, patting his knee. "You're a lucky little fellow, and I can use some luck. My sisters saw me leaving the garter about last night, and that wasn't lucky at all."

Effington shuffled, taking his time because the markings on the cards were subtle and not easily read. Yorick leaped into Mannering's lap, and looked entirely happy to be there.

"A gentleman occasionally keeps a garter as a memento of a pleasant encounter," Effington said. He'd had an encounter or two with Mannering's sisters, and what they lacked in scruples, they made up for in stamina and inventiveness.

While all of the virtue and coin and none of the brains in the Mannering family sat across from

Effington, now wearing dog hair on a beautifully tailored pair of doeskin breeches.

"Keep a lady's garter?" Mannering asked. "What a peculiar notion. Anyhow, I'd put the garter on a bust of some old Roman fellow—Socrates, I suppose— and here come the harpies, full of questions and sly remarks. If we're to play cards, hadn't you ought to deal a few my way?"

Effington had been shuffling in hopes of putting a poor combination before his guest. He ended up dealing Mannering a pair of sevens.

"I'm sure you told your sisters to mind their own business, and Socrates was Greek." Two kings smiled up at Effington, hearts and diamonds.

"Poor fellow's dead, in any case," Mannering said, scratching Yorick's shoulders. "My sisters, by contrast, took a keen interest in why their brother was leaving garters about other people's corridors. Nosy pair, those two."

Nosy, but not overly concerned with propriety. "Another card, Mannering?"

"Yorick, what do you think? Shall Uncle Lyle have another card?"

Yorick gazed adoringly at Mannering, tail wagging.

"Yorick says one more card, please," Mannering said. "As I was saying, my sisters got to pesterin' me, and there we were in the corridor, and rather than be found arguing with a pair of perishin' females, I told them you had instructed me to leave the garter about, and it was all in aid of gaining a good match for Lady Della. They got quiet then. When those two get quiet, a man should worry."

Effington tossed a card across the table. A two, by the feel of the edge and the design along the border.

"Mannering, you will not get your vowels back at this rate. In fact I ought to double the interest rate on your debt."

"Interest? Now see here, Effington. Those vowels ain't thirty days old, and they're debts of honor, not a mortgage on the ancestral pile. Let's have no mention of interest. Yorick doesn't like nasty talk like that."

More tail wagging, drat the beast, but Effington was nothing if not resourceful, and the Mannering twins were well placed to aid his cause.

"You may tell your sisters whatever you please," Effington said, "as long as you remind them that old friends generally guard one another's interests if they know what's good for them. Does Trudy still have that darling mole on her right hip?"

Mannering put down his cards and covered Yorick's ears. "How the deuce should I know? Really, Effington. My sisters aren't exactly nuns, but a gentleman ought never to tell. Will you have another card?"

Effington made a show of perusing his kings, though he'd be a fool to try for an ace when Mannering was holding sixteen points. The chances were greater that Mannering would go over twenty-one, or do no better than tie the dealer, who won all draws.

"Shall we make this round interesting?" Effington said. "If you win, the amount you owe me is cut in half. If I win, it doubles."

Mannering held Yorick up before him. "What say you, lucky dog? Shall I chance my fate on the turn of a card?"

Yorick yipped and squirmed.

"Yorick says I'm lucky today. I accept the wager and with what I have in my hand."

"A deal then," Effington said, smiling at his kings. "I have a pair of handsome fellows, for a total of twenty. When shall I expect payment?"

"I'll send my man around tomorrow," Mannering said, "for I've twenty-one." He kissed Yorick's head. "Three sevens. What could be luckier than that?"

Well, damn. Either the seven of hearts had acquired an extra nick along the edge, or Effington's focus had been distracted by the memory of Trudy Mannering's ample breasts.

"The loser gets a boon," Effington said, collecting the cards. "You had the benefit of my lucky dog, after all."

"We can be generous in victory, can't we, Yorick?" Mannering asked, holding the dog to his cheek. "Yorick says yes. What boon would you like?"

Half an amount paid in the next day was, at present, better than the whole amount paid at a future date, and some favors were worth more than money.

"Tell your sisters that I don't care what venom they spew regarding Lady Della, provided they spew it in Jonathan Tresham's direction. I don't trust him, and can't think he means well by my intended. If he takes Lady Della into dislike, she's the better for it."

Mannering cuddled Yorick against his chest. "Damned confusing, if you ask me. You don't protect a lady by spreading talk about her. If you put your ring on her finger, then Tresham wouldn't have anything to say to it, would he?"

"Tresham is a ducal heir, Mannering, and reportedly

quite wealthy. His interest in the lady does not bode well for my plans, or for her future."

What boded ill for Effington's plans was the notion that Tresham might become fond of Lady Della, or worse, enamored of her. Tresham could afford to be indifferent to the settlements, while Effington could hardly afford good black tea anymore.

"I'll say something to the twins," Mannering allowed. "They'll be at the Henningtons'. See that you dance with neither of them, if you please."

Mannering's tone was pleasant, his caresses to Yorick's head gentle, and yet Effington was touched to think genuine fraternal protectiveness had inspired that warning. The twins, oddly enough, could turn up protective of Lyle too.

"You are a good brother," Effington said, rising. "And you shouldn't begrudge the ladies a bit of fun. It was all long ago, and hardly worth mentioning now."

Mannering stood and set Yorick on the chair by the card table. "Then don't. Mention it, that is. My sisters need marrying too, Effington, and sooner rather than later. Yorick, thanks for your assistance." He blew the dog a kiss. "See you tonight, Effington."

Without so much as a bow, Mannering was on his way, Yorick trotting to the door in his wake.

"You were no help at all," Effington informed the dog. "Three sevens, indeed." He aimed a halfhearted kick in Yorick's direction, but the little beast was nimble.

"You'll have to be quick when I turn you over to the badger pits," Effington said, snapping his fingers. "Come along, for tonight I must look my best. I've a lady to woo, or ruin, or perhaps both."

Twelve

"Quimbey's heir is handsome," Susannah said, swaying slightly to the music. "Or he would be if he didn't look perpetually serious."

Jonathan Tresham was in conversation with his uncle several yards away, and while Tresham didn't smile, he was clearly fond of Quimbey. Della thought *protective* would be a better description—a more inconvenient description. Harder to confront a man who was protective of his elders.

"You still can't recall where you met Mr. Tresham?" Susannah asked. "He looks familiar, but I can't place where I've seen him."

"Perhaps he resembles Quimbey?" Della suggested, silently crossing her fingers behind her back.

"That must be it. Same nose. Quimbey puts his hands behind his back when he's launching into a discussion, as Mr. Tresham does."

Della brought her wrist corsage up for a sniff. "Nicholas has the same habit."

No, he did not, but Susannah was distracted, searching the ballroom for Mr. Willow Dorning, and any response from Della would have placated her.

The musicians had embarked on a break, and Della and Susannah had retreated to the benches among the potted palms and tipsy dowagers. Tresham had spotted Della, of that she was certain.

"Are you hiding," Ash Dorning asked, "or avoiding me?" He moved too quietly, and looked entirely too handsome in his evening finery.

"Neither," Susannah said, offering him her hand. "We're resting our feet. Somebody has seen to it that Della gets very little opportunity to sit of an evening."

"A woman of wit and charm will always be in demand," Mr. Dorning replied, bowing over Della's hand. "Perhaps that same woman might like a turn on the terrace before she's besieged with eligibles again?"

Ash Dorning was no fool. He complimented Della prettily, while subtly implying that he was not among the eligibles.

"I'd go if I were you," Susannah said. "As the Season progresses, the ballrooms become stifling, while the gardens are increasingly attractive. I'll find Leah, and—Mr. Dorning, good evening."

Between one pleasantry and the next, Susannah bloomed. Where a cordial, slightly bored older sister had been, a demoiselle emerged, one with a shy smile, bashfully lowered lashes, and a glow about her. Della was honest with herself: she never glowed that prettily, had never had anybody to glow *for*.

"Mr. Dorning," Della said, rising. "Your brother has been kind enough to offer me his escort to the terrace. I leave Susannah to your kind offices."

And…*yes*. Will Dorning's expression blossomed too, from handsome gentleman to besotted swain.

"Come along," Ash Dorning said, tucking Della's hand over his sleeve as he led her away. "He's seen you, and noted my handsome, doting presence. You may thank me later."

Della glanced about, expecting Effington to be among those watching her process with Mr. Dorning. Effington had once again signed up for the good-night waltz though, which meant he'd likely spend the rest of the evening in the card room.

"He's seen me? I don't know who you mean," Della said.

"Tresham, glowering piratically on the starboard side of the largest palm tree. If you look put upon, he might forgive you for bearing me company. You're the first woman he's stood up with this Season, and you're entitled to gloat over that."

Della did not want to gloat. She wanted to yank her arm free, wrench off her corsage, and stomp it to bits with her dancing slippers.

"I danced with Mr. Tresham once, and during that dance, Mr. Dorning, he said nothing more than, 'try not to look so murderous' and 'stop attempting to lead.'" And the whole time, Della had been too flummoxed to come up with what she should have said.

"Give me the letters or you'll regret it," had only occurred to her as Tresham had bowed over her hand in parting.

And then, as he'd walked away, the useless thought, "Oh, please just give me the letters. *Please*." A man of Tresham's consequence could not be trusted with pleading, and the middle of a ballroom was the last place Della would make a spectacle of herself, even to gain Tresham's notice. She meant him no harm, but he hadn't given her a chance to say even that much.

Mr. Dorning led Della to the terrace in silence, a blessedly cool, quiet oasis only one-quarter as crowded as the ballroom.

"Let's avail ourselves of the conservatory," Mr. Dorning said. "You can rest your feet, and I can steal a peach."

An excellent notion, for the conservatory was quieter still, sitting as it did a distance from the Henningtons' back terrace. A few couples roamed its paths, and torches illuminated most of the interior. The scent within was benevolent—earthy, green, fresh, and floral.

"This place makes me homesick," Della said. "I miss Kent." Missed the peaceful, uncomplicated life, but not the boredom.

"Homesick for the country? Willow was wilting on the vine until your sister came along. Town is a tribulation for him, but we couldn't let Cam loose without at least two of us to watch over him. The peaches are down here."

"Down here" turned out be a deserted corner of the conservatory, where a full-grown peach tree had anticipated the growing season by several months.

"The poor trees get confused," Della said as Mr. Dorning plucked a ripe fruit. "I've been confused since my papa died."

Or maybe Della had been at a loss since she'd learned the late Earl of Bellefonte was not her father, though he'd been in every way a loving and doting papa. She missed him terribly, and wished he'd never passed along to her the late countess's diaries and correspondence.

"Are you—?" Mr. Dorning's expression in the dim light was thunderous. "You are. Are those tears for Tresham? If he was rude to you, I will offer him a lesson in manners he won't forget. Perhaps you're crying for that Effington buffoon? He has fine manners, but is an utter dolt over cards. Have a seat, and tell me who I must thrash."

"N-nobody," Della said, touched by the offer of violence. "I want to thrash them, though. Since coming to London, I'm always tired, and there's been talk, and Susannah suggested we might return to Kent, but I can't leave now, and—"

Mr. Dorning produced a folding knife and cut a slice of peach, which he held before Della like a talisman.

"Eat," he said, coming down beside her on the bench. "My brother Sycamore claims life always looks gloomy on an empty stomach."

Della took a bite of peach, and Mr. Dorning watched her chew as if she'd consumed some magical fruit that might change her hair to the required Haddonfield blond.

"Thank you," she said. "My brother Ethan grows peaches. I fancy them. This one's quite good." For being out of season. Ethan was actually a half brother—a bastard, nominal half brother, whom Della also, abruptly, missed terribly.

Ethan would have thrashed Tresham for Della first, and asked for explanations later, if at all.

"Town has given you the dismals," Mr. Dorning said, cutting another slice of peach. "Willow would understand. I'd miss you if you hared off to Kent, but I couldn't blame you. I console myself that if Willow and Lady Susannah ever plight their troth, I might see you from time to time."

In the shadowy light, Della couldn't read Mr. Dorning's expression, but her ears were in excellent working order.

He popped the bite of peach into his mouth, and together, they demolished their stolen fruit.

"You'd like to see me from time to time?" Della asked, when she'd used Mr. Dorning's handkerchief to wipe her fingertips. Her gloves lay beside her on the bench, Mr. Dorning's gloves atop them.

"Well, yes. Rather frequently, from time to time."

"I'd like to see you too, Mr. Dorning."

He wiped off his knife blade with the handkerchief, then wrapped the peach pit in the cloth.

"I'll plant this," he said, "a reminder of a pleasant moment in an otherwise long and tedious Season. You're not setting your cap for Tresham?"

Della shuddered. "I don't even like him." A howling disappointment. Effington, by contrast, was merely pompous, and entertaining his overtures at least gave Della a reason to attend social gatherings.

"Effington's your choice then, my lady?"

How had life grown so complicated in such a hurry?

"Lord Effington has not offered for me. I'm not faced with a choice yet, am I?" Though if Effington offered, Della would probably accept out of sheer exhaustion. She could not endure another Season with Susannah hovering, Tresham sneering, gossip swirling, and her feet aching.

Mr. Dorning tucked the peach pit away, an odd, sentimental gesture, though a bit messy.

"If you are faced with a choice, I want you to consider something before you give Effington his answer."

"I am listening, Mr. Dorning." And Della wasn't crying. A moment of undemanding quiet, a stolen peach, and she was fortified against the rest of the evening, though the rest of the Season remained a daunting prospect.

"Consider this," he said, sliding his bare hand across Della's nape. Ash Dorning's touch was warm, unhurried, and shocking for its presumption, and yet Della closed her eyes and savored the contact. In the ballroom, all was smiles and gaiety, but nobody *touched*.

Beautiful clothing, pristine gloves, and relentless propriety meant Della moved through her evenings as she had her tea parties as a little girl. The other attendants had been dolls, stuffed bears, and imaginary princes. Polite Society had less animation than those toys, and for Della, less interest.

"Do that again," Della whispered.

Mr. Dorning's fingers slid into her hair. "Consider this as well." The brush of his lips was deliberate, warm, and peach flavored.

Oh, gracious angels. Della would never merely fancy peaches again. She was abruptly ravenous for the scent and taste of fresh, stolen fruit. She kissed Mr. Dorning back, uncertainly at first, then his grip on her firmed, and she got a fistful of his lapel.

"I shouldn't—" he managed, but Della had other plans for his mouth. She plundered the taste of him, learned the contour of his lips and teeth and tongue, then invited him to reciprocate. Ash's approach was more delicate, teasing instead of demanding, delighting where Della had ransacked.

"You'll drive me daft," she said, resting her forehead against his. "You look like such a...a normal, handsome fellow, but you kiss like a prince."

"You've kissed princes, then, to make an informed comparison?"

He was short of breath. Della loved that he was short of breath. She loved that Ash Dorning could appear to be just another tall, dark, handsome bachelor, albeit one with interesting eyes, when in truth he was a dashing, peach-pilfering knight of the stolen kiss.

"I haven't kissed anybody," Della said, "until now, that is, but when you kiss me, I feel like a princess."

His lashes lowered and he patted his pocket. "That's something, I suppose. When you're making that choice, recall how you felt now. Whoever you bestow your hand upon, he should make you feel if not like a princess, then like a queen."

Sadness muted the glow of their kiss, because again, Ash was reminding her that he was not among her suitors. He was not asking for her hand. His kiss had not been an overture, but simply a kiss.

"Would you cut me another peach?" Della asked.

He rose and selected another ripe fruit. In a few deft strokes of the knife, he'd reduced it to slices and a bare, hard pit with a few scraps of flesh clinging to it. As Della sat on the bench, he stood before her and presented the whole on a second, plain handkerchief.

"First selection goes to the lady," he said.

Della chose the pit and wrapped it in her own

handkerchief. "I should get back to the ballroom. Susannah might be looking for me."

Mr. Dorning held up a slice of peach to Della's mouth. She took a bite, he finished the slice, and tossed the rest into the undergrowth.

A sad waste, and somehow Della's fault. She passed Mr. Dorning his gloves, drew on her own, and with a peach pit secreted in her skirt pocket, accepted his escort back to the ballroom.

❦

"Effington has emerged from the card room," Will said as he and Susannah made their way toward the punch bowl.

The ice sculpture had at one time been a unicorn, but the poor beast had wilted, rather like Susannah's patience, and now resembled more of an ice-rock with an odd, dull sword sticking into it.

"Why must Effington leave his cards now, when Della has gone for a breath of air?" Susannah asked. "Do you suppose he saw Tresham glowering at Della and Ash?"

Will's hand at the small of Susannah's back was no comfort. She was not a dog, to be guided at all times by its master.

"Tresham wears a perpetual glower," Will said. "When next I work with Quimbey, I'll inquire as to the reason for Mr. Tresham's disposition. Susannah, are we in a hurry?"

She was in a *taking*, tired of socializing that only seemed to dim Della's prospects instead of enhance them. Of all the bad luck, Effington was apparently intent on a glass of punch as well, for he met them when they'd gained the end of the line at the punch bowl.

"My lady, good evening. Mr. Dorning, is it?"

They exchanged the required pleasantries while the line inched forward, and Susannah's impatience strained closer to exasperation. She did not want to make small talk with the world's most indifferent, arrogant suitor.

But for Della, she would be pleasant and agreeable. This was the man whom she must impress with her dog-loving skills, after all.

"Is your pug with you at the card tables, my lord?" Susannah asked. "Della claims Yorick is a lucky dog."

"Of course he's a lucky dog," Effington replied. "He's *my* dog, and thus has only the best of care. He'll not disappear like those other unfortunates, you may depend on that."

Susannah seized on the topic like Georgette with a favorite stick.

"My lord, as a dog fancier, what do you make of these disappearances? All three dogs from aristocratic households, all sizable animals whose owners esteemed them greatly."

Effington fluffed the lace of his cravat, which upon examination, had several snags in it, perhaps Yorick's doing.

"One supposes the owners were careless," Effington drawled. "I never let Yorick roam, for example, because I'm the protective sort. I don't suppose Mr. Dorning would allow his beasts to stray, though they're much larger than my Yorick, more mature, and probably quite capable of looking after themselves."

Effington smirked at Susannah, as if the larger, more mature sister ought to be able to protect herself too. Several people nearby smiled—as he'd doubtless intended—while Willow's silence took on the quality of a growl.

"Mr. Dorning has explained to me some of the simpler aspects of dog training," Susannah said.

Effington's fluffing paused. "Has he now?"

"Lady Susannah is diligent," Will said. "She grasps intuitively that canines benefit from order, calm, and frequent praise."

"Much as most women do," Effington replied, "save for the occasional stubborn soul in need of firmer discipline. Though as a rule, the ladies smell ever so much nicer than the dogs."

The couple ahead of them in line smirked at Susannah, and that pair of arch smiles touched a chord, such that Susannah was again a shy seventeen-year-old, her stays too tight, and her ability to recall dance steps nowhere to be found. She *wasn't* seventeen though. She was wise enough to see the sheer spite in those smiles, to feel a circle of malicious interest gathering around her like drunks around a cockpit.

This time, she would not retreat to the garden in tears.

"Like most women?" Susannah retorted. Will's hand was at her back again, a warning that only goaded her past manners, past her own good intentions where Effington was concerned.

"I'd say men are more often the ones who need order, calm, and frequent praise," she went on, "and many can't even manage a pleasant fragrance. They expect a lady's hand in marriage in exchange for a few waltzes, and then she's to content herself with bearing the heir and spare while the fellow carries on with his gaming and vice as if he had no wife at all. I can understand why many a dowager prefers the company of her dog to that of another husband."

Silence rippled out from where Susannah stood, and across the ballroom, Della came in from the terrace on Mr. Dorning's arm.

Oh God. Della. *What have I done?* But even as Susannah worried for her sister, she remained standing before Effington, barely restraining the urge to slap him.

Effington picked a dog hair off his sleeve and flicked it in Susannah's direction.

Her hand drew back of its own volition, only to be gently drawn into Will's grasp.

"So that's what I've done wrong," said a jovial male voice. "I've neglected to pant and wag my tail at the ladies. Who would have guessed it's so simple? Perhaps a fellow ought to go courting with a stick in his mouth and a lavender sachet about his neck."

The Duke of Quimbey winked at Susannah, and beside her, Will relaxed.

"Of course, Your Grace," Effington said, bowing. "Though most fellows do provide the lady a ring, their good name, a home for life, and children to love."

Jonathan Tresham appeared at Susannah's elbow. "Some fellows, you mean. Other men live off their wives' settlements, and provide the woman nothing but misery, as Lady Susannah suggests. My lady, Mr. Dorning, good evening. My uncle tells me he's learned a great deal from Mr. Dorning about training my late father's pet. How do you know where to start when the wretched beast has no care for basic manners? He's handsome enough, and has all the breeding in the world, but one despairs of his deportment."

Currents of male power and innuendo shifted around Susannah. Tresham didn't turn his back on Effington—who had little care for basic manners— but Tresham, Quimbey, and Will excluded him from the conversation nonetheless. Will held forth about rewards and attention, successive commands, and patience, while Quimbey beamed good-natured boredom in all directions.

And Susannah's pride wrestled with her common sense.

She'd spent hours in the park with Will, much of that time focused on learning to communicate with a species she didn't even like. She'd been as pleasant to Effington as she knew how to be, and still he was condescending, mean, snide…

And Susannah was trying to *win his approval*?

"Mr. Dorning, will you excuse me?" Susannah said. "I forgot to mention something to Della."

"Are you well?" Will asked, very quietly.

Susannah loved him for asking, for having only concern in his eyes, not reproach or chilly disappointment. For gently and discreetly stopping her from turning a bad moment into an awful one.

She still wanted to wallop Effington and all of his ilk. "Yes, but…I need to talk to my sister. I'll be on the terrace."

"I'll bring your drink to you."

Susannah wanted to kiss him, wanted to surrender to his embrace with half of Polite Society gawking.

"I'll escort the lady to the terrace," Mr. Tresham said.

"Off with you, then," Quimbey said. "Be patient with him, Lady Susannah. He has much to learn yet about panting and wagging his tail."

Susannah accepted Tresham's escort, though he exuded about as much warmth as the unicorn stranded in the punch bowl.

"I thought Effington was on the verge of making an offer for Lady Della," Tresham said.

"I did too," Susannah replied. "Now, I'm not sure what to think. One doesn't court a woman by insulting her sister, or the entire feminine gender."

"Some of us can't help ourselves, my lady," Tresham said. "Quimbey was born charming, while I was born unable to trust others unless they are acquaintances of long standing. You might convey that sentiment to Lady Della."

Why couldn't more men be like Willow Dorning? He said what he meant, he didn't indulge in stupid posturing, and he was kind.

"You may tell her that yourself, sir," Susannah said. "Della is tolerant and sensible, though she does not suffer fools."

"Bodes ill for Effington, doesn't it?"

Whatever that meant. "My thanks for your escort." Susannah curtsied. Tresham bowed and left her several yards short of where Della stood talking with Ash Dorning.

"Is Tresham not speaking to me now?" Della asked as Tresham disappeared among the crowd.

"I think he's shy," Susannah said. "Certainly slow to trust, but you should ask him about that. Mr. Dorning, would you excuse us for a moment? I need Della's assistance with a sagging hem."

Mr. Dorning was a less substantial, younger version of Willow, and his eyes were not such an intense violet. He was nonetheless a handsome fellow, and he made a pretty picture bowing over Della's hand.

"I'm to be denied my dance again," he said. "I'll keep instead the memory of a stolen peach, and claim the dance another night."

And off he went in the direction of the card room, the same direction Tresham had taken.

"Do you suppose they'll exchange words?" Della asked. "They're both fierce, each in his way, but Mr. Dorning has more…"

"Yes," Susannah said. "More." Of Della's interest. "Would you join me on the terrace, Della?"

"What about your sagging hem?"

Susannah linked arms with her sister, and smiled blandly at the Mannering twins lurking beneath a sconce. The flickering shadows made them look like something out of a discarded scene from *Hamlet*.

To perdition with the both of them. The Bard would have found a better way to say it, but Susannah simply—surprisingly—no longer cared what the Mannering twins, what anybody besides her friends and family, thought of her.

Are you well? Willow had asked. Susannah was *different*, and perhaps even well too.

She returned Trudy Mannering's simper with a steady gaze, not offering a cut direct, but visually conveying the utter indifference of a mastiff who knows her own strength and is on her own territory.

Trudy tried for an arch smile, which wilted around the corners then disappeared. Susannah held her gaze until Trudy looked down, studying the toes of her dancing slippers. Her sister took to inspecting some portrait or other.

"Bother my sagging hem," Susannah said, moving along, and bending close to Della as if imparting a confidence. "I want to know what, exactly, you're doing with Effington, because I've only now realized you have no intention of marrying him."

Thirteen

"I BUNGLED THAT," WILL SAID WHEN HE AND QUIMBEY were both holding glasses of pink punch. Quimbey set his cup on a marble side table, took out a flask, and tipped a liberal portion into each serving.

"You were supposed to call Effington out?" Quimbey mused. "Maybe that's what he sought. I'm surprised you didn't interrogate him yourself about the missing dogs. Considers himself quite the authority on canines."

Susannah had gone gamboling down that path, much like Georgette on the scent of a rabbit.

"The missing dogs are unfortunate," Will said, "though I have no idea where they might be found. Very odd, that three dogs should go missing from wealthy households in such a short time."

Quimbey took a sip of punch, grimaced, then set his glass aside. "Hostesses who demonstrate their wealth by heavily sugaring every dish and drink are an abomination. I wish some of the ladies were sweeter and the punch less so. You're not attempting to locate these missing dogs?"

Will did not mistake the situation for small talk.

Quimbey was genial, benevolent, and tolerant, but this was an interrogation.

"Are you concerned for Comus, sir?" Or perhaps concerned for Tresham, or some other wellborn fellow who'd taken up trafficking in dogs to cover gambling debts?

"Let's enjoy the night air, Mr. Dorning."

Will wanted to keep Susannah in sight, to ensure she didn't take it upon herself to question anybody else about missing dogs or found garters. He and the duke chatted about the upcoming race meets, and who was betting on which horse, until they'd reached the garden walkways.

Smokers congregated on the downwind side of the terrace, leaving the garden to those inclined to stroll.

"The roses ought to be showing some color," Quimbey observed.

The roses were at least three weeks from blossoming. "I do enjoy a precocious bloom," Will said.

He and the duke admired daisies and snapped off sprigs of lavender, and still Quimbey remained merely convivial.

"Shall we sit for a moment, Mr. Dorning? Early mornings in the park take a toll on old bones, as does keeping up with a nephew new to the blandishments of Polite Society."

Tresham likely had trouble keeping up with Quimbey, much as the old hounds could outhunt the younger fellows. Will twirled his sprig of lavender into a circlet.

"About the missing dogs," Will began. "I'm not comfortable investigating the situation in any obvious way, but my brother Sycamore has come across a stray who might be Lady March's missing pet. We've yet to lure the dog close enough to catch him, though if we do, I'll have Cam simply adopt the dog as his own."

Quimbey perched on a low wall, no longer the duke, but the hounds and horses man in excellent condition—for any age.

"The damned beast is better off in your brother's care, or even on the streets," Quimbey said. "Ernestine March is a dithering, flirting disgrace to her gender. Tried to get herself compromised with me even before she was properly out, then put her own daughter up to the same tactic years later."

Will liked Quimbey, and more to the point, Comus liked the older fellow, and Comus was in a position to assess character more accurately than Will could.

"Do you suspect Lady March is involved in the disappearances?" Will asked.

"She undoubtedly sold her dog, Mr. Dorning. I'm sorry if that behavior doesn't comport with your estimation of the fairer sex, but I hold some of Lord March's vowels. I don't expect to collect on them anytime soon. I've recently learned that large dogs eat large quantities, and they absorb the time and efforts of at least a footman."

Will had not considered that Lady March herself might be stealing dogs—or having them stolen.

He propped himself against the wall, common sense, honor, and regard for Lady Susannah making a hash of what ought to be a pleasant social evening.

"If the dogs have been stolen," Will said, "and mind you, Your Grace, I'm not admitting they have been—then somebody is letting the thieves know which households can afford a reward—or a ransom—and which households have large, reasonably well-trained canines. I am loath to court the enmity of a person placed well enough to provide that knowledge. The Dorning family name is respected, but we have neither wealth nor extensive connections to lend us consequence."

Will had his dogs, though, and they were enough to keep him happy—almost.

"Prudent of you," Quimbey said. "Dogs are one thing, the family escutcheon quite another."

The garden was quiet, but not silent. Laughter and the low hum of conversation came from the terrace, a carriage jingled past in the nearby alley, and in the ballroom, a violinist was repeatedly practicing an ascending scale that turned into an aggressive glissando.

Quimbey was not finished with Will though, so Will waited, wondering where Susannah had got off to, and if he'd have a chance to dance with her before the evening ended.

"Do you know," Quimbey said, "Comus has taken to napping in the evening when I'm working on my accounts. He curls up by the fire and closes his eyes. Let me get up from my desk, or even open a drawer, though, and he's awake."

"Dogs have very acute senses, Your Grace." Will stripped another sprig of lavender and tied it in a circle. "I sometimes believe Georgette can hear me thinking."

"Comus is barely half-grown, I know, but last night, I was remembering my brother Harold, how he despaired of Jonathan, how he regretted not being a steadier father to the boy. Comus brought me a leash, and put his chin on my knee."

Good boy, Comus. Every dog had strengths, and areas that did not come easily in training, but Will had yet to find the dog born with a cold heart.

"Georgette interrupts me similarly when I'm at my accounts," Will said. "She seems to know when I'm at my limit with the figures, and in need of fresh air."

Quimbey pitched his lavender into the bushes. "Right, and because you insist that I care for my own dog, or my brother's dog, I took Comus out to the garden. He led me straight to the honeysuckle. Such a lovely, soothing scent."

A hint of the same scent lingered beneath the smoke of the torches, and the lavender Will had crushed with his fingers.

"Perhaps honeysuckle is soothing to the dogs too," Will said.

"Howard adored honeysuckle, said it reminded him of the love of his life, of the happiest spring he'd ever spent in Town. I recalled my brother's regrets, and Comus reminded me of Howard's joys. I would hate for anything untoward to happen to my dog, Mr. Dorning. He's been through enough for a young fellow of limited intellect, and is settling into the household very nicely."

My dog. Quimbey had referred to Comus as *the dog*, or *my brother's dog, the canine ruffian, Howard's dubious bequest.* In the space of one walk in the garden, Comus had become the Duke of Quimbey's dog, and a lonely old man's friend.

A high calling, indeed.

"As long as you have Comus at your side," Will said, "he should be safe from thieves and miscreants. Not many would steal from you, sir, and Comus won't leave your side willingly."

Except for a juicy steak, perhaps.

Or true love.

Or a slow rabbit on a boring afternoon.

Comus was young, and his training far from complete. Once again, Will pushed aside the thought of Caesar in the hands of the bear-baiters. The Duchess of Ambrose had earned Caesar's trust only slowly. Subjected to rough treatment, he'd soon lose heart all over again.

Unless Will found him first. Him, Alexander, and who knew how many others.

"I've been thinking," Quimbey said, shoving off the wall. "D'you suppose Tresham could do with a dog? The boy is lonely, and you've had good luck attracting a lady through your canine friends. Jon's like Comus, unsettled, too handsome for his own good, but basically a good-hearted fellow."

Will's estimation of Tresham would not have been half so charitable. "I place dogs only with people who want them, and with people who will return them to me if the dog doesn't settle well with the new owner."

Quimbey dusted off his backside as unceremoniously as Cam might have. "If you pursue your courting as conscientiously as you do your canine business, Lady Susannah ought to be wearing your ring directly, Mr. Dorning. Best of luck, but if you'll take the advice of an old hound, there's a time for stealth and subtlety, and a time to leap into the chase."

Also a time to kiss among the ferns. "Yes, sir, and, Your Grace?"

The duke tucked his hands behind his back. "Mr. Dorning?"

"Arabella, Duchess of Ambrose, knows a lot about training dogs, and has a soft spot for the larger breeds. A visit from Comus might console her on the loss of her Caesar."

"Now that is a woman of sense and wit, and you say I'm to take Comus calling?"

"He's ready, sir." And so was the duke. With his heir finally putting in an appearance in the ballrooms, and even dancing, Quimbey could afford to make a few social calls.

"I'll talk it over with the pup," Quimbey said. "Boy might need a bath first, and a new collar. Doesn't do to go calling on the ladies in anything less than one's best finery. Good night, Mr. Dorning. Comus and I will see you Tuesday at eleven in the usual location."

His Grace strode off into the night, leaving Will to ponder whether Samson was ready to take on a new owner, and whether Will trusted Jonathan Tresham to rise to such an honor.

❧

Will had gone strolling by with the Duke of Quimbey several yards from where Susannah sat. The men had been deep in a discussion of horse racing. The topic reminded Susannah that the Season, in its exhausting, interminable fashion, was inching forward, and time was running out for Della to make a match.

Or not.

"Why do you say I've no intention of marrying Effington?" Della asked, keeping her voice down. "He's eligible."

This discussion wasn't one anybody should overhear, and yet, if Susannah didn't press Della now, with Effington's nasty remarks still making the rounds in the ballroom, Della would likely continue to prevaricate.

"Come with me to the conservatory," Susannah said. "Quimbey is more eligible than Effington. Jonathan Tresham is more eligible. Casriel is more eligible. Eligible has little to do with anything unless you're enamored of the fellow."

While Willow Dorning did not consider himself eligible, and Susannah was certainly enamored of him.

"Not the conservatory, please," Della said. "I notice you don't mention Mr. Ash Dorning among the eligibles."

The omission had been deliberate. "But you do, so why this nonsense with Effington?"

"One needs a gallant," Della said, wandering away from the lighted path. "One needs a flirt, a fellow to walk with in the park, to stand up with for the waltzes. I look like a child dancing with our brothers because they are so blasted tall. Effington isn't overly tall, he isn't quick. He's so absorbed with himself and his little dog that I needn't do more than smile and say 'yes, my lord' or 'whatever you think best, my lord.'"

Susannah followed Della into the shadows until they came to a secluded fountain. The swan sculpted in the middle sat serenely under a perpetual delicate cascade of water. The sound of the trickling water soothed the soul, the moonlight on the water pleased the eye, and yet Susannah longed to be away from this contrived replica of nature.

"You're using Effington as a decoy?" Susannah asked. "As long as he's sniffing about your skirts, you're escaping the notice of the other fellows."

Except for Ash Dorning, apparently.

Della sat on the edge of the fountain, not a graceful settling of skirts, but an inelegant perching of tired bones on a handy seat.

"I hate London," Della muttered. "I thought I would, and I was right, but you, Kirsten, and Leah were excited for me to make my come-out, and Nicholas was determined, and so here I am."

Susannah dusted off a spot on the fountain's rim and sat beside her sister. "You didn't protest, Della Haddonfield. With Kirsten and Nita finding their fellows, you could have waited another year."

"I wanted to get the business over with," Della said, toeing off a dancing slipper and crossing her ankle over her knee. She commenced rubbing her silk-clad arch, while the fountain trickled quietly, and a violinist practiced a cadenza inside the ballroom.

"Matters have grown complicated," Susannah said, feeling elderly, but also glad to be beyond the ordeal Della was enduring. "You've allowed Effington to develop expectations, and that will have consequences."

Della switched feet. "My feet hurt, that's a consequence. I'm an object of gossip, which we knew might happen. You've met Willow Dorning, and taken to spending time with him and his dogs. I think that's more a blessing than a consequence."

That dog, as Willow might say, would not hunt.

"You are not enduring this Season for me, Della. I've known Will Dorning for years, and been through this exercise a half-dozen times. Nobody remarks my presence in Town at all."

Della wiggled her feet back into her slippers, her demeanor young and bored. "I needed to come to Town, you're right. To see what a Season was, to meet the eligibles and dance. I will be glad to get back to Kent, though. I'm told Kirsten managed to turn her ankle one year and develop a cough another. I understand why."

Such self-absorbed drama missed the point. "Della, if you have no intention of entertaining Effington's suit, then make your feelings known as gently and as soon as you can. Toying with his affections—or his expectations—is not simply a matter of having somebody to stand up with."

Della finished tying the bows on her slippers. "We walk in the park, he's tried to kiss me a few times. What of it?"

A great weight fell from Susannah's shoulders as Della sniffed at her wrist corsage and tugged at a sleeve. All those years ago, when Lady March's tea dances had turned into a miserable gauntlet of ridicule and heartache, Susannah had felt stupid.

As if she lacked some fundamental instinct every other girl had been born with. As if what others grasped intuitively, Susannah could only comprehend by ponderous logic and lumbering explanations.

And that was *wrong*, for Della, a canny, intelligent young woman with more than a normal sense of self-preservation, was apparently just as ignorant of

Society's labyrinths, just as lost in a jungle of innuendo and influence.

I was simply young. The realization came on a flood of compassion for that younger woman, for her bewilderment, and for *how hard she'd tried* to decipher codes written before Shakespeare had set pen to paper.

I was young, and I did the best I could. No absolution was required for being young and bewildered, and yet Susannah felt an easing in her heart. She had needed time and guidance to find her balance, the same as Della did now, the same as any young lady did. Willow had tried to assure her this was so, though the truth of his perspective was only now sinking in.

Della was doing her best too, yet a warning was in order. "That you don't let Effington kiss you ought to tell him a lot," Susannah said, "but, Della, you've created a problem nonetheless."

"Because you've had to spend time with Willow Dorning? I know you're not fond of dogs, Susannah, but I thought you enjoyed those outings nonetheless." Della stood, her smile smug.

"I have enjoyed those outings, for the most part, but your situation is precarious. If you don't want to marry Effington, then you're about to make an enemy of him. His lordship will look a fool when you refuse his suit, and he doesn't strike me as a man to endure humiliation stoically. He'll retaliate against you, or against those you care about."

Della's smile faded, like the moonlight when clouds crossed the night sky. She quit brushing at her skirts, and her shoulders slumped.

Susannah had stood in Della's slippers, when a Season was a great trial, not a privilege.

"I want you to be happy," Susannah went on, meaning it from the bottom of her heart. "We'll get you through this Season, Della, but please be careful. You might be able to endure Effington's version of revenge, but I don't trust him to limit his wounded pride to nasty talk and vile rumor. He can be cruel, and he has the ear of the gossips. Watch your every step."

Susannah hugged Della and accompanied her back to the lit walk, then surrendered her into the company of the Duke of Quimbey, who came striding up a side path.

"Will you come back to the ballroom with us, Susannah?" Della asked.

"No, thank you," Susannah said. "I'll enjoy a little more fresh air. The violinist has mistaken the ballroom for a concert hall, and I'm in need of quiet."

Susannah needed Willow Dorning, in fact, and he was somewhere down the path Quimbey had just traversed.

❧

"I am turning into my brother Sycamore," Willow announced as he slipped into her ladyship's bedroom.

Susannah had kept her word and left her balcony door unlocked, and as she'd promised, a sturdy maple had made climbing to that balcony a moment's work. Thank heavens for a Dorset boyhood that had included climbing many a tree.

"I chose this bedroom so that my sister Della wouldn't have it." Susannah reclined on a chaise, a branch of candles at her elbow, no other illumination in the room, a book in her lap.

The picture she made was full of contradictions, dark and light, demure and seductive, alert and idle. Her hair was in a single golden braid, her nightclothes delicate white silk, white-worked hems, and frothy lace. Her expression when she set her book aside and rose boded ruin for Will's good intentions.

"Why shouldn't Lady Della have this room?" Will asked, even as he knew he was taking the first bait cast at his figurative feet in what could become a difficult game of fetch the stick.

"Della is reckless," Susannah said. "Not on purpose— I'm about to be reckless on purpose—but because she simply doesn't know any better. Della can't see the dangers lurking behind the potted palms, for all she herself has a talent for dissembling. Hold still."

Everything in Will—including the protestations he ought to be sputtering—remained silent and unmoving while Lady Susannah took his evening coat and then unknotted his cravat.

"Susannah, what are you doing?"

"Seducing you, or preparing to seduce you," she said, fingers busy at his throat. "My experience is limited, but suggests fewer clothes portend greater success. This is a lovely pin."

Fewer clothes portended greater pleasure—also greater foolishness. "A gift from my late father that even my brothers haven't the nerve to steal. You are not seducing me."

"Not yet," she said, draping the cravat over Will's shoulder. "First we must have the discussion you were unwilling to have in the Henningtons' garden. I commend you for your prudence, because one never knows who's lurking behind a lilac bush. The clasp is loose on this sleeve button."

"Sycamore took my good pair, Ash my second best. These are Ash's, because Sycamore's have probably gone to the pawn shop."

Susannah's fingers brushing over Will's throat and wrists were like a fresh breeze to a well-rested hound. They tempted Will to slip the leash, to bound off in search of forbidden adventures, no matter the consequences his disobedience might earn.

No matter *anything*.

"You would not discuss the missing dogs, the rewards, or Effington's ill luck at the tables," Susannah said. "But as it happens, I wanted to discuss something with you."

If she started—

She started on his falls.

"Stop," Will said, stilling Susannah's hands with his own. "In the first place, a man can't think, much less carry on a lucid conversation, when a lovely woman is undoing his falls."

Susannah kissed him on the mouth. "In the second place?"

Merciful devils, the feel of her, soft, unbound, silky and sweet, pressed right against Will. No stays, or petticoats, barely any clothing...

"In the second place...I forget what's in the second place." Will kissed Susannah back, seized the initiative from her, and spent a few moments reacquainting himself with the glory of Susannah Haddonfield in an amorous mood. She was a smoldering conflagration of bad ideas and lovely sensations.

Her hands, disarranging the hair he'd troubled to comb to rights before scaling her maple tree; her breasts, pressed against his chest with shameless generosity; her sighs and the way she smiled against Will's mouth when his hands cupped her derriere.

Delight surged as he drew Susannah closer. "We fit. I love how we fit," he muttered. "Like coming home, like every happy Christmas, and—"

He dropped his hands and stepped back, because whether she'd intended to or not, Susannah was seducing him.

Sit, he commanded himself.

But where? his last functioning particle of common sense wondered. Not the bed, not the chaise. Will took the cold, hard stones of the raised hearth.

Stay.

Susannah came down beside him, her bare toes peeking out from her hems. "I do enjoy kissing you, Willow. You can't know what a relief that is. I thought something was wrong with me, that I could not be warmed by the kisses of a man on the verge of offering for me."

Like cold water thrown on a barking dog, her observation cooled Will's desire.

"I am not on the verge of offering for you," he said, a reminder to them both. A Riot Act read to the mob rule clamoring behind his half-buttoned falls. "I wish my circumstances were different, but at the present time, my expectations do not allow me to offer for anybody."

Susannah shifted, so the toes of one foot were covered by a lacy hem, while the toes of the other remained delectably in view.

"But if you were to offer for anybody, that anybody would be me," Susannah said. "I'm not a schoolgirl, Willow. I'm not a virgin, I'm not anybody who needs to hear your warnings and remonstrations. Have you made any progress locating the missing dogs?"

Back to this. Susannah was tenacious, while Will was besotted. He should never have climbed to her balcony. He should have stood in the garden like that idiot Romeo, declaiming verse and keeping his falls buttoned.

Though declaiming verse in a garden had little to recommend it, compared to Susannah Haddonfield's bare toes. Look how old Romeo had fared in the end, after all.

"I am in pursuit of Alexander," Will said. "My brothers and I saw the same dog in the park this evening, but he was unwilling to extend his trust under the circumstances. Time and patience will likely see him safely into our care."

"You won't give him back to Lady March and claim the reward?"

Susannah was unplaiting her braid, and the play of the candlelight on her hair—antique gold, burnished bronze, diamond white—reminded Will of what flames did to brandy in crystal. Beauty and danger, a visual song of temptation.

"Cam's heart would break if we returned that dog to a negligent owner," Will said. "I had Cam in mind for Samson—Hector is not ready—but Quimbey asked me about a dog for his nephew."

Susannah shook her head, like a fit canine after a
good swim, her hair spilling around her in casual glory.

"What about the other missing dogs? If Lady
March is unlikely to pay the reward, then keeping
her dog is no great loss, but what about the other
dogs? They're reported to be good-sized, protective
beasts, and I've a notion we should look for them in
the bear gardens."

"I hate to hear those words, especially from you,"
Will said, drawing Susannah's hair over her shoulder.
Her profile was lovely. The weight of her hair, warm
and soft as sunshine against his fingers, was the stuff of
reason's ruin.

"I can wear a disguise," Susannah said, with alarm-
ing assurance. "I'm tall enough to pass for a man, slim
enough to be a young man. Della would be proud—"

Will settled a hand on Susannah's nape and shook
her gently. "No. No bear gardens for you. The violence is disgusting, the crowd pathetic, and the specta-
tors as dangerous as the wretched beasts they've come
to see tormented. If I let you attend a bear-baiting,
you'd never forgive me, and I'd never forgive myself."

Cam, however, had recently been, and would likely
go again if Will asked it of him. Ash would accompany
him, and even Casriel's presence wouldn't be unusual.

"I'll send my brothers, if you insist." Will could
make that promise, but what then? If he saw Caesar
among the pack turned on the bear, would he hold his
tongue? Alexander? The Duchess of Ambrose would
insist on paying the reward, and that would only stir
up notice and talk.

"You will send your brothers, and they will report

back, and you will tell me what they learn," Susannah said, resting her head on Will's shoulder. "I have one more topic to discuss before I finish seducing you."

Her head fit perfectly—

"You'll not seduce me." If Will joined her in that big, fluffy bed beckoning from the shadows, it would be of his own free will, and hers too.

Though he wouldn't. Join her in the bed. At that moment.

"What will you do with yourself, Willow, when you've seen your brother the earl safely married?"

Susannah's fingers drew a pattern on Will's knee, a many-petaled daisy, perhaps. Her touch was soothing and distracting at once.

"I have five other brothers. Some need marrying, some need constant supervision, one in particular needs a daily scolding on general principles." Yes, a daisy. The schoolgirl game came to mind: he loves me, he loves me not.

Except there wasn't any *not*. Will loved Susannah. Had loved her courage and tenderheartedness years ago, loved her self-reliance and fortitude now. He loved her toes too, and her touch, and her kisses.

"You cannot make a career out of being your brothers' matchmaker, Willow. You must have some life of your own, some…" Her finger slowed—"I thought marrying Della off was my responsibility, but that's presuming of me, isn't it? I've never been married. Never truly been courted, so who am I to see to Della's happiness?"

Somewhere in Susannah's musing lay a point, probably a valid point. Will would ponder her words later, if his mind ever resumed functioning. Susannah's single finger had drifted higher on Will's thigh, blossoming into a bouquet of gentle erotic impressions—he loves me, he loves me, he loves me—while the gears of his mind ground ever more slowly.

Until a single concept meshed with every detail and sent Will's imagination whirling forth in eight different happy directions.

"Are you concerned for your own happiness now, Susannah? One can see why you would be, when all you hear from me is that I'm not proposing, and I can't propose. Remiss of me, when I can see no future without you in it. I cannot offer you a proposal, but I can offer you *an understanding*."

The finger of diabolical feminine designs paused. "An *understanding*, Willow?" She beamed at her toes, at Will's knees, at her own hand, and Will abruptly felt like the juiciest, most succulent treat ever to wear breeches and a half-unbuttoned shirt.

Also like the luckiest dog.

"An understanding," Will said. "I will not tender my suit to another, I will not share my kisses with another. I have insufficient means to offer you marriage at the moment, but I can give you my loyalty and fidelity, and assure you they're yours for all time."

Fidelity was an intimate concept, and Susannah clearly sought an intimate understanding. The part of Will that knew he ought to have lingered in the garden also knew he'd just complicated matters terribly. A woman who shared an understanding with a fellow might reasonably expect that fellow to collect any available rewards posthaste.

Susannah leaned forward, resting her cheek against Will's knee. "We have an understanding, then, Mr. Dorning. I forget what else I was supposed to tell you. Something about Ash and Della."

Oh, how quietly delighted she looked, nuzzling Will's knee. He could almost feel the pleasure of their bargain purring through her.

"Ash and Della would suit, but he lacks means," Will said. "A common condition in the Dorning family. I'll address my own shortcomings in this regard as diligently as hard work and good luck allow."

Will stroked Susannah's back, his resolve settling into relief. Their understanding was a compromise, and he excelled at the reasonable compromise. He'd give Susannah his promise of a proposal, and all the pleasure she sought, and she'd give him time to earn a tidy amount of coin through decent, prudent means.

Susannah straightened and aimed a smile at Will that made him pity all the Romeos in their lonely gardens, baying at the moon, sonnet by hopeless sonnet.

Let those poor louts have their poetry, for he and Susannah had an understanding.

Fourteen

IF SUSANNAH MARRIED WILL IN JUNE, THEIR WEDDING would distract all the tabbies and gossips from whatever tempest Della's Season provoked.

That cheering realization was Susannah's last coherent thought before Will drew her to her feet and straight into his arms.

Their discussion had settled something for him. Susannah could feel the confidence in him where wary hesitation had been.

Perhaps her suggestion of a visit to the bear gardens had inspired his hopes of earning the rewards, perhaps her ready acceptance of his *understanding* had reassured him.

Unattached women were prone to insecurities, but single men weren't to admit to the same vulnerability. Susannah kissed Will, rather than tell him how his offer of an understanding had reassured her.

"I could stand here all night kissing you," Will said, "all Season. Do you keep lavender sachets in your wardrobe? You smell like a sunny garden, and all my best memories of Dorset."

They'd live in Dorset, a beautiful place, and just far enough away from all of Susannah's dear, meddlesome siblings.

"Tell me about Dorset," she said, though one swift embrace had confirmed for Susannah that not all of Will's attention was on pleasant memories and sunny gardens. Part of it was on her, and on what would happen in her bed.

Will's hands settled on her shoulders, his thumbs making gentle circles below her collarbone, and Susannah's knees nearly gave out.

"Dorset is good land for sheep, and far from London's stink and bustle. I love it, and I hope you do too. Tell me about your nightclothes, my love. Do they stay on and risk injury to their seams, or do we remove them now?"

From Dorset to endearments was quite a leap, but Susannah was ready for leaps. She'd spent years observing, considering, pondering, and soothing her spirits with Shakespeare, but now, she and Willow Dorning had an *understanding*.

"Let's get you out of your finery," Susannah said, for she was determined to enjoy herself, and waiting for Will to guess her thoughts and preferences was simply a waste of time. "Do you need help with your boots?"

He didn't need help with anything, being a younger son who managed without a valet. Susannah's role was to stand and marvel as waistcoat, shirt, boots, and stockings were handed to her one after another.

Willow Dorning was fit, as an active man would be, a man who preferred country life to Town idleness. As he shed each article of clothing—all sober, well-made Town attire—he seemed to relax, and become more the calm, confident fellow who'd taken Susannah's situation in hand years ago and steered her past gossip and meanness with a smile, a bow, a wink, and a minuet.

Perhaps a special license would be better. A few weeks was plenty of time to find some missing dogs, collect rewards, and arrange a quiet wedding.

"You are impressive," Susannah said, when only Will's breeches remained on his person. "And you are not shy."

"But you are both shy and impressive," Will said, leaning over to blow out all but one candle. "Come here, Susannah."

In the near darkness, Susannah heard invitation rather than command in his words, and she complied. Deft male fingers undid her bows—she'd tied each bow loosely, after all—and silk whispered down her arms.

"The nightgown too?" Will asked.

"Your breeches first."

Will didn't even undo all the buttons, just a few more on each side, a shove and a step, and there he was. *Gracious*.

"I desire you," he said, his fingers wrapping around a part of him Susannah had felt but not seen previously. "I hope you want me as well, but you can change your mind, Susannah."

Susannah stepped closer and kicked Will's breeches aside. "Are you daft? I've wanted you since you first found me in Lady March's garden, weeping into my handkerchief and despairing of my future. Every time another fellow would come fawning and simpering over my hand after that, I measured him against your example. Was he kind? Was he honest? Was he considerate of a lady's feelings?"

Susannah hadn't even realized what a lodestone Willow Dorning had been for her, until halfway through her first Season, she'd caught a glimpse of him leaning against a marble pillar, watching the dancers twirl past. As stalwart as that pillar, he'd stood in her imagination for the consideration a true gentleman showed others at all times.

"I have missed you, Willow," she said, closing the distance and wrapping her arms around his waist. "I have missed you through Seasons, and summers, and sonnets and plays. Take me to bed, for I've had enough of missing you."

Susannah's silk nightgown was all that came between them, so Will's body heat warmed her. When he scooped her up against his chest, she could feel the strength and suppleness in him, the male competence. He set her on the bed gently, and then climbed in right over her.

"I've missed you too," he said, crouching above her. "I'd see you, looking cool and elegant in the park, or graceful and pretty on the dance floor, and I'd wonder: Is she happy? She looks happy, but also wistful. She'd rather be reading Shakespeare, but I'm glad she's here, where I can reassure myself that she's well."

Well. A tame, tepid word for the heat building inside Susannah. To know Will had watched for her—watched over her—asking nothing in return, made her heart sing and ache at the same time. She twined a leg over his flank.

"I want to gobble you up," she said. "I want to possess you—"

Will did not gobble, he silenced Susannah with delicate, easy kisses to the corner of her mouth, to her brow, to her chin. She'd seen his patience in action—with the rambunctious Comus and the impatient duke, with *her*—and knew she was in for a siege.

Well, so was he.

Susannah kissed him back, arched against him, drew her toes up his muscular calves, locked her ankles at the small of his back. She wanted his scent on her skin, his passion in her blood.

And then she got serious, tugging on his ears, gently, easing control away from him. She set up a rhythm with her hips, until Will braced over her, his breath a soft rasp against her cheek.

"I have no…"

"You have no prayer of withstanding my determination, Willow Dorning. Stop playing and love me." For Susannah loved him, had loved him for years as a girl. Now she loved as a woman loves, with heart, mind, soul, *and body*.

"I have no *sheath*," he muttered. "No goddamned sheath to protect you from conception, to—damn it, Susannah. That feels so good."

She'd got hold of him and traced the pad of her third finger around the tip of his member. Delicate touches for delicate flesh.

"You like that?"

"Much more of that, and I won't need a sheath."

Will would spend, in other words, and then he'd be finished and want to nap. Susannah's previous experiences had taught her that simple sequence, so she left off tormenting him.

"I'll withdraw," Will said. "I will die fourteen thousand deaths, but I'm dying fifteen thousand right now. Do you understand what I'm saying, Susannah?"

He was saying he desired her nearly as desperately as she desired him. "I understand."

Susannah left the rest up to Will, because her grasp of intimate activities fell far short of competence, much less confidence. He eased closer, so his arousal teased at Susannah's damp sex, and at her sanity.

"Willow, I'm not a—" Ah, God. A firm, short thrust that sent pleasure reverberating through Susannah.

"If you remind me again that some other fellow had the gall to sample your charms, then disappoint you, I will be cleaning my pistols, Susannah Haddonfield."

Willow Dorning was a different creature without his clothes, an entirely more primal and forceful beast, and Susannah gloried in his intimate acquaintance.

"I'm not a delicate flower," she said, taking his earlobe between her teeth. "Nor at this moment am I a patient lady."

Susannah was no sort of lady at all, she was simply Willow Dorning's lover, his woman. While he could restrain his passion with endless self-discipline, Susannah wanted no part of such sophistication. Will had shown her how to lure satisfaction closer, how to ignore volition and thought, and follow instinct to pleasure upon pleasure upon pleasure.

Just as Susannah might have bit Will for his measured, maddening lovemaking, he shifted over her, and increased his tempo.

For a few luminous moments in Will's arms, Susannah Haddonfield, spinster in training, bluestocking, and literary glutton, was made of pleasure's fire. The entire firmament glistened dully compared to the sensations shimmering through her, and the rays of the sun were cool when measured against the warmth Will inspired in her heart.

Susannah lay beneath him, spent, undone, unmoving. "*All done*, Willow," she managed. "All done forever. I cannot convey—"

He moved, the beast, and sensation ricocheted out from where he and Susannah were joined.

"Not all done," he growled. "Not nearly. Not by half, not by a quarter. My lady may have as many treats as she pleases."

"Again?" Susannah marveled as the sun blossomed anew inside her. "Again, Willow?"

"And again, and again, and again."

❧

Will's balls probably matched his eyes in color, but he'd subject himself to the last two hours all over again, simply to see Susannah Haddonfield stretching naked and replete by the guttering light of the single candle.

He'd let himself spend, after he'd withdrawn, though a man's singular pleasure was a vulgar, messy conclusion to the soul-boggling intimacy of becoming Susannah Haddonfield's lover.

"Will you nap with me?" Susannah asked, her toes trailing up the side of Will's calf. She could provoke riots with those toes, convey glee, mischief, passion, determination.

"I don't dare nap," Will said, turning on his side to face her. The bed was wide and comfortable, and somewhere in its vast depths was Susannah's nightgown. Will fished around with his foot, found a promising hint of silk and embroidery, and snagged it by a hem.

"Your nightgown," he said, passing it over.

Susannah stuffed her garment under the pillow. "My sister Kirsten has recently attached the affections of a clergyman. I hadn't realized how convenient that will be, for weddings, christenings, and so forth, assuming Daniel remains with the Church."

"You are capable of thinking and holding a conversation," Will said, tracing a finger along Susannah's lips. "This is unfair. I will be tripping over my own tongue for the next week, but it's too soon to make wedding plans, my love."

Not too soon to dream, though. Will didn't begrudge Susannah her dreams.

"Nonsense," Susannah said, sitting up. The covers gaped and a tantalizing view of a full, rosy breast flashed in the candlelit shadows.

Down. Will was sore—oh, happy state—and that meant Susannah was likely sore, and he hadn't a damned sheath, and—

"What do you mean 'nonsense,' Susannah? My prospects are no better now than they were two hours ago, and while I am hopeful, and strongly motivated to improve those prospects, that will take time."

A year, two, possibly more. Fortunately, Susannah was a patient woman—when dressed—and Will was nothing if not tenacious.

She smoothed a hand over the covers, and Will felt her caresses all over again—on his back, his chest, his hair, his—

He should get out of the bed and get his sore, weary, not-quite-engaged arse down the maple tree and into the dark, lonely, *safe* garden. Quimbey's nephew needed a dog, and might want training services as well. The Duchess of Ambrose might do for Hector, in another month or two, because she was patient and calm.

Susannah scooted back against the headboard, which caused jiggling in Will's brainbox and other places. Truly, he was a brother to Sycamore Dorning.

A litter mate.

"I can understand why you're reluctant to send Alexander back to Lady March," Susannah said, "but we can call on the Earl of Hunterton—you do know his dog's gone missing?—and you'll send your brothers to the bear gardens. I've been thinking, and if you implied to the right parties that you know of some large dogs that need good homes—"

Will wanted to cover his ears, but they were probably sore too. "Susannah, I am not pursuing those rewards. My business depends on having a good reputation among the wealthy and titled. The training is but a small part of it, a sort of advertising. The greater income results from breeding collies, but if a peer buys a pet from me, then he's very likely to buy his collies from me as well. Do you know how many sheep a man like Quimbey owns?"

Worth Kettering shamelessly discussed his business ventures with Jacaranda, and relied on her instincts as much as his own when it came to investment choices. The female of the species, despite societal platitudes to the contrary, was often more observant and shrewd than the male.

Susannah was entirely capable of grasping Will's point.

"You are convinced somebody is stealing the dogs for profit," she said, "and that same somebody is well-placed enough to ruin your business. I'm not convinced theft is involved."

Will extracted Susannah's nightgown from her pillow, for she would not give up on this topic.

Though she might well give up on *him*. He dropped the nightgown over her head and helped her find the sleeves, then, in defense of his jiggling sanity, he tied a single bow at her throat.

More fool him, for silk only emphasized what a man longed to again touch and taste and fondle.

"If the dogs are willingly surrendered, that's worse," Will said, shifting to sit beside Susannah. He wanted to cuddle up, his head in her lap, while they dreamed together of a country wedding and large litters of puppies, but that wasn't to be.

"Maybe the scheme falls somewhere in between," Susannah said, slipping an arm around Will's waist. "The lady of the house, or possibly the dog's owner, is assured the dog will have a good home, and they want to believe that. No stealing required, only lying. The dogs are bought here in London for a pittance, then sold elsewhere—trained, mature, handsome dogs—for good coin."

If Will were not exhausted, if he weren't muddled, if he hadn't handled the very silk now lovingly clinging to Susannah's breasts, he might have kept his thoughts to himself.

He *was* exasperated, and needed for Susannah to grasp the magnitude of the quagmire she expected him to leap across.

"Susannah, the plan you imagine sounds plausible—dogs purchased openly then resold to good homes—but to enact it, whoever is procuring the dogs would need to know where in the hinterlands—a different hinterland for each dog, lest anybody grow suspicious—such dogs are in demand, when most every market town has a few dog breeders. Moreover, this dog-pawning business would need the means to transport large dogs all about the realm, and that is not a cheap or simple proposition."

She turned her head and pillowed her cheek on her up-drawn knees. "You would know about that. You've brought Georgette up to Town a time or two, haven't you?"

"I could not endure Town without her," Will said. "And the journey from Dorset is tedious, indeed, for even one mastiff won't fit in the average dog cart. We must alternate having Georgette travel in my brother's coach, and run beside my horse, stopping frequently to let her into the coach, then to let her back out. Then she decides she doesn't care to travel in the coach, or traveling in the coach upsets her digestion."

"So the stolen dogs haven't left London," Susannah said.

The ensuing silence was accusing, as if the dogs were simply tied outside the nearest posting inn, and all Will had to do was snap his fingers, toss some cheese, collect a few rewards, and recite his wedding vows.

The reality could be so much worse than that.

"The dogs are in somebody's mews," Will said, "if they haven't been sold to the pits already. The baiters can pay excellent coin, they're discreet, and they need a constant supply of big, healthy dogs. Moreover, a man of position and consequence could move easily between the best households and the lowest entertainments. You're asking me to risk my livelihood, Susannah, rather than assure our future."

Perhaps the common sense of his argument was penetrating her enthusiasm for orange blossoms. She sat up and tugged the hem of the coverlet higher. The candle flame flickered, a prelude to guttering, and a reminder that Will should exit the premises sooner rather than later.

He ought to quit the premises immediately, and prowl the alleys searching for missing dogs with his brothers. He could not claim the rewards, but neither could he live with the knowledge that innocent animals would be sent into violent situations because he'd failed to intervene.

"That's what I forgot to tell you," Susannah said. "Della is likely to refuse Effington's suit, should he tender a proposal. If your brother Ash was waiting for the lists to clear, his opportunity might be in the offing."

Dogs could not speak, could not explain to an owner this baffling behavior or that persistent bad habit. Will had often wrestled with the mysteries of the canine mind, occasionally going so far as to get down on his hands and knees, sniff, and consider the world from a dog's-eye view.

These flights on his part were sometimes forays into

the ridiculous. Other times, taking a moment to view the world from a canine perspective had illuminated a problem. Georgette had repeatedly moved her puppies from the whelping box because it had been positioned in a draft obvious only when a man sat on the floor next to the box.

Between one flicker of the candlelight and the next, insight shot through Will, with the stealth and rapidity of instinct.

"For Della to refuse Effington would be a disaster," Will said, climbing off the bed. For a moment, he could not remember where he'd put his clothes, then he recalled that Susannah had gathered up his clothing for him.

"On my vanity stool," she said. "I thought you disliked Effington."

"I dislike him," Will said, sorting his breeches from the rest of his clothing and pulling them on. "I loathe him, in fact. He cheats at cards, beats his dog, uses his dog to cheat at cards if the talk can be believed, and gossips. Where is my—?"

He found his shirt and pulled it over his head.

Susannah plucked at the coverlet, and the quality of the gesture was reminiscent of a cat flicking the very tip of its tail before pouncing.

"Do you want Della to marry such a paragon?" she asked.

"Of course not." *Susannah* had wanted that very outcome, at least until recently. Will shrugged into his waistcoat rather than remind her of that. "But when Effington realizes his courting has come to naught, he'll look about for somebody to blame his failure on, and for a means of getting even with the woman who led him a dance."

If not the man who intended to wreck the dognapping scheme *Effington* had very probably set up.

Susannah pushed the covers aside and slid off the bed, subjecting Will to a glimpse of pale knees and muscular thighs.

"I warned Della the situation could get messy," Susannah said, taking Will's cuff in her hands and accepting a sleeve button from him. She did up his cuffs, left then right, then began on his shirt buttons.

"Susannah, messy isn't the half of it." Will didn't want to say the words aloud, much less to Susannah, as if speaking them would turn his hunch into a certainty. "Effington is mean, but he's not stupid. If he can't have the bride he wants, he'll not only ruin her chances of a good match, he'll ruin who or what she cares about."

The rest of Will's suspicions, he kept to himself. A hunch was not proof, a guess was not certainty.

Susannah tied Will's cravat in a tidy mathematical. She'd make an attentive and comfortable wife, when she wasn't loving him witless—except he'd never have the opportunity to marry her if his instincts proved correct.

"Della will retire to the country at the conclusion of the Season," Susannah said, patting Will's cravat. "Or she'll attend house parties with a grandmamma or auntie. I've endured many a house party, and will attend a few more if necessary."

The image of Susannah, loose among the ne'er-do-wells and scapegraces who frequented house parties, nearly had Will sinking back onto the bed, but a worse disaster loomed closer at hand.

"Effington doesn't like you, Susannah, not that he likes anybody, and he'll turn on Della like a rabid cur. When she refuses his suit, his only decision will be whether to accuse me or to accuse Ash of stealing the missing dogs. Perhaps he'll accuse us both and Sycamore too."

❧

Will tucked in his shirttails and buttoned his waistcoat, and with each article of clothing, he became less Susannah's lover and more the mannerly gentleman who'd brought her a purple parasol and an apology weeks ago.

Not her Willow, but some quieter, more reserved fellow who'd forgotten how to smile.

"I want to say you've taken leave of your senses," she muttered, passing him his cravat pin. "But Effington isn't... He isn't a credit to his antecedents. He's calculating. Shrewd and nasty."

Like the Mannering sisters, to whom Susannah had given too much deference.

"Effington is also in want of coin," Will said, sitting on the vanity stool to yank on his boots. "That combination bodes ill for all in his ambit."

Two hours ago, Susannah had been pleased with life, enjoying a sense of newfound calm and clarity. She'd excused herself from the duty of seeing Della married off, and had instead focused on ensuring Willow Dorning remained a part of her own future.

"What are you planning?" Susannah asked.

Will stood, all buttoned up, and produced a comb from a pocket. He put his hair to rights without even glancing in Susannah's folding mirror, then tucked the comb away. He looked ready for a hand of cards at the club.

Maybe even ready to walk out of Susannah's life.

"I face choices, my lady, none of them to my liking. If I leave matters alone, I'm essentially waiting for Effington to come along and snatch my business prospects, my good name, and possibly my blameless brothers away."

"But Ash hasn't stolen anybody's dog. Effington would have no witnesses, no proof."

The look Will gave Susannah was chilling in its pity. "My dear, Effington will regretfully swear, under oath, that he saw Ash Dorning leading Alexander away from the Marches' mews. Effington will recollect Sycamore in conversation with a notorious bear handler, and recount money changing hands along with a large dog. Others will corroborate that testimony, or important parts of it. Effington is a rotter, and the more rotten he plans to be, the less we'll grasp what he's about until it's too late."

Will spoke as if it was already too late. As if they were helpless but to read their lines in a tragedy, the ending of which had been fated before the curtain had gone up.

"Then I will swear that Ash Dorning was with me," Susannah said, "and Effington must have been mistaken."

Will's palm cradled Susannah's cheek. "Your testimony won't hold up, because you are a paragon who could not possibly lie convincingly, but I love you for offering to protect my brother at the cost of your own reputation."

Dread swept away the pleasure Susannah took in having Willow Dorning in her bedroom avowing his love.

"Are you saying Della must marry this cur?"

"For her to marry Effington is one alternative, though I can't, as a gentleman, support it."

Relief coursed through Susannah. Will was a gentleman, of that there had never been the slightest doubt. The truest gentleman she'd ever met.

"Even if a marriage between Della and Effington would assure our own future, I can't support it either, Willow."

This was…not how Susannah had felt even that very morning. Then, she'd been willing to ignore her own instincts regarding Effington, and she'd regarded any match for Della as better than no match. That's how desperately she'd sought to put an end to her own social ordeals, how badly she'd craved the safety of spinsterhood.

"So if Della isn't to marry Effington," Susannah said, "what other choices does that leave?"

Susannah would loathe these choices. She knew that by Will's shuttered expression, and how his hand fell to his side.

"Ash, Cam, and I can leave London immediately. When dogs continue to turn up missing, we'll have some evidence to exonerate us. Perhaps Effington would go after Casriel next, but that would require more boldness than even Effington has."

"Why can't Effington simply marry some other

young lady, one with fat settlements and a fondness for new bonnets?" Susannah asked, slipping her arms around Will's waist. He'd already departed, in some sense, already gone over the balcony rail, into the dark night without her.

Damn Effington and all his mangy ilk, for taking advantage of helpless dogs, who asked for little enough in life. For ruining honorable men because of a lack of coin. For destroying a young woman's future out of simple spite.

"Willow, I want you to know something."

His arms came around her, solidly, snugly. "I want you to know something too."

If he said he was leaving her, running back to Dorset with his tail between his legs, Susannah would…

Try to let him go, though scurrying away would be wrong—for them, and also for him. Very wrong for the dogs nobody cared about the way Will did.

"I want you to know, Mr. Willow Dorning, that the moments I've shared with you, on the dance floor, in the park, in that bed, I have felt more alive, and more like myself, than at any other time. I love you, I will always love you for those moments."

She felt the shock of her words go through him, and they'd surprised her too. Her declaration lacked the Bard's finesse, but she'd never expressed herself more sincerely.

"I want much more than moments with you, Susannah."

She hadn't expected Will to say that, and for the space of a sigh, Susannah simply basked in his assurances. His embrace was firm, his words unhesitating.

This was the true Will too. Tenacious, relentless, tirelessly patient.

"If Della isn't to marry Effington," Susannah said, "if you're not to take your brothers back to Dorset, and Effington isn't to ruin anybody, then what are we to do?"

For Will had made a choice. Susannah could feel that in him too. The certainty he enjoyed about so much of life had not failed him now.

"The course is simple, though not easy. All I have to do to thwart Effington is find the dogs and ensure that the guilty party is held responsible for stealing them, and I must do this before Effington suspects Lady Della's affections are not engaged."

He was quivering with eagerness to begin that quest, ready to bound away in hot pursuit of a nearly impossible goal.

"Willow, it might already be too late. Della was prepared to give Effington a rousing set-down before she left the ball tonight."

⁂

In Effington's opinion, last night's ball had ended well. Lady Della had been tongue-tied and unforthcoming during their waltz, such as a lady might become when growing uncertain of a suitor's affections. That notion cheered him considerably, but not enough for him to overlook a serious lapse on his housekeeper's part.

"What do you mean, we've not a single headache powder in the house?" Effington asked pleasantly. The menials knew to be terrified when he scolded in mild tones. Yorick crouched beside Effington's slipper, the poor fellow nearly shivering with dread.

Wentworth did not so much as twitch at her skirt. "When we ran out of chocolate on Thursday, your lordship, your mother decided she'd pay a visit to Lady Mannering, and her ladyship has been there since. She took the last two headache powders, and the only bottle of Godfrey's Cordial."

Wentworth's tone suggested Mama might also have made off with the silver. Mama would do it too. The viscountess was a right bitch when she was in a taking, which generally lasted until her allowance ran out.

"Then I suggest you either retrieve that bottle of Godfrey's Cordial from her, or procure more," Effington said, picking up Yorick. "A household without remedies is a household with a lax housekeeper."

He stroked the top of Yorick's head and met Wentworth's gaze. She was desperate to retort that the marketing money wouldn't cover an excursion to the apothecary, desperate to suggest that her employer retrieve the medicinals from his wayward mother. Too bad for Wentworth, a lax housekeeper was one step away from being turned off without a character and without the wages due her.

"I'll send a note to Lady Mannering's housekeeper, your lordship, and let the viscountess know you're asking for the return of a few small items."

Cleverness was tedious in the help. "You're excused, Wentworth. Send Bolton to me, for it's time I tended to my social obligations."

Wentworth was a tall, thin woman, all bustling energy and nervous disposition. She looked like she was about to wet herself in her desire to quit the room.

"Mr. Bolton is apparently under the weather, your lordship."

Bolton was an indestructible terrier of a valet, and if his skill with a needle and his knowledge of fashion weren't faultless, Effington would have tossed him out on his presuming ear long ago.

"What sort of under the weather, Wentworth?"

"He went to visit his mama this morning, sir, it being his half day. He didn't come back at midday, which is his usual habit. We've sent a note inquiring after his health."

Yorick whined, for which Effington smacked him on the snout, and that passing gesture of reproof caused the housekeeper to flinch.

None of which would soothe a suffering man's pounding head.

"Send another note, and tell Bolton his services will no longer be necessary. That will be all."

She curtsied and scurried out, while Effington poured himself a tot of brandy. "Hair of the dog that bit me," he muttered. "The most useful of the canine allusions."

Yorick didn't so much as wiggle to be let down, but hung motionless on Effington's arm. He set the dog on the carpet, which needed a good beating, much like his mother and half the help.

"You're for the badger pits," Effington informed his dog. "You're losing your lucky touch, my boy, for I lost last night."

Before Effington had settled in at his club, he'd made arrangements to call on Lady Della, which had been prudent of him. He'd lost every penny due him from Mannering, drat the luck.

The time had come to plight his troth. Mama's defection was inconvenient, but if word got out that Viscount Effington was managing without a valet, or reneging on debts of honor…

"Not to be borne," Effington said, downing his brandy and pouring another. "At least Lady Della assured me she'd be home this afternoon, should I care to call." Assured him emphatically, almost as if she were desperate to have a private moment with him.

Which she ought to be. The time had come to sample Lady Della's charms. One didn't buy a horse without trying its paces.

The second brandy was the last available, some incompetent having forgotten to refill the decanters.

"Just as well," Effington said. "Something I ate last night disagreed with me, or something I drank."

He'd drunk rather a lot, otherwise that Tresham fellow with the cold gaze wouldn't have won so much from him. Ash Dorning had won a fair bit too. Bothersome vermin, younger sons, and the Dornings had those odd, overly blue eyes.

"I'll steal his brother's dogs," Effington said, downing the second brandy. "That enormous creature who tried to piss on my leg is due for a comeuppance, and the earl's town house is not three streets over. They won't be posting any tiresome rewards, either, because all the world knows the Dornings need every coin they can beg, borrow, or steal."

Or marry. That thought, for reasons the brandy put just beyond Effington's reach, was not cheering.

"Out of my way," he said, shoving Yorick aside with his foot. "I've arrangements to make and calls to pay, and when I'm done, you, my boy, and those other canines eating me out of house and habiliment will find your situations vastly changed for the worse."

While Effington's would change for the better. He upended the brandy bottle, delivering the last, sweetest drops straight down his gullet, snapped his fingers, and repaired above stairs, where he'd puzzle out how to tie his own cravat.

How hard could that be, after all?

Fifteen

Dogs survived as a species, despite wars, disease, famine, and man's violence, in part because dogs naturally gravitated toward their own kind. In the wild state, they dwelled in packs, so the best hunters were free to hunt, the young were protected, the alert stood guard, and the powerful did battle.

Will came to this realization watching Samson and Georgette play with Hector in the town house garden. That Hector could play at all was progress, for the dog had been the slowest to trust, the most ready to see every overture as at threat. Hector's own kind could coax him into playing again far more quickly and exuberantly than Will could.

"At the rate you're going, we'll have you to the park before the Season is out," Will said when all three dogs were panting on the grass. "Samson once wanted confidence, as you do, and he's coming right."

Lady Susannah had a lot to do with that, for she settled Will in a way he could not settle himself, and when the owner was settled, the dog could be calm.

Last night had left Will both settled and unsettled. At peace and ready to go to war.

"She is part of my pack," Will said. "Has been for years, but we're only now realizing that."

"Ah, so I'm not the only man who talks to my dog."

The Duke of Quimbey stood several yards away on the terrace. Comus was with him, looking well-groomed and very much on his manners.

"Georgette, Samson, come. Hector, sit." Will shook the treat bag, because Comus was not a stranger to Hector, but they hadn't seen each other for some time and Hector was focused on the newcomer.

"You could pull a curricle with those three," Quimbey said. "I don't recognize the fawn-colored fellow. Is he new?"

Hector stared straight at Comus, who glanced from Will to Georgette to Quimbey. Hector's staring was the behavior of a dog who intended to remain in charge of a situation, and Comus, without a growl or a bark exchanged, signaled his willingness to allow Hector the upper paw, as it were.

"Hector, sit," Will said, making the hand sign.

Hector remained on all fours.

"Hector's training isn't very far along." Will fished out a treat and held it before Hector's nose. "Hector, sit." Will drew the treat up to a point between Hector's ears.

The dog ignored the treat and growled.

"I can't chide Hector for his behavior, because Comus is arguably an intruder," Will said. "If Your Grace will wait for a moment, I'll put Hector in the stables."

Will put a leash on Hector, who grumbled at that

indignity as Will led his fractious beast across the alley to the stables. The stable boys did not handle Hector—nobody handled Hector save Will—so it fell to Will to put Hector in his stall.

"Hector, sit," Will instructed when the leash was off.

Hector sat. No tail thumping, no embellishing the moment with pleasantries. The dog was well aware of Quimbey and Comus over in the garden.

"Good boy," Will said, "and for today, that's enough. You weren't exactly top wrangler for social skills, but you didn't disgrace your training, either. I'm proud of you, and we'll play again before supper. *All done*, Hector."

Hector offered a single thump of his tail in exchange for a final treat, some commands being easier to learn than others.

Will rejoined the duke, who'd taken a seat by a dry fountain.

"You can let Comus off the leash," Will said. "Samson and Georgette will enjoy more playtime."

"We all enjoy playtime," Quimbey replied. "One tends to forget that. Tresham has certainly forgotten it."

"You're worried about your nephew," Will said, touched that the duke would confide such a woe to a mere trainer of dogs. Comus sniffed noses with Samson and Georgette, then various other parts were sniffed, until Comus lowered his front end and woofed.

Several hundred pounds of overgrown puppies soon went rolling and yelping across the grass, a sight Susannah would have enjoyed.

"I am worried about Tresham," Quimbey said, "and

you're the canny sort who notices more than others. I trust your discretion to the utmost, Mr. Dorning."

"And well you should," Will replied as the dogs started a game of chase-my-neighbor around the sundial at the center of the garden.

"You know I've admonished Tresham to take a wife. He's my heir, I'm getting on, and he's lonely."

Will knew no such thing. "I've suggested Casriel find a countess, Your Grace. He needs an heir other than myself, and he's lonely too." Though Will hadn't realized that until the words had left his mouth.

"So, there I am," Quimbey said, getting up to pace, "exhorting the boy to marry posthaste, and the only woman he takes an interest in is Lady Della Haddonfield. I tell myself this is of no moment, for Lady Della is all but spoken for by that Effington buffoon."

Will hoped that as he and the duke were speaking, Susannah was having a delicate conversation with Lady Della. The younger Haddonfield sister must play out the line with Effington, neither making promises nor rejecting his offers. A note from Susannah at breakfast assured Will that Lady Della had yet to send the viscount packing, though Effington could be paying a visit that very afternoon.

"Effington has shown an interest in Lady Della," Will said. "Nothing more—yet."

Georgette caught up with Comus and began the game of catch-me-if-you-can all over in the opposite direction, with Samson woofing encouragement from the rear.

"I saw Lady Della last evening with your brother, Mr. Ash Dorning," Quimbey replied, turning on his heel and putting his hands behind his back. "Effington doesn't stand a chance, Mr. Dorning, and I hope Lady Della's family is relieved as a consequence. I cannot see Mr. Ash Dorning making an offer, though, being the impecunious extra spare, and a gentleman."

Will felt a growing urgency to call on the Haddonfield ladies, while Quimbey seemed content to pace off the metes and bounds of ballroom gossip.

"Ash hasn't confided any plans to me," Will said, "but he knows my own circumstances are constrained by a lack of coin. If I'm not proposing marriage in the near future, I doubt Ash would be."

"Precisely!" Quimbey rocked forward on his toes, then settled back into his pacing. "Precisely, Mr. Dorning. I knew you were the perceptive sort. You saw to it that Comus and I got off to a good start, after all. So, there we have it. Lady Della will reject Effington, she won't get an offer from your brother, and the only other fellow who's up to her weight, so to speak, is my nephew. He's set a man to keep an eye on Lady Della, and that does not bode well at all."

Susannah would do Will an injury if he pulled that sort of maneuver, and yet a ducal heir needed to exercise caution where his private affairs were concerned.

Quimbey pivoted again, and an image came to Will's mind: Tresham, in the same posture, hands behind his back, speechifying, every inch a duke in training.

Then another image: Lady Della, hands behind her back, every inch a lady from birth, speechifying... And Susannah confiding that Lady Della was the product of their late mother's indiscretion.

Oh dear.

"Cousins occasionally marry, Your Grace," Will said cautiously. Was this why Quimbey had remained single? Because he'd harbored a *tendresse* for Della and Susannah's mama?

His Grace wilted onto the bench across from Will. "Cousins might marry, Mr. Dorning, half siblings do not. My brother was a hopeless romantic, his wife a hopeless thespian. They were in some senses well suited, but their son deserved steadier parents. I did what I could for Jonathan, but now… I did not foresee this situation with Lady Della, and yet Jon seems interested in her. It's nearly farcical, but also unnerving, and something must be done."

Will recalled Tresham expressing a wish that Della would leave London, just before glowering at the lady for the duration of an entire waltz.

"Tresham suspects some connection," Will said, "though you needn't worry he's smitten. I'd bet Georgette on it, and I do not bet my dogs lightly. Lady Della might suspect a connection as well, but neither is she enamored of Mr. Tresham."

Instinct said that was the case. Prudence suggested the matter was too delicate to leave to chance. Indifference could turn to fondness, as it had with Susannah and the dogs.

Georgette let out a rare bark, which set the other two off. Hector gave a few plaintive echoes from the stables.

"Georgette, come," Will called. "Samson, you too. Come, now."

Georgette trotted over, snout in the air, Samson following.

"Do I call Comus?" Quimbey asked.

"Yes, and praise him for obeying, though he's simply aping his elders." Will passed over a piece of cheese as Georgette leaned against his knee.

Comus sat at the duke's feet without being asked, and Quimbey gave the dog a treat and a pat.

"Good fellow, Comus. You were a good boy when we called on the Duchess of Ambrose too, weren't you?"

"*All done*, Georgette," Will said, surrendering the cheese, then repeating the instruction with Samson. "*All done*. Down and stay. Good girl. Good boy."

And *good boy*, Comus, for charming the duchess.

"Can't you simply explain the facts to Tresham?" Will asked. "He had to know of his father's amorous tendencies, and now that I consider the matter, Tresham and Lady Della have similar coloring."

Similar coloring, similar glowers, similar gestures. Will would not be the last to remark the similarities. Even Effington might notice a resemblance—God help them all.

"You and Tresham have similar coloring," Quimbey scoffed.

"I have more muscle, I'm taller, and I have the Dorning eyes," Will said. "Shall I warn Tresham away?"

The notion was no more burdensome than paying off Cam's vowels, or having a word with the housemaid in Dorset who'd taken a fancy to Cam. Part of looking after a pack mate.

"One doesn't want to unnecessarily shock the young people," Quimbey said. "Couldn't you intimate to Jonathan that Mr. Ash Dorning has an

inheritance that will allow him to offer for a young
lady in a year or two?"

"I'm not comfortable dissembling, Your Grace.
What if Tresham confronted Ash about this nonexis-
tent inheritance? The truth is usually the best choice."

"Spoken like a man with a clear conscience," His
Grace muttered. Comus put his chin on the duke's
knee, Georgette sighed, and from the stables came a
lone, melancholy bark.

"My conscience is mostly clear," Will said, "and
I'm happy to have a private conversation with Mr.
Tresham, but I'd like your views on another delicate
matter if you have a moment." Only a moment, for
this new development made it imperative that Will
return to Susannah's side.

"I can be discreet too, Mr. Dorning. One can't help
but notice that Lady Susannah has caught your eye."

"When did one notice this?"

"She nearly knocked me from her path last night.
Like her mama, Lady Susannah knows what she wants
and goes after it—or after him. My brother had occasion to admire Lady Bellefonte's determination." And
Quimbey didn't judge a woman for being determined
on an objective, even if that objective had been his
fickle brother.

"I esteem Lady Susannah above all others," Will
said, "but matters have grown complicated." Will
explained his marital aspirations, his suspicions regarding Effington, and the need to find the dogs. "As soon
as my brother Sycamore is awake and sentient, I'll
explain the situation to him, Ash, and Casriel too."

Sycamore had reported no dogs answering to

Caesar's description at the bear garden as of last evening, which meant the missing dogs might be as close as Effington's mews.

"Good fellows, your brothers," Quimbey said, rising. "Though I'm sure the younger one, Sycamore, will give you some bad moments. Puts me in mind of myself as a lad. You're off to scour London for missing mastiffs, then?"

As soon as Will called on Susannah. "I am, and if you have suggestions, I'm happy to hear them."

"Suggestions. Here's what I suggest, Mr. Dorning: find the dogs, the sooner the better. Effington was at the club last night, making bold proclamations about securing the succession and filling his nursery."

Georgette, in the manner of dogs, unceremoniously deposited the contents of her belly at Will's feet.

"I'll also have a very quiet word with Tresham," Will said. "Excuse Georgette, Your Grace. Her digestion becomes unsettled when she plays too hard."

Quimbey fastened Comus's leash to a handsome braided collar. "Georgette has the right of it. A man who cheats at cards and enlists the aid of an innocent dog in his chicanery ought not to have a chance to fill a nursery. Comus agrees with me. Come, Comus. We must pen the duchess a note thanking her for this morning's hospitality."

༄

"I'm here to pass along something you should know," Ash Dorning said as he stood beside Della, looking out over a back garden coming to its glory.

To Della, his eyes were his most interesting feature.

Their color was intriguing, more purple than blue, between lilac and gentian, like the pansies growing in pots at the top of the terrace steps. Those beautiful eyes held Della's attention, not for their hue, but for their sincerity.

"I know I like kissing you, Ash Dorning."

"I more than like kissing you, but that was... I'm not here to kiss you, my lady."

He at least sounded regretful, though he looked far too handsome in the midday sunshine. Susannah would join them any minute, and that would end even talk of kissing, so Della made her words count.

"I would like to kiss you again, sir, and then some. You'll think me bold, but kissing you was illuminating."

He looked down, possibly hiding a smile. "Illuminating in what sense, my lady?"

"You were right," Della said, plucking a pansy and threading it through the buttonhole in his lapel. "I deserve to feel like a queen when somebody kisses me. I am not responsible for my antecedents, and I should stop feeling as if I owe my family a quick exit from Polite Society's stage. I want more kisses from you, Mr. Dorning, and I want to walk in the park with you, debating the merits of reform or Mrs. Wollstonecraft's theories, instead of hanging on your arm and hoping everybody sees me there."

Mr. Dorning removed the pansy from his lapel and tucked it behind Della's ear. "I'm in favor of reform, actually, in moderate degrees. The alternative is revolution, and we've seen the state that left France in."

For a moment, the sensation of Mr. Dorning's fingers brushing against Della's hair robbed her of rational thought. Warmth trickled through her, and remembered joy. Mr. Dorning had kissed her, thoroughly, and here he was, not twenty-four hours later, calling upon her without benefit of his brothers' company.

"My point," Della said, taking his arm and leading him down the steps, "is that I can't sacrifice my happiness for anybody's convenience, and with that in mind, you should know that I intend to pester Jonathan Tresham until he returns certain letters my mother wrote to his father."

Mr. Dorning said nothing, so Della plowed ahead, though she knew she might be forever ruining her chances of having more of his kisses. That would be sad—very sad—but not a tragedy.

"Certain very personal letters, Mr. Dorning."

"That's what you're about with Tresham, my lady? You're bothering him to return some old correspondence?"

"Not even that," Della said as they descended into the knot garden. This part of the garden was near the alley, but visible from the house too, so propriety would not be offended if they tarried here. Della took a seat on the marble bench, lest she escort Mr. Dorning behind a huge, leafy maple. "I intend to offer Mr. Tresham a trade, if he'll ever condescend to have a discussion with me. Brothers are the very worst when they're feeling stubborn."

Mr. Dorning flipped out the tails of his riding jacket and came down beside Della uninvited. She liked that he didn't stand on ceremony with her, for a man who stickled over manners was a man who'd avoid the company of a countess's by-blow.

"I have six brothers," Mr. Dorning said. "One of them is Sycamore, and he ought to count triple. Tresham is your brother?"

Four little words, and from Mr. Dorning, they were only mildly curious words. A weight eased off Della's heart and fluttered away on the spring sunshine.

"Tresham is my half brother, considerably my elder, and I gather my existence has been kept from him. He did not respond to my letters, has refused my conversational overtures, and glowers certain death at me when our paths cross."

Della waited, though waiting was hard. Mr. Dorning could still bow politely and stride out of her life, or change the subject.

"Tresham may not have all the puzzle pieces," Mr. Dorning said. "Have you told him you're his sister?"

Or Mr. Dorning might get to the very heart of the matter. Della pulled the pansy from behind her ear.

"One doesn't put that in writing," she said, twirling the flower by its fragile stem. "I informed him I had some documents written by a late member of his family, and asked him to make an opportunity to discuss them with me. He's been dreadfully stubborn, and unforthcoming. Also nimble as a hare at eluding my company."

And that…hurt, that her own brother, the only brunet sibling she had, the only one who wasn't a shining blond giant or giantess, should turn his back on her without even a fair hearing.

Della had waited years to make Jonathan Tresham's acquaintance, only to find he was a condescending blockhead. How like a brother.

"You've frightened the poor man," Mr. Dorning said. "He probably thinks you're a by-blow of Quimbey's, or an avaricious blackmailer. He's not thinking you'd like to give him letters his father wrote, despite what you told him."

"Tresham's father was so proud of him," Della said, which was more unfairness. "I want to know what Mama wrote to our papa, if she even told him I was on the way. There's much I don't know."

Mr. Dorning's arm came around Della's shoulders. "Your Haddonfield family has no idea you've carried these questions on your own, all these years. Your looks are deceptively slight. I told Tresham that last night."

Tresham who? Della was too pleased to find herself in Mr. Dorning's embrace, too soothed and comforted by his affection. She'd fret over her idiot half brother some other time, or maybe give up on him as a hopeless case.

"Effington took issue with my estimation of you," Mr. Dorning went on. "That's why I'm making so bold as to call on you, my lady."

Della wanted Mr. Dorning to hush, to simply hush and let her enjoy the sense of acceptance he offered.

Or maybe he could kiss her again?

"I honestly do not care one whit for what Lord Effington says, Mr. Dorning. He's a buffoon who has made the early weeks of my Season tedious in the extreme. I made excuses for him—he's reserved, he's busy, he has much on his mind, he's a convenient escort—but mostly he's a bully who singled me out for his attentions because he grasped how insecure I was."

"You're not insecure," Mr. Dorning said, nuzzling

Della's temple. "You're cautious. There's a difference. I ought to be cautious too, but you smell of honey-suckle and mischief, and I've spent too much time with Sycamore to be on my best behavior."

Bless Sycamore.

"I would have remained in Kent," Della said, "except I wanted to meet my brother and my uncle. Quimbey is a dear old fellow, though Mr. Tresham lacks charm."

The arm fell way from Della's shoulders. "Tresham is a fine card player," Mr. Dorning said. "He and I ended up at the same table with Mr. Effington, and you will please not kiss me again until I tell you the rest of it."

"Speak quickly, Mr. Dorning." At any minute, Susannah would come out of the house, and then nobody would be kissing anybody.

"Mr. Tresham and I decided you should be told that Effington cheats at cards."

This confidence was significant and shocking, such as might restore a blockheaded brother a bit in Della's eyes. Men called each other out over such foolishness, and the ladies were never given any details. A "mishap with a gun" befell a man, and in a young lady's hear-ing, nothing more was ever said.

"This is bad, isn't it?" Della asked. "That Effington cheats, and that both you and Mr. Tresham realized it."

"Sooner or later, Effington will be called out. Fortunately, he's a bad cheat, and both Tresham and I won significant sums from him, though I doubt Effington will pay. We thought you should be warned, because if he'll cheat at cards, then his honor is not to be trusted."

That observation was another sort of kiss, a declaration that Della deserved to be treated with respect and honesty. She kissed Mr. Dorning's cheek in agreement.

"Thank you, Mr. Dorning. I suppose I'm in Tresham's debt as well."

"If you have the letters his father wrote, I can take them to him, and explain the situation, if you like. He won't avoid me, and he can give me your mother's letters more easily than he can pass them along to you."

Sitting beside Mr. Dorning in the sunny garden, Della felt a piece of her heart come right, and yet she ached too, because this offer of assistance had been so freely given.

"I had never thought to enlist another's aid." She wanted to tuck the pansy back with the other blossoms before it wilted, but of course, that would not serve. "You make this exchange of letters sound easy. A quiet chat. No drama, no scandal, which is all I wanted and what I was sure I couldn't have."

"Sycamore says being near the bottom of the sibling heap is hard, that one must cultivate drama simply to assure any notice at all."

"I like Sycamore." Della liked all of the Dornings she'd met so far, including Georgette. "If you would be so kind as to explain matters to Mr. Tresham, I leave it to him whether he and I converse, or whether he gives me Mama's letters. I'll bring my father's letters to Mama along with me when—Susannah, good day."

Mr. Dorning stood and bowed, his movements elegant and unhurried. "My lady, good day. Is that the infamous parasol of apology?"

"Mr. Dorning, greetings. I brought it for Della, if

she insists on sitting in the sun. The day is so pleasant, I might tarry here for a moment myself before seeing to an errand."

Bless Susannah, she was being conspiratorial, asking if Della wanted company, not insisting on chaperoning at close quarters.

"I will take my leave," Mr. Dorning said. "Lady Della, I trust we'll speak further soon."

"I'll see you to your horse."

Susannah pretended to absorb herself in the intricacies of opening the parasol, but Della knew a sisterly smirk when one was barely contained. Della nonetheless walked Mr. Dorning to the garden's back gate and across the alley, where he signaled a groom to bring his horse around.

"Please do speak to Mr. Tresham," Della said. "And call again soon, Mr. Dorning."

"Ash," he said. "When we're private, I invite you to call me Ash, though my brothers will refer to me as Ash-heap or Ash-pidistra."

"Brothers can be inventive."

So could Della. She went up on her toes and kissed Mr. Dorning on the mouth, knowing she'd ambushed him. He tasted good, of peppermint and promises, and his arms around Della felt like home.

"Mischief," he said, pulling on his gloves when Della had stepped back. "I have no immediate prospects, I come simply as a friend, and I find myself subject to irresistible mischief. For shame, my lady."

He kissed her nose, and went whistling into the stables.

"Why is it," Della asked the lovely spring day, "Lord Effington's conceit and condescension, his title and all his silly manners, appeal to me not at all, while Mr. Dorning, who has a good heart and no immediate prospects, has stolen my fancy?"

She twirled once, for the sheer joy of making her skirts bell around her ankles, then scampered off to rejoin Susannah in the garden.

❧

Effington's horse was a plodder, but because his lordship's afternoon had started with a jaunt to Knightsbridge, and the next errand after proposing to Lady Della would take Effington all the way to Bloomsbury, Effington was on horseback as he came up the alley behind the Haddonfield town house.

In Knightsbridge, he'd negotiated a tidy sum to be paid to him upon delivery of several big, nasty dogs who could take on the nasty job of regularly worrying a big, nasty bear. The expense of keeping the dogs in Bloomsbury would be eliminated for the nonce. Jasper and Horace, a disgracefully greedy pair, could then—at Effington's direction—find or steal more big, nasty specimens for eventual sale in Knightsbridge.

A profitable day thus far, and marriage settlements would go even further toward relieving the monetary anxieties that played such havoc with Effington's nerves.

Effington's horse chose that moment to relieve itself, and being a plodder who did not appreciate a day spent dealing with London traffic, this equine trip to the jakes meant coming to a complete stop. The horse grunted, lifted his tail, and deposited a steaming pile of manure on the cobbles.

The gelding was not the sort to hurry even that

indelicate process, and thus Effington was standing in his stirrups in the shade of a plane tree when up ahead, across the next intersection of alleys, Lady Della emerged from a back garden on the arm of Mr. Ash Dorning.

Her ladyship was affixed to Mr. Dorning in a most familiar manner, though Effington didn't begrudge any woman her flirts. Life was tedious, and flirting was harmless.

Mr. Dorning looked rather well put together for a morning call, and he certainly wasn't objecting to Lady Della's presumption. Perhaps the fool didn't understand that her ladyship could compromise his honor with a word.

Though, of course, she wouldn't. Della Haddonfield tried to hide it, but she was a shrewd little baggage. She knew the value of a title, and did not expect hearts and flowers from a prospective spouse beyond what was required by appearances.

The horse grunted again, and dropped one last, damp, stinking addition to the pile on the cobbles. The innocuous scents of a shady Mayfair alley acquired an acrid pungence.

Rather than urge the horse forward, Effington let the beast stand a moment, for a bit of spying was in order, and neither Lady Della nor her caller had taken notice of Effington—of anything, save each other.

She said something, then plastered herself against Mr. Dorning and kissed him. Mr. Dorning kissed her ladyship back, and because the horse had stopped groaning and shuffling about, Effington caught the last few words.

"Mischief," Dorning said *smugly*. "I have no

immediate prospects, I come simply as a friend, and I find myself subjected to irresistible mischief. For shame, my lady."

Dorning kissed her nose on that towering understatement, and strutted into the stables whistling a snippet of the Hallelujah Chorus.

Dorning had no prospects at all, as every member of Polite Society knew, so perhaps he'd simply humored a forward young woman.

Effington was about to signal his horse to walk on—the lazy beast usually ignored any command the first three times it was given—when Lady Della turned her face up to the dappled sunshine pouring from the heavens.

"Why is it," she asked nobody that Effington could see, "Lord Effington's conceit and condescension, his title and all his silly manners, appeal to me not at all, while Mr. Dorning, who has a good heart and no immediate prospects, has stolen my fancy?"

She twirled, her words twisting a dagger into the belly of Effington's future, and flitted away, back to the garden from whence she'd come.

Ash Dorning emerged from the stables a few moments later, blew a kiss across the alley, mounted his horse, and trotted off, probably to steal kisses from other men's fiancées, all the while claiming mere friendship.

Effington sat in the saddle for some minutes, sorting alternatives, debating whether he might that very instant confront her fickle ladyship with an offer of marriage.

But no. She'd shown her true colors, and Effington had been patient long enough.

A prudent man, especially one in want of means,

always had a strategy in reserve for those unfortunate times when matters did not unfold as that man had planned them. The dogs would disappear into the baiters' pits before sunset.

That much hadn't changed.

Effington would then attend the subsequent bear-baiting, and identify one of the unfortunate canines as stolen property—the duchess's mastiff would do—and raise a hue and cry to pillory the fiend or fiends responsible.

The horse evidenced its usual inattention to its master's wishes, so Effington jerked the beast's head around and gave it a stout swat on the quarters. The horse tossed its head and planted its front hooves, which display of pique Effington thwarted with another smart whack with the crop, for the contingency plan was taking on an urgency.

Ash Dorning was ideally situated to steal dogs from aristocratic houses. His brother was a dog trainer, and Dorning had just admitted to a lack of funds. Ash Dorning thus had a motive for kidnapping canines either to sell them or to collect any offered rewards.

How...convenient.

"And then we'll see who is kissing whom," Effington muttered as he sent his recalcitrant horse trotting off in the direction of Bloomsbury.

Sixteen

Della returned to the garden looking entirely too pleased with herself, though her grin was a reproach to Susannah, who'd forgotten that Della *could* look pleased with herself.

"Please tell me Mr. Dorning didn't kiss you in the very mews, Delilah Haddonfield," Susannah said.

"He didn't," Della replied. "I kissed him. He bore up manfully under my shameless behavior. Susannah, I am in love."

Susannah rose and collected her reticule. "Not a very dignified condition, is it?"

"You are in love too," Della said, taking the place Susannah had vacated on the bench. The sun had warmed the stone, and if Susannah weren't in a hurry, she would have tarried with Della and indulged in the literary pastime of describing what it meant to be in love.

Only the Bard had come close, and even he had occasionally struggled.

"Where are you off to?" Della asked.

"I am expecting Mr. Willow Dorning to call, but my favorite version of the sonnets is growing worn. I thought I'd step around to Hanford's bookshop and see if they know of somebody who can repair a binding grown weary with overuse."

For the first time Susannah could recall, she had no plans to borrow more books for reading.

Another symptom of having fallen in love.

"Don't tarry," Della said, passing Susannah the purple parasol. "Effington is to call on me, and I'll need to regale you with a recounting of that ordeal the instant I've sent him on his way."

Susannah had been frank about Effington's ability to damage innocent lives. "You will ask for time to consider your situation, and imply that if I can bring Mr. Dorning up to scratch, then you'd like my nuptials to precede your own."

Della kicked off her slippers and sent them sailing across the grass. "I thought I was the devious sister. Off with you, and hurry back."

Barrisford crossed the terrace, his gait stately, and yet conveying a sense of urgency. "A gentleman has come to call, my ladies. I've put him in the family parlor."

Not Will, for Barrisford would have mentioned Georgette.

Della rose. "I know, Suze. Simper, bat my eyes, be flattering and inoffensive, but don't commit to anything." Off she marched to her fate.

"Della Haddonfield," Susannah called. "Your slippers, dear. Martyrdom is more convincing if one is properly shod for the ordeal."

Della stuck out her tongue, retrieved her slippers, and accompanied Barrisford into the house.

Susannah let herself out through the garden gate,

the alleys being a much quicker route to Bond Street. Della hadn't chastised her for going without a maid, which was fortunate when Jeffers had claimed to be suffering a megrim, and Willow would soon call.

Time was of the essence.

Had Susannah not taken a moment to fiddle with the mechanism of the parasol, she might have missed the commotion at the north end of the alley. A gentleman on horseback was having an altercation with his mount, who apparently did not care to deal with the heavy traffic on the main thoroughfare.

"Ouch," Susannah muttered as a riding crop came down on the horse's quarters with significant force. The horse kicked out with both back legs and hopped sideways across the alley.

The dialogue continued in that fashion—bad behavior from the horse followed by an application of the crop, followed by more bad behavior—while a nagging sense of familiarity stole through Susannah.

"Effington," she whispered, shrinking back against the garden wall. Della and Mr. Dorning had been kissing in this very alley not five minutes past, and there was Effington in a serious temper not a hundred yards away.

Oh, Della. Oh, no.

"God rot your stubbornness!" Effington bellowed as the horse came to a quivering standstill. "Take the damned alleys then, but get me to Bloomsbury or it's the knacker's yard for you."

Bloomsbury, where Sycamore had last seen the dognappers.

Find the dogs, Will had said. Find the dogs, or risk

injury to multiple reputations, and injury or worse to several beloved pets. Susannah tucked the parasol under her arm and stole after the viscount and his fractious horse.

❧

"Mr. Dorning!" Lady Della beamed at Will across the parlor as if he'd brought news of Wellington's victory at Waterloo. "I was expecting Lord Effington."

While Will had expected Susannah to greet him. "You don't seem disappointed, my lady."

"Your brother Ash was here not fifteen minutes ago. He has a very cheering effect on a lady's disposition. Disappointment is beyond me, though I'm to simper and sigh and blush when Effington tenders his suit."

Georgette sighed and sat at Will's feet.

"Then Lady Susannah has acquainted you with my suspicions regarding your—regarding Lord Effington?"

And where was Susannah? The last time Will had fallen prey to this nameless, pulsing dread, he'd come upon a missive from Jacaranda, informing her brothers she'd gone into service, where—according to her note of farewell—being a drudge for an ungrateful household would at least earn her some coin and a half day off.

Will had not seen his sister again for months afterward.

Lady Della went to the window which looked out across the back garden. High walls separated the earl's property from those on either side, but from a second-floor vantage point, Will could see a milkmaid coming up the alley separating the garden from the mews.

"Susannah had a blunt talk with me at breakfast,"

Lady Della said. "I have been a very great fool, but I had my reasons for coming to London, Mr. Dorning. We'll resolve the situation with Effington, and then I'll return to the countryside. I hope you and Susannah will invite me for frequent visits at times when your brother Ash is likely to call."

The midday light revealed fatigue about her ladyship's eyes, but determination about her mouth. Will suspected he knew why.

"Quimbey asked me to have a word with Tresham," Will said. "We can discuss that topic later, my lady, but right now, I feel a pressing urgency to speak with Lady Susannah. Might you ask her to join us?"

Please.

"Susannah isn't here, Mr. Dorning. She popped out to Hanford's hoping to have a book rebound, but she knew you were coming, and said she'd be right back. Through the alleys, it's only a few streets over."

"She took a footman, I trust?" Three footmen would have been better, or Georgette.

"Susannah didn't want to miss your call, Mr. Dorning, so she left without taking Jeffers with her. Jeffers is not exactly fleet of foot."

The dread gnawing at Will's belly grew claws to go with its teeth. Dognappers prowled Mayfair's alleys, Effington's proposal was about to meet with a less-than-enthusiastic response, Sycamore had gone off hunting for Alexander again, and Will needed to know Susannah was safe.

"Don't feel compelled to sit here with me swilling tea and getting crumbs on the carpet," Lady Della said. "Effington is late, though he's been none too reliable in the past. If he appears, I'll keep the door open, and ensure Barrisford alerts my brother and sister-in-law to the identity of my caller."

"Don't leave the house with Effington," Will said. "Plead sore feet, a megrim, female indisposition, anything, but don't let him take you from the safety of your brother's home."

Will kissed Lady Della's forehead, and with Georgette at his heels, ran for the door.

The milkmaid, fortunately, had stopped outside the stable to flirt with the Haddonfield groom, and Will quickly discovered that, yes, Lady Susannah had gone haring off alone, right after the toff on the cranky gelding had raised such a ruckus closer to the street.

The groom didn't speak as if he'd been raised in London, but rather, had Kent in his vowels and into-nation, suggesting he was staff who traveled with the family. The horse had been tired and troublesome— "truu-blesome"—but the gent whackin' and whalin' on the beast hadn't helped.

Della had said Effington was late to call on her. Effington was a toff, and he'd be stupid enough to beat a tired horse in expectation of making it more obedient.

Worse and worse. "Can you describe the gentle-man?" Will asked.

"Blond, not overly big, fancy gold waistcoat, and lots of lace," the groom said. "Told the beast to get him to Bloomsbury. Half Mayfair would have heard the row."

Effington, then, damn and blast the luck. "Did Lady Susannah hear the altercation?"

The groom squinted down the shady lane. "She might have. I was sitting on yon bench, and I heard it.

I don't think her ladyship saw me but from where she stood, she would have seen down the alley."

Had Susannah followed the viscount, or kept to her original itinerary and gone to Hanford's? Will had told her finding the dogs was the imperative next step, but would she have trailed Effington on her own?

The Haddonfield mews sat on the corner of two alleys, one route leading northeast to Bloomsbury, one southeast to Bond Street. While Will debated in which direction to travel, Georgette nosed at the weeds along the northbound alley.

"Georgette, we haven't time to explore now."

She ambled back to Will's side and dropped a printed page at Will's feet.

"Come, Georgette," Will said, taking the southeast direction. "I will be much more willing to admire your treasures when I know our Susannah is safe and firmly—"

Georgette picked up the paper again and brought it to Will. "Woof."

Will wanted to speak very sternly to his dog indeed, for now was not the time for her to cast aside years of training, and yet—

Instinct, or something like it, prodded him to study the mastiff. Georgette was looking at him the way he often looked at Sycamore. *Will you never learn?*

"What have you got there?" Will asked, crouching to take the page from Georgette.

Love is not love
Which alters when it alteration finds
Or bends with the remover to remove.

Oh no, it is an ever-fixed mark
That looks on tempests and is never shaken;
It is the star to every wandering bark,
Whose worth's unknown, until his height be taken.

"Woof." Georgette had found this page of sonnets several yards in the direction of Bloomsbury rather than Bond Street, which meant...

Susannah had gone after Effington without an escort, but she'd brought both the Bard and a full ration of cleverness, for this page had been neatly parted from its binding.

"To Bloomsbury, then," Will said, giving Georgette a pat and addressing the groom. "Would you please have Lady Della send a note asking my brother Ash to meet me at the King's Comestibles."

"Your brother Ash," the groom repeated, "the King's Comestibles. Aye, sir."

Will strode off along the alley leading north. "Georgette, come."

But the dog was already several yards ahead of him.

❧

Susannah was destroying her most treasured book, page by page, even as she knew that paper lying in an alley was probably the least obvious means of leaving a trail for Will.

She tore out number sixty-five—"In black ink, my love may still shine bright"—as Effington paused to sample the contents of a silver flask. Either his horse was tired, or Effington himself lacked fitness for travel on horseback, because Susannah had

managed to keep up with him through several turn-
ings and crossings.

Effington knew the alleys, and he had a specific
destination in mind.

Find the dogs, Will had said. Everything depended
on finding the dogs before Effington could use the
poor beasts to hurl accusations and lay information.

Or just as bad, consign innocent pets to a brutal,
undeserved fate.

Effington gave his horse a stout kick, and the gelding plodded on.

Susannah's doubts and misgiving were proceeding
at a dead gallop: *I should have sent for Willow. I should
have let Della know what I was about. I should have alerted
Nicholas—no, that could not have ended well.*

Effington was working his way north and east, and
though Susannah was tiring, though she was second-
guessing herself, though Will would be wroth with
her, the thought of the feckless dogs, consigned to
suffering they did nothing to deserve, drove her on.

> *When, in disgrace with fortune and men's eyes,*
> *I all alone beweep my outcast state,*
> *And trouble deaf heaven with my bootless cries,*
> *And look upon myself and curse my fate…*

"I do not curse myself, or my fate, but I am heartily
out of charity with Effington," Will said.

They'd come to another crossroad, and Georgette
had again found the requisite evidence before Will
could spot it. Effington was heading straight for the

neighborhood of the King's Comestibles, which, as luck would have it, was where Sycamore was likely searching for Alexander.

"When we find them, no heroics from you, my girl," Will said, stroking Georgette's head. She was panting, but also clearly eager to continue this new and interesting game. When Will paused, Georgette went looking for Shakespeare, and thus another leg of the journey was saved from turning into a goose chase.

They'd crossed Soho, and Oxford Street lay ahead, but still, Will hadn't caught a glimpse of either Susannah or Effington.

He stuffed the page into a pocket along with all the others and continued his pursuit.

⁂

"Move the dogs today, he says," Jasper mumbled, crumpling up a note from his High and Mighty Lordship. "I'm not paying you to sit on your arses, he says. Horace, I sometimes feel exactly like these poor brutes, damned if I don't."

The dogs were consuming what was probably their last meal in Jasper's care, because his lordship had snapped his fingers and all creation must jump to obey.

"You ain't as mean as this big brute," Horace allowed, using a bucket to dump fresh water into the dog's bowl. The big brute was at his supper, so the bowl in the corner of his stall could be safely filled, and then the top half of the door re-closed.

"I'm not as mean," Jasper said as the sound of voracious dogs consuming inadequate rations filled the stable. "But his lordship must think I'm as stupid. He says we're not to collect the money—he'll do that—but we're to deliver the dogs before sunset."

"Today? When all the Quality is sashayin' about and waving t'each other?"

Jasper could go around the Kensington Palace side of Hyde Park, but that would take an age, and traveling that distance with a lot of crated-up, unhappy dogs would attract notice.

"I told him we ought to drug the poor beasts, deliver them at night, same as usual, but himself is in a taking."

"Oh, the Quality," Horace muttered as an empty food dish went thumping against a stall wall. The big dog, the one they'd stolen from the duchess, was in truth a bright animal.

Also furious and perpetually hungry.

"I like most dogs, but I do not like that dog," Jasper said. "He's plotting revenge, and all we ever done is feed him and keep him outta the wet."

And take him from his home, and knock him about a bit. Only a bit.

"I do like the little pug," Horace said. "Poor little mite won't last a day with the badgers. Hasn't a mean bone in his body."

The poor little mite sat in his wooden crate, head bowed, staring at the ground as if he could hear a gibbet being built for him in the alley.

"The big dogs cost a pretty penny, and the baiters try not to let 'em get hurt too bad," Jasper observed. "Little ones has it hard."

"We 'ave it 'ard," Horace said. "I say we tell old

man Dickerson to give us the money same as usual, and I'll take the pug home to me missus. Little fellow will keep her company and he won't eat much."

Jasper took out his flask, which would soon need a refill from the King's Comestibles, and passed it over to Horace.

"You are a good man, Horace," he said, "and every once in a while, you come up with a brilliant idea."

Fortunately, Horace had muttered his brilliant idea before the sound of iron-shod hooves clopping up the alley came to a halt outside the stable.

"Drink up," Jasper said. "His Royal Highness is here, and it's time we show him how well we can sit up and beg."

❧

Susannah's side throbbed, sweat made her straw hat stick to her forehead, and she'd stepped in something disagreeable while crossing Oxford Street, but the distinctive odor of kenneled hounds told her Effington had finally reached his destination.

His lordship clambered off his gelding not one sonnet too soon. Fifty yards downwind from Effington, Susannah tore out number ninety-two—"But do thy worst to steal thyself away"—and tucked it between two bricks at about waist height.

In this part of London, shabbier and smellier than Mayfair, a lone page of poetry did not command attention. Old newspapers, handbills, and worse littered the ground, and clearly, the alley hadn't been swept since Charles II had reopened the theatres.

Something more noticeable was called for, but not too noticeable.

Two large, unkempt fellows came out of the stable, and one of them took Effington's horse. The other stood in the middle of the alley, pushing at the cobbles with the toe of a dusty boot, while Effington gesticulated to the stable and peppered the afternoon with foul language.

Susannah tore off a length of purple lace from the parasol, rolled up the page of poetry, and tied the lace around it. She stuck the sonnet back between the bricks closer to eye level, and let the purple lace trail down the crumbling wall.

Then she crept closer.

❧

"Don't move. Don't make a sound or you'll wish I'd killed you when you were eight years old and you spent my coin collection at the market day sweets booth."

Cam nodded, and Will took his hand from his brother's mouth.

"Sycamore, you must be more alert. If I could sneak up on you, Georgette panting at my heels, then Effington's men could do the same." All they'd have to do is grow curious about the two men lounging around the back entrance to the King's Comestibles, loitering in the shade of the shed set between the inn and the alley.

Georgette was out of sight, behind an overturned barrel at Will's side.

"Effington's men couldn't sneak up on a deaf granny," Cam replied. "What are you doing here?"

"What's Effington doing here?" Will asked as Effington continued to berate one of his minions. Will and Cam were thirty yards upwind of the stable, and Susannah was nowhere in sight. The alleys in this neighborhood were not peaceful, shady thoroughfares between one tidy stable and another; they were mean, crooked, narrow, and dirty.

And Susannah had braved all of this, for the sake of a few unfortunate dogs?

"Effington's in a lather about something," Cam said. "I saw Alexander about an hour ago and left him a wedge of ripe cheese near the mouth of the alley. Now I wish I hadn't."

Will was working on a blister on his right heel— riding boots were not intended to be worn hiking all over London. He hadn't eaten since breakfast, and Georgette needed water, but what filled his mind was pride in Susannah's courage—and worry.

A great deal of worry.

"We might be able to use your bait to our advantage," Will said, swatting a fly away. "Have you seen Susannah?"

A scrap of purple fluttering in the breeze halfway down the alley suggested Susannah was nearby. Very nearby.

Cam offered him a glower worthy of Casriel when the housemaids were revolting. "You brought a *lady* into this situation? *Your own lady?* Willow, I raised you better than this. Effington is mean, stupid, and arrogant, and unless I mistake the situation, that stable is full of mean, smart, and determined dogs."

"Susannah brought herself into this," Will said,

"despite claiming she doesn't even like dogs. My lady and I will have a pointed discussion regarding her affinity for canines, assuming we survive this adventure. We're here to rescue the dogs and put an end to Effington's bad behavior, for if those are the kidnapped dogs, Effington's hand in matters is undeniable."

In the next instant, a large dog came trotting into the mouth of the alley, and only Will's grip on Cam's arm kept the younger Dorning from charging headlong down the alley.

"That is *my dog*, Willow," Cam hissed. "That is my Alexander who has once again put himself in harm's way, and those foul excuses—"

"It's too late," Will said, shoving Cam back into the shadows. "They've spotted him, and with Effington on hand, those men couldn't ignore that dog if they wanted to."

While Cam aired vocabulary that singed even Will's ears, Effington's second henchman, the one who'd taken the gelding into the stable, reemerged with a net draped over his shoulder.

"They'll hurt him," Cam said, shoving at Will. "Alexander won't go without a fight, and they'll take up where they left off, giving him more scars and injuries."

Who was this passionate fellow, who'd spend days searching for one dog, squander coin he didn't have, and risk his own neck to save the dog a beating?

"Sycamore, compose yourself," Will said. "Three men with a net shouldn't have to hurt the dog to subdue it. This is our chance to get to the others."

Georgette whined softly, clearly feeling as frustrated

as Cam, and Will had not a single piece of cheese to give her.

"Quiet, Georgette, please. All we need do is wait, and while Alexander provides the diversion, we'll slip in and retrieve the dogs."

Effington sent one minion around to the street, while the other slowly ambled down the alley, the net looped over his arm. His lordship remained closer to the stable, passing within three yards of where Cam and Will stood.

"Another moment," Will whispered.

"We haven't a single weapon," Cam whispered back. "There are three of them and only two of us, and you tell me Lady Susannah is flitting about somewhere. How do we retrieve several large, unhappy dogs, Willow, without ending up caught in a net ourselves?"

"We have Georgette," Will said, "and we have the element of—God save us."

A flash of purple, a glimpse of pale blue skirts, and just like that, Susannah had stolen across the alley and into the stable.

From which, a furious barking immediately ensued.

❧

For half the breadth of London, Susannah had argued with herself: she was a fool to pursue Effington on her own. He was ruthless, cunning, nasty, and angry. He enjoyed watching innocent creatures torment each other, and she was the last person to take on such a bully.

Even before her come-out, Susannah had learned to tread carefully, to keep to the sonnets and stage plays, to never give anybody another chance to turn her life into drama.

And yet, as she'd developed a stitch in her side, and torn one page after another from her keepsake volume of Shakespeare, another perspective had suggested itself.

Effington could destroy Will's business, swear out charges against Ash or Cam, toss unsuspecting dogs into the pits, and gossip about Della.

He could not touch Susannah. After the debacle at the hands of the Mannering twins and their friends, Susannah had kept nothing of value for herself, not suitors, not a reputation for cleverness, not a fat dowry, not much of a social life, not even dreams. She'd comforted herself with books, and Effington could not destroy her pleasure in reading if he set fire to all of Mayfair.

Will would come, but first, Susannah, whom Effington could not impugn, would assure herself she'd found the dogs. Though how she'd defend them from whatever plans Effington had for them, she did not know.

A commotion in the stable yard had her slinking behind a gnarled oak that cast much of the alley in shadow. Last year's acorns were still wedged between cobbles at her feet, and whatever she had stepped in an hour ago was drying on the sole of her half boot.

"Oh, Alexander, you poor dear."

For that large, skinny dog with the healing gash had to be Alexander. He'd found something to investigate, probably something to eat, and hadn't taken notice of the men intent on his capture. One went around by way of the street, one had fetched a net, and Effington presumed to direct both on how to catch the doomed beast.

Susannah seized her moment, sidling into the dimly lit stables. The scent of neglected canines was a fetid stench, and Effington's horse stood with one hip cocked in cross ties at the far end of the aisle.

A dog resembling a very sad Yorick looked up when Susannah dashed into the stables, and his little tail started wagging against the slats of his crate as if he'd seen his dearest friend in the whole world.

"Shhh," Susannah whispered. "Quiet, Yorick. Be a good boy. I can get you out of that crate but only if you—"

Yorick yipped, and from his end of the stables, came a chorus of much deeper barking.

Susannah had found the dogs, but she could not allow Effington to find her.

She unlatched the door of the nearest stall, ducked inside, and pulled the stall door closed. She could not latch the door from the inside, so she crouched down in a front corner, where somebody walking past would have to look very closely to notice her.

The stink of the straw bedding was unbelievable, enough to make Susannah's eyes water and her nose run. No dog, with its sensitive faculties, could have tolerated such poor conditions for long. Thank goodness the stall was empty, and thank goodness she was safe.

And then, from the back of the stall, came a low, very unpleasant growl.

⁓

"We can't just wait here," Cam fumed. "Lady Susannah's in there, they've got Alexander, and you might be willing to sit on your arse and let that cretin—"

"Am I too late for the party?"

Ash strolled over from the back of the inn, Casriel on his right, Tresham on his left.

"Sometimes, Sycamore, a moment's pause can save the day," Will said. Cam, of course, elbowed him hard in the gut and muttered something about saving the dogs. "Tresham, my thanks for your presence. A ducal heir will lend a certain cachet to the situation. Here's what's afoot."

As the barking went on across the alley, Will took half a minute to sketch the particulars, which were simple enough: several large unhappy dogs, one defenseless woman, a conscienceless scoundrel, and his two bullyboys all needed sorting out.

Immediately.

"Seems straightforward enough," Tresham said, taking off a signet ring and slipping it into a pocket. "I want him"—he nodded at Cam—"at my back."

"Because I'm quick?" Cam asked.

"Because you're so obnoxious, you'll draw their fire, and my face won't be the one they rearrange," Tresham replied. "And you're quick."

"That's all right then," Ash said. "Will, say when."

The horse was whinnying, and apparently capering about on the cross ties if clattering hooves were any indication. Effington's shouts only made the dogs bark more loudly, and the two other men were having difficulty keeping Alexander wrapped in his net.

Will stepped out of the shadows. "*Now.* Georgette, come. *Play*, Georgette. Grab any handy villain and teach him to *play* nicely."

Seventeen

OH GOD. OH GOD. OH GOD.

Fear paralyzed Susannah as she huddled in the stall. Not three yards away, the largest dog she'd ever seen crouched as if to spring at her and rip her throat out. Its lip was curled back to reveal enormous teeth, and while Yorick yipped and created a ruckus at the far end of the stable, this great mastiff growled so deeply Susannah could feel the menace vibrating in her chest.

Effington could not hurt her, but this dog could kill her.

She had only her reticule, which was at least weighted with the remains of the sonnets. Effington was shouting at all and sundry, probably upsetting the dogs more, and the horse was unhappy as well.

"Hush," Susannah whispered. "There now, it's all a lot of bother caused by stupid men taking advantage of poor creatures who can't help themselves. Are you Caesar? You look like a Caesar."

The growling stopped, but the commotion was dying down too. Only Yorick continued to yip and bark, drawing Effington's ire for his continued noise.

Susannah held out a hand to the dog and looked away, as if she fully expected her fingers to be where she left them after a thorough sniffing over.

Delicate, damp breath caressed her hand.

"Good boy," Susannah whispered. The dog licked her fingers and crawled closer. "Good boy, Caesar," she whispered again.

A great tail began to thump against the straw, and Caesar barked once.

Oh God, oh God, oh God. Susannah tried tugging on a large, doggy ear. Slowly, repeatedly, and the tail only thumped faster.

"Make that damned dog shut his mouth," Effington said. "And get that other damned dog into a stall before he chews through the net."

Caesar barked again, a joyous bark that Alexander answered.

"Hush," Susannah whispered as Yorick added to the conversation. She had only one possible treat left, and pulled the remains of the sonnets from her reticule. She tore out the page bearing her father's handwriting, and shoved the remains of the book at the dog, whose tail was beating a regular tattoo against the straw.

Caesar sniffed at the leather, which would have born Susannah's scent, also the scent of the glue holding the book together. Enormous jaws opened on some of the finest prose ever penned in the English language, and commenced a happy chewing.

"Good boy, Caesar," Susannah whispered, stroking the dog's ear. "Enjoy them, for I certainly did."

"What the hell!" Effington roared as another

commotion ensued at the far end of the stable. Susannah rose enough to see that more men had rushed into the building, along with another enormous dog.

Georgette! Susannah had never been so happy to see a big, loud, barking dog.

As much scuffling and swearing went on, Susannah ducked back down, more relieved than she could say. Will would be upset with her, of course, but they'd found the dogs, and all would be well at last.

Relief washed through her, and she was planning on exactly what she'd say to explain her presence when a shot rang out.

"He has Georgette," somebody yelled. "The bastard has his gun trained on Georgette."

❧

A gun. Why hadn't Will assumed that a man who didn't take the time to learn how to communicate with his animals would resort to violence if necessary to remain safe around them?

"Effington, really," Will said as his brothers and Tresham arranged themselves at his sides. "Shooting a dog? Shoot me instead. Georgette has done nothing to hurt you, and if you destroy my property, I will bring suit."

The pistol had two short barrels. Not very accurate over a distance, but up close, it could do lethal damage.

"Anybody can destroy a dangerous stray," Effington said, chest heaving. "I'm a peer, I'll be tried in the Lords if you can even get me charged, and you're trespassing."

Ash shot his cuffs. "You're up to date on your rent at this fine establishment? The signed lease is available for inspection by the courts? When one has read law, such details plague one's curiosity without mercy."

The larger handler wrestled Alexander into a stall, net and all. The other one led the horse out to the yard and tied it there.

The animals, with the exception of Georgette, were safe.

"You do know," Will said, "I could command Georgette to attack you, and she'd probably get in a couple of good bites even if you managed to hit her with your single remaining bullet?"

"Give the poor pup food poisoning," Sycamore muttered. "She doesn't deserve that."

Will would die to know his dog had been shot, likely killed, for no reason. Effington would not pay for that crime, not if he was tried in the House of Lords.

Will would hold him accountable just the same.

"I think you should let him shoot the dog," Casriel remarked. "I will enjoy retelling the tale of how a peer of the realm, a man who paid others to steal pets from aristocratic homes, fired at a helpless dog who had the great effrontery to merely pant at his feet. Such courage and integrity should be the subject of endless discussion even if the courts don't intervene."

"I never stole anybody's dog," Effington snarled. "I relieved the streets of Mayfair of a few dangerous strays."

Effington's gun was pointed at Georgette, but the viscount himself remained two yards away from the dog. All Will needed was for Effington's attention to waver for an instant, and Will could knock the gun aside, or put himself between Georgette and the bullet.

"I saw this fellow ridding the streets of Mayfair

of Lady March's pet," Sycamore sneered, gesturing to the man at Effington's left. "Poor dog was on a stout leash and being beaten about the head. Tends to make me more dangerous, when I'm subjected to gratuitous violence."

"Lord March gave me that dog," Effington shot back.

"How inconvenient," Tresham drawled. "His lordship must have neglected to inform Lady March of the dog's good fortune. Did Lord March give you the Duchess of Ambrose's dog too? The Earl of Hunterton's?"

They'd keep Effington talking, while Will waited for an opening, for the slightest indication Effington's attention was not on—

Behind Effington, the stall at the end of the aisle cracked open three silent inches, and Will's heart lodged in his throat.

"Was *Yorick* among those strays imperiling the good folk of Mayfair?" Will asked, knowing the pug would respond to the use of his name. "Did *Yorick* threaten the King's peace, to deserve a remove to that wretched crate? *Poor Yorick?*"

The dog's whining escalated to barking, which would at least keep any creaky stall doors from notice.

"Yorick must have lost the knack of cheating at cards," Tresham mused.

"Is Effington's complexion puce?" Sycamore asked. "The ladies are always going on about puce, and raspberry, and such, and I've wondered what exactly puce is."

One of the minions snickered, while Susannah crept silently down the aisle. Not by a flicker of an eyelash did Will, Cam, Ash, Casriel, or Tresham reveal her presence behind Effington and his men.

"I believe that qualifies as puce," Casriel remarked. "Gin-soaked puce, perhaps. Not sure what to call that waistcoat, though."

"Cowardly puce for his lordship's complexion," Will replied, desperate to hold Effington's attention. "Miser's gold for the waistcoat. I'd hazard these stout fellows haven't been paid their wages, and the stolen dogs likely haven't been given enough to sustain poor Yorick."

The pug's frenzy had escalated to shaking his entire crate as he threw himself at the door repeatedly in an effort to win free.

"Who names their dog after a damned skull?" Ash asked. "Gives the little fellow a bad opinion of himself."

The other dogs were growing restive, and Georgette was looking at Will as if he'd forgotten the treat bag.

Susannah had the damned parasol in her hand, as if she might bring it down on Effington's head, or his arm, either of which could result in a bullet striking Georgette.

Then she shifted her grip, and swept the parasol in a swift, silent upward arc. Effington's wrist took the brunt of the blow, being knocked high as the gun discharged. Will dove for Effington, pinning him to the nearest post with his gun-hand pushed above his head.

Dogs barked madly, while from the open stall door an enormous mastiff came bounding forth with the remains of a book in its jaws, and both of Effington's handlers took off at a dead run.

"Georgette, Caesar, drop 'em!" Will yelled as Cam,

Ash, Georgette, and the mastiff all bounded off after the departing pair.

"I'll fetch you a rope," Casriel said. "Don't let Effington go until we have him bound hand and foot."

Safe, was all Will could think through the rage and relief misting his vision red. His lady, his brothers, Tresham, Georgette, the stolen dogs, all safe.

Susannah came swishing into his line of sight, her expression severe. Her hat had come loose, and her blond hair streamed about her in glorious golden disarray.

"Mr. Dorning, apologies for my unseemly display," she said. "I see you have matters in hand, as usual."

"My lady."

Casriel bustled over and secured Effington's hands as Yorick's fussing muted to whining and worrying his crate door.

"Mr. Dorning," Susannah said, "if I recall your training methods, when a dumb beast has misbehaved, it should be corrected immediately. A sharp word will usually do, but for the particularly dim souls, a more explicit lesson is in order."

"I would never argue with a lady," Will said, especially not this lady, with that light in her eyes. "And I've yet to meet the dog who benefited much from repeated displays of violence."

"Nor have I," she said, slapping the parasol against her palm, "but a peer of the realm who takes advantage of *unsuspecting* households"—whack! A blow landed on Effington's shoulders—"and betrays the loyalty of *trusting* beasts"—whack! Another blow, this one to his middle—"and houses those poor animals in *deplorable*"—whack!—"*conditions*"—whack!—"while he tarnishes the good name of an innocent young lady"—whackity, whack, whack, whop!—"clearly cannot grasp even the simplest concepts of honor without having them beaten into him."

She swung the last blow hard, connecting with a portion of Effington's anatomy Will could not have envisaged the prim, bookish Lady Susannah Haddonfield aiming for.

Effington went down in a ball of suffering viscount, his complexion shifting toward dyspeptic green. Will stepped over him and took Susannah in his arms.

"My lady, I could not have put it better myself."

Yorick's cage door burst open, and the little dog capered around Susannah's skirts, then trotted over to Effington.

"Yorick," he gasped. "There's my little—"

Yorick lifted a stubby back leg and relieved himself right on the viscount's gold waistcoat, then trotted away, tail held high.

Susannah had grown up around older brothers. She was accustomed to their noise, to how their sheer size could make even a large space feel crowded and a mere sister off in a corner reading Shakespeare insignificant.

Only a ducal family parlor was spacious enough to house the gathering surrounding Susannah now, and thus she found herself in Quimbey's town residence.

Her hair had come down, and her braid had disintegrated. Her boots had been consigned to the dogs, and on her feet were a pair of men's wool stockings.

Her hems bore testimony to the alleys she'd traversed earlier that day.

Susannah was exhausted, disheveled, drained, and hungry, and yet no queen enthroned among her courtiers had ever felt more cherished.

Casriel had sent a footman to procure the wool stockings from Bond Street, and Will's coat was about her shoulders. Quimbey had found her a cashmere lap robe that had belonged to the dowager Duchess of Quimbey, and Sycamore Dorning had poured Susannah's tea from a service that had once belonged to the King of France.

"It's good to be the heroine, isn't it?" Susannah whispered to Georgette, who sat panting gently at Susannah's side. Caesar was stretched out at their feet, while Alexander, Comus, and Yorick lounged beneath an open window across the parlor. Hunterton's Alsatian had been taken to the garden by two stout footmen.

"Hunterton will be along shortly to claim his pet," Worth Kettering announced.

Sir Worth had apparently been hosting a meeting between Casriel, Tresham, and Quimbey when Ash Dorning had tracked them down. Will had sent his sister, Jacaranda, to retrieve the Duchess of Ambrose, then he'd dispatched Tresham to fetch Della to Susannah's side.

"Much to-ing and fro-ing," Will said, stepping between and around dogs to take the place next to Susannah. "How are you?"

Nobody ever asked Lady Susannah Haddonfield how she was, but after she'd wielded her parasol in that Bloomsbury stable, her welfare had apparently become the concern of every person in the room. She and Georgette had been bundled into Tresham's crested barouche, Will on one side, Casriel on the other, and the ducal heir himself at the reins.

They'd trotted through Mayfair at a smart clip, collecting stares and curious glances, though Susannah had been too busy holding Will's hand to care.

"I am—" She'd been about to say she was fine. Lady Susannah Haddonfield was always fine, unless she'd gone for an entire day without sticking her nose in a book, in which case she was fidgety and cross.

I am in love. Susannah hadn't read anything to speak of for nearly a week.

"I am happy," Susannah said, kissing Will's cheek. "Also relieved, tired, pleased for the dogs, and so very impressed with you, Mr. Dorning."

Will was exhausted too. Susannah would never forget his expression when Effington had trained a gun on Georgette, and Will had remained so outwardly casual and civil. His eyes had told a different tale, silently pleading with Susannah to be careful, to preserve her own welfare even if it meant the dog—or the man Susannah loved—took a bullet.

"I merely made small talk with a scoundrel," Will said, "while you plotted his downfall, my lady. You will be the toast of the Season after this. Hunterton has already sent you flowers."

Will's words were pleased and proud, though his gaze was on the bouquet of irises Susannah hadn't noticed on the sideboard.

"I beg you to spare me the ordeal of being toasted,"

Susannah said. "Once upon a time, being the toast of the Season would have been a dream come true. Now that fate looms as a tedious waste of time."

She'd surprised Will, but just as the first glimmer of a smile bloomed in his eyes, the Duchess of Ambrose burst into the room, Lady Worth at her side.

"Oh, my dearest, dearest Cee-Cee. Come to Mama!"

Pandemonium ensued of a variety Susannah was coming to know. Large barking dogs, effusive emotions, flourished handkerchiefs, concerned gentlemen, and an eventual lessening of the din.

Sycamore Dorning—"what a dear, darling young man"—served the duchess two restorative brandies and had poured her a third by the time every dog was back to sitting or lying on the carpet.

"Quimbey, I won't have it," Her Grace said. "You will not return such a dear puppy to that dreadful Ernestine March. Her idiot of a husband will simply sell the dog again and tell his imbecile wife the dog has run off. Alexander has already been through enough of an ordeal."

Sycamore, in a display of reticence Will probably had to see to believe, merely petted Alexander's head.

"You are not to worry, my dear," Quimbey said. "I hold Lord March's vowels and will accept Alexander in payment for some of them. Comus will adjust, if need be, but I suspect Alexander has other options."

Sycamore's ears turned red.

"I'll just take Alexander to the garden for a moment," Sycamore said. "Ordeals leave a fellow with a need to stretch his legs. Yorick, come along."

"Take Comus too," Quimbey said. "Make sure

the footmen haven't been licked into oblivion by Hunterton's pet."

Quimbey took a nip of Her Grace's brandy, which earned him a swat on the hand. Caesar exchanged a look with Georgette suggesting humans were tiresome but dear.

Some humans.

"What about Effington?" Susannah asked, tugging gently on Georgette's ear, when she wanted instead to tug on Will's. "He deserves to be pilloried."

Susannah had wanted to put an end to the Effington succession, and this, as much as anything else, had apparently earned her the approval of every man, dog, and horse in the Bloomsbury stable.

Bullies understood blunt displays of authority, a lesson Susannah wished she'd learned earlier.

"Effington shall be pilloried," Her Grace said. "No hostess will receive him, and no young lady of any means will accept his addresses. His debts will come due immediately, and he'll either pay them, be called out, or take a repairing lease on the Continent."

Beside Susannah, Will shifted.

"Mr. Dorning, have you something to add?" Susannah asked.

"We'll have the sworn statements of his two henchmen," Will said. "Even the baiters apparently had little regard for him. Effington won't return to England, ever. I know several large dogs and a half-dozen fellows who'll be happy to remind him what a purple parasol can do, when wielded by the right hands."

The parasol held pride of place on the mantel, though it was missing some of its lace.

"Such a lovely shade, that parasol," Susannah said. The same shade as Will's eyes, when he was content or amorous. He was neither at the moment, which was the pea under the mattress of Susannah's happiness.

"Oh, Suze! Suze, you are all right!" Della cried, dashing through the parlor door. "You saved the day, and the dogs, and, oh, I am so proud of you, and so jealous. *Are* you all right? Of course you're all right. I want to hear every detail, from the beginning. Hold nothing back, and use as much colorful language as you dare."

Della held out her arms, clearly expecting a sisterly embrace, so Susannah left Will's side, stepped over Georgette, and hugged her sister.

Ash Dorning hovered on Della's right, smiling indulgently. Tresham stood on Della's left, hands behind his back.

"I'm managing," Susannah said, hugging her sister tightly. "There isn't much to tell. Effington was a scoundrel of the first water. Willow gathered up these good fellows to take Effington and his dognappers in hand, I assisted in wresting Effington's weapon from him, and the dogs are fine."

"All's well that ends well?" Della said, sniffing and blinking.

"A volume of the sonnets suffered a noble end," Susannah said, "but I saved Papa's dedication page. I also have five other copies, and had memorized the ones I enjoy most. Shall you have a seat, Della?"

"I shall have a brandy. Jon, if you'd oblige?"

Jon? Well, apparently yes, *Jon.* For Tresham was soon passing Della a glass while Ash Dorning took the place beside Della on the settee.

Della drew the gentlemen into a discussion of the afternoon's events, the duchess had Quimbey's staff bring around trays of ham, buttered bread, cheddar, and—in honor of the momentous day—sliced pineapple, while Susannah resumed her place at Will's side.

He was unsettled, as was she, but simply being beside him, feeling his warmth, breathing in synchrony with him, restored her spirits. Dogs did this, kept close company, no need for words, no need for activity. They had each other, and that was pleasure enough.

And yet Susannah could sense in Will a discontent too. She kissed his cheek as Della prattled on and on—Della was in fine form today—though Susannah wanted to tug gently on his ears, and wanted him to once again tug on hers.

Eighteen

GRATITUDE, FATIGUE, PRIDE IN HIS LADY, AND IMPA-
tience dogged Will's steps as he accompanied Susannah
up the walk to her home. He once again carried the
purple parasol, though Georgette had elected to
remain at Quimbey's, where the shameless beast cast
die-away glances at any who'd toss her a bite of ham—
and at Caesar.

Will knew how that felt, to be the one going
hungry at the feast.

"I gather Mr. Tresham and Della are in charity with
each other?" Susannah asked.

"I haven't all the details," Will said. "That appears
to be the case." He and Susannah would discuss what
details Will had on some other, less fraught day, if
Lady Della didn't make familial announcements soon.

The door opened, the butler bowed, and Will
accompanied Susannah upstairs, though he might have
bade her farewell at the door. He'd taken a moment
when changing his clothes and washing to tend and
bandage the blister on his heel, but that meant his
boots chafed in other places.

Susannah hadn't dismissed him, though, so up the steps he trudged.

"You are so quiet," Susannah said, wrapping her arms around him at the top of the stairway. "I was furious, Willow, to see Effington holding a gun on an innocent dog. Come with me, please. I cannot part with you just yet."

Nor did Will want to part with Susannah, ever, and yet the sun was setting and much was still unresolved.

Susannah led him not to the family parlor, but in the other direction, through a quiet house to her sitting room.

"I thought I'd put all that nonsense when I was younger behind me," Susannah said. "The nasty gossip, the sly tricks, the spilled punch, and the way all that made me feel."

"You rose above it." Seven years ago, Will had also had a word with Susannah's brothers. They'd mustered their friends to fill her dance cards, and made sure she was escorted in the ballrooms at all times.

Guard dogs of the titled variety.

"You lifted me above that pettiness," Susannah said, closing the door, locking it, and returning to Will's embrace. "I still carried the memories, and the feelings."

Desire stirred, despite Will's fatigue, and despite the fact that Susannah wanted to *discuss* the past. They hadn't really. Not yet. They'd referred to it, alluded to it, mentioned it.

But they hadn't put the pain to rest.

"I'm loyal and protective by nature," Will said. "I can't help that. What those girls tried to do to you was unfair. My honor was offended on your behalf."

He'd been enraged. Debutantes on the verge of marriage were not a litter of puppies, mere weeks old, picking on the runt out of blind instinct. Susannah had been singled out because she threatened those less well-placed—or those less decent.

"I was ready to give up before I'd been presented," Susannah said. "I hadn't realized that in addition to the hurt, fear, and bewilderment, I was also furious. You're right—I was treated unfairly. I think all girls who are treated unfairly should be given purple parasols, and allowed to lay about with them, holding bullies accountable for their cruelty."

That's what Will had seen in Susannah's eyes as she'd crept down the barn aisle. Her gaze had blazed with righteous fury, and even he had felt a frisson of uneasiness. In those moments, clutching her parasol and intent on thwarting Effington, Susannah had been without fear. She'd been pure, incandescent righteousness, and woe to him who had earned her ire.

Nonetheless, she'd restrained herself with Effington. Susannah Haddonfield had a lot of experience with restraining herself.

Her ladyship wasn't restraining herself now.

"My dear, what are you doing?"

"Unbuttoning your falls. I'm still a mess, while you are all tidied up. I'm in the grip of a compulsion to untidy you. All of the boldness and passion I've kept between the pages of my Shakespeare for the past seven years is refusing to come to heel and sit quietly, Willow."

And Susannah's hands had gone exploring.

"I'm feeling somewhat bold and passionate myself," Will said, kissing his beloved. "Somewhere among my treasured possessions is a lecture on dignity and gentlemanly something or other, but Susannah—"

She kissed him, a naughty, tantalizing reproof to lectures of all varieties. "We have an understanding, Willow Dorning. Right now, that entitles me to also have *you*."

Will's conscience wasn't troubled—he and the woman peeling his clothes away had a very clear understanding—but his heart was burdened. His situation was fundamentally unchanged from when he'd awoken, unless falling more deeply in love with Susannah counted as a change.

As clothes piled up on the floor, Will sensed Susannah turning upon him all the focus she'd previously reserved for her literature, memorizing him with her touch, underlining endearments to his various attributes—his hands, his eyes, and his heart.

In bed, she offered him sonnets of tactile pleasure—caresses and kisses, her breath breezing across his chest, her legs embracing his flanks.

"I was so frightened," Susannah whispered as Will rose above her. "I should not have followed Effington. I should have sought help instead, should have let others face him who were better equipped, but I could not."

Will could barely make sense of Susannah's words, he wished so badly to join with his lady, to be with her in the place beyond even the most beautiful words.

"You are brave," Will said, finding her heat, finding his home. "You have endless courage."

"All the way across London, I was afraid, Willow. I've been afraid. I feared to pay the wrong compliment, wear the wrong dress, cast the wrong glance."

"Chained in a pit," Will whispered, "no hope of escape." Save her damned sonnets, written by a dead man who'd understood both captivity and freedom.

"But I thought, 'Willow will find me, Willow will come. I'm afraid, but he will not fail me.'"

Will had been born to find her, born for this moment, when Susannah's trust, her courage, her love poured through him and became a sharing of limitless joy and passion.

"I will never fail you, Susannah, and I will always love you."

The room became silent, save for the gentle rustle of lavender-scented sheets, the slide of flesh on flesh, a giggle.

A sigh.

A groan.

When even those had ebbed on the tide of gratified passion, Susannah fell asleep beside Will, her breath tickling his shoulder. She had offered him everything she had, her courage, her fears, her past, her future, her love, and she deserved more than an understanding in return.

Will rose from the bed, dressed, kissed his beloved's brow, and left her dreaming. He'd made her a promise, and he intended to keep it.

He would not fail her, not ever.

৵৽

"The reward money must go to Ash and Sycamore," Will said, stroking a hand over Georgette's head in a gesture Worth had seen countless times before. "For I've been told in no uncertain terms, the rewards will be forced upon me. Even Mannering has babbled something about restitution, and Yorick—Fortinbras as he's to be known—never suffering want in Mannering's care."

The evening was mild, crickets chirping on Worth's back terrace. Upstairs, Jacaranda was tending to the baby, while Meda dozed at Worth's feet.

Though Willow appeared a figure of quiet repose in the last of the day's light, Worth was reminded of when he'd first made the acquaintance of the woman running his country seat more than a year ago. Jacaranda had striven mightily to present herself as a mere housekeeper, but her violet eyes had flashed lightning at Worth's flirtation, and her muttered asides had been the first rumblings of thunderbolts.

One underestimated a Dorning at one's peril. Reliable sources said the Mannering twins were off on an extended repairing lease in Paris, to the relief of every debutante, hostess, and bachelor in London.

"Ash Dorning will have no need of coin," Worth said, because somebody had to speak sense to Willow. "He'll have steady employment with me, at least. Lady Della's association with Quimbey and his nephew will also apparently result in a sizable, if quietly conveyed, dowry."

A trust account here, some lawyerly obfuscation there, an obliging Earl of Bellefonte nodding benignly as he appended signatures to a few documents at a private meeting or two. Worth had handled similar situations for many wealthy families, a resolution of the equities—and the requirements of honor—far from the sight of Society.

"Lady Della's to be well dowered?" Will asked,

crossing an ankle over his knee and wincing. "Then I leave to Ash what he does with his half of the rewards. He might turn the funds over to Casriel, invest them on behalf of our other brothers, or consider investing them in a venture I'm intent on beginning myself."

Worth did not consider himself any sort of hounds and horses man. He was a pounds and pence fellow, *after* he was Jacaranda's devoted swain and tireless lover. And yet, at the mention of the word "investing," Worth knew exactly how the hounds felt when they raised the scent of old Reynard.

"Say on, Willow. I'm a papa, you know, and my precious princess likes to hear my voice as she drops off to sleep."

Meda cast him a look at that bouncer, but kept her chin on her forepaws. She'd be up in the nursery when the child was laid in her crib, though how the dog knew when to assume guard duty was a mystery.

"Jacaranda can spare you for a few more moments," Willow said, shifting to prop a foot on the low table before them.

Jacaranda was Worth's queen, and their daughter the princess. Worth let the distinction pass, because Willow Dorning talked dogs, training, cheese, and rewards without ceasing, but in Worth's experience, investments had never earned more than Will's fleeting notice.

"You mentioned a venture involving money," Worth said. "I know a few things about ventures involving money, and can tell you the Dorning men-folk as a tribe are sadly in want of that knowledge. You will please hound Casriel on this topic at every opportunity. My brother's finances are finally coming right, and that's after generations of neglect."

"May I take off my boot?"

Worth exchanged a look with his dog. "I work financial miracles, and you want to take off your boot. Only the one?"

"Yes," Willow said, tugging his footwear off and setting it out of Georgette's sight. "I tramped too far in the wrong boots, you see."

Georgette licked her master's hand, as if she'd clearly heard the metaphor Worth had barely noticed rustling among the undergrowth of Willow's usual reserve.

"Then let's get you in the right pair, Willow. Have you a monetary scheme in mind?"

"Georgette and Caesar are likely to become parents this summer," Willow said. "That can happen, when a dog and a bitch spend time together. If he's the right fellow for her, he can bring her into season, despite all calendars and convenience to the contrary. Quimbey saw them in the garden, and wants to give the pick of the litter to Tresham. I want my funds to have puppies too."

The day had been harrowing from all accounts, but Willow Dorning was a stouthearted creature.

"Willow, can you speak English instead of Doggish? Coin of the realm does not have offspring."

"Coin produces interest, Kettering. The hardest-working coin produces compound interest. I can continue to train the occasional aristocrat, two or three a Season, on how to be an ideal owner for their pets. It's enjoyable work and helps me find deserving homes for some of my hounds. But I ought to be training others to be trainers, training the masters of foxhounds, the shepherds."

Worth's mind was attracted to numbers the way some women were attracted to shoes and bonnets, the way other men were fascinated by games of chance.

"You can train one Duke of Quimbey, or two dozen of his chief shepherds, in other words. One Earl of Hunterton, or all four of his masters of foxhounds."

Compound interest, indeed.

"And I can explain to those fellows how to train their inferiors, perhaps over the course of several summers. The result will be I'll have a volume of trained dogs to sell or otherwise distribute as a result of my students' work with them. I will have a reputation throughout the realm as opposed to a slight cachet in one corner of Dorset and one clearing in Hyde Park. I will see more quickly and with my own eyes which puppies have great promise as working dogs, which are better suited to life as a pet."

Willow leaned back, hands linked on his flat belly, his gaze on the stars coming into view above.

"I will operate the equivalent of Oxford University," Will said, "for the people whose livelihood and dearest diversion is dependent on the canine. The dog has long been a best friend to many Englishmen, from King Charles's spaniels, to an aging duchess's companion, to the Yorkshire shepherd who may go days without hearing another human voice but is in constant conversation with his collie. Those dogs are my countrymen, Kettering, and I intend to take my place among them."

Not the Duke of Dogs, as Will's brothers referred

to him, but king of an entire empire that could yield significant returns in a very few years.

Better still, nobody that Kettering knew of had had the vision to undertake such a project. England had world-renowned stables, and was exporting sheep and wool products, cheese…but why not export first-rate collies to go with the sheep?

"Willow Dorning, you have impressed me. Better still, I know of at least two dukes who will be similarly impressed, if you're looking for investors."

Please let him be looking for investors. Casriel, at least, ought to back this venture, Tresham and Quimbey had been casting around for something to undertake together, the earls of Westhaven and Hazelton were canny fellows open to unusual opportunities, and Hazelton's seat was in the sheep-infested north.

Willow wiggled his toes inside a large wool sock. His feet were similar in their proportions to Jacaranda's, something only family would know.

And Will and Worth were family.

"I must discuss this with Lady Susannah," Willow said. "I wanted to discuss it with you first, though, for a commonsense assessment of its feasibility. I'll undertake this project even if you tell me it's doomed, because it's all I know to do, Kettering. Lady Susannah might be willing to extend me some patience, but I cannot be so generous. I have promised I will not fail her."

Jacaranda appeared in the French doors, the baby in her arms.

"My ears deceive me," she said, strolling out onto the terrace. "I might have heard Willow discussing business. Good evening, Georgette."

"Woof." The dog apparently knew not to raise her voice around the baby.

"Willow, why is your boot off?" Jacaranda asked, passing her brother the baby. "I hope you are not setting this sort of example for Sycamore."

The baby was perfectly happy in her uncle's embrace, and Kettering had a premonition, then, or a vision of life as it would unfold for Willow Kettering.

"Willow wore the wrong footwear for the job," Worth said, pulling his wife down beside him. "Haring all over London in riding boots wasn't well advised. Willow will soon be wealthy enough to have a new pair made every day though."

"Woof." Even more quietly, but surely a vote of agreement?

"The rewards were that sizable?" Jacaranda asked, tucking herself beneath Worth's arm.

"Willow's imagination is that sizable," Worth said. "You look entirely at home with an infant in your arms, Dorning. Shall we schedule a meeting with a few fellows I know next week?"

Worth might as well not have spoken, for Willow was nuzzling the baby, and she was cooing and waving her arms about in a manner that did queer things to Worth's heart.

Willow would do very well with his enterprise. Very well indeed. He cared for those around him, he paid attention, he worked hard. Worth was proud to call him a friend, prouder to call him family.

"Never underestimate a Dorning," Jacaranda whispered, kissing Worth's cheek.

"Schedule the meeting no later than the first of the

week, please," Will said, passing the baby over to her father. "I'd say we hold this gathering tomorrow, but I must convince Sycamore that it's time he became at least a nominal scholar, and I've a few other errands to tend to."

"What do you suppose Lady Susannah will make of this venture, Will?" A man not yet married might neglect to consider his wife's reactions, and that man would learn to regret his oversight.

"Lady Susannah is the one who convinced me I should attempt this," Will said, offering Georgette a gentle tug on each ear. "You should have seen her ladyship, Kettering. My prim, bookish, retiring daughter of an earl came stealing down the barn aisle armed with nothing more than a tattered parasol. She was more menacing than a Highland regiment in battle regalia, and all because Effington was threatening Georgette."

The dog whined gently, as if she knew exactly the scene Will referred to.

"Georgette is a lovely dog," Worth said, though a few months ago, he would have felt silly calling any dog lovely.

"She's only a dog," Will said, scratching the mastiff's shoulder. "A pet, a lowly beast, and that is why Susannah was so determined to protect her. Effington was victimizing the most loyal, blameless creature in the stable. From the start, Georgette has known she could trust Lady Susannah. *I can too*. Whether my business succeeds or fails, my lady will be content with what we have, provided we have each other, and that, oddly enough, is what compels me to undertake this venture."

On that profundity, Will pulled his boot back on.

Georgette rose with her master, and with a final pat to Meda, and a kiss to Jacaranda's cheek, the Emperor of Canine Enterprise went sauntering into the night.

"What sort of errands do you think he must tend to?" Jacaranda asked.

"That particular Dorning is hard to read," Worth replied as contentment and gratitude settled around him. His wife, his daughter, his loyal hound, and all coming right for nearly half of Jacaranda's brothers gave a lowly knight of business much to be grateful for.

"Is he off to procure a special license tomorrow?"

Well, of course. "Very likely." Or perhaps a helpful family member would see to that errand for him.

"Shall we go up to bed, Husband?"

"Never let it be said I refused my wife's invitation to go to bed, but might we bide here for a moment first, Jacaranda? The baby's content, the night is lovely, and I'm endlessly happy simply to spend a few minutes enjoying it with you."

Meda rested her chin on the toe of Worth's boot, and Jacaranda cuddled closer. "I love you," she said. "We'll get Willow and Susannah a hammock for a wedding present. They have everything else they need to be happy already."

"A hammock," Worth murmured. "Perfect."

❧

"Willow, you need not have done this," Susannah said, gazing at the ring in the little box.

Will had run about like a March hare all morning, fetching the special license, choosing a ring, answering notes from Quimbey, Tresham, and Casriel, and opening

a deluge of correspondence from people either congratu-
lating him on solving the London dognapper crimes or
imploring him to work with their brilliant, beautiful,
tireless, et cetera, et cetera, dogs starting immediately.

Some of them had named sums too, which was
damned silly. Susannah had been the one to trail the
dognapper to his lair and foil his worst intentions.

"I wanted something that went with your eyes,"
Will said, slipping the ring on her finger. "Something
as blue as a perfect sky over a perfect Dorset summer
day. I've always loved your eyes."

Loved her.

"But sapphires and diamonds cost *money*,"
Susannah wailed, collapsing against him. "You think
money is important, though I know what you did,
Willow Dorning."

He'd paid his five pounds to procure a special
license, the sum of the day's important transactions.

"I fell in love with you," Will said, holding
Susannah's hand out, so the sunlight caught the fire in
her ring. "I fell in love with you years ago, like a loyal
hound devotes himself to a worthy lady, but I also love
you as a man loves the woman he was meant to be
with. Will you marry me?"

Her ladyship commenced crying, scolding him for
being such a ninnyhammer, kissing him, holding him
tightly, then pushing him away to stare at her ring and
tear up some more.

"I am an expert at interpreting communication
that doesn't rely on words," Will said, getting in as
many kisses of his own as he could. "I will take your
response for a yes."

"Yes, of course yes," Susannah said, flinging herself at him again. "But you're s-sending Cam to Oxford, and Ash was closeted with Nicholas this morning and then with Della, and you haven't kept any of the reward for yourself, have you?"

"I've kept the best part of the reward for myself," Will said, picking Susannah up and spinning around with her. They were in the Haddonfields' family parlor, and if Will had had a tail, he'd probably have knocked over half the breakables in his unbounded glee.

"You must put me down," Susannah said, looping her arms around Will's neck and laying her head on his shoulder. "Ash told me. You've turned over all the money to your brothers, but, Willow, I don't care. We can live in a shepherd's hut with Georgette and I'll be happy. I don't want to wait for your fortunes to improve, I don't want an understanding. I want a *husband*, and only you will do."

Will kept hold of his treasure and sat with her in his lap on the red settee. "I quite agree. I'm the husband for you, you're the wife for me, and I have a special license in my pocket. Name the day, my lady."

She bawled in earnest, to the point that Georgette might have been concerned, except that shameless creature was paying another visit to Caesar in Quimbey's spacious gardens.

"I'd say today, but I look a fright," Susannah replied some minutes and more than a few wrinkles to Will's cravat later. She sat beside Will, stroking his knee, alternately dabbing her eyes with his handkerchief and peering at her ring.

"You look beautiful, though I hope you won't be

too disappointed when I explain that we won't be living in a shepherd's hut."

"I would, you know," she said, all seriousness. "Though a hut might soon become crowded, between Georgette's puppies and other developments."

Everything inside Will came to a still point, poised to soar. "Susannah?"

She nodded, and a blush crept over cheeks. "It's early days, emphasis on the days, but I have hopes. I feel different."

Will scooped her back into his lap, his joy muting to the incandescent glow of a sunset that would become only more glorious as the tribulations of the day surrendered to the comfort of the night.

"My love, my love," Will said. "We shall be married tomorrow, if you like, and then there's a meeting we must discuss—perhaps you'd like to attend?— before we go on our wedding journey. We'll need to find a property, and you must hear what I'd like to do with that property, if you're amenable?"

Susannah squirmed around, so she was straddling Will's lap. "Married tomorrow, Willow? Do you promise?"

Susannah had plans for him in the nearer term. Her gaze and the way she already had his cravat undone assured Will of her intentions.

"Tomorrow," Will said. "And about this meeting…" As clothing fell away and was pushed aside, Will explained his venture to Susannah, and explained about dogs and the people who are devoted to them, and puppies, and his brothers playing a role, and then he explained—both with words and without—that he loved Susannah without limit and that, no matter what else befell them, when it came to loving her, he would never, ever be *all done*.

Not ever.

They were married the following afternoon, with a duke, a duchess, several earls, and any number of winking, well-dressed siblings in attendance, and both Georgette and Caesar barking their good wishes to the happy couple—the other happy couple.

Read on for an excerpt from

Gareth

"A Young Person to see you, milord."

The old butler's very lack of expression was eloquent: beyond doubt, a lady—unchaperoned and uninvited—awaited Gareth Alexander, Marquess of Heathgate, in the smaller formal drawing room.

Again.

Gareth walked into the drawing room still dressed in riding attire. That in itself was a bit of rudeness, but merciful saints, what could any decent woman be thinking, to call upon *him* in broad daylight?

His visitor stood with her back to him, and his immediate impression, based on the tension in her spine and the set of her shoulders, was that this was, indeed, another desperate female looking to him to forgive her husband's, brother's, or cousin's debts of honor.

The worst kind of helpless female too, he concluded as she turned—a *virtuous*, helpless female.

At first she did not meet his gaze, but aimed a martyred stare at his least favorite Axminster carpet. Her dress was an ugly, serviceable gray; her gloves faded black; and her person without adornment. Her brownish hair was pulled back into a large, simple knot at her nape. She was altogether pathetically unremarkable.

Until she looked at him.

Amber eyes, slanting above high cheekbones and a wickedly full mouth arrested Gareth's dismissive perusal. He'd refuse what she would offer as collateral for some man's debt, though he was... tempted. She had a feline cast to her fine features, an intelligence and alertness that made him want to keep his eyes on her. Watching her for a progression of silent instants, he gained the impression she could move like a cat, think like a cat.

The serious gaze she turned on him suggested that she probably, in keeping with solid English propriety, did *not* purr like a cat.

He approached her with a slight bow. "Heathgate." He'd purposely neglected to append the courteous "at your service."

She curtsied. "Thank you for meeting with me, your lordship."

She did not offer her name, though she had a pretty voice. Gareth's brother Andrew would call it a candlelight voice.

"Shall we be seated?" He gestured to the settee then ordered a tea tray—to appease his hunger rather than convention—and turned to find his guest once more staring at the carpet.

"So, why have you come to see me, madam? You must know propriety is not served by a meeting under these circumstances."

To his surprise, that blunt opening comment earned him a fleeting smile.

"Propriety is a luxury not all of us can afford." Her accent was crisply aristocratic, but musical, as if there might be some Welsh or Gaelic a few generations back. He paid attention to voices, to dress, to the tidy stitching on the index finger of her glove, to the details relevant when dealing with opponents in any game of chance. Hers were a challenge to add up.

"Propriety is a necessity if a young lady is not to lose her reputation, as others have done in similar circumstances."

At that salvo, the lady removed her worn gloves—probably without realizing the symbolism of the gesture—to reveal pale, elegant hands. The hands—God help her—of a true lady.

The tea arrived, and as the footman withdrew, Gareth closed the door. That got the woman's attention, for she leveled a questioning glance at him.

He mustered his miniscule store of patience. "You come to see me without invitation or chaperone; you will not tell me your name. I can only conclude you do not want the servants to overhear what you discuss with me. Will you pour?"

She gave a dignified little nod from her perch on the edge of the sofa. "How do you take your tea?"

"I like it quite strong and with both cream and sugar."

Her movements were confident and graceful; she knew her way around an elaborate tea service. She was a lady fallen on difficult times.

Oh, hell, not again. What was wrong with the young men of England?

"Shall we let it steep a bit, then?" she asked. "I wouldn't call it strong yet."

"As you like, but you will please disclose the nature of your errand. This appointment was not on my schedule." He wanted to get this over with, though his rudeness did not seem to perturb his visitor.

"I am without relations, your lordship, except for a younger sister. My other nearest relation, a distant cousin, has recently passed away. Her will left me with a substantial source of income, provided I meet certain stipulations. The stipulations involve you. Should I fail to meet the conditions of her will in the immediate future, I am without a means of supporting myself, which is no great inconvenience. I could work as a governess or become a lady's companion. My retainers, however, are elderly, and my younger sister—"

She fell silent and poured a splash of tea into a cup. The lady must have decided it wasn't strong enough even yet, for she sat back and regarded him with steady topaz eyes.

He saluted her mentally for meeting the challenge: they were quite down to business, thank you very much.

"How do the stipulations involve me?" Clearly, she wanted him to ask, to show some curiosity about her situation, while he wanted to leave the room at a dead run.

"My distant cousin was a… madam, sir, and the source of income she left me was her brothel."

She had his attention, drat her. He spotted a mahogany bay horsehair on the cuff of his riding jacket and focused on plucking it away. "And the conditions?"

"There are essentially two. First, I may not sell the

business for at least one year. During that time it is to be held in trust for me, and the profits available to me for my personal maintenance. That condition is problematic in itself." She paused, peering at the tea again. This time she poured as she continued speaking, then doctored his tea according to his stated preferences. "If it becomes public knowledge I am living off the proceeds of a brothel, my future is ruined—though that matters little. My younger sister, however, is blameless, and deserves some happiness from this life. She cannot be tainted by this association."

He accepted the tea and took a sip. This difficult, inconvenient woman had made him a perfect cup of tea. Against all probability, he found his goodwill modestly restored. "The second condition?"

The lady looked briefly away—toward the white roses on the piano—and he had the sense this mannerism was how she gathered her courage, though none of her trepidation was betrayed in her expression.

"I am to spend at least three months under the personal tutelage of the trustee, learning the skills necessary to manage what I am told is a high-class sporting house. I am to learn what the... employees know, how the business works, how to gamble, and how the courtesan's trade is"—she searched for words with a delicately lifted eyebrow—"undertaken."

Gareth stood as genuine surprise—a rare emotion for him and unwelcome—coursed over him.

"Did your cousin dislike you so intensely, to put this choice before you?" Her cousin's generosity would be the ruination of her, whoever she was.

"She hardly knew me," came the reply. "She had

chosen or been forced into her profession when I was but a girl. The family no longer received her, nor did she appear to want their acknowledgment. She probably felt entitled to her anger, if in fact this bequest is a display of anger."

Gareth lowered himself beside his guest on the settee. He did not ask permission, and she did not shift away.

"How could this not be a posthumous tantrum? You appear to be a decent woman, and your cousin has made sure if you accept this bequest then you won't be, nor, by association, will your sister be. I call that mean-spirited, particularly when your alternatives are what? To go into service, where your safety is none too assured anyway? It's a diabolical gift, this bequest."

The lady regarded him steadily, measuring him with cool, feline eyes. "My cousin was Callista Hemmings."

He leaned back against the settee, feeling a stab of loss. Callista had been the quintessential *grande horizontale*, and she'd treated him honorably. When all London had been fawning over the newly invested Marquess of Heathgate to his face and laughing at him or accusing him of murder behind his back, Callista had been honest. She'd taken him on as a project, educated him, refined him, shown him skills and weapons that had needed only the sharpening influence of time to see him into the peerage on his own terms.

She'd passed along tidbits about this peer, or that bit of business that had allowed him to make some brilliant investments. Then she'd dumped him flat, telling him she chose her clientele, and she was unchoosing him.

In hindsight, he'd seen the kindness in what she'd done. Untried as he was, he'd been in danger of losing his heart to her. She was shrewd enough to know that wouldn't have been in her interests—or his. He was in her debt, and now she was gone. He'd felt the loss of her months ago, and felt it anew at the mention of her name.

"You knew her," his visitor observed dryly.

"My dear lady, much of London's titled male population knew her, and the remainder could only wish they had. Your cousin was... quite a woman. Quite a lady."

"She was not a lady," his guest countered, the first hint of heat in her words.

He let that observation hang in the air while he took another sip of wonderfully hot, sweet, strong tea. "You resent this choice."

"I resent it, yes, even as I am grateful it gives me options. Penury would likely cost me my virtue at some point, in any case. I am resigned to traveling a safer road to ruin. Were my sister older, I could get her married posthaste then slide into obscurity, but she is seventeen, and that is..."

Her faltering resolve was interesting. "Seventeen is...?"

"Seventeen, in her case, is too young."

Gareth's guest busied herself sipping her tea, apparently oblivious to Gareth's perusal. He sipped along with her, waiting to see where she was heading with her disclosures. At seventeen, without the first clue what present company was getting herself into, *she* would have married to protect her sibling, had it been an option for her. He had no doubt of that.

"I am not the only one who might resent the way my cousin has arranged things," she said. She had pretty hands, but as she set her teacup down, Gareth noticed a minute tremor in them.

"I expect the ladies in Callista's employ are not particularly pleased, and the trustee might find himself in a bit of a bind." The poor bastard would be in one hell of a bind, in fact.

She looked at him directly, and he realized all her previous glances and gazes had been oblique in comparison. Foreboding prickled up his neck.

"Do you?" she asked evenly.

"Madam?"

"Do you find yourself in a bit of a bind?"

"Why would I do that?"

"Because Callista named you as the trustee of her estate, my lord, and thus the guardian of my virtue."

Bloody, rubbishing, perishing... Gareth stalled discreetly, calling for more tea and some cakes while his internal world righted itself. He was too taken aback at Callista's scheming to puzzle through the reasons for it—unpleasantly taken aback. Shocked, even, and it took a great deal to shock him—now.

While his guest nibbled away at a chocolate éclair, Gareth held his peace and found consternation growing into monumental resentment. Miss Shabby Dignity eventually finished her tea and turned her unnerving regard on him once more.

"So, my lord, do you resent the task requested of you? Callista named an alternative trustee should you decline the position."

Reprieve. Maybe there was a way out—if he wanted one. "Whom did she name?"

"Viscount Riverton."

"I see." Callista must have truly hated her cousins. Riverton was a confirmed deviant, sick at best, and evil, more likely.

No damned reprieve whatsoever.

"Riverton will not do." Did he detect a slight relaxation in her shoulders? "Any provisions for a substitute of my choosing?" And to whom could he delegate this project anyway?

She considered her empty teacup, very likely some of the finest china she'd ever see, much less touch. "None. You take on the job or Riverton will, and I can tell you I do not relish the thought of his personal tutelage one bit."

His guest was a martyr with some discernment, then. How flattering.

"What exactly does personal tutelage involve?" Because unless his distant recollection of Chancery law was in error, the will would have to be carefully worded to successfully skirt the illegalities of passing along a house of ill repute.

She remained perched on the edge of the settee, while Gareth suspected she was longing to get up and pace. "It isn't complicated, my lord. I am to learn to be a madam. Your job is to teach me at least the rudiments of that profession, and the will stipulates that I have only so long to complete this education. Make no mistake: my cousin's solicitors were quite careful to explain that if I want the benefits of Callista's generosity, I have approximately ninety days left to learn to whore."

The vulgar term in the midst of her polite diction landed like the sound of breaking glass in a quiet library. Gareth sat forward, resting his elbows on his knees and mentally sorting through curses in French, though being a *lady*, she'd probably understand those too.

First things first. "Do you *want* me to teach you to whore?"

"I do not want to starve, and I do not want my sister to starve. I hope to undertake this… apprenticeship for the next several months. One year from Callista's death you can sell the business for me, and then this episode in my life will be over. The only one who will know of it besides me and the solicitors is you, and I am hoping to rely on your gentlemanly discretion."

Gareth took a moment to digest her little speech. The course she proposed was probably the most sensible, from her point of view. And he could be discreet. A man on familiar terms with all manner of vice had to be faultlessly discreet if he wanted to maintain his privacy.

Which he did.

"Why do I not simply lie to the solicitors, tell them you have fulfilled the terms, and let us go our separate ways in peace?"

She wrinkled her nose—and it was a pretty nose, in perfect proportion to the rest of her features. "The solicitors are to test me, using a list of questions and answers Callista devised, and if they suspect I've not surrendered my innocence to their satisfaction, they implied they could have me examined by a midwife. They would have me believe myself fortunate that I was not asked to entertain a customer before witnesses."

Gareth's eyebrow shot up, because he knew Callista could be ruthless, and he'd damned near loved her for it, but this was beyond ruthless. This was cruel, and not a legacy any court would have a part in enforcing.

Not that the lady would obtain the property or its income in the next decade by bringing suit in the courts of law.

"To summarize, then," Gareth said, "you want me to spend three months teaching you how to please a man, how to run a brothel, how to play various games of chance, and so on. I am to at least relieve you of your virginity, and I am to complete these tasks without anyone being the wiser? Moreover, I am to sell the brothel for you at the end of one year, all with utmost discretion. What do I get out of it?"

If this woman knew anything about him at all, she'd know to expect that question from him.

"My guess is Callista chose you for her own reasons, believing you would accept. I can't see that you get anything out of this other than the trustee's portion of the proceeds, which I doubt you need." She cocked an eyebrow, perhaps mocking him, perhaps inventorying his physical assets. "If Callista's faith in you is not misplaced, you will get the free services of a well-trained whore, won't you? I doubt you need those either."

He suppressed a flinch at her continued use of the word "whore." There were so many other ways to say it—soiled dove, courtesan, lady of the night, fashionable impure. His guest seemed to want to shock him, and maybe herself.

Two could play at that. He stood and locked the door.

"Why don't we gather a little more information before we decide what to do with this situation, hmm? Would you oblige me by standing?" She did, watching him warily as he stalked toward her. "Over here, away from the window, if you please." He took her cool, bare hand in his and guided her across the room.

"What are you about, my lord?" She put some indignation in her tone, but not enough to cover the unease.

Good, he wanted her unnerved. So unnerved and angry she'd stomp right out of the house and never want to lay eyes on him again. Let her swallow her pride and move in with dear old Aunt Besom or eke out a living on piecework from the modistes.

Though piecework would ruin those pretty eyes and her pretty hands.

"Before you accept me as the guardian of your virtue, to use your words, you should have some idea whether you can even accept my touch on your person. Losing one's virginity involves a great deal of touching, under ideal circumstances. You have to know that much at least?"

She nodded once, suggesting that was the limit of her understanding.

"I will take on this trusteeship if you conclude you can indeed find pleasure in my carnal touch. I will not force you." He would not force any woman, ever. To know he could still speak with conviction in this regard was a relief. "You decide if you can allow me to seduce you."

He purposely stood too close to her, letting her physically experience his six-foot-four inch height, the scent of horse and sandalwood about his person, and the sheer masculine strength he had in abundance. Her pulse beat rapidly at her throat, and she was back to staring at the carpet.

He dropped his voice to a near whisper and leaned in even closer.

"You must be sure, my lady, because once your innocence is compromised, you will never regain it, whether your virtue is intact or not." He picked up her hand and massaged his thumb slowly across her knuckles.

Her eyes clamped on their joined hands, depriving him of her gaze. "Do you seek to take my virginity now?"

Brave lady. He awarded her points for that, and for amusing him—his reputation would suffer terribly if he allotted her deflowering only the few minutes available. "No time for that today, my dear, but I would ask of you a kiss to seal our bargain and begin your education. We have, after all, but a short time to complete it."

She glanced up long enough for him to see relief in her eyes, though such a proper lady could have no idea what manner of kiss he contemplated. His hands settled on her waist, and he tugged her closer.

"Close your eyes, my dear, and relax. You have nothing to fret about today."

She didn't immediately close her eyes, but watched him as he took both her hands in his, kissed each palm, then slipped them around his neck. He slid his hands around her waist, resting them at the small of her back. She was close enough to him now that he could hear the catch in her breath as his hold grew more firm.

She wasn't as cool as she wanted him to believe, and that realization gave Gareth a pause in his determination to rattle her. He started off by nuzzling her temple with his lips, and even that caused her to flinch. He repeated that caress, doing nothing more than inhaling the lavender scent of her hair until she relaxed minutely against him.

"I'll make you a promise." He moved on as he spoke, breathing against her hair, the curve of her ear, the silky skin of her neck, even as his hands went questing over her back in long, slow strokes.

"I will promise you if at any point you want me to stop, no matter what we're doing, then I will stop. You have only to tell me." He'd begun kissing her, sipping at the spot where her shoulder and her neck joined, and Gareth had to wonder if speech were already beyond her. Her scent was lovely, fresh and clean, without paint, powder, or the slightly singed odor of the curling tongs.

Despite her prim and proper airs, despite the mad scheme she'd brought to his door, despite the niggling itch of what remained of his conscience, his body at least was enjoying itself.

"Kiss me," he whispered against her cheek. "Kiss me now."

She turned her face toward him, tensing up for what she no doubt expected would be a grinding, wet, teeth-bumping awkwardness. She was too pretty not to have suffered the attentions of a callow swain or two.

So his lips were feather-gentle as he played at her mouth and invited her to trust him for the duration of one soft, sweet kiss. His mouth parted over hers, and he was rewarded when she sighed, her body finally losing its starch against his. Her fingers drifted through the hair at his nape, and Gareth realized she didn't have to go up on her toes to fit him perfectly—more's the pity.

He traced his tongue over her lips, thinking not

only to steal a taste of her, but also to distract her from the hand resting due north of her derriere. He molded her against the length of his body and continued plying his tongue along her mouth. Tentatively, she touched her tongue to his, provoking him to growl in satisfaction at her overture.

She shyly tested the contours of his lips, and he let her explore while his hands stroked her back. Gareth sensed she was just becoming aware of the ridge of male flesh rising against her belly, when his instinct for self-preservation had him easing out of the kiss and letting his hands fall still on her back.

Her breathing was slightly accelerated as she curled against his chest and rested her head on his shoulder. He tucked his chin on her crown and held her, unable to locate a compelling reason to let her go.

"My dear woman, I should at least know your name."

She remained quiet against him, and he brought one hand up to massage the nape of her neck in slow circles.

The kiss had gotten a bit out of hand was all. Spinsters were, on the whole, a courageous lot, but he hadn't been expecting this particular variety of courage from her. This variety of honesty.

She stood unmoving for another moment then stepped away.

"You'll do it then—take on the trusteeship?" Her eyes were a little unfocused, which pleased Gareth inordinately.

"I'll take on the trusteeship for now, and I will be as discreet as possible. You must realize, though, if word of this gets out, I can do nothing to protect you from the scandal that will result from the terms of Callista's will. I doubt her solicitors want anyone knowing they've created such a bequest—one Chancery would scoff at, mind you—but given who I am, I won't be able to repair your reputation, nor will I try."

She nodded at him soberly. "If this becomes public, nothing will save my reputation, and I don't suppose you want people knowing you've taken on a spinster protégé, either. Such a liaison hardly flatters you." She stepped back farther and put her gloves on, donning another increment of reserve as she did.

She was wrong, of course. She would be ruined, while Society, being stupid, venal, and easily entertained, would regard this as another one of his titillating larks, nothing more.

"So how shall we go about this?" he asked, his voice holding a detachment his body did not feel.

"Don't scowl at me, your lordship. This situation is not of my doing or yours. I appreciate your willingness to comply with the terms of the bequest, but just as you asked me if I were willing to be seduced, you must be a willing seducer."

The women who would scold him were few in number. That this pretty, proper spinster might be one of them suggested their dealings could grow… interesting. "I can assure you, my dear, I am a willing seducer, enthusiastically and often. When do you next have your courses?"

"Wha… I beg your pardon!" She gaped at him, her self-possession gratifyingly absent. "What can that have to do with… why would you ask such a thing?"

"How much do you know about the mechanics of copulation?"

He'd chosen one of the more polite terms, and yet it raised a magnificent blush against the lady's fair coloring.

"It... It involves sleeping in the same bed, and probably some kissing, and... touching. I know there is a maidenhead." Her blush deepened, so he gave her a moment to compose herself by unlocking the door and retrieving her wrap. He returned with her cloak and slipped it around her.

Without thinking, he turned her by the shoulders to face him and fastened the frogs of her cloak under her chin. Such caretaking was an intimacy, one he took completely for granted with any woman he'd kissed— until he noticed how stiffly *this* lady was standing.

"Intimate business between men and women involves a bit more than you perceive," Gareth said, finishing a bow off-center beneath her chin, "and it will be my pleasure to educate you. I would remind you, though, I have promised if you at any time want to desist from this project, you have only to say so. I can probably find you and your dependents decent employment on one of my estates."

"That is generous of you, my lord, but having imposed on you to this extent, I would not seek employment from you. I have no doubt my mortification is just beginning, and you will be the last man I ever want to spend more time around once this situation is resolved."

He nodded, relieved, because having her in his employ didn't sit well at all. She'd then be under his protection in the *unavailable* sense, and that could only be awkward as hell. She ducked her chin and said in a low voice, "I will likely... *start* Monday next." She looked around self-consciously, as if afraid of being overheard by the very furniture.

How long had it been since a woman had blushed in his company? "And how long are you indisposed?"

"Three or four days." Her answer was barely a whisper. She donned a bonnet that was the same color as old horse droppings, not at all flattering in its style and years out of fashion.

When he taught her how to be a madam, surely he could dress her, too? He took her elbow and walked her toward the door.

"If you will send your direction to me, I will have my coach pick you up Monday afternoon at two of the clock, sharp. Expect to spend the balance of the afternoon with me, and at least several afternoons each week thereafter."

She paused at the door to the hall, making an intense study of her gloves. "Will you give me some idea what to expect?" she asked, very much on her tattered dignity.

He considered the brim of a very unprepossessing bonnet. The only decent women he consorted with frequently were his dear mother and her aging friends, and even they—veterans of years of genteel warfare in the best ballrooms—knew not to reveal their emotions.

The lady in the ugly bonnet and mended gloves was scared. Also affronted, humiliated, and many other things—likely including outraged—but under it all, she was afraid.

Of him, of what he would ask of her.

Gentlemanly sensibilities chose that inconvenient

moment to rouse themselves from a nap of years' duration. Of course she was frightened. Terrified— what if he'd refused her? What if he'd raped her? God in heaven, what had Callista been thinking?

Long ago, grieving, guilty, and bereft, hating the lofty title that had made a laughingstock of him, Gareth had been scared. As young men will, he'd used other terms for it: daunted, challenged, or when things had been particularly bad, overwhelmed. In truth, he'd been terrified, and Callista had been his one ally against that fear.

He scowled at his visitor, resentment resurging at her and at the bargain he'd been inveigled into honoring. "Remember my promise, madam. You hold the control, no matter what I or Callista's solicitors have planned. Considering your indisposition, why don't we start next week with the business aspects of the operation? The expenses, suppliers, ledgers, household budget, and so forth. Have you seen the property?"

"I drove by it in a hackney."

Did everything make her blush? "Well, then we'll find things to keep us busy next week. Shall I notify Callista's solicitors I've taken the post?"

"If you'd contact them, I would appreciate it. They make me... uncomfortable," she replied as he escorted her to the front door. She stopped before taking her leave. "My lord?"

Didn't *he* make her uncomfortable? "Yes?"

"Thank you. Riverton was not a prospect I could have endured."

Her gratitude was surprising, and some part of him also found it... insupportable. Repugnant. "I know."

Neither could I. "There's just one more thing, if you would be so kind?"

"My lord?"

"Your name."

She turned to go and beamed a smile at him over her shoulder. Her smile embodied benediction, relief, and pure female beauty all at once. Had he been a less experienced man, it would have bowled him over.

He was a very experienced man, and still, her smile stunned him momentarily witless.

"I am Felicity, your lordship. Miss Felicity Hemmings Worthington."

Andrew
The Lonely Lords

by Grace Burrowes
New York Times and *USA Today* Bestselling Author

He'll do anything to protect her...

After a tragic yachting accident leaves him wracked with guilt and despair, Andrew Alexander is certain he doesn't deserve to be around his own family, let alone the beautiful, forthright Astrid Worthington. He wanders for years, only allowing himself respite from his self-imposed exile when he thinks Astrid is safely married. He returns home to find instead that the only woman he's ever loved has been recently—and mysteriously—widowed.

...especially from himself

When Andrew leaves, Astrid finds a husband and contents herself with a cordial, if unexciting, marriage. But after her husband's sudden death, Astrid finds that Andrew will do anything to protect her not only from her enemies, but also from the truth of his dark past.

"Burrowes's unique ability to make each book stand alone yet connect to the other books in the series amazes me. Andrew engages the reader's emotions and senses from start to finish—a joy to read." —*Long and Short Reviews*

For more Grace Burrowes, visit:
www.sourcebooks.com

Douglas
The Lonely Lords

by Grace Burrowes

New York Times and *USA Today* Bestselling Author

———— ✍ ————

Douglas needs a home for his aching heart

Douglas Allen, Viscount Amery, has arrived to his title without knowing how to manage his properties, so he reluctantly puts himself in the hands of Guinevere Hollister, the estate's steward. He's surprised to discover beneath her prickly exterior a woman of passion and honor. Yet despite the closeness they find, she will not marry him.

And Guinevere needs a champion

In Douglas's eyes, Gwen deserves to make her own choices, and he will take on family, a meddling duke, and Gwen's own lonely, stubborn heart to ensure his lady's happiness.

———— ✍ ————

"I was certain by the end of Douglas's book, Grace Burrowes would have me melting and falling in love! She not only succeeded in that, but made it happen in the first chapter." —*The Reading Cafe*

"It's a joy to read. Can't go wrong with a Lonely Lord in your hands." —*First Page to Last*

For more Grace Burrowes, visit:
www.sourcebooks.com

David

The Lonely Lords

by Grace Burrowes

New York Times and *USA Today* Bestselling Author

— ✍ —

David, Viscount Fairly, has imperiled his honor…

Letty Banks is keeping a secret that brought her, a vicar's daughter, to a life of vice. While becoming madam of Viscount Fairly's high-class brothel is a financial necessity, Letty refuses to become David's mistress—though their attraction is harder to resist the more she learns about him…

Perhaps a fallen woman can redeem it

David is smitten with Letty's beauty, but also with her calm, her kindness, her quiet. David is determined to put respectability back in her grasp, even if that means uncovering Letty's secrets—secrets that could take her away from him forever…

— ✍ —

For more Grace Burrowes, visit:
www.sourcebooks.com

About the Author

New York Times and USA Today bestselling author Grace Burrowes's bestsellers include The Heir, The Soldier, Lady Maggie's Secret Scandal, Lady Sophie's Christmas Wish, Lady Eve's Indiscretion, The Captive, The Laird, The Duke's Disaster, and Tremaine's True Love. Her Regency romances and Scotland-set Victorian romances have received extensive praise, including starred reviews from Publishers Weekly and Booklist. The Heir was a Publishers Weekly Best Book of 2010, The Bridegroom Wore Plaid was a Publishers Weekly Best Book of 2012, Lady Sophie's Christmas Wish and Once Upon a Tartan have both won RT Reviewers' Choice Awards. Lady Louisa's Christmas Knight was a Library Journal Best Book of 2012, and What a Lady Needs for Christmas was a Library Journal Best Book of 2014. Darius: Lord of Pleasure was an iBooks Store Best Book of 2013. Two of her MacGregor heroes have won KISS awards, and five of her titles have been nominated for Romance Writers of America's RITA awards. Grace is a practicing family law attorney and lives in rural Maryland.